D1340139

PRAISE

'A dream of a book you'll want to savor and share'
Lisa Wingate, author of *Before We Were Yours*

'A captivating and insightful backstage pass into a timeless classic'
Candis

'*Finding Dorothy* pulls back the curtain on a fascinating
relationship behind the making of *The Wizard of Oz*'
Martha Hall Kelly, author of *Lilac Girls*

'A magical tale about a classic book and movie'
Melanie Benjamin, author of *The Aviator's Wife*

'An unflinching journey between hardship and hope,
with a catch-your-breath ending'
Pam Jenoff, author of *The Orphan's Tale*

'A well-researched, Technicolor delight'
Eowyn Ivey, author of *The Snow Child*

'Engrossing . . . This is a crowd-pleasing,
thoroughly satisfying novel'
Publishers Weekly

'A riveting read'
Yours

'An endearing novel'
Choice Magazine

'An absorbing read'
Kirkus

700044308748

Elizabeth Letts is the #1 *New York Times* bestselling author of *The Eighty-Dollar Champion* and *The Perfect Horse*, which won the 2017 PEN Center USA Literary Award for research nonfiction, as well as two previous novels, *Quality of Care* and *Family Planning*. A former certified nurse-midwife, she also served in the Peace Corps in Morocco. She lives in Southern California and Northern Michigan.

elizabethletts.com
Facebook.com/ElizabethLettsAuthor
Twitter: @ ElizabethLetts

By Elizabeth Letts

FICTION

Family Planning
Quality of Care

NON-FICTION

The Perfect Horse
The Eighty-Dollar Champion

FINDING DOROTHY

ELIZABETH LETTS

Quercus

First published in Great Britain in 2019 by Quercus
This paperback edition published in 2020 by

Quercus Editions Ltd
Carmelite House
50 Victoria Embankment
London EC4Y 0DZ

An Hachette UK company

Copyright © 2019 Elizabeth Letts

The moral right of Elizabeth Letts to be
identified as the author of this work has been
asserted in accordance with the Copyright,
Designs and Patents Act, 1988.

All rights reserved. No part of this publication
may be reproduced or transmitted in any form
or by any means, electronic or mechanical,
including photocopy, recording, or any
information storage and retrieval system,
without permission in writing from the publisher.

A CIP catalogue record for this book is available
from the British Library

PB ISBN 978 1 52940 345 9
EB ISBN 978 1 52940 342 8

This book is a work of fiction. Names, characters,
places and events portrayed in it, while at times based on
historical figures and places, are the product
of the author's imagination.

10 9 8 7 6 5 4 3 2 1

Book design by Barbara M. Bachman

Printed and bound in Great Britain by Clays Ltd, Elcograf S.p.A.

MIX
Paper from
responsible sources
FSC® C104740

Papers used by Quercus are from well-managed forests and other responsible sources.

For
Susanna Porter

There is a word sweeter than Mother,
Home, or Heaven. That word is Liberty.

—*Matilda Joslyn Gage*

The story of "The Wonderful Wizard of Oz" was written solely
to pleasure children of today. It aspires to being a modernized
fairy tale, in which the wonderment and joy are retained
and the heart-aches and nightmares are left out.

—*L. Frank Baum*

I tried my *damndest* to believe in the rainbow
that I tried to get over and I *couldn't*.

—*Judy Garland*

HOLLYWOOD

October 1938

IT WAS A CITY WITHIN A CITY, A TEXTILE MILL TO WEAVE THE gossamer of fantasy on looping looms of celluloid. From the flashing needles of the tailors in the costume shop to the zoo where the animals were trained, from the matzo ball soup in the commissary to the blinding-white offices in the brand-new Thalberg executive building, an army of people—composers and musicians, technicians and tinsmiths, directors and actors—spun thread into gold. Once upon a time, dreams were made by hand, but now they were mass-produced. These forty-four acres were their assembly line.

Outside its walls, the brown hills, tidy neighborhoods, and rusting oil derricks of Culver City gave no hint of magic; but within the gates of M-G-M—*Metro,* as it was known—you stepped inside an enchanted kingdom. A private trolley line that cut through the center of the studio's back lots could whisk you across the world, or back in time—from old New York's Brownstone Row to the Wild West's Billy the Kid Street to Renaissance Italy's Verona Square—with no stops in the outside world. In 1938, more than three thousand people labored inside these walls. Just as the Emerald City was the center of the Land of Oz, so the M-G-M Studios were the beating heart of that mythic place called Hollywood.

———

MAUD BAUM HAD BEEN waiting on foot outside the massive front gates of Metro-Goldwyn-Mayer for almost an hour, just another face among the throngs of visitors hoping for a chance to get inside. Every now and again, a gleaming automobile pulled up to the gate. Each time, the studio's guard snapped to attention and offered a crisp salute. Whenever this happened, the fans waiting around the entrance, hoping to catch a peek of the stars, would leap forward, thrusting bits of papers through the car's windows. As Maud observed this spectacle, she couldn't help but feel a pang for Frank: his doomed Oz Manufacturing Film Company, a single giant barn-like structure, had been just a short distance away from the current location of this thriving metropolis of Metro. In 1914, when Frank had opened his company, Hollywood had been a sleepy backwater of orange trees and bungalows, and filmmaking a crazy venture seen as a passing fad. If only he could have lived to see what a movie studio would become over the course of the next two decades: another White City, a giant theater stage. This fantastical place was the concrete manifestation of what Frank had been able to imagine long before it had come to pass.

At last it was Maud's turn. As the guard scribbled her a pass, her stomach fluttered. Inside her purse, she had the small cutout torn from *Variety*. She didn't need to look at it; she had long since memorized its few words: "OZ" SOLD TO LOUIS B. MAYER AT M-G-M. As the last living link to the inspiration behind the story, she was determined to offer her services as a consultant. But getting access to the studio had not been easy. For months, they had rebuffed her calls, only reluctantly setting up a meeting with the studio head, Louis B. Mayer, because the receptionist was no doubt fed up with answering her daily queries. Today she would make her case.

If Maud's suffragist mother, Matilda, had taught her anything, it was that if you wanted something, you needed to ask for it—or *demand* it, if necessary. True, Maud would far rather be reading a book at Ozcot, her Hollywood home, but she had made a promise to her late husband that she aimed to keep.

The guard pushed her day pass through the glass-fronted window and gave her a nod.

"Where is the Thalberg Building?" she asked.

He jerked his head to the left—a gesture that could have pointed anywhere. "White Lung? Just head that way. You can't miss it."

White Lung? What a peculiar name for a building. Maud was about to ask him why, but as she'd aged she'd learned to keep her thoughts to herself so as not to come off as a doddering old fool.

Inside the studio's gates, the paths and private roads were crowded with people and vehicles. A knot of actors hurried by, costumed in elaborate ball gowns, paste jewels, and powdered wigs, followed by painters in splattered coveralls, a man humming a tune to himself, and another fellow, likely a writer, with a furrowed brow and a pencil tucked behind his ear. Maud leapt out of the way as three girls whizzed past on bicycles. Having spent much time in the theater, she was reminded of the bustle of backstage, but this—this was such an immense scale—*all the world's a stage!* Frank had loved to quote Shakespeare. Here, it seemed to be literally true.

The Art Moderne Thalberg Building was dazzlingly white, its fresh exterior paint as clean as snow. A few scaffoldings still crept up one side—the building was clearly brand-new. When she stepped inside the polished lobby, she felt a chill prickle her skin and heard an odd wheezing sound like an old man breathing. She pulled her cardigan tighter around her shoulders as the receptionist gave her a sympathetic look.

"It's the air conditioner," she said. "Like a heater for cool."

Maud suppressed a smile. Such a Frank-like idea. A heater for cool. He was always saying backward things like that.

"May I help you?"

"I am here to see Mr. Louis B. Mayer." Maud made sure that her voice conveyed no hint of hesitation. *She who hesitates is lost.* That was another of Matilda's expressions. Seventy-seven years old and Maud sometimes still felt as if her mother were perched just behind the wings, whispering stage instructions.

The receptionist was a young woman with a well-coiffed platinum bob. "Actress?" she asked.

"Most definitely not."

The girl raised a stylishly penciled eyebrow and gave Maud the once-over, from her gray curls down to her sturdy brown pumps.

"Are you . . . ?" She leaned in. "His mother?"

To her credit, Maud did not show her irritation. "Mrs. L. Frank Baum. I have an appointment."

The young woman narrowed her eyes, the rubber tip of her pencil ticking down the list. "I'm sorry, Mrs. Baum. You aren't on Mr. Mayer's schedule."

"Check again," Maud insisted. "One o'clock. I made this appointment weeks ago." She wouldn't let them turn her away now. She'd been waiting too long for this day to arrive.

"You'll have to speak to Mrs. Koverman . . ." She dropped her voice. "Mount Ida. No one gets to Mr. Mayer without going through her first."

Maud smiled. "I'm quite adept at going through people."

"Take the elevator to the third floor. Mrs. Koverman's desk will be right in front of you."

As Maud waited for the elevator, her blurry reflection looked back at her from the shining brass of the twin doors. She hoped that her expression reflected a resoluteness of spirit, rather than the trepidation she was now feeling as this important meeting was at last upon her.

"Third floor," she said to the uniformed elevator man, stepping inside.

When the doors slid open, she faced a secretary's desk with a plaque that read MRS. IDA KOVERMAN. A stout matron with bobbed brown hair inspected Maud.

"Maud Baum," Maud said. "I have an appointment with Mr. Louis B. Mayer."

"On what business?"

"My late husband . . ." Maud was horrified to hear her voice squeak.

Mrs. Koverman looked at her with no trace of sympathy.

"My late husband, Mr. L. Frank Baum, was the author of *The Wonderful Wizard of Oz*."

Mrs. Koverman's expression did not soften.

Maud had long since noted that there were two kinds of people in the world: fans of Oz—those who remembered their childhoods—and those who pretended that they had never even heard of Oz, who believed that adults should put away childish things. From the look on her face, Mrs. Koverman fell into the latter category.

"Have a seat." She cut off any further conversation with a vigorous clacking of her typewriter keys.

Maud sat, feet crossed at the ankle, handbag and a well-worn copy of *Oz* balanced on her lap, hoping to convey that she wasn't planning on going anywhere.

Every now and again, Mrs. Koverman would stand up and rap upon the door with the brass plaque on it reading LOUIS B. MAYER, then enter with a piece of typed paper or a phone message. Each time she emerged, Maud looked at her steadily while Mrs. Koverman avoided her gaze. Once in a while, Maud glanced at her wristwatch. Soon one-thirty had come and gone.

The two women might have remained in their silent test of wills had not a large commotion ensued from the elevator bay—a loud *thwack* and a cry of "Bugger all!" filled the room. Maud was astonished to see a giant young man—well over six feet tall—rubbing his head, then bending over to gather up a scattered pile of papers from the floor. Most surprising, a brand-new edition of *The Wonderful Wizard of Oz* had skidded across the floor, landing almost at Maud's feet.

She picked it up and approached the man. "I believe you've lost this?"

"Right," he said with a British accent. "Just give me a minute. I'm a bit dazed."

Maud watched with alarm as the lanky man swayed like a tall pine on a windy day. But after a moment, he straightened his tie, took the book from Maud, and held out his other hand in greeting. "Noel Langley. Scenarist."

He noted the faded clothbound volume Maud held in her other hand. "Doing a little homework, I see."

"Homework?"

"Let me guess. Are you playing Auntie Em?"

"Auntie Em?" Maud was startled. She peered at the man, confused. "But how could you . . . ?"

"Clara Blandick," Langley continued, not seeming to notice Maud's reaction. "I presume . . ."

"Oh, the actress?" Maud said, gathering her wits. "You mean the actress?"

"Yes, the *actress*," Langley said, louder this time. Maud blinked in irritation.

"Not at all. I'm not an actress," Maud said firmly. "I'm Maud Baum—Mrs. L. Frank . . . ?"

Langley returned a blank look.

"My late husband, Frank—L. Frank Baum? Author of *The Wonderful Wizard of Oz*?" Maud held up her book and pointed to the author's name.

Still looking puzzled, he scrutinized Maud as if seeing her for the first time. She twisted the emerald she wore on her fourth finger and smoothed the folds of her simple floral dress, aware how out of place she must appear to this elegant young man.

"But the book was written before I was born . . ." Langley said slowly, as if trying to solve a difficult math problem in his head. "Surely his wife must be . . ." As he spoke, his head cocked progressively more to one side, until with his long limbs and small tilted head, he looked like a curious grasshopper.

"I'm seventy-seven years old," Maud said. "Not dead yet, if that's what you were thinking."

"Certainly not, of course not," Langley stammered, his face now beet red. "It's just that I imagined the book was published years ago? I guess, I assumed—oh, never mind what I assumed . . ."

"Not to worry," Maud said soothingly. "*The Wonderful Wizard of Oz* was published in 1900. The turn of the century."

"Ah, yes . . ." Langley said. His blush had faded, but the tips of his auricles remained pink.

"Must seem like ancient history to a young man like you." Maud's heart sank at the thought.

Langley nodded in agreement.

"Which brings up a good point," Maud said. "It's a lucky chance I've run into you. You see—"

Before Maud had a chance to finish, the elevator doors slid open again and a brown-haired man seemed to blow out as if pushed by a strong wind.

"Langley!" he cried out.

"Hello," the tall fellow answered. "Look what we have here . . . if you can believe it. It's Mrs. L. Frank Baum. Mrs. Baum, this is Mervyn LeRoy. He's the producer."

LeRoy skidded to a stop in front of the pair and looked Maud up and down.

"Well, I'll be," he said, appearing mystified at her presence.

LeRoy's gaze fell upon the faded green book Maud clasped in her bony, spotted hands.

"Well, now, look at this." LeRoy reached out. "This looks like the exact same edition I had when I was a kid . . . sat on the shelf right by my bed. Loved that book so much."

Maud sensed an opening. "Would you like to take a look?"

She held out the worn volume, the color leached from its cover and its edges frayed. Before cracking it open, LeRoy inhaled its papery scent, then reverently brushed the palm of his hand across the stamped green cloth. Flipping it open, he perused the color illustrations one by one, a half-smile on his lips.

"I grew up reading this book. Loved it! It's hard to explain. I almost felt as if the characters were part of my own family."

"I am glad to hear you feel that way. So you'll understand why it's so important to stick to the author's vision."

LeRoy tore his eyes away from the volume in his hands and returned his gaze to Maud, whose corporeal presence he still seemed to find puzzling. "The author's vision? Tell the truth, I never gave a moment's thought to the person who wrote it. Oz always seemed so timeless—eternal, really. Funny to think it started out as the idea of an unknown person with a pen in his hand."

"I assure you, my husband was a very celebrated man in his day.

The newspapers used to be full of stories about him. Headlines. Mr. L. Frank Baum, celebrated author of *The Wonderful Wizard of Oz* . . ." She looked at LeRoy expectantly, but he maintained the same bland expression. Even though this one wasn't as wet behind the ears as Langley, he had most likely still been in knee britches when Frank Baum's name was on every lip.

"Perhaps a young man like you wouldn't remember . . ." Maud was unable to hide the discouragement in her voice.

"No, ma'am. This is all news to me. But I promise you, it doesn't matter one bit. I may not recall anything about the author, but I'll definitely never forget that story!"

It pained Maud terribly to think that Frank could be forgotten, and yet, she wasn't entirely surprised. Now, almost twenty years after her husband's death, many people didn't recognize his name, but was there anyone, big or small, who didn't know Dorothy and the Scarecrow, the Tin Man and the Lion? Frank's creations had grown more celebrated than their creator, bursting out of the confines of the pages to which Frank had entrusted them. Of all people, Maud knew best that none of it—the Wizard, the Witches, the Land of Oz itself—would have existed were it not for the real flesh-and-blood man who had walked this earth, who had lived and laughed, and sometimes suffered . . .

"Mrs. Baum?" LeRoy was holding the book out to her. Maud realized she had been lost in her thoughts.

"Well, it's been a pleasure." He turned to go.

"Mr. LeRoy?" Maud held out her hand.

"Yes?"

"Do you think that you could . . . Well, it's just that . . . You see . . . I'm the last link to the author of this book, and yet I can't even get permission—"

"*Mister* LeRoy," Ida Koverman interrupted.

He pivoted to Mrs. Koverman as if surprised by her presence. "Well there, Ida," he said jovially. "Do you know who we have here?" He held up the book. "This is Mrs. L. Frank Baum! Can you believe it?"

Mrs. Koverman's eyebrows remained fixed in a straight line,

matching exactly the cast of her mouth. "Mr. Mayer will see you and Langley now."

At the mention of Mayer's name, the two men were suddenly all business. Langley muttered, "Good day," LeRoy tipped his hat, and Maud realized that their brief conversation was over. The two men hurried inside the confines of Louis B. Mayer's office without a backward glance, leaving Maud no choice but to return to her seat. Half an hour later, when Mayer's door pushed open and the two men emerged, Maud stood up expectantly, hoping to engage them once again, but this time, deep in conversation, the men barely nodded to her as they passed, and she soon found herself alone with Mrs. Koverman, who was typing with a rapid-fire *clickety-clack, clickety-clack, zing.*

After what seemed an eternity, Ida Koverman stood up and beckoned. The door swung open upon an office so vast that Maud could have ridden a bicycle across it. At one end stood a pearly grand piano; at the other was a massive white semicircular desk. Behind the desk sat a round-faced, bald-pated man with equally round spectacles. To Maud, he looked like a prairie dog just emerging from his hole. He seemed to take no note of her at all but was rummaging around on his desk, leafing through some papers that might have been a script. Behind her, Mrs. Koverman exited, leaving the door open. Maud stood still, waiting for some sign of acknowledgment; at last, certain that none was forthcoming, she approached.

Louis B. Mayer looked up, as if startled to see her there. "Mrs. L. Frank Baum," he burst out, jumping up from his seat. "Mrs. Oz herself." He stood up and reached across the desk, pumping Maud's hand warmly, then dropped it suddenly, taking a step back as if seeing her for the first time. "So tell me, Mrs. L. Frank Baum. What can I do for you today?"

"I'm here to offer my services," Maud said. "I called the moment I saw the announcement in *Variety.*" Maud did not mention that the studio had been rebuffing her overtures for months. "I want to be a resource to you. I can tell you all about Oz, and about the man who created him. Nobody knows more about the story than I do—"

Mayer cut her off, calling through the open door.

"Ida?"

Mrs. Koverman popped her head in.

"Mr. Mayer?"

"Bring that box of letters in here, will you?"

A moment later, the secretary deposited a large box on the desk.

"Be a doll and read us a couple."

She sifted through the box for a minute and pulled out an envelope, from which she extracted a letter.

"Go on," Mayer said.

Mrs. Koverman began to read in a high-pitched singsong: " 'Dear Mr. Mayer, please make sure that you don't change anything in the book. Sincerely, Mrs. E. J. Egdemane, Sioux Falls, South Dakota.' "

Maud sat up straighter in her chair. "Ah yes, the mail. We used to receive it by the wheelbarrowful. The fans are so passionate. Did you know that my husband used to incorporate suggestions from children into the storyline whenever he could?"

Mayer sat impassively, hands folded on the desk in front of him. Maud couldn't decipher his expression.

Mrs. Koverman rummaged around and plucked out another, as if picking numbers for a game of Bingo. "This one's from, let's see . . . Edmonton, Washington. 'Dear Mr. Mayer, Nobody can play the scarecrow like Mr. Fred Stone from the Broadway show. Please see to it that he is cast in the movie.' "

Mayer grinned. "No matter that old Fred Stone has hardly been able to walk since he got wrecked in that airplane stunt, never mind dance."

"Stone is quite recuperated," Maud said tartly, but Mayer was still nodding for Mrs. Koverman to continue with her recitation.

" 'Dear Mr. Mayer, My name is Gertrude P. Yelvington. I've been reading the Oz books since I was a young girl. Judy Garland does not look like Dorothy. P.S.: Please see to it that the characters look like the illustrations done by W. W. Denslow . . . I like those the best.' "

She dropped it, fluttering, back into the box.

"You see what I'm up against," Mayer said. "Everyone has an opinion. I've been told that more than ninety million people have read one or more of the Oz books. Of course I don't need to tell *you* that, Mrs. Baum. Oz is one of the best-known stories in the world. That's both our blessing and our curse. So, you have opinions about how the movie should be? Well, take a ticket and stand in line."

Maud tried to keep her composure. She had not known what to expect from Mayer, but she had not contemplated such an abrupt and thorough disregard.

"But, Mr. Mayer—"

"Is that all, Mrs. Baum? I'm a very busy man."

Maud looked at him steadily, her mother's daughter, even now. "No, Mr. Mayer, I'm not finished. Please hear me out. You need to understand that you have an obligation. To many people, Oz is a real place. . . . And not just a real place—a better place. One that is distant from the cares of this world. There are children right now who are in difficult circumstances, who can escape to the Land of Oz and feel as if—"

"Of course, of course." Mayer waved his hand dismissively. "The story is in the best hands. You have nothing to worry about, Mrs. Baum. Thank you so much for visiting today—if something comes up we'll call. . . . Ida, take Mrs. Baum's phone number, would you?" He had already disengaged.

So much was riding on this encounter, Maud found herself grasping to explain. She wanted to say that she was the only person who could help them stay true to the spirit of the story, because she was the only one who knew the story's secrets. Yet it was difficult to articulate such an imprecise thought, especially to such an abrupt and dismissive little man. So, instead of making a reasoned argument, Maud defaulted to the truth.

"I'm here to look after Dorothy."

Mayer regarded her skeptically.

"Dorothy?"

Maud nodded. "That's right."

Mayer chuckled. "Judy Garland has a mother, Ethel Gumm, I'm sure you'll find she's quite involved in taking care of her daughter. I'd suggest you not get in her way. She's a real fireball, that one."

"Well, it's not the actress I'm concerned with . . ." Maud said. "It's Dorothy."

"The character?"

"Without Dorothy, the story is nothing."

"Mr. Mayer—" Ida Koverman interrupted, glancing at her watch. "You wanted to see Harburg and Arlen? They're working in Sound Stage One. If you leave right now, you can catch them."

Mayer jumped up and spun from behind the desk. "Why don't you come with me, Mrs. Baum?" he said. "I'll introduce you to our star. One look at our Dorothy and I'm sure your mind will be set at ease. I'm telling you, she's divine."

HOLLYWOOD

October 1938

M AUD COULD BARELY KEEP UP WITH THE SMALL MAN as he bounded onto the elevator. When the twin doors slid open, she raced after him as he crossed the polished lobby floor. They emerged into a crowded alleyway where the air was, thankfully, a bit warmer than inside. After waiting for so many weeks, rehearsing her speech in her mind, she had clearly not gotten through to him. How could she explain that she wanted to be a governess to Frank's unruly ménage of fictional creations and to fulfill her long-ago promise that she would look after Dorothy?

But she didn't have long to dwell. Mayer was ducking in and out of the throng, striding past four costumed centurions carrying shields and swords, darting around a group of jaunty sailors, and whizzing past two ballerinas walking flat-footed in their ballet slippers and pink leotards, their pointe shoes slung over their shoulders. Soon Mayer led Maud to a large building with STAGE ONE emblazoned on the door.

"The girl is going to sing," he said. "Big star, big star. Biggest voice you'll ever hear. She'll knock your socks off."

On a stage at the far end were two men. One held a pad of paper in his hands and had a pencil stuck behind his ear; the other sat at a piano tapping out chords.

Mayer showed Maud to a seat near the back—there were rows of empty chairs, each faced by an empty music stand. He then hurried up the three steps onto the stage. He looked over the shoulder of the piano player, fidgeted with some papers on top of the instrument. He did not take a seat. His sudden appearance in the building seemed to fluster the musicians. The piano player fell silent and his head sank down on his neck, a half-submerged vessel between the oceans of his shoulders.

At first Maud thought they were alone in the room—piano player, pencil-behind-the-ear man, Louis B. Mayer, and herself—but then her eye was drawn to one corner of the stage, where a bored-looking teenage girl straddled a stool, one arm tightly folded across her chest, as if she were embarrassed by the suggestion of breasts that showed through her blouse. Could this really be Dorothy?

"Shall we take it from the top then? A one, two, three . . ."

The piano player warmed up with a few bars, and the girl squinted at a pad of paper she held in her hand, then put it down on her lap. The man with the pencil behind his ear looked up and caught Maud's eye—as if he had not noticed the old woman's presence until now—then turned back to his notepad as the piano player continued.

For a small girl, she had a big mouth, and when she opened it, the sound she made was twice as big as she was.

The notes started low and then took flight, showcasing the girl's voice as it ascended. Maud could feel it vibrating deep within her chest, an emotion as much as a sound. She was so struck by the tone that at first she didn't think about the words, but as she tuned into the lyrics, her face flushed. The song was about a rainbow? Where on earth had those lyrics come from? There were no rainbows in *The Wonderful Wizard of Oz*. Nobody knew about the rainbow—besides herself and Frank. She felt a momentary flicker—that there was something familiar in this girl, in this tune—but the piano hit a false note, the girl frowned, and the sensation faded.

The piano player stopped, trying out several chord progressions. Maud looked around the room, half-expecting to see Frank.

Wouldn't that be just like him? Popping his head out from behind a doorway, eyes a-twinkle. Maud loosened her collar, slipped off her sweater. Of course, Frank was not going to appear here, at *Metro*, in 1938. He'd been gone for almost twenty years; Maud knew that perfectly well. She was not crazy. Her mind was sharp as ever. She shifted in her seat, corrected her posture, folded her hands in her lap.

After several false starts, the piano player went on, sounding out complex, resonant chords that shifted through elegant progressions. The girl's big voice effortlessly filled the room. When she stopped singing, the silence that followed seemed like the plain sister of a beautiful girl.

Peering at Mayer from under her dark fringe of lashes, the girl was clearly hoping for a note of affirmation.

"Oh, my little hunchback can certainly sing! Come over and give Daddy a hug," he said.

She slowly uncoiled from her stool, unveiling a glimpse of the woman she would soon become; then, younger again, she rushed toward him, flinging her arms around the short man, so that she knocked his glasses askew. Maud watched the spectacle uncomfortably. The girl looked to be at least fifteen and was surely too old to be quite so affectionate to a grown man. Who wasn't her father.

"And the song?" the piano player interjected.

Mayer dropped his embrace of the young actress and turned to the fellow at the piano as Judy, suddenly subdued, slunk back to her perch on the stool.

"Perfect. Excellent. Very good. Everything she sings is perfect."

"I think the song isn't quite right," Maud said.

Mayer turned and stared at her, as if he had forgotten she was there.

"Perhaps just a little bit faster next time," Mayer said.

"Not faster," Maud said, annoyed that her voice had emerged like a mouse's soft squeak. She cleared her throat. She had never had trouble speaking her mind—but the devil of old age was that sometimes she sounded frail when she didn't feel it in the least.

"The song," Maud said. "Where exactly did you say it came from?"

"Where exactly, didja say?" The piano man stood from the bench and crossed the stage, shading his eyes and peering into the darkness. "I can tell you where. I was in the car, idling at the corner of Sunset and Laurel, right in front of Schwab's . . ."

Maud was instantly intrigued. "Go on."

"That's where it came from . . . popped right into my mind. I scribbled a few bars on a receipt—right there on the dashboard of my car—and as soon as the light changed, I rushed back to the studio."

"Sunset and Laurel?" Maud said. "That's the last trolley stop."

"With all due respect, there's no trolley there," the man with the pencil behind his ear said. "The Garden of Allah Hotel is on that corner. Never seen a trolley near there."

"I'm quite aware there is no trolley there *now*. I'm speaking of the year 1910. My husband and I got off the trolley there on our first visit to Hollywood." An image of Frank rose up in front of Maud: his dust-covered white spats, crumpled gray suit, and the impressive fountain of his brown moustache as he stepped off the trolley car, onto a dirt road surrounded by orange groves, and crowed, "So this is Hollywood!"

The girl turned and stared, blinking into the dark. "Who are you?"

"Oh, we have a visitor from the Land of Oz itself—this is Mrs. Maud Baum. Her husband wrote the book," Mayer said. "Mrs. Baum, meet Judy Garland. She is going to be a huge star!"

"My *late* husband wrote the book," Maud corrected, the vivid momentary vision of Frank already fading.

"And, of course, being the widow of a man who wrote a book does not give you the slightest expertise in music," the piano man muttered, just loud enough for Maud to hear.

But the girl seemed interested. "Why? Why do you say the song is not right?" Judy stood up from her stool and walked to the edge of the stage, peering into the shadowy hall.

"Well . . ." Maud breathed in slowly to calm herself, collecting her thoughts. "It's lovely, it's just . . . something about the manner. There's not enough wanting in it."

"Not enough wanting?" the piano man said. "That's preposterous." He played a few bars, heavy on the pedal, for emphasis.

But the girl was listening. Maud could tell.

"Have you ever seen something that you wanted more than anything, but you knew you couldn't have it? Have you ever pressed your nose right up to a plate-glass window and seen the very thing you're longing for—so close you could reach out and touch it, and yet you know you will never have it?"

The girl's eyes narrowed. A faint blush crept along her cheekbones, and one corner of her mouth tugged down. She twirled a lock of hair around her finger.

"Sing it like that."

Maud studied the girl's expression. Would this girl, this would-be Dorothy, understand? Could she understand?

"She can sing it however you want!" a woman's voice called out from the shadows behind the stage. "Just say it, and she'll do it. Do what the lady says, Baby. Sing it with more wanting."

The girl's forehead puckered, and her mouth pinched into a pout. She whirled around and hissed, loud enough for Maud to hear, "Be quiet, Mother! I'm trying to listen to the lady."

"Just trying to help," her mother stage-whispered back.

Maud could now make out a middle-aged woman wearing a pink blouse and white pedal pushers, standing in the shadows at the side of the stage.

"Pardon me, ma'am," the fellow with the pencil behind his ear said to Maud. "What was it you were saying? I'm Yip Harburg, lyricist. I wanted to hear what else you had to say." The pencil man had a shock of dark hair, and the warm flash in his brown eyes was visible behind his spectacles.

"Well, about the words . . ." Maud said softly. "When she sings 'I'll go over the rainbow,' isn't that a bit too certain?"

"Too certain?" Harburg said. "I'm not sure I follow."

"Shouldn't a song about a rainbow have a little more doubt in it?" Maud said, starting tentatively but getting a little louder as she spoke. "Just because you can see a rainbow doesn't mean you know how to get to the other side. Think about it. That pot of gold—you can't ever see it, right? You have to take it on faith."

The pencil man nodded, then slipped the orange stub from behind his ear and scratched a few words on his pad of paper. "You know, I hadn't thought of it quite like that, but you could be on to something."

Maud turned back to the girl, to see if she understood, but the girl's mother now stood next to her on the stage, fussing with her hair and whispering to her in an agitated hush.

Louis B. Mayer clapped his hands twice. "Splendid! Splendid! We must be going. Keep working on it. Just continue to do as you do. . . . Don't you worry, Mrs. Baum. Chances are this song won't even make it to the final cut. No reason to think about it now."

Mayer put his arm through Maud's, directing her toward the door. As he hustled her out into the bustling alley, Maud craned her neck, trying to catch a last glimpse of the girl as the heavy sound stage door swung shut behind them.

"L.B. . . . !" someone was shouting.

"A moment, please!" Mayer said, then hurried away from Maud without even saying goodbye, leaving her alone in the crowded alley.

"But, Mr. Mayer!" Maud called out to his receding back.

"Come around whenever you like!" he called out to her. "Just don't get in the way."

Maud headed home, feeling unsettled. She'd known from the moment she'd seen Judy that she was too old to play Dorothy, who was but a girl in pigtails, forever young. But that soaring voice . . . somehow this girl, a stranger to Maud, had conveyed exactly what it felt like to be just spreading her wings, waiting to fly. Even now, in her eighth decade, Maud had not forgotten those complicated emotions: the desire to escape, to get away, to grow up—the fate of every girl.

Every girl except Dorothy.

Something had pierced Maud deep down. Was it the girl? Or was it the song, whose odd melody had burrowed into her ear and now seemed to play in the background? She drove home unable to forget the tune's haunting effect, like a Broadway overture teasing at what was to come.

FAYETTEVILLE, NEW YORK

1871

MAUD WAS TEN YEARS OLD WHEN SHE FIRST DISCOVERED that possession was nine-tenths of the law. She was hitching up her infernal skirts, hightailing it away from Philip Marvel, who had just lost his precious amber cat's-eye marble to the neighborhood's fiercest girl. Maud clutched the marble in her sweaty palm, her rawhide marble pouch banging against her wrist as she ran. Now, as always, she longed for the pockets that all the boys had. She had long been a faster runner than anyone on the street, and this in spite of her greatest handicap—her petticoat and skirt. Philip and the rest of her schoolmates were jeering at her. She could hear their footsteps pounding behind her, and the sound of their familiar taunts. She was still half a block away from home, lungs burning, but she kept running. She had won the amber cat's-eye fair and square; she knew Philip and his gang were hoping to take it back through their advantage of numbers and brute force. She had no intention of giving it up.

The Gage house in Fayetteville sat on a street corner next door to the dwelling of Mr. Robert Crouse. The fastest way to the safety of her own back porch was across the corner of his garden—but she didn't like to take this route. Perched in the center of the neighbor's kitchen garden was a scarecrow clad in a long black frock coat, a floppy black preacher's hat shading its terrifying face of straw. Maud was not generally a fearful sort, but the scarecrow bore a strong resemblance to his daunting owner, Mr. Crouse, so much so that when she was younger, she used to confuse the two. At night, before Maud fell asleep, she often imagined that the scarecrow had escaped from his perch, climbed up the rain gutter, and was peering through her bedroom window.

Maud ran on. The boys' footsteps were getting closer. Rounding the corner, she reached the bushes that ran along the side of Crouse's garden, where she caught sight of the frightful face of the scarecrow staring down at her. The boys had almost reached the corner, so she darted through a hole in a hedge of lilac bushes. Hidden among the leaves, Maud panted silently as they ran straight past. From her vantage point, she saw them slow to a walk and stop, looking around but unable to see her in her hiding place.

"Where's Maud?" Philip called out. "Gone to vote with her mother?" The boys tittered. Encouraged by the reaction, Philip raised his voice, looking around, hoping to catch sight of Maud. "At ten a little pet, at twenty a sweet coquette, at forty not married yet, at fifty a suffragette!" The boys exploded in laughter.

Maud's face flamed, and her fist closed tight around her marble. Unable to rein herself in, she called out from her retreat in the bushes, repeating every word she'd heard her mother say at home: "Women will vote! And we'll never vote for a dumbskull like Philip Marvel or his boring, long-winded, small-minded Methodist anti-suffrage father!"

At the sound of her voice, the boys whirled around. Knowing they would discover her hiding place momentarily, Maud had no choice. She had to cross Mr. Crouse's garden and climb over his side fence. If Crouse saw the girl in his yard, he'd give her a good scolding. Holding tight to her marble, she counted to three, then burst from the bushes, into Crouse's yard.

A few paces into the yard, she heard a strangled cry. She jumped back, heart pounding in her throat. At first she saw nothing, but when she crouched down to see from a different vantage point, she came face-to-face with a beak and two bright blue eyes.

It was a baby crow, hopping awkwardly across the grass, injured and probably too young to fly—ready prey for the many cats who roamed the neighborhood. Maud squatted lower to get a better look, then quickly glanced back toward Mr. Crouse's house. The door was shut, and the windows were blanks framed by curtains.

Very slowly, Maud reached out her hand. The crow peered at her with his blue eyes, as if he were considering whether or not he wanted to be Maud's friend.

Maud watched without moving until she started to feel pins and needles in her legs, but still the little black bird just stood there, cocking his head, yet not trying to escape, either.

"Maud," her mother's voice called out the back door. "Maud, it's close to supper."

Maud glanced up at Mr. Crouse's house; there was no sign of movement, so she set her marble down on the grass, then gently coaxed the injured bird onto her skirt, flipping up the cloth so that the bird was caught in its folds. Just then, she heard the creak of a door, followed by Mr. Crouse's voice calling out, "Young lady, stay out of my garden!"

Maud skedaddled fast as she could across his yard, making a beeline for the stockade fence, which separated the Gage and the Crouse properties. She had reached its wooden slats and grabbed hold, ready to climb, when she realized that something was wrong. Her hand was empty—she had set her marble down to retrieve the bird and, in her haste, had left it there. Her heart was pounding in her chest, and she could feel the tiny bird restlessly scratching the inside of her skirt.

"Maud?" Her mother's voice was just over the fence. So close to safety! She spun on her heel and ran back across the yard to the spot near the lilac bushes where she had left her marble.

Maud pounced on it, then—skirt in one hand, marble in the other—bolted back across the yard. When she got back to the fence, she faced another dilemma. With one hand clutching her skirt and the other holding the marble, how was she to scale its boards?

Mr. Crouse was crossing the yard toward her at a rapid clip. Now was not the time to hesitate. She popped the marble into her mouth and, one-handed, climbed the fence.

Just as she straddled it, Mr. Crouse reached her. He tried to catch Maud's sleeve, but it was too late: she was already sliding down the Gage side of the fence—only as she slid to safety she felt her petticoat catch, followed by a loud tearing sound. By the time she arrived, red-faced and winded, at the back door, she was wearing only her pantaloons—her skirt was still folded up, the crow scrambling inside. Maud spit the marble back into her hand. Triumph!

She looked up to see her mother peering sternly at her, but Maud couldn't miss the merriment in Mother's eyes.

"What have you got in your skirt, and where, mind you, is your petticoat?"

Maud turned to gesture at the fence, but no sooner did she point it out than mother and daughter saw the crinoline and lace disappearing as if being yanked from the other side.

Gently, she unfolded her skirt, and there was the baby crow, looking startled but none the worse for wear.

"Stealing crows from the Crouses' scarecrow?" her mother asked, with obvious amusement.

"I think he fell out of his nest. We need to feed him and find him a place to sleep."

Without a word about Maud's dirty skirt, unbraided hair, or lost petticoat, Matilda set to work with utter seriousness. She found an empty flour crate and helped Maud fashion a bed from straw. After bringing up some dried corn from the cellar, she gently placed some kernels next to the bird.

Matilda then pulled out one of the old medical volumes from her grandfather and mixed up a syrup of cane sugar and water. "If it's good enough for human babies, it is most likely to be good enough for crow babies, too."

Mr. Crow was quite settled and comfortable when a sharp rap sounded on the front door.

Matilda, smooth as always, glided across the room and opened the door.

There stood Mr. Crouse. In his hand, he held Maud's lace petti-coat.

"Mrs. Gage," he said, tipping his hat. "I'd like to speak with Mr. Gage."

"Mr. Gage is not at home right now," Matilda replied. "But I'm standing before you, so please speak your piece."

Just then, the baby crow decided to open his beak and let out a loud squawk. Maud giggled.

Mr. Crouse peered over her mother's shoulder as Maud strug-gled to put a serious expression on her face.

"Your youngest," Mr. Crouse said, "was not behaving in a man-ner that is suited to a young lady."

Maud's mother raised her chin and snatched the petticoat out of his hand.

"Good afternoon, Mr. Crouse," she said. He tipped his hat again and had not even turned all the way around when she shut the front door firmly.

Matilda was not a woman to be trifled with, and she did not ap-pear amused. She said nothing about Maud's petticoat—just tossed it in a heap on the table.

"The simplest way to avoid needing to speak to Mr. Crouse about your petticoat," she announced, "would be for you to stop wearing them." She marched upstairs and shortly came downstairs with two pairs of T.C.'s old short pants.

"From now on, why don't you simply wear these?"

It did seem like a splendid idea. Maud envied the boys their short pants and despised the skirts that slowed her down, but she got teased enough already and she couldn't imagine what would happen if she went out wearing her brother's hand-me-downs.

"Oh, Mother! Are you sure that's wise?" Maud's sister, Julia, had just entered the room, a basket of mending balanced on her hip. "Everyone will call her a terrible tomboy. Doesn't Maud get tor-mented enough?" Even though she was a decade older than Maud, she was not much taller. Her long, fawn-colored hair was twirled in an enormous coil atop her head, with a few curls pulled out to frame her face. Now her eyebrows slanted down like a line of geese heading south. "You've ripped your petticoat, Maudie? Again? I just mended it last week."

Sorry! Maud mouthed, putting a finger across her lips to indicate that she did not want Julia to tell Mother how much the boys already teased her.

Matilda waved her hand dismissively. "Mr. Crouse believes that I'm not raising your sister to be ladylike," she told Julia. "For the record, let it be known that this is true. Too much control can stunt a girl, sap her of courage, and render her weak." Maud cast a furtive glace at Julia, and sure enough, she saw her sister's mouth pucker in frustration. This was one of Mother's pet theories, that girls needed to be free in order to learn to be strong, but to Maud, it always sounded like a backhanded insult to her sister, who had left school years ago.

The front door pushed open and Papa entered. Maud flung her arms around his legs so hard that he pretended his petite daughter had almost knocked him over. Scattered across the dining room table were straw, corn husks, twine, brown paper, and all the rest of the makings of the crow hospital.

"Oh!" Matilda said, sniffing a slight burnt odor in the air. "I've forgotten entirely about our supper! Julia, quickly!" Obediently, Julia set down the mending basket and ran into the kitchen, the torn petticoat at last forgotten.

Papa's eyes crinkled as he removed his coat and hat while listening to Maud's story. He spent a long moment admiring the crow. Then Maud remembered the very best thing about the day: her cat's-eye, which she had put in a small box on the window ledge for safekeeping.

Papa held it up to the light of the gas lamp, catching its amber sparkle.

He got down on one knee and pressed it back into his daughter's hands.

"Boys will be looking to win it back," he said. "Keep your skills sharp and I trust you won't let them."

———

MATILDA SET ABOUT NURSING that crow with the same determination she brought to every task. Maud's crow grew rapidly, and soon she let him outside, where he perched on the fence, showing a fearlessness in the face of Mr. Crouse's scarecrow that Maud quite envied. Every morning, she brought him corn, and though he had learned to fly, he still stayed nearby, seeming happy with the arrangement. Maud was certain that he recognized her. He made a loud *caw-caw* sound whenever he saw her.

A few days after Mr. Crow's emancipation, however, Mr. Crouse showed up on their doorstep again. Matilda went out onto the porch, closing the door behind herself. Maud didn't hear much of the short conversation between Mother and the neighbor, but as soon as Matilda came back inside, she burst out laughing, until she was bending over and tears were rolling down her face.

"What is it?" Maud asked.

Finally, her mother caught her breath enough to tell Maud what had happened.

"It seems that our neighbor believes that our crow is mocking him," she said, wiping the tears from her eyes.

"Mocking him?" asked Julia. "What ever can he mean?"

"Apparently," Matilda said, "he believes that our crow has learned the English language, and instead of the normal cawing of a bird, our crow is taunting him by calling out his name: *Bob Crouse! Bob Crouse!*"

MAUD SAT CROSS-LEGGED IN the grass, wearing her new knee-high pants, which were ever so much more comfortable than a skirt and petticoat, and carried on a long one-sided conversation with her avian friend until he answered: *Bob Crouse, Bob Crouse*. And then Maud would reply to him, in her best crow voice: *Bob Crouse, Bob Crouse*.

One Saturday morning, Mr. Crow was in the backyard squawking when the loud crack of a shotgun sounded outside, followed by silence.

Thinking her pet crow might have been frightened away by the sound, Maud went out to the yard to investigate and saw Mr. Crouse staring out his second-story window. He waved and smiled.

Mr. Crow lay on the grass near the fence with a bullet hole straight through his heart.

"Mother!"

Maud ran across the backyard, through the kitchen, and into the parlor. Mother had her glasses on and was writing something. Maud knew not to interrupt when her mother was working, but Matilda must have heard her daughter's sobs and seen her tearstained face and was at her side in an instant.

Mother's face drained white when she saw her daughter's pet lying in a pool of blood in the grass.

"This is murder!" she said. She scooped up the crow, blood and all, and grabbed Maud's hand. They went straight down the walk and marched up onto the Crouse front porch, where Mother pounded on his brass knocker with a fury of which only she was capable.

The door opened, and there stood the offender himself, still with a big grin on his face.

Without a word, Mother unfolded her skirt to reveal their poor tortured crow. His still, glassy eye stared out at Maud, piercing her heart.

"Looks like you've got dead vermin, there, Mrs. Gage."

"This was my daughter's pet. You had no right to do what you've done."

"I'd say that was a good riddance," he retorted.

"What could you possibly have had against this poor crow?" she said. "He was no danger to your garden. He took corn straight from the palms of our hands."

"His noisy cawing kept me up all night," Mr. Crouse said. "I couldn't get a wink of sleep."

"Killing him was completely uncalled for."

"And what are you going to do about it?" He chuckled. "Are you going to write the Declaration of the Rights of Crows? 'I hold these truths to be self-evident,'" he tittered, looking down his long, bony nose. "'That all men, women, vermin, critters, and creatures of the field are created equal . . .'"

Mother's voice was steady. "I believe that to be true, Mr. Crouse. Good day." Mother's chin raised up another few inches, and from the way she grasped her daughter's hand, Maud knew that she better look proud too, even though inside her heart was breaking. Back at the Gage house, Maud burst into tears again, and Matilda reached over and pinched her arm, hard.

Maud gasped. "What did you do that for?"

"That's what *I* do," Matilda said. "You're old enough to learn that crying gets you nowhere. If you pinch yourself, it will remind you that it's better to be strong—when you're strong, then you can fight."

It was raining and blood-red maple leaves were falling in clumps later that day when they buried Mr. Crow in their backyard. Dry-eyed, Maud carried the crow's casket, which Papa had carefully fashioned out of scraps of wood. Papa dug a narrow hole in the ground just under the apple tree. Maud lowered the small box into the hole and solemnly covered it with a flat rock. Papa spoke the eulogy, and Mother added a few words about how crows were loathed for eating people's corn and dressing in black feathers but that even so, they deserved equal protection, for they possessed inalienable rights. Maud thrust her hand into the pocket of her short pants and pulled out her amber cat's-eye marble. At least she had managed to hold on to that prize. They sang "All Things Bright and Beautiful." Once they had finished up with the amens, Maud called out a loud *caw-caw* that sounded suspiciously like she was saying *Bob Crouse, Bob Crouse*. Pretty soon, they had all joined in, even Mother and Papa. That was how the funeral of Mr. Crow ended up with peals of laughter.

After that day, Maud felt better about the demise of Mr. Crow, but she soon realized that the crow's funeral had done nothing to set her mother's ire to rest. Matilda took up a crusade, writing letters to the state legislature. She was up in Albany all the time anyway, doing her business as the president of the New York State Women's Suffrage Association, and she could talk a legislator's ear off whenever she wanted something enough.

Not much later, Matilda retrieved a letter from the mail slot and fluttered it at Maud triumphantly. The New York State Legislature had passed a bill making it illegal to kill a wild animal that was being kept as a pet.

"You see, this is what the law can do. You're going to study to be an attorney. With a diploma in law, you will be able to right this wrong and many others. You will grow up to be strong and brave, and you will protect the crows of the future," she said. As Mother had assured her many times before, every man, woman, and child, Negro, believer, unbeliever, and even the critters of the field deserved an equal shot at happiness.

Maud clasped her hand around the cool surface of the cat's-eye in her pocket, but she felt, deep inside, that her mother was wrong. All the laws in the world couldn't bring her crow back, nor make her forget the forlorn look in his eye. And how was she so certain a girl could earn a degree in law? She'd never heard of any woman achieving such a thing—not even her formidable mother, not even Auntie Susan, her mother's dearest friend, the famous Susan B. Anthony! A diploma for a woman seemed even more impossible than a crow getting a fair shake in the world.

ITHACA, NEW YORK

1880

NINE YEARS LATER, MAUD GAGE STOOD ON THE PLATFORM of the train depot in Fayetteville as the steam engine pulled in, black, belching, and majestic, drowning out her words, sweeping up her skirts in a gust, and blowing wisps of hair into her mouth. Maud's hair was rolled and pinned up in the latest style, and she wore an elegant blue traveling dress. Now nineteen, she had long since folded away her hand-me-down boy's clothes. Her father stood on one side of her, her mother on the other. In the din of the approaching train, Maud could see her mother's mouth moving but was unable to hear her words. For the first time in Maud's life, the giant iron horse, the rattling clacking sounds of the rails, the deep hoot of the whistle, even the blue sky itself seemed to work together in concert to diminish her mother. Maud was leaving home to attend Cornell University, and Mother was staying behind.

Papa escorted his daughter onto the train and ushered her into a seat next to the window before settling into the one beside her.

"Big day!" he said gruffly, reaching out to envelop Maud's hand in his.

Maud felt an unexpected tug of sadness. She had already sensed how much her father was going to miss her, but these last few days she'd hardly given him a thought, packing and repacking her trunk, counting the hours and minutes until her departure. She blinked resolutely, determined not to let her feelings show. Papa continued chatting in his mild manner—making comments about the passing scenery, the fine weather, and naming merchants he did business with in the towns they passed through. But Maud was too excited to listen, answering her father's conversational gambits with monosyllables until, at last, he nodded off to sleep. Left uninterrupted, her thoughts clattered in her head like their passenger car over the tracks. She stared out the window, noting the station platforms— Homer and Cortland, Freeville and Etna—marking off a path that took her farther from home. With each passing depot, more weight lifted off her shoulders. By the time the train arrived in Ithaca, she felt so light she could float upon the air. She stepped out onto the platform certain that she was going to love her new life.

The buildings of Cornell University crested a high hill. At the college's center rose the brick-fronted form of Cornell's new women's dormitory, Sage College, its central tower jutting like an accusing finger into the sky. Maud could imagine Mother pointing at the colossal edifice and saying, "Women are equal, and here is the proof." But not everyone was as convinced of this as Matilda Joslyn Gage. In spite of the beautiful new building dedicated to women's education, the young coeds were not fully equal, not yet.

Eager to start her new life, Maud had tried not to dwell on her mother and brother T.C.'s discussions about the storms of controversy that had ensued in the male student body over the admittance of young women—the furious debates in the school's newspaper and around the dining tables in the refectory, the young men, soon to be her classmates, who had spoken out vociferously against the new policy, the faculty members who had argued that women would bring down the standing of the fledging Cornell. Maud's mother had fought hard for women to win the right to earn a diploma— something that Matilda herself had been denied. Maud's older sister, Julia, had borne the agony of her mother's dashed expectations, enrolling at Syracuse only to return home, unable to keep up due to her sick headaches and nerves. Maud understood that she had been anointed—she was not to let her mother down.

———

PAPA COULD NOT STAY LONG—the last train out of Ithaca gave him little time to linger—and so once he had seen to it that her trunk was delivered safely into her new room, they said their goodbyes. Maud clung to Papa for a final moment, burying her face in his wool coat, breathing in the scent of him, his cigar smoke and his soap. After a moment, she let go, but he held her at arm's length a bit longer. "Don't let anybody steal your marbles," he said, his voice cracking, then let go and turned away, although not fast enough for Maud to miss the tears glistening in his eyes.

Through the window she saw him retreating back into the carriage and tipping his hat before disappearing from sight. Maud realized that she was alone, for the first time in her life.

But she had not been alone for a quarter of an hour when she heard a gentle rap on the door of her new room. She opened it to find a smiling young woman whose aureole of red-gold curls was lit up by the sun streaming in the window.

"Oh, you're here! How delightful!" the girl said, walking into the room without stopping to ask her leave. "You must be Miss Gage? How do you do? I'm your roommate, Josie Baum."

Miss Baum had a freckled complexion and eyes that looked like bright blue buttons in her face. Their room, which was situated along a long corridor on the third floor, faced the quadrangle, and the window afforded a pleasant vista of its green expanse. Her new roommate, a sophomore, knew all about life in Sage, and Maud took the opportunity to ask her many questions.

"Let me take you on a tour," Josie offered. "You need to be able to find your way around."

Sage College, christened just five years earlier, in 1875, had been constructed with no expense spared; it was a three-story building with three large wings, and everything the coeds could have needed or wanted was provided for them. There were modern water closets on every floor, and bathrooms where hot water came straight from the taps. Josie toured Maud around its vast expanses, the corridors and stairways, the drawing rooms with the silk striped

wallpaper, elegant wicker upholstered armchairs, and thick Orien-
tal rugs. Each common room was equipped with its own grand
piano. There was a gymnasium for healthful exercise, an indoor
swimming pool, and an infirmary for when they were sick, a library, countless classrooms, and, of course, a large dining room
that served three hot meals a day. All that was missing were girls.
The cavernous building was mostly empty, its long hallways flanked
by empty rooms. Mr. Sage had designed the college to be large
enough to house more than two hundred young women, but fewer
than thirty brave souls had enrolled as coeds. Maud's own class
consisted of only nineteen women among a class of more than two
hundred gentlemen.

Maud spent the rest of the afternoon unpacking her trunk, while
Josie sat on her bed. Each dress Maud unfolded required a full inspection from her new friend, who was enthusiastic about all things
dress-related. This was a surprise to Maud. Mother, though particular in her own toilette, thought discussion of dresses and ribbons and lace frivolous. Besides, she seemed to assume that Maud
was the same girl who had been happy wearing boy's clothes, when,
in fact, she'd developed quite a liking for pretty frocks.

"Oh, you must wear this one to dinner tonight!" Josie said when
Maud pulled a pale yellow dress from her trunk and smoothed out
its wrinkles.

"Do you like it?" Maud asked. "I just picked it up from the dress-
maker. It's brand-new."

"It's lovely," she said. "And you simply must make a good first
impression. The young men join us for dinner. First night, you
know, everyone will be looking at the new hens."

"Hens?"

"Oh, that's what they call us," Josie said, as if it didn't bother her
at all. "You'll get used to the way we talk here, soon enough."

THE TWO WOMEN DESCENDED the broad staircase of Sage College
arm in arm. In the dining room, large tables laid with crystal and
silver glowed in the soft light of the gas lamps. Clusters of young

men were gathered on the sofas and at the small tables, and a group had gathered around the piano, where someone was playing "When 'Tis Moonlight." Maud couldn't help but focus on a tall young man with hair the color of late autumn straw standing near the piano. His solid tenor floated above the other voices; he turned to watch Josie and Maud enter.

"That's Teddy Swain," Josie said. "He's an upperclassman."

The song ended and the piano player launched into a rollicking version of "My Grandfather's Clock," sending everyone's feet tapping. Maud saw the giant expanse of polished dance floor in front of her and swirled right out into the middle of it, twirling so that the yellow skirts billowed out around her. She spun until she started to feel so dizzy that she staggered to a stop. As the room swam back into view, she saw Josie standing before her. Maud tugged on her new friend's hand.

"Come on," Maud said. "Come dance with me." Josie's face was pale, and her mouth looked carefully arranged to appear completely neutral—just her eyes, normally merry, betrayed her sense of alarm. Only then did Maud notice that the music had stopped and that all eyes were upon her. She caught sight of Teddy Swain, still standing alongside the piano, a slight smile curling his lips. This was not the time to show embarrassment. That was a lesson the taunting neighborhood boys had taught her well. So, she laughed and did another twirl. She heard a smattering of applause, and saw that Teddy Swain and some of the other boys were clapping. Turning toward them, she curtsied low. Some of the girls looked away with pained expressions; others tittered behind their hands.

"That one's lively!" a young man commented.

Josie came to Maud's rescue, locking arms with her and marching her out of the common room and down the long polished hallway, until they stopped outside the library, where no one was about.

"Miss Gage. What were you thinking? Would it not be prudent to start your introduction to society here a bit . . . well, more sedately?"

Maud was stung that her brand-new friend was criticizing her, but she could plainly see that Josie's expression was kind.

"We have a way of doing things here," Josie continued. "We girls come in for so much attention—you have no idea. You might avoid bringing attention to yourself."

"But I wasn't trying to bring attention to myself," Maud said, puzzled. "I heard the music, I saw the dance floor, and my heart was just full to bursting with the excitement of it all." She looked curiously at Josie. "Aren't you excited to be here? Oh, I mean, I know this is your second year, but we are away from home and on our own . . ."

Josie laid her hand on Maud's forearm. "You are away from home. Away from the guiding attention of those who love you. But, Miss Gage, if you wouldn't twirl like that in your own parlor, in front of your own mother and father, pray why would you choose to do it here?"

Maud stared at Josie, still confused. "Why would I not twirl in front of my own mother and father? Why, I've twirled around my own parlor more times than I can count. Is there a rule against twirling . . . ?" Maud peered at her friend. "Are you a cranky old Methodist?"

Josie's expression softened. She looked as if she was struggling not to burst out laughing.

"I'm *not* a cranky old Methodist," Josie whispered. "I'm not cranky. I'm not old. I'm not even a Methodist," she said. "I love dancing. But there is a time and a place for everything . . . and dancing is fine when others are dancing and you have been asked . . ."

"You need to be *asked* to dance?" Maud asked.

"You know, you are a most unusual person."

Maud's face crumpled. "I don't try to be unusual. I don't feel unusual. But no one has ever suggested to me that it might not be a good idea to dance when you have a dance floor in front of you and someone is playing the piano."

"Well, let me tell you something," Josie whispered. "Here at Sage, you might want to watch the other girls and see what they are doing, and try not to call too much attention to yourself."

Maud frowned. "I'm going to try to learn. It is very important that I acquit myself well here."

Josie patted her new friend on the arm. "Here are a few rules I suggest that you follow. When the gentlemen are about, don't bring up any subjects to talk about. Let them lead the conversation. If there is an awkward pause, in a pinch, you can comment on the weather."

"But why would I do that?" Maud asked.

"You truly don't know?" Josie said.

Maud shook her head.

"I can see that you have a lot to learn."

"Will you teach me?" Maud asked. "I don't mean to seem unusual."

"Have you seen the aspidistra plants, one in each corner of the common rooms?"

Maud nodded.

"You see how they stand in the corners, and you don't really notice them?"

"Yes . . ."

"That is how you want to act. If someone looks at you, they will admire your shiny green leaves and the erect way you hold yourself, but if someone is not looking at you, they might forget that you are there."

"You want me to emulate the behavior of a potted plant?" Maud said.

"I think a potted plant would be a good place to start," Josie said.

"And should I hop about?" Maud asked, hitching up her skirts and bunny-hopping down the corridor. "Because it will be most difficult to walk normally if both of my feet are planted in a pot."

At that, Josie hitched up her skirts and the two of them proceeded to hop down the empty hallway toward the dining room, their laughter ringing out.

As they reached the far end, they almost hopped right into Teddy Swain. Somehow, in a miracle of quick transformation, Josie managed to drop her skirts and reassemble her face into an expression of quiet repose, but Maud forgot to let go of her skirts and exclaimed, "Oh!"

The gentleman bowed gracefully, though Maud could see that he did so partly to hide the smile on his face.

"May I make the honor of your friend's acquaintance, Miss Baum?"

Maud, coming to her senses, let go of her skirts, smoothing them under her palms, which suddenly felt sweaty, as she looked up into the hazel eyes of Teddy Swain.

"Miss Maud Gage, may I introduce Mr. Theodore Swain."

"How do you do," Maud replied, aggravated when she heard a small squeak in her voice. She must get hold of herself.

Teddy Swain nodded. "Pleased to meet you, Miss Gage. Are you by any chance one of the Fayetteville Gages? My uncle's family has spoken of a family of that name."

"Yes," Maud said, smiling. "My father is Henry Gage. And who is your uncle?"

"We are related to the Marvel family, on my mother's side. Pastor Marvel is my mother's brother."

Maud couldn't believe it. Of all the luck that she should arrive in Ithaca to be reminded of her former tormentor. But she didn't want to let on how she felt. She thought of the potted plants and tried as best she could to emulate their expression.

"Well, I'm very pleased to make your acquaintance," she said. Teddy Swain tipped his head and held the door open for Maud and Josie to pass into the dining room.

"He's so handsome," Maud whispered to Josie, after they were seated.

"He's a big man on campus," Josie said. "President of the student body. He makes *quite* an impression on all of the girls."

AS THE WEEKS PASSED, Maud began to settle into her new life. When she walked across campus, such a wide swath of the world was in view—august brick and stone buildings crowned the top of a large hill. In the distance, she could see the rooftops of the buildings in the village of Ithaca spread out below them, the multihued autumn trees, the wide dish of the valley. The campus's broad green lawns were crisscrossed by pathways crowded with students. But as Maud hurried from building to building with her books tucked under her arm, she could not miss how much easier things were for the young male students. They controlled all of the school's institutions—the newspapers and social clubs, the sporting activities and academic groups. They clustered noisily outside the buildings, calling out to the girls as they passed. After nightfall, the girls rarely ventured outside, but they could hear the young men carousing freely across the campus's dark expanses.

The days grew shorter and colder, the sky was brilliant blue, and the red, yellow, and gold leaves brightened the campus quadrangle. Maud had not made much progress in behaving like an aspidistra. She introduced topics of conversation when young men were present. She never mentioned the weather, and she thought nothing of interrupting her male classmates in class discussions, which always caused the line of female heads (the coeds always sat in the front row) to turn and pivot toward her as if she were a squirrel and they were a line of eager hunting dogs. She had not yet had the opportunity to speak again to Teddy Swain, although she sometimes imagined that he was looking at her, and she always felt a blush form at the base of her neck as she quickly glanced away. She noticed that groups of boys sometimes stared and whispered behind their hands when she passed, but Maud tried not to let that bother her.

But one day, Maud tarried too long in the library and did not notice that it was time to leave for her botany class. She rushed pell-mell across the campus, pushed through the classroom door, and winced as it banged shut behind her. Maud could feel her bun pulling loose, and when she reached up to smooth her hair, her Latin book slipped out of her grasp and landed with a loud *thwack*, skidding along the polished floor in front of her.

To her horror, Maud spotted Teddy Swain, the corner of his lip bent up in a smirk, and she watched as if in slow motion as he began to slowly clap, until soon all the boys in the class were clapping, and hoots and whistles soon filled the air.

Maud saw Josie surreptitiously lean over and pick up the errant textbook and tuck it in her lap, and Maud ducked her head and aimed toward her seat like an eagle streaking down toward its prey, muttering to herself, "Potted plant, potted plant." But then she caught the eye of Teddy Swain, whose fingers were tucked in the sides of his mouth as he wolf-whistled, and she felt rage bubbling up inside her. Didn't the men often come in late, in twos and threes, laughing and talking as they did? Had anyone ever whistled or applauded or jeered at them? And yet the coeds were always bent on getting to all their classes early so that they could take their seats up front and avoid the spectacle of walking down the aisle with a hundred young men's eyes trained upon them.

Maud stopped dead in her tracks. She threw her shoulders back and rose to her full height. She stopped directly in front of Teddy Swain.

"Have you got something stuck in your teeth?" she asked him. "As I see you have your fingers in your mouth."

Teddy Swain appeared startled at the unexpected confrontation. He pulled his fingers from the corners of his lips and dropped his hands into his lap.

"And as for the rest of you . . ." Maud's voice rang out across the length and breadth of the hall, and the room suddenly went silent.

Maud never had a chance to decide what it was that she was going to threaten, as into the silence, the botany professor, a shrunken man with wisps of white hair that clung to his collar, injected a small cough, then a slightly bigger one, before he said, "I believe that we are turning to the phylum of the fern species today."

Maud took this chance to skid across the front of the room and plop into the seat Josie had saved for her.

"Thank you," she whispered. "That was dreadful. Why can I not learn to arrive at class on time?"

"Boys are horrid," Josie said. "Or most, anyway, or whenever they're in a group."

Maud pulled out her pencil and notebook and tried to concentrate on the professor's dry voice as he discussed the species of fern native to the Cayuga region, but all she could hear were the jeers and whistles and applause that had greeted her entrance. She did not want to learn about ferns; she wanted to be a fern, with no purpose greater than waving a bit in the wind. Was this truly the equality that Mother had searched for so dearly?

From that day on, Teddy Swain would fall silent and look away whenever she happened to pass him on campus, and when he dined at Sage College, he appeared to take great care to sit on the far side of the room. One evening, not long after the incident in the classroom, she caught sight of him across the crowded dining room, engaged in animated conversation with Clara Richards, a raven-haired sophomore who was as pretty as she was reserved. Her head was tipped up, and she was listening intently to whatever Teddy was saying to her, as if it were the most fascinating thing in the world. Maud felt a slight twinge—not quite regret, but almost. Would things have worked out differently if she could have learned the manner the other girls seemed to master so effortlessly? Would she be seated with Teddy Swain, raptly looking into his handsome face as he lectured her about weighty matters? Maud sat up straighter and resolutely shifted her gaze away from him. In truth, though she longed to fit in, she felt more compelled to be true to herself. If she were to have any hope at love, she'd have to find a man who could love her as she was, even though there seemed little likelihood that such a man existed.

ONE FRIDAY EVENING NEAR the midterm, Maud's sleep was interrupted by the sound of pebbles rattling against their third-floor window. Josie didn't stir, so Maud crept out of bed and across the room. She shoved the sash until the heavy window pushed open, and a handful of pebbles flew in and skittered across the floor. Maud leaned her head outside, hoping to see who was below.

Confused, she beheld a group of women gathered below her window. Who were these people, and what did they want? But a second later, she heard the rich tenor of Teddy Swain, slurred with drink, soon joined by his compatriots. This was no group of women—it was eight boys dressed up in women's clothing, and they were dead drunk and singing at the top of their lungs.

> *"There is a gay maiden at Sage,*
> *Who flies into a terrible rage*
> *If one says in a crowd,*
> *In a tone a bit loud,*
> *'Matilda, may I ask your age?'"*

"Oh!" Maud exclaimed, loud enough to wake Josie, who now joined her at the window.

"Close the window!" Josie whispered frantically. "You should never have opened it."

"They were throwing stones," Maud said.

"You *never* open when they throw stones," Josie said, grabbing the window and slamming it shut. "It just encourages them."

But Maud could still hear their loud, drunken voices through the closed window, and she knew that all the other girls were likely awake and could hear it, too. And she had not missed the point: they had used her mother's Christian name instead of hers. If Maud had thought that she was striking out on her own here, she had been foolish—the colossus of Matilda had come along with her. She had never really stood a chance at all.

It wasn't enough to push open the doors. You had to change minds. How could girls truly make their mark if their role models were houseplants, if their fashions scarcely allowed them to breathe? If any expression of opinion on any subject was considered by young men to be a threat? And even more so, how could they escape the basic fact that no matter how horrid the boys were, the young women still wanted to please them—because what choice had they, really? Where could they go besides back to their own homes, where they would rest under the heavy thumbs of their own mothers, or into the home of a man—with the hopes that this man would be indulgent, like Papa, and not oppressive or cruel, like so many others?

Maud was beginning to understand that she would never be like the other girls. Here at Cornell, she would always fight with her own nature just to fit in, and she would always be seen not just as herself, but also as her mother's daughter. Matilda Gage, the controversial advocate for the rights of women. In some ways, living here was more constraining than life at home, where, she had come to realize, she had been indulged in her eccentricities. The heady sense of newfound freedom she had felt on first arriving here had started to ebb away. The beautiful campus of Cornell, which had seemed so open, so vast, started to close in on her, and Maud began to understand that finding her own way here would be more elusive than she ever would have guessed.

CHAPTER
5

ITHACA, NEW YORK

1880

THE WEATHER TURNED SUDDENLY SHARP AS THE TREES AROUND
campus faded from brilliant red and orange to a wan straw color.
The young men's voices grew loud with talk of upcoming revelries
as their secret fraternities geared up for Hallowe'en, a night of
drunken rituals that were never talked about in front of the young
ladies. But it was widely known that the women of Cornell would do
best to stay indoors and learn of the men's exploits only through the
dormitory windows.

For their part, the girls could not help but think about magic
prognostications—apple peelings, egg yolks, and lighted candles
held in front of mirrors—for All Hallows' Eve was the night on
which, according to common superstition, their future husbands'
names might be revealed.

Now that the girls were settled into their routines and felt fully
comfortable around one another, they had begun to go about Sage
in loose tea gowns, without their corsets. The same girls who maintained a strict air of composure while conducting their scholarly
life on campus could be lively and gay inside the confines of the
henhouse.

The day before Hallowe'en, several girls gathered in Maud and
Josie's room, and the talk soon turned to boys. Everyone, of course,

was talking about their future husbands, but no one wanted to be the first to suggest that they try any of the rituals for themselves.

"I think I would simply faint if I looked into a mirror with a candle and saw an image appear over my shoulder. I would collapse so quickly from fright that I wouldn't ever be sensible enough to know what I saw." This from Josie Baum. Everyone knew she was sweet on her beau, Charlie Thorp.

"It would be dreadfully wicked to do such a thing," Jessie Mary said. She was a strict Presbyterian.

"I can promise you," Maud said, "that if I looked in the mirror, I know exactly what I would see."

"Oh, Maud, do tell!" Her friends leaned in with interest. Up until now, Maud had never breathed a word about having a beau. Josie thought that Maud had seemed interested in Teddy Swain before their disastrous encounter in the botany class, and Maud had never mentioned anyone in particular since.

"I would light a candle and look in the mirror, and over my shoulder"—Maud spread her hands wide, lowered her voice, and widened her eyes—"an image would appear . . ."

"Tell! Tell!" Josie said. "Who would appear in the mirror?"

"And there over my shoulder," Maud continued, "I would see a ghostly image, first faint, then bolder, and then, finally, crystal clear." She paused for effect, holding her two friends spellbound.

"Tell us!" Josie cried.

"Over my shoulder would appear—MY MOTHER!" Maud cried. "Saying, 'Maud Gage, I did not send you to get a degree in holy matrimony. I sent you to study for a diploma. You will most certainly *not* be married by Hallowe'en next. Now, get back to your studies!'"

With that, the girls collapsed in laughter.

Maud flipped over onto her stomach and stared at everyone.

"I have an idea," Maud said. "We should form our own secret society—females only." From the corner next to her wardrobe, she grabbed a broom, brandishing it high above her head. *"In hoc signo vinces!"* Maud cried. "In this sign, we conquer, and in this room, we all have a vote! Who votes that we revive the all-secret, all-female Cornell Women's Society of the Broom?"

Maud kept the broom held aloft as she looked around the room, meeting the eye of each of her friends. All of them knew the story of the super-secret all-female society. It had long been rumored that in 1872, when the first sixteen women enrolled at Cornell, the men had refused to enter into any social intercourse with these new coeds, shunning them in classes, ignoring them as they walked across campus, and banning them from ever entering in the all-male fraternities that controlled the campus's social life. To fight back against this slight, this intrepid group of young women had formed their own clandestine organization—naming it the Society of the Broom and taking as their motto *In hoc signo vinces:* "In this sign, we conquer." Of course, the men did not fail to notice the symbolism behind their choice—the broom, witches, the dark arts of women. No one discussed it publicly, but in private, the campus was scandalized that the women were being so radical.

If the group had indeed once existed, as rumored, it had long since been disbanded, but the legend of the Broom Society continued.

The relations between the sexes, while not exactly warm, had since thawed enough that the rumored society was no longer necessary, and the girls had become more interested in joining one of the nascent sorority organizations that were already being founded in other universities, particularly in the West. But the significance of their predecessors' secret society was lost upon none of them.

"Let's reconvene the Society of the Broom," Maud said. "We can hold a séance."

"Oh, Maud!" Jessie Mary breathed. "Are you a *medium*?"

"Of course not," Maud said. "But tomorrow is Hallowe'en, so why not try it?"

"I don't think it's a good idea," Josie said.

"It won't be a real séance," Maud insisted. "We're just doing it as a lark. The boys have all kinds of fun in their secret fraternities—this will be our secret ritual. We won't breathe a word about it."

"Sorcery . . ." Jessie Mary murmured, as if bewitched by the mere sound of the word.

"We all know that witchcraft and sorcery are nothing more than superstition," Maud said decisively, lowering the broom. "But I say we have a right to a little bit of fun while the boys are outside making mischief."

THE NEXT NIGHT, a few minutes before midnight, nine intrepid girls were crowded into Maud and Josie's room. Maud had placed a small table in the center of the room, and she told the girls, who were pressed shoulder to shoulder, to each place both hands on the table.

"I will act as the medium," she announced. "Because I'm not afraid of the supernatural, and I don't believe in it, so if anything happens, we'll know that it's true."

The girls all nodded their assent. No one but Maud would be bold enough to try to act as a medium.

The night of Hallowe'en was frigid and still. Sharp pinpoints of starlight shone through the window. The gas lamps were extinguished, and the girls' faces were shadowed, but their white dressing gowns glowed in the dark.

"Silence," Maud said in a firm voice. "No laughing, no giggling, no talking. We must all be perfectly still." Maud struck a match and lit a wax candle, placing it in the center of the table. The girls stared solemnly at the flame.

Matilda had always maintained an interest in the occult and spiritualist practices. But Maud herself knew little about any of it except what she had picked up from her mother. She thought this was all just playacting, though she knew from the attitude of the other girls that many of them were inclined to believe.

"On this All Hallows' Eve," Maud intoned. Josie giggled. Maud nudged her under the table. "We summon the spirits. . . . If you hear us, please give us a sign."

The room was quiet, but filled with the muffled sounds of young bodies trying to stay still: the shuffling of feet, cleared throats, loud breathing. The silence went on and on until Maud sensed that their concentration was just about to break.

Without giving any outward sign, she pushed up on the table, very slightly, until the side she was holding levitated just above the ground.

The change in the room was electric. The table seemed to move even higher now, as if several of the girls were buoying it into the air. Their faces were shadowed, so she couldn't read their expressions, but she decided to continue to play along.

"We have received a sign!" Maud said in her most dramatic voice, channeling Susan B. Anthony as she whipped up a lyceum crowd.

Maud heard Jessie Mary's audible gasp and felt her startle beside her, which only made the table shake more.

"Can you answer some of our questions?" Maud asked, in the same portentous tones.

This time, Jessie Mary didn't move, so Maud surreptitiously rocked the table herself.

The girls sat perfectly motionless, their attention rapt. Maud was enjoying herself. "Who has a question for the spirits?" she intoned, her voice grand.

The air of expectancy in the room was palpable.

Josie coughed, and a half-strangled word died on her lips.

"Josie? Do you have a question? Be bold! Speak up!"

"Well . . . I . . ."

"Spirits, Miss Josie Baum would like to ask a question. Do you agree to accept her question?"

Maud waited to see what would happen, but nothing did.

"Give us a sign." Again, silence. Maud slowly raised her knee and bumped the underside of the table, taking care not to jostle the candle too much.

The startled cries around the table satisfied Maud. It pleased her to know that the girls could get up to their own mischief without having to carouse outside like the boys.

"Miss Josephine Baum, please state your question."

"What is the name of the man I will marry?" The girls all giggled, the table jostled, and the candlelight flickered around the room.

Now Maud had to improvise. She had a strange feeling deep in the pit of her stomach: Did all the girls know she was just fooling? Or had she swept them up into something without really thinking about the consequences?

She looked around at the faces of the gathered girls, wondering what should happen next, but soon her sense of fun overtook her. With her index finger, she began a series of knocks under the table. She tapped three times, then stopped.

"Why, I believe that the spirits are spelling," Jessie Mary cried out.

"One-two-three. It must be *C*!" one of the other girls said in a hushed voice.

Counting on her fingers, Josie exclaimed, "It's *C*!"

"Charlie Thorp!" the girls cried in unison. Of course everyone knew that he was Josie's beau.

"Ask him when we will marry!" Josie said excitedly.

Maud quickly did the math in her head, figuring out when Charlie would graduate before tapping the numbers 1-8-8-3.

Soon the room was filling with questions, and Maud stopped worrying so much about whether it was obvious that she was answering everything herself.

IT WAS PAST ONE in the morning, and the girls were finally starting to tire. The candle was burning down to a stub, and the air of heady excitement was tapering down to yawns and fatigue. Maud herself was worn out. As the night had gone on, the girls had heard more shouting and revelry as packs of drunken boys had carried on below their windows. At one point they even heard the windows rattling—as if someone had thrown up pebbles—but when they looked below, they saw nothing and heard only the sounds of distant laughter. Maud was glad that the boys had seen the lights flickering and known that the girls also had secret cabals of which the men could have no part. At the same time, she wished desperately that she were outside, in the cold night and wide-open air, instead of trapped inside this stuffy room where all of the girls seemed to have anointed her as the purveyor of vital information about their future lives.

"We thank you, kind spirits, for revealing the secrets of the other world," Maud said, hoping to wrap it up for the night.

"But, Maud!" Josie cried. "We haven't asked a question for you!"

Maud had been hoping that this omission would pass unnoticed. She dreaded the indignity of asking her question only to have the question remain unanswered, because she couldn't answer it. She did not know whom she would marry.

"Yes, Maud! We must ask for Maud," cried a chorus of voices.

"No," Maud said. "I don't want to know. I don't want to ask the spirits about myself."

"Well, then I'll ask," said Josie. "Oh, spirit, please tell us the name of the man that Miss Maud Gage will marry."

Now Maud was biting her tongue. She wanted more than anything to put a halt to all this and confess that the only spirit in this room tonight had been her own—the one that no one ever tired of telling her was far too lively. The silence had grown so long that Maud thought she would die of embarrassment when into the silence a muffled rapping sound started at the window: 1 . . . 2 . . . 3 . . . 4 . . . 5, then a lengthy silence, then one more: 6.

Maud leapt up from her seat at the table so quick that she almost knocked over the candle.

"The wind is blowing," she said. "It's just a pine bough batting up against the window." She pushed open the heavy sash and frigid air rushed inside, making her shiver violently. Outside the window, she could make out the outlines of a pine tree, which was now utterly still.

"Close the window, Maud, we're all freezing in here!" Jessie Mary said.

The girls had all lost interest and were overtaken by yawning, and the stub of their candle finally sputtered out, leaving them in darkness. Tired but full of new gossip and speculation, everyone except Josie and Maud departed for their own rooms.

The two girls settled under their covers, but Maud lay awake in her bed, thinking about her own deception. She was in so deep that she couldn't possibly confess. And what of the six taps of the pine bough upon the window when the air was still outside? A sudden gust of wind, she told herself, had moved the branch—that was all. She tossed about until her bedclothes were rumpled.

At last she could keep quiet no longer. "Do you believe in spirits?" she whispered, thinking that if Josie had already fallen asleep, her friend would not hear.

But Josie was also wide-awake. "I do, I do, of course I do," Josie replied. "You heard the sounds as well as I did."

"Perhaps . . ." Maud thought again of confessing her role as a "medium," only she didn't quite dare. "Perhaps one of the girls was knocking the table?"

"But why would anyone want to do that?" Josie sounded mystified. "What good would it do to make up stories when we want real answers?"

The question hung in the air between them. Maud wasn't sure what to say. From where she sat, people often preferred made-up stories to real answers. Hadn't she spent her whole life around her mother's suffragist friends, women who always had their eyes set one hundred years in the future, imagining the welfare of their daughters' daughters' daughters while they sometimes seemed too busy to pay attention to the flesh-and-blood girls who stood before them? Was imagining that you could see the future really any different from knocking on tables in the middle of the night?

Maud lay in silence for a while, thinking about the six faint scratches against the window. *A, B, C, D, E, F*—according to superstition, she should be marrying a person named *F*. Only what if it wasn't *F* for someone's name but, rather, a big fat *F* for failure?

"Guess what?" Josie was still awake. "I suddenly realized that I know exactly who would be perfect for you. You want me to tell you?"

Maud rolled over and propped her chin up on her hand, peering at her roommate's silhouette in the other bed.

"Not at all. It doesn't interest me in the least."

"Oh come on, sure you do." Josie yawned and rustled in her bed.

"What girl doesn't want to know the name of the man she'll be married to by next year?"

"Well, you can tell it's all nonsense just from that," Maud said. "One year from now, I'll be right here where I am now, studying at Sage College."

"Oh, I can't resist telling you. I can't believe I didn't think of it right away. I know someone who is just as peculiar as you!"

"Oh, 'peculiar'! That is some compliment!" Maud said. "You've been on the lookout for a boy who is just as peculiar and odd and strange as Maud Gage?"

"No," Josie said. "That's not how I mean it. This is someone quite wonderful—he's handsome and kind, and he's funny, and ever so interesting."

"Funny and kind," Maud said. "Now, that *is* peculiar!"

"But there is something about him that's—oh, you'll just have to meet him. Come for a visit at Christmastime and I'll see that he comes to call. He's my cousin. His name is *Frank*. Frank Baum."

Frank. Maud could almost hear the faint scratching of the tree branch, although now all was silent. *A, B, C, D, E,* then *F.*

HOLLYWOOD

1939

"MRS. BAUM?"

The phone rang at Ozcot at ten o'clock on a Thursday morning. The switchboard operator's nasal voice said, "Metro-Goldwyn-Mayer Studios is on the line. Can you please hold?"

Maud gripped the receiver, frowning in concentration. This was the first time anyone from the studio had gotten in touch with her. Had Louis B. Mayer decided to enlist her help after all?

"Mrs. Baum, this is Mary Smith—I'm the unit publicist for *The Wizard of Oz*? Can you come over to the lot this morning? We have something we want to show you."

"Come over to the lot?" Maud tried to suppress the note of enthusiasm that leapt into her voice. She was thrilled to be asked but didn't want to fawn—she should not need to beg to be involved.

"We'll send a car," the woman said.

An hour later, Maud was being driven through the front gates of the studio. This time, the guard behind the glass didn't stop them at all—just issued a jaunty wave. The car pulled up in front of the sound stage. Inside, the light was dim, and it appeared that they were doing something with costumes. As her eyes adjusted to the light, Maud saw a determined young woman with a mass of blond curls hurrying toward her.

"Mrs. Baum?" she said. "I'm Mary Smith, the one who phoned you? It is *such* a pleasure to meet you. You must be wondering why we brought you here?"

"Indeed," Maud said, her tone cool as she studied the young publicist's overly bright expression. She had not forgotten the repeated snubs that had preceded this morning's abrupt invitation.

"It's just that we've had the strangest—well, let me just show you," Mary said. "We've found something that we think may be of interest to you. . . . It's just the gosh-darnedest thing . . ."

Mary Smith darted away, leaving Maud standing on the set alone—with only a bridge and a wooden wagon. On the side was painted PROFESSOR MARVEL in big gilt letters. Maud could not place this scene in Frank's book. She had expected to feel elated to finally set foot on the set of *The Wizard of Oz*. Instead, she felt disoriented, and puzzled about why she was here.

"Here it is," the publicist clucked. "This is the one!"

Curly-haired Mary had returned, now holding a faded old coat—hanger in one hand, the rest draped over her arm. Evidently, it was a costume of some kind.

Maud groped around in her handbag until she found her glasses, perching them on the end of her nose, but even with sharper vision, she did not see what was special about this garment. It was just an old suit coat with prominent lapels.

"Isn't it amazing!" the publicist shrilled, clapping her hands together in delight.

Her exclamation was loud enough that it caused a small crowd to gather around them, some people wearing costumes and makeup, others in paint-splattered coveralls, others carrying clipboards. Some of the cameramen had clambered down from their high stools. Toward the back of the group, Maud caught a glimpse of the young actress playing Dorothy.

"The costumer sent an assistant to look for old jackets in a local secondhand store. She bought up a whole rack of them. We've been testing costumes for Mr. Morgan."

Maud recognized the actor cast to play the wizard, Frank Morgan. She had kept up with the casting decisions by reading *Variety*.

He pushed toward the center of the circle, bringing with him the scent of whiskey.

"There was a hole in the front pocket," he said. "And when I pulled the lining out . . ." The actor appeared quite shaken, his face white around the edges of his makeup.

The publicist was now groping along the outside of the jacket, a huge heavy garment made of faded black broadcloth so aged it had acquired a greenish tinge.

"Here!" she said. "This is what we found. What Mr. Morgan found, to be precise."

"I pulled out the pocket," Morgan went on, seeming to have regained his composure. He now spoke in his booming theater voice: "And at once, I beheld the name. . . . A name I would never forget, mind you, as it graced the cover of the most delightful Christmas present I ever received when I was but a lad, a gift from my father, a brand-new copy of *The Wonderful Wizard of Oz*. When I saw the tag, I realized, to my utter amazement, that this jacket had once belonged to the great author himself."

He pointed to a faded name tag stitched onto the breast pocket lining.

"As you can see, it reads L. FRANK BAUM!" Morgan pronounced triumphantly.

"L. Frank Baum?" Maud was bewildered. She leaned in closer, close enough to catch the jacket's scent, hoping to pick up a trace of Frank there, but all she smelled was mothballs.

"Says so right here," Morgan repeated, holding the garment out for Maud's inspection.

Maud reached out, rubbing her finger over the tag, turning it so that one of the bright spotlights shone more directly upon it. She could make out an *L* and an *F* and a *B,* but not much else. And the jacket—now that she saw it up close, there was something familiar about it. It was a turn-of-the-century style, a long Prince Albert jacket—it was true, Frank had once worn that style. A wave of confusion suddenly washed over her. Closing her eyes, she could clearly imagine him standing vividly beside her. How could this old garment compete with the bright memories that still danced in her mind?

"It's startling, isn't it?" the publicist said, looking at Maud with round blue eyes.

Maud stared at the faded tag. Most of the printing had been rubbed off—seeing her husband's name required a squint and a good bit of fill-in-the-blanks. More clear was the tag that read, BOSTWICK & SONS, the name of a large Chicago haberdasher.

"I remember Bostwick & Sons . . ."

"So did it belong to your husband?"

Maud reached out, feeling the cloth in her hand. Many men had worn those Prince Albert jackets around the turn of the century. Bostwick & Sons had been a popular haberdasher—half the salesmen in Chicago had probably had a jacket like this one at that time.

She looked up at the publicist, trying to read her expression. What did she want from Maud?

"We were hoping you could authenticate it," the publicist insisted.

The rest of the faces gathered around her were looking at her expectantly. Maud tried to think.

Then suddenly it was as if Frank himself were standing there before her in their Chicago kitchen, his face gray with fatigue but his countenance still lit up with a sunny smile. He was back from a two-week trip selling china, and on his last stop, in Galena, Illinois, he had set the heavy trunk down on a street corner as he awaited the arrival of his livery carriage, just for a minute, and a mule had kicked it over, breaking all of the fine china inside. The cost to replace the samples was twenty cents more than he had earned during the entire trip.

She could see this scene, more than forty years past, as if it were just earlier that day, the way the light was filtering in from the window behind him so that a shadow fell across his face.

"I've got a hole in my pocket," he had said, flipping out the two waist pockets at the same time as if performing a magic trick. Several folded bits of paper flipped out, too, skittering across the floor like the secret notes kids passed in grammar school. Maud bent over to pick them up.

"And what is this?" she had asked, uncrumpling one. She flattened it out against the table where her mending basket sat.

"Nothing," Frank had said. "I'm just scribbling a few lines. It gets so dull sitting on the train that I make up stories."

"Made-up stories and holes in your pockets! That's all you've got to show for yourself, Frank Baum?" Maud's mother had called from the other room.

A moment later, Matilda had come into the kitchen with a swish of heavy skirts; she'd leaned over, plucked one of the crumpled pieces of paper from the floor, and read the words that Frank had scribbled there.

"You are clever, Frank. You should write some of these down."

Standing in that kitchen in 1892, Maud had had more important things to worry about than made-up stories and writing things down—she'd needed to get supper on the table.

"Mrs. Baum? Would you like to sit down?"

Maud snapped back to the present, noticing that everyone was staring at her.

By this time, Judy had jostled her way to the front of the assembled group. The last time Maud had seen her, she'd been wearing no makeup. Today, her skin was covered by a layer of foundation with darker lines of contour visible on each side of her nose. Her brown eyes, highlighted by heavy eyeliner and fringed with false eyelashes, glowed brightly. The layer of thick cosmetics made her look older, but her hopeful expression made her seem even younger.

"The coat belonged to the man who wrote the book?" She stared wonderingly at the jacket. "How did it end up here? Did *you* bring it?"

"Bring it?" Maud looked out at the small knot of people clustered around her. She peered over her glasses. "I most certainly did not. I'm seeing it for the first time right now."

"But what about the tag?" people were murmuring. "Does it really say his name?"

Mary Smith was looking expectantly at Maud. "It does say his name, doesn't it?"

It was starting to dawn on Maud what was going on here. Did they think that because she was old she was dim-witted?

"You know, I've been in Hollywood for thirty years now," Maud said. "And in the theater even longer . . ." She paused for effect. "You call me to the studio to see an old coat. You want to make me believe that you just happened upon an old coat that once belonged to L. Frank Baum?"

The young publicist nodded.

"Well, I think I know a publicity stunt when I see it," Maud said. "I'll allow that it's clever. The book and its author have millions of fans. If you connect the jacket to the author and the author to the moving picture, it should make for some nice press. Well done, I say."

"Oh, no, Mrs. Baum." The blonde shook her curly head like a retriever just emerged from a swimming pool. "I assure you, this is no stunt. The costumer's assistant went to a secondhand shop. She brought back a pile of old men's jackets." She gestured to a motley rack of coats of all shapes and hues. "This was just the only one that fit Morgan."

Maud tried to imagine how this would be going if Frank or her mother were here. Their worlds were full of mystical connections and wild coincidences—beautiful twists of fate that unfolded to give one's life a shape as graceful and parabolic as a perfectly plotted book. But it was Maud's blessing—or her curse; she'd never been sure which—that she could usually see the pedestrian facts behind the seemingly wild coincidences, the ropes and pulleys that held up the sets, the actors' makeup that covered age and fatigue, the dreams of lighted marquees that ended in half-filled theaters in tiny two-horse towns.

She remembered her days with the Baum Theatre Company, when it was her job to give out news—sometimes good, like payday, though other times disappointing, like a canceled show. Back then, she had decided that it was an occupational weakness among theater people to be quick to believe in magic. But, perhaps as a con-

sequence of the hard life they all led, they were also quick to become cynical once the slightest bit of humbug was exposed. Indeed,
the assembled group now looked at Maud with expressions of eager
hopefulness admixed with suspicion.

But not Judy. Her brown eyes glowed. "It must be some kind of
sign, don't you think?"

The young star was wearing a brown wig, curled into ringlets.
Her lips, painted with red lipstick, were parted. She had an open
quality, full of childlike wonder. It was not unlike the chief charac-
teristic Maud had seen in Frank himself.

"Oz itself has a magic to it," Maud said, following her instinct to
tread lightly on this girl's openhearted hope.

Judy reached out and rubbed the sleeve of the jacket. "I'm sure
this will give us good luck."

"Okay, everybody!" a man wearing chinos and a white button-
down shirt called out. "We've got to get a move on here."

"You'll stay and watch, won't you?" Mary Smith lightly touched
Maud's arm. "Let me show you where you can sit without getting in
the way." She led Maud to a viewing platform set up atop a scaffold,
with a flight of wooden stairs leading to it. Maud settled on a wooden
folding chair to watch.

In her younger days, Maud had spent many hours in the back of
darkened theaters watching rehearsals, but she soon realized that
this was quite different. The set was not a stage but, rather, a large
area broken up into several different regions—a bridge with real
water under it was on one side, and a wooden caravan with a small
burning campfire next to it was on another. Dozens of people
milled around, several clusters of cameramen perched on high
stools, men fiddled with the thick power cords that snaked everywhere, clipboard-carrying assistants darted to and fro. Judy's
mother, Ethel Gumm, leaned against a far wall, lips pursed in concentration.

The scene they were filming involved the girl crossing the
wooden bridge, an empty basket in one hand, a suitcase in the
other, as Toto followed at her heels. The bright-eyed terrier looked
as if he'd leapt straight out of the pages of the book. As Judy crossed

the bridge, the dog had to walk just behind her, and then, at just the right moment, run down the path toward his handler, who stood just off camera with a small bag of treats. Girl and dog were patiently enduring endless takes of the same short series of actions. Each time, something seemed to go wrong, which necessitated more fiddling with the lights, the power cords, and the cameras. When the cameras were rolling, Judy was the focal point of everyone's attention, but as soon as the cameras stopped, everyone ignored her. Between takes, Judy knelt down and stroked the dog, the only one who paid her any mind.

After a while, even this repetitive action ceased. It appeared that one of the cameras wasn't working, and Judy waited, speaking to no one, while the key grip and gaffer conferred. Judy was standing alone, her back to Maud, holding Toto, when a dark-haired man approached the girl from behind and tried to slip his arm over her shoulders. As he did so, the little dog growled, then let out a series of short barks. The man quickly retracted his arm.

"Now, Toto," Judy said. "Don't do that! That's not nice!" She turned bashfully to the dark-haired man. "I'm sorry, Mr. Freed."

The dog's trainer snapped his fingers, and Toto leapt down from his perch in Judy's arms and jumped up into his trainer's. Freed stepped back in, slipping his arm around her waist this time and leaning in close. Judy edged a step away, but he drew her nearer, whispering in her ear. Maud couldn't hear what the man was saying, but there was something about the heavy drape of his arm around the girl that bothered her.

The well-behaved terrier hadn't moved from his trainer's arms, but Maud noticed that the dog was watching Judy and the man carefully. When the director called out that the cast was breaking for lunch, Maud hoped to catch up with the girl, to have a private word with her and tell her something about the character of Dorothy—perhaps something she could use to help her develop the role—but Maud had no chance of reaching her. Judy, not even five feet tall, was dwarfed between the full-grown men who hurried her out the sound stage door.

FAYETTEVILLE, NEW YORK

1880

MAUD PLACED HER BAGS ON THE SIDEWALK, RAN UP THE front steps, and threw her arms around one of the big white pillars on her front porch. How odd that she had flown out of this house just a few months earlier with scarcely a look back and now felt her heart leap at the sight of it. There was something so solid and comfortable about its square frame with the four white columns out front, the wide porch, the beveled windows. The house looked anchored to the ground, the street, the neighborhood. Home. She opened the front door.

It was Christmastime, and the place was bedecked. Evergreens hung from the mantel and looped up the banister. The scent of a baking chicken floated in from the kitchen. In a sudden flood of relief, she felt her entire body go limp. It was so good to be home, away from all the worries and exhaustions of school.

With a rapid bustle of skirts and petticoats, Matilda swept into the front hall as if transported by a secret force. She was diminutive but such a strong presence that, as always, she seemed to fill the room with her aura. Maud flung herself against her mother as Matilda gathered her in her warm embrace.

"My coed is home at last!" Matilda exclaimed. "I can hardly wait for you to tell me all you've learned."

Maud blew at her bangs with a puff of breath from between pursed lips.

"I've learned a great deal about mankind," Maud said. "None of it good."

"You'll have to share every detail," Matilda said happily, seeming not to notice Maud's bleak tone.

"Let's let Maudie get herself settled before we pepper her with questions, shall we?" suggested Julia, and Maud flashed her older sister a grateful glance.

"Where's Papa?" Maud asked.

"Sleeping," Matilda said.

Maud felt a flicker of worry. "Fevers? Again?"

Matilda nodded. "I'm afraid so, but he's been a bit better these last few days. He's been waiting eagerly for your arrival. Now, let's have some dinner, shall we? You must be tired and hungry!"

JULIA SAT AT THE FOOT of Maud's bed, watching as she unpacked her traveling bag. Maud's older sister had a small head and ears that stuck out a little too far from the sides of her head. Her hair was very long, below her waist, and she always braided and coiled it, taking care to cover her ears. Somehow, the combination of the top knot, protuberant ears, and ruddy round face had always reminded Maud of a jolly teapot just about to boil. Right now, her beautiful hazel eyes, her best feature, were lit up with enthusiasm at Maud's return.

"What was it like?" Julia asked. "Tell me everything!"

"I guess that depends on what you mean."

Julia leaned forward, her face full of interest. "Did you meet any special young men?"

Maud sighed. "'Special' might not precisely be the right word for it . . ."

"I imagine that there must be quite a social whirl? Parties and dances?"

Maud, seeing her sister's eager face, did not want to disappoint. "Well, they call Sage College 'the henhouse,' and the young men do come around quite a bit. They join us for dinner—and some of them aren't so bad . . ."

Maud flounced back onto her bed and stared at the ceiling. "The truth is, most of them are horrid. The classes are interesting, and I wouldn't mind school so much if it were just us girls. Do you know how hard it is not to bring too much attention to yourself?"

Julia tucked a lock of Maud's hair behind her sister's ear. "I suppose we've all indulged you," she said. "Mother and Papa both—they've always let you be such an unfettered spirit."

"I'm an *unfettered spirit*? I've been *indulged*? What is that supposed to mean?" Maud sat up again, and with her stocking-toed feet sticking out in front of her on the bedspread, she looked like a child about to start a tantrum.

"Nothing, my beautiful. You are perfect the way you are—the beautiful lark of the Gage family."

Maud's lower lip trembled. She pinched her arm. "Do you mean to tell me that everyone *even in my own family* considers me to be a flighty bird? Did no one think to share this with me before sending me out on my own?"

Julia closed her eyes and drew a slow breath. "Maud, you are not a flighty bird—not at all. You are like a beautiful canary with all its shining plumage, and everyone delights at the sight. Mother never clipped your wings. I think she simply couldn't bear to do it. . . . I wasn't sure that was wise."

"Brilliant plumage? Clipped wings? If you are trying to make me feel better, rest assured that it is not working! Maud Gage, odd bird!"

"When you are a girl, it is a good idea to have a firm grasp of your expectations. Our lot in life is restricted, no matter what Mother and her friends might say. Sometimes it's better to know that and learn to live with it."

Maud kicked her heels against the bedspread, her brows knit in frustration. "You must be mad. A bird with clipped wings can't fly. It just hops around in the most pathetic sort of way, and when a cat comes . . . !" Maud made a loud gulping sound, pretending to be a cat swallowing a meal. "You don't want to be that bird, and neither do I! Can I tell you the most incredible thing? My dearest friend, Josie, once gave me the advice to try to act like an aspidistra plant that stands in a pot in the corner of one of the rooms."

Julia's eyes sparkled with laughter, and the hand resting upon her lap began to shake. Her sister was trying desperately not to laugh—so Maud poked her in the stomach. "Oh, go on. . . . You think it's funny!"

Julia laughed out loud. "An aspidistra plant. Now, imagine that!"

Maud leaned in and whispered earnestly: "I don't think that's the answer—clipping our wings and planting our feet. Why, if we do that, how are we any better than the heathen Chinamen who bind their ladies' feet?"

"Well, you've got nothing to worry about. You just can't be repressed—believe me, I've tried."

Maud was about to snap back another retort, but when she focused on her sister's face, she bit her tongue. Had her sister always had those fine lines around her eyes? And was that a single silver strand cutting through her fawn-brown hair? At nineteen, Maud felt just barely grown up, but Julia was twenty-nine, and how much smaller was her world, here at home, with Papa sick and Mother too busy with her suffrage work to handle the family affairs? Couldn't she tolerate her sister's chiding on her first day home from school?

"You know what?" Maud said, changing the subject. "Josie—my roommate, you remember—has invited me to come to her house for a Christmas party. She wants me to meet her first cousin."

Now Julia looked interested. "A young man?" she asked.

"Yes, indeed," said Maud, but then her cheery face was taken over by storm clouds. "I'm sure he will hate me! Or laugh at me!"

"But why would you think that?"

"You have no idea. The Cornell boys despise me—they hate me once for being Maud, and twice for being Matilda's daughter."

Julia picked at an imaginary piece of lint on the counterpane and then smoothed the front of her dress. Maud noticed just the slightest shadow crossing her sister's face, so fleeting that no one but a sister would have caught it. It had never occurred to Maud that Julia also might have had trouble finding suitors because of Matilda's reputation.

Maud regarded her sister's funny face, framed with a frizz of loose curls that never seemed to want to lie right. As she took in her intelligent eyes and her short broad nose, she felt a familiar stab of emotion. Deep down, she knew that her sister wanted nothing more than what any maiden wanted: a household of her own to run. And yet this ordinary dream seemed so elusive for Julia.

"I suppose we're not particularly marriageable!" Maud said with sudden conviction. "Who wishes to take the hand of the dog who tries to bite it!"

"Maud!" Julia exclaimed in mock horror, but then she couldn't help laughing.

"Neither of us married," Maud said. "From what I hear, there are not enough women to go around out in Dakota . . ." Maud pushed her sister's arm. "Perhaps you should go visit T.C.!" Their brother had moved to Dakota Territory several years ago. "You might make quite an impression out on the frontier."

Julia covered her mouth with her hand, but not before Maud saw that she was hiding a smile.

"I *have* a beau. His name is James Carpenter. He's trying to get enough money together to stake a claim in Dakota."

"Julia!" Maud flung her arms around her sister in excitement. "This is the most wonderful news! Do you think you'll get engaged?"

"I'm not sure. I don't want to leave with Papa so ill, and James doesn't have a lot of money. He's a bit younger than I am," Julia whispered. "Don't be shocked."

"Younger?"

"Just twenty," Julia said.

Maud tried to hide her surprise. "You have almost a full decade on him? Why, he's closer to my age than yours!" Maud placed her hand on her sister's arm. "Are you sure that's wise? It's much more usual for the age difference to fall in the other direction."

Julia's face took on a stubborn cast. "I don't find you to be so

worried about conventions when it's your own life you're considering. Has it occurred to you, my beautiful baby sister, that my op-
tions have dwindled, that I might have to make the best of what is
offered? I do love Mother, but she is so *trying*."

"Oh, but what difference does it make how old he is!" Maud
said. "Of course you need your own household. Let us not to the
marriage of true minds admit impediments! It is a marriage of true
minds, my sweet Julia, isn't it?"

Julia continued to pick at the counterpane.

"He's not got much capital, but with what I bring along it will be
enough to start up a small farm in Dakota. You won't stand in the
way of my happiness, will you, Maudie darling? You've no idea what
it feels like to have you gone and be left here behind. It's time for
me to lead my own life!"

Maud fell silent, contemplating her sister's serious expression.
"If you love him, I love him, too. What do Mother and Papa say?"

Julia held a finger up to her lips. "Mother doesn't know. We
won't tell her until our plan is almost set. As for Papa . . ." Julia
turned and looked out the window.

"Is Papa truly so ill?" Maud asked. "Why didn't anyone tell me?"

"Mother didn't want to worry you and distract you from your
studies."

So much had happened since Maud's departure. Julia with a
beau and Papa so sick. How could everything have changed in that
short time?

"Come now," Julia said. "What about this young man you are
supposed to meet?" Clearly, Julia didn't want to dwell on Papa's illness, so Maud did her best to answer. "I don't know much about
him—but listen to this: He's in the theater. He travels all over, putting on plays."

"The theater? That hardly sounds appropriate. Mother won't
want to hear of it. She wants you to focus on your studies."

Maud looked out the window. "I try so hard to be grateful. I know
how much Mother and Papa have sacrificed to send me to the university. I wish I liked it better, but I just don't."

"You won't quit, will you? Mother would be crushed!"

Maud picked up her feather pillow and swatted her sister so that bits of feather floated out and caught the amber afternoon sunlight beaming in the window. "Don't breathe a word to Mother." Maud whacked her sister with the pillow again. "I'm desperately trying to like it. I really am!"

ON CHRISTMAS EVE, the weather was cold and snowy. Josie's family was sending a sleigh to fetch Maud the eight miles to Syracuse. At half past four, the Baums' driver reined the two-horse team to a halt in front of Maud's house, helped her settle in her seat, and tucked her in warmly under thick layers of robes. Maud greeted her fellow passengers, some relations of the Baums who lived in the neighboring town of Manlius. Sleigh bells chimed as the party glided along the road that led from Fayetteville to Syracuse. Thick white flakes swirled through the air, and her breath came out in white puffs. Her hands were encased in a fur muff, resting on top of the heavy wool robes. Bundled in a thick wool coat and scarf, with the luxurious folds of her crimson velvet dress hidden underneath, she was warm, but she still shivered in anticipation of the evening's festivities.

Maud had convinced herself that she was not interested in meeting a young man, any young man. She had spent more time avoiding the gentlemen at Cornell than getting to know them. Meeting this itinerant theater man—such a peculiar profession— was certain to be awkward, and no matter how much Josie had boasted of her cousin's charm, Maud was sure she wouldn't fall for it. She was not in the market for a suitor. Her job was to pursue her studies.

A large pine wreath hung on the door of the Baum residence, a comfortable Italianate-style house on one of Syracuse's most beautiful streets. Through the front door's beveled glass, shadows moved, and then the door swung open with a tinkling of bells. Josie greeted Maud and her traveling companions warmly, helped her off with her coat, and admired her Christmas dress. Over her friend's shoulder, the room was crowded with revelers.

"He's in the front parlor," Josie leaned in to whisper conspiratorially. Then, louder: "Come in, come in!"

Josie led Maud into a spacious parlor. In the corner stood a giant, richly scented northern pine, festooned with sugarplums, ribbons, tin cutouts, and glowing candles. A gentleman was playing Christmas carols at the piano, and a group was singing; others stood in clusters, chatting gaily. Josie stepped away to greet a new group of guests at the door. Maud felt suddenly shy—she did not know any of the Baum family—but a moment later, a large woman with a shiny red face, dressed in emerald velvet, took Maud's arm in hers.

"You must be Maud Gage. You are just as pretty as my daughter said. She has told me so much about you!" Maud took an instant liking to Josie's mother, and she followed her deeper into the parlor.

"There is someone Josie wants you to meet."

The room was so crowded that the pair had to work their way around the cluster at the piano and through several conversational knots. At last they reached the small group of people her hostess had been looking for. A tall man was standing with his back toward them. Maud suddenly regretted that she had agreed to this introduction. What had she been thinking? She started to pull her arm loose of Josie's mother's grasp, but Mrs. Baum held tight. With her other hand, she reached out and tapped the gentleman on his arm, and he spun around. Maud found herself face-to-face with a slender brown-haired man with bright gray eyes and a thick, dark moustache. She felt a streak of something dark and hot plunge from her throat down through her belly.

Mrs. Baum gently pushed Maud toward him.

"This is my nephew Frank. Frank, I want you to meet Miss Maud Gage. I'm sure you will love her."

The young man tipped his head toward Maud, and a slow smile spread across his face. "Consider yourself loved, Miss Gage."

She could see a twinkle of merriment in the gentleman's eye. Was he making fun of her? He looked at her as if expecting a response.

"I consider that a promise," Maud answered tartly. "Please see that you live up to it."

She whirled away quickly, without giving him any chance to answer, only to see Josie hurrying toward her, her eyes dancing.

"So? What did you think?" Josie whispered. "Good-looking, isn't he?"

Maud clasped her hands in front of her stomach, attempting to compose herself.

"Well?" Josie said, looking at her friend with great interest.

Before Maud could decide what to say, she was interrupted by Josie's mother, who gestured them over to the piano to join the carolers.

Maud linked arms with Josie as they sang "The Holly and the Ivy." Over her shoulder, she heard one of the voices, a silvery, floating tenor, separate itself from the group, chiming in a melodic descant, but she did not turn around to see whose it was. The pianist flipped through a book of popular carols, and Maud and Josie sang joyfully, calling out the names of their favorites, still arm in arm. Maud was so caught up in the singing that she didn't think of Josie's cousin at all. By the time they had finished caroling, the young man had disappeared from sight.

SHE WAS SEATED IN another room, chatting with a small group of girls, when she looked up to see that Frank Baum had come in to join her.

"Do you mind?" he asked, gesturing to a nearby chair.

"Please," Maud said.

"I'm afraid I may have offended you," he said.

"Not at all," Maud replied. "If you offend me, you will know it immediately."

"And how will I know?" he asked, evidently amused.

"Because I'll tell you."

"My cousin Josie thinks the world of you. She has told me so much about you."

"And what kind of things did she tell you?" Maud blushed at the implication. He clearly did not know that Maud heard far too often that people were talking about her.

"Let me see if I can remember. . . . Ah, no need to remember," he said. "I have it right here!"

He fished into his breast pocket and pulled out a letter, which he began to read aloud.

" 'We had a most agreeable time on Hallowe'en,' " he read, in a warm, musical voice. " 'We girls decided to conduct a séance—' "

"She didn't!" Maud exclaimed.

Frank smiled, his expression amiable but not entirely free of mischief.

" 'All of us got clues about our future husbands—' "

Maud stood up and tried to snatch the paper from his hand, at which point he smiled and handed it to her.

" 'Except for Maud. The knocks and raps entirely ceased when we asked about her future husband.' " He was now reciting from memory. " 'I should think that the spirits were more terrified of her than she was of them!' "

Maud's temper was about to erupt. How could Josie have written to him about the séance? This was certainly not going the way she had expected it to.

" 'And then,' " he continued, still reciting from memory, " 'a tree branch started rapping on the window, and it spelled out the letter F.' "

Maud wished she could back up to the beginning of this entire meeting and start over. Every time he looked at her, she felt like a loud whirring sound started up in her ears, as though their entire conversation were taking place in a railroad car.

"So, ever since," Frank concluded, "I've been dying to meet you. I wanted to meet a young woman of whom the very spirits are terrified!"

By this point Maud was certain that he was teasing her, even if she couldn't read it in his expression.

"The spirits are not terrified of me," Maud said. "Nor I of them. I don't believe in spirits."

Appearing amused by this proclamation, the gentleman just stroked his generous moustache with the tip of one slender index finger and said nothing.

Maud was growing frustrated, but she was determined to be cordial, at least for Josie's sake, so she tried again: "So, tell me, Mr. Baum. What line of work are you in?"

"Actor," he said. "Director, stage manager. Oh, and writer. Perhaps writer should go first. I'm the principal everything in the Baum Theatre Company. It's a small company. We travel from town to town putting on our shows. It's a vagabond's life, but I couldn't ask for anything more."

"Oh," Maud said. "I don't know the first thing about theater. How does one go about becoming a theatrical man?"

"Well, I wasn't fit for anything else," Frank answered, his eyes crinkling up into a smile. "Not a whit of business sense, I'm afraid—unless that business is magic."

"Magic?"

His eyes lit up. He spread his arms wide, as if, with his long, tapered fingers, he could cast spells right in front of her.

"Isn't that what the theater is? You conjure up something out of nothing—you build a whole world from the ground up out of nothing but the images that dance around in your mind. Nothing like it. As to how I got started, my father built a theater for me—down in the oil country. I'm not ashamed to admit I was the beneficiary of his extraordinary largesse—but the plays are all mine. I do it all: the acting, the songwriting, the dancing. I even use the latest fandangos to rig up the sets. But it's all in the service of the spellbinding, transformative, elusive, otherworldly quest for magic. That's why I was so eager to meet you, Miss Baum." He peered into her eyes. "So few young ladies seem interested in this kind of thing. And here is my own cousin's friend leading a séance—you must be a most intrepid individual."

His discourse was so odd that Maud was not sure what to make of it, and yet there was something in his manner that had captured her fancy.

"I hate to disappoint you, but I'm not afraid of spirits because I don't believe in them—not because I'm so intrepid. Although, I daresay, I'm not easily scared."

Frank was gazing at her with much interest. "You're not afraid of anything?"

"Well . . . I didn't say I wasn't afraid of *anything*. I don't care for scarecrows—and I can't abide to be teased. Because I lose my temper. I guess I'm a bit afraid of my own temper."

"Scarecrows?" Frank asked as if this was the most wondrously fantastic statement he had ever heard. "Why don't you like scarecrows? They can hardly scare a crow—much less a person. Why, I've seen scarecrows who were so friendly with crows that they seemed to invite them into the cornfield for company!"

Maud tried in vain to suppress a smile before she burst out laughing. "Our neighbors had a scarecrow in their yard. I could see him from my bedroom window, and I was convinced that he was going to climb down off his perch and come after me!" she admitted.

"You must have been something as a young girl!" Frank said. "I wish I had known you then."

"Oh, you would have despised me," Maud blurted out. "I was a terrible tomboy—my mother let me run around in my brother's cast-off short pants. I climbed trees and shot marbles . . . the boys teased me, and so did the girls!"

Frank laughed and leaned closer. "I'm certain I would *never* have despised you!" he said.

"I'm so glad that you two are getting to know each other." Only now did Maud notice that Frank's aunt Josephine Baum had been hovering nearby, seeing how the matchmaking was going.

"Miss Gage was just telling me she's not fond of scarecrows," Frank said genially. "While I'm rather partial to them—the straw men and I have had some pleasant conversations through the years."

Josephine beamed at her nephew. "Frank does say the most unusual things, doesn't he? Why, I could listen to him all day. One time, we were driving to Onondaga and the whole way he told me a story about the horse who was pulling the buggy. He was just an old nag, but the way Frank told it, he had an entire life story. Remember that, Frank dear? You called him Jim the Cab Horse? You had us in stitches. Oh, I wish I could have remembered it so I could have told it to other people . . ."

Frank laughed. "I don't remember Jim the Cab Horse, Auntie, but I've found that most cab horses have quite a lot to say. They've got interesting lives, you know. They travel all over the place, seeing all kinds of things."

"Oh, Frank." His aunt smiled indulgently. "Always so fanciful. Come on into the dining room," she said to both of them. "We're about to serve dinner now."

A crimson damask tablecloth covered the table, and the place settings gleamed with silver. A goose, its golden skin crackling, was at the table's center. There was a silver tureen of oyster soup and fluffy mashed potatoes, two kinds of pudding and a beautiful mince pie. But Maud could scarcely eat. She was seated at the far end of the table, where she tried to keep herself from throwing glances toward Mr. Baum. She was hoping to have a chance to speak to him again after dinner, but then she saw him excuse himself just as the dinner was ending.

"I'm so sorry to leave early," he said to the assembled group. "But the snow is coming down hard. I need to go now, before it gets too deep for my buggy to pass."

He hurried out of the dining room with a genial wave but didn't even glance in Maud's direction. Maud followed him with her eyes, and felt her face freeze. The meeting had clearly been a failure.

The plates were cleared and the group had moved back to the piano when Maud looked up and saw Frank, now dressed in his hat and topcoat, in the doorway, a sprinkling of snow whitening his shoulders. He beckoned to her. Maud looked around. No one was watching.

Extricating herself from the group, she passed into the front foyer. "I thought you had already left," she whispered.

"I couldn't leave without speaking to you again," he said.

Maud's heart beat faster.

"I want to call on you. Tomorrow? The day after? Next week?"

"Tomorrow is Christmas Day. You can't come tomorrow!"

"I have to return to Pennsylvania with my theater company on New Year's Day."

"I'm going back to school then. I won't be home until March." She tried to sound as if she didn't care.

"I want to call on you," he repeated, then turned his head at the sound of harness bells in the street outside. "Please. I have to go— my horse is getting restless. I'm sorry to leave so suddenly like this. Please, I want to call on you before you return to Ithaca. May I?"

Maud tried to say no but found herself nodding. His face unfolded into a brilliant smile, and then tipping his hat, he opened the door and disappeared into the falling snow.

MAUD WOULD RETURN TO Fayetteville early in the morning to celebrate Christmas at home, but tonight, she was staying over at Josie's. Upstairs, after the guests had left, the two girls helped each other unbutton their Christmas dresses, unlace their corsets, and unpin their hair. At last unfettered in their loose nightgowns, they lay down next to each other in the bed.

"So, what did you think of him?" Josie asked.

Maud was flustered, for once not knowing what to say. With his talk of chatty cab horses and friendly scarecrows and magic, he seemed more than anything to be a bit strange—and yet, her memory of his face, his slow smile and steady gray eyes, seemed to float in front of her even now.

"I don't know. Yes, no, I'm not sure," Maud answered. "I don't know what happened to me. I couldn't seem to carry on any kind of sensible conversation with him."

"Oh, Frank always says the oddest things, doesn't he? I always thought you'd go together. You're both so different from other people!"

"In any case, I'm not looking for a beau," Maud said. "And I'm sure he didn't like me anyway."

The girls lay in companionable silence for a few minutes. "He did have a nice smile," Maud said. She heard Josie breathe a contented sigh.

"I knew it!" she said.

ON THE THURSDAY FOLLOWING Christmas, the Carpenter family, distant cousins on Matilda's side, were coming to call. Julia whispered to Maud that among the visitors would be her secret beau, Mr. James Carpenter. Color high and eyes shining, Julia put on her Black Watch plaid with the deep blue velvet trim. Maud worked on Julia's hair, coiling her long braid with pins to her crown, covering her ears, then smoothed the frizzy flyaways and pulled a few tendrils loose, to frame her face.

"You look beautiful!" Maud whispered.

Julia patted her hair nervously, her cheeks flushed pink. "Oh, no . . . I know I'm plain . . ." She looked anxiously in the mirror, tugging at the waistband of her dress. "I would have made a good schoolteacher, if I hadn't suffered so from nerves."

"Don't say that," Maud remonstrated. This was a familiar topic, and one that grated on Maud. She did not find her sister plain—she was petite in stature and had blunt features, but her hazel eyes sparkled with wit, and her tawny hair was beautiful. Mother had always had a plan for Julia. She would study to become a schoolteacher. But Julia, smart and bookish as she was, was not well-fitted for higher education. Her studies had been too much for her. Julia was content in the home, but Maud hated how Mother bossed her sister around. Today, Julia looked beautiful, Maud genuinely thought, and she was expecting a visit from her beau. She pinched her sister's cheeks to pinken them, then slipped her arm around Julia's waist and gave it a reassuring squeeze.

Mr. James Carpenter was thin and knobby, with a baby face that made him look even younger than his years. Maud could not help but draw an immediate comparison between this young man and the one she'd met the previous week. Whereas Frank Baum's eyes had been warm and lively, Maud found something slightly unsettling about James Carpenter's demeanor. At first she couldn't quite put her finger on it, but after seeing him return to the rum punch several times, she realized that he was intoxicated.

She was seated on one of the divans in the parlor, next to Julia, when he made his way toward them.

"You are studying at the university?" His manner seemed not completely friendly.

"I am," Maud replied. "I'm taking a degree in literature."

The young man seemed to have no reply for this, and an awkward silence followed. "And what about you? What line of work are you in?" Maud asked, trying to be polite.

"I intend to explore the field of agricultural cultivation," he said grandly. "I am currently amassing the necessary funds," he added. "I plan to depart for Dakota Territory within the year."

Without so much as a tip of the head, he spun on his heel and walked away.

"What do you think of him?" Julia whispered.

"Well, I'm not sure," Maud said. "We've only just met. But I think he's rather abrupt—and very young!"

Julia frowned. "He's not abrupt. Just ambitious! He has such a fire in him. I'm sure he'll make a success in Dakota."

"I think his passion leans more toward the rum punch," Maud muttered, but Julia did not appear to hear. She was following his form as he cut across the room.

"He's very handsome, don't you think?"

Maud was mystified that her sister could be smitten with this young man—still wet behind his ears, and not at all pleasant in his manner. But she did not want to hurt her feelings, so she simply murmured her assent.

Maud soon grew weary of the visitors and wished nothing more than to go upstairs to her room, change into a loose house dress, and read a book. At least in the henhouse she could retreat into the solitude of the library. Here at home, she was constantly forced to dress up and chatter with people who seemed dreadfully dull to her. From time to time, her thoughts floated to the strange young man with the gray eyes.

He must be waiting to see if he would receive an invitation to call at the Gage home. Maud knew that he could not come to visit unless invited—and if Matilda invited him, Maud would be signaling her interest in him. But Maud had not yet figured out a way to speak to Matilda about this. If she told her mother that she wished to receive a visit from Frank Baum, then her mother would no doubt besiege her with a lecture about focusing on her studies instead of on young men. She was so fixated on Maud's diploma that sometimes it seemed as if she wanted it for herself.

Maud was so lost in her thoughts that she barely registered that her mother had approached her.

"Maud?" she said. "Can you please help me out for a moment?" She held a piece of twine with a large iron key suspended on it.

"Of course, Mother."

"Would you fetch a gallon of cider from the cool storeroom? Cook is busy stirring the custard and can't leave the stove."

Maud nodded, pleased to have something to do besides sit like a lump in the middle of the convivial guests.

James Carpenter was leaning up against the wall near the window, speaking with Julia, but Maud had the uncomfortable sensation that his eyes were upon her as she passed.

Maud entered the kitchen, where Mary O'Meara, the Irish cook, was standing in front of the stove. Maud passed out of the kitchen and into the hallway that connected to the back storeroom. The iron key was tricky to insert into the lock; Maud was fiddling with it when she felt a presence.

"Can I give you a hand, Miss Gage?"

Startled, she dropped the key, which clattered on the brick floor. She turned to see James Carpenter standing directly behind her.

He bent down and scooped up the iron key, bending uncomfortably close as he inserted it into the lock. With a click, the door swung open, releasing a puff of colder air scented with potatoes, carrots, and straw.

"I heard your mother say that you needed to retrieve something for her, and I thought I could help you carry it." His tone was ingratiating, but his fleshy pink lips hung slack, and she could not bring herself to meet his eyes. Just inside the hallway, she was only steps away from the cozy kitchen filled with the warm scents of vanilla, sugar, and scalding milk, but she had closed the door behind herself to keep the chill from the kitchen, and she saw that in following her, he had done the same. Hadn't anyone noticed? Certainly someone would have thought that it was odd and overly familiar for a guest to follow her into the narrow hallway. But as Maud had passed through the kitchen, Mary had been concentrating on her stirring.

"Thank you kindly, Mr. Carpenter, but I'm not in the least in need of assistance," Maud said, her voice firm. "I suggest that you return to the party. Everyone will be wondering where you have gotten to."

Keeping her eyes averted, she turned and walked through the open door into the cold storage room, passing quickly across the small dark space to the shelf where the fresh jugs of cider were kept. Behind her, the storeroom door clicked shut. The room plunged into total blackness. Inside the confined space, Maud heard breathing, and she realized he had entered behind her. She turned to face toward him, backing up slowly as her eyes adjusted to the darkness.

"I am not in need of your assistance." Maud couldn't hide a slight quaver in her voice.

"I'm just here to help a pretty girl." He took a step forward.

"Please leave!"

He barked a laugh. "I would think you are used to being alone with men, as a coed . . ."

Maud's eyes had adjusted to the dim light leaking in around the hallway door. She picked up the heavy earthenware jug and assessed the distance she had to cross to reach the exit. The room was narrow, and she wasn't sure she could dart to either side of him. She took a small step forward, hoping that he would move aside, but instead he stepped toward her.

"Pray, Mr. Carpenter, leave me alone and return to the house," Maud said. "I do not need your assistance."

His laugh had an edge of rum punch in it. "Ah, Miss Maud Gage, daughter of the famous suffragette. Perhaps I'd prefer to stay and enjoy your company!" He lurched toward her.

Without thinking, Maud pitched the heavy jug as hard as she could. It caught him on the chin, sending him reeling a step back before it shattered on the bricks. Maud seized the opportunity, rushed past him, and pushed open the heavy door. She plunged with relief into the cool back hallway, and in moments she was standing in the kitchen, where she found Matilda gazing at her reproachfully.

"It's taken you so long, and you've come back empty-handed?" Matilda said.

Maud was flustered, grasping for words to describe what had just happened.

"Your dress is all wet!" Matilda said.

"I'm sorry, Mother—I dropped the jug, and the cider splattered."

At that exact moment, James Carpenter stepped into the kitchen with a heavy jug of cider in each hand.

"Here you go, Mrs. Gage," he said. "I was just giving Miss Gage a hand."

Matilda looked mystified.

"Why, Mr. Carpenter, I believe you've hurt yourself," she said.

He set the jugs on the counter, rubbed his chin with one hand, and looked startled to see the blood on his fingers.

"I must have cut myself leaning over to pick up the jugs." He caught Maud's eye as he said this, as if daring her to call his bluff.

Maud was gathering her wits to respond when Matilda said, "Maudie darling, why don't you run along upstairs so you can change?"

Maud narrowed her eyes and glared at James, hoping to communicate that her choice to say nothing would in no way let him off the hook. But James slunk out of the kitchen, avoiding her gaze. Blinking back tears, Maud cut through the crowded parlor and hurried up the stairs. In her bedroom, she took off her cider-stained dress, unlaced her corset, and threw herself on her bed. She had decided not to return to the party.

After some time, she heard the tinkle of crockery and the tread of footsteps in the hallway, and Julia came in, carrying a tray of warm custard and chamomile tea. Afraid that her sister would subject her to an interrogation, Maud picked up her novel and began to read. She hoped that Julia would recognize that she was hiding something. She had yet to figure out a way to broach this painful subject with her sister.

Julia sat on the edge of her bed, and when Maud looked up, a soft smile lit up her sister's face. From beneath the fold of her skirt, she pulled out her left hand, revealing that a thin band of gold now crossed her fourth finger.

Maud stared at the ring in horror.

"Julia? What have you done?"

"What have I done?" Julia blanched.

"Have you thought this through? I'm not sure this is wise."

Her sister's eyes glinted, now with an edge of defiance.

"Your best wishes are welcome. I'm not interested in your opinions."

THE NEXT AFTERNOON, MAUD TRIED once again to speak to Julia, when she found her alone in the front parlor.

"Sister, are you absolutely certain? Do you know enough about this young man's character?"

Julia sighed and clasped her hands in her lap, silently spinning the gold band around and around on her finger.

"How can we know the future?" Julia said. "All I know is what my life is like now. I desire to escape it." She looked Maud straight in the eye. "I've made up my mind, sister. I don't wish to speak of this matter ever again."

Matilda sat in her study, facing away from Maud, her watercolors arrayed in a brilliant palette in front of her. A half-finished painting of a vase full of forget-me-nots stood before her.

"Might I have a word with you, Mother?" Maud asked.

Matilda turned around, greeting her with a distracted air.

"What is it, Maud?"

"In the matter of Mr. James Carpenter . . . do you not have any reservations?"

"I'm not sure what you mean."

"He is closer to my age than Julia's," Maud began, trying to decide how best to articulate her reservations. "He seems—"

Matilda sighed, and Maud noticed the violet blotches that encircled her mother's eyes. Matilda was tireless, indefatigable, the author of books and speeches, the ruler of the household, the person on whom all responsibilities lay, from watching over the cooking to educating her children to saving the fate of all womankind. Maud always thought of her mother as entirely invincible, but here, in this quiet moment, Maud got a glimpse of the fact that Mother needed a rest sometimes, too.

"He has ambition, and he appears to be in good health. Would you really let the matter of age interfere in your sister's happiness? Most women marry men old enough to be their own fathers and then end up caring for the cranky and querulous men in their old age, only to find themselves widowed and obliged to move in with their children for relief."

Maud had certainly observed that this was true, even in her own family. Papa's bouts of fever confined him to bed more and more often, leaving Mother to shoulder the family's burdens alone, and though she wrote her fingers to the bone, and talked often of royalties, money never seemed to follow. Her mother's closest allies in the suffrage movement faced no such difficulties. Matilda, Auntie Susan, and Mrs. Stanton were writing a series of books together, a multivolume history of the women's suffrage movement. They'd been working on it for years, and, frankly, Mother did most of the work. Auntie Susan said that she could think but she couldn't write, and Mrs. Stanton was often too busy to help. Maud could not avoid noticing the differences in their circumstances. Auntie Susan, a single woman with no children, made large sums of money giving speeches, and Mrs. Stanton was a wealthy woman who traveled to and from the Continent without a care. But Mother had to manage the family and its finances, her own work, and all her work for the movement without much help.

"I'm getting older," Matilda said. "It would be a help if Julia were situated. . . . I'm sure you realize that she has not had the prospects that you have had."

"It's better for her to stay at home than to be married to the wrong man. How many times have you said that yourself?"

"But what possible evidence do you have against this young man?" Matilda asked. "If you have something to say, please speak your piece now."

Maud opened her mouth, intending to tell her mother about the incident in the storeroom, but before she spoke, she thought of her sister's face: her defiant expression, her certainty that she was making the right decision. What right had Maud to set Mother against Julia? Since the day Julia had quit her studies, Mother had never treated her the same. The great Matilda Joslyn Gage was impatient of weakness, intolerant of those who lacked resolve in the fight. Maud was certain that Matilda, had she been born a boy, would have taken up arms to fight for the Union, stood on the battlefield, faced down the cannons and artillery, and spurred on her comrades to fear not in the face of the fight. Alas, Mother had had to content herself handing out flags and giving speeches—cajoling the young men of her generation to fight against the evil scourge of slavery. Her battlefield was her own home, her daughters her soldiers. Julia, in Mother's view, was a deserter to the great cause of women's emancipation. And Maud knew that this was a heavy cross for her sister to bear. Maud balled her hands into fists in the folds of her skirt, blinked, swallowed, and decided, after all, to say nothing.

"Speak up, Maud. Do you have something to say?"

Instead of speaking of her sister's situation, could she not be courageous on her own behalf?

"Maudie?"

"I do have something to say, Mother, but it's on another matter."

"Your studies?" Matilda said, suddenly eager. "Have you chosen your field of concentration?"

"Not my studies, Mother. Believe it or not, I do think of other things from time to time."

Matilda frowned, but then immediately softened. "Of course, my dear. What is it that you want?"

"I'd like to receive Josie's cousin Frank Baum. Can you please invite him?"

Matilda's forehead wrinkled slightly. "Josie's cousin Frank Baum—is that Benjamin Baum's son, the proprietor of the Rose Lawn estate in Mattydale?"

Maud nodded encouragingly. "Yes, the very one. He's Josie Baum's first cousin."

"I understand that the Baums' business concerns have considerably dwindled . . ."

"I know nothing about that," Maud said.

"And what line of work is the young man in?"

"He is an actor," Maud said. "And a playwright."

Matilda paused reflectively.

"You return to Cornell in two days. I think it would be best if you continue your studies for now without the distraction of a visit from a young man—especially one in such a flighty and unstable profession. First, for you, a diploma, and second, a learned man. You deserve no less."

Matilda, certain that their interview was finished, turned her back to Maud and dipped her paintbrush into the small pot of water, carefully dabbing it against the pot's side.

"But, Mother!" Maud said.

"We'll see about it later," Matilda said. "Perhaps once the school year has ended."

"But, Mother!" Maud protested again. "That is months from now. Perhaps he will have forgotten me by then."

"And perhaps you will have forgotten him by then as well. I see little point in pursuing this. He seems like an entirely unsuitable match."

Maud could read the set of her mother's shoulders. She would engage in no further discussion.

Maud's thoughts kept circling back to the rushed conversation in the hallway at Josie's house—he had pleaded for an invitation. How would he respond to this silence? Most likely, he would simply move on, and their brief meeting would be forgotten.

By the time her school vacation had come to an end, Maud could hardly wait to return to Cornell. In spite of the difficulties she had faced there, in comparison, home had come to seem stifling and intolerable. And perhaps Josie would have some news of Frank Baum.

HOLLYWOOD

1939

A FEW DAYS AFTER THE INCIDENT WITH THE SECONDHAND-store jacket, Maud returned to M-G-M Studios, hoping to catch the young actress alone. Since the last time she had seen Judy, the thought of the girl had never been far from her mind. At odd moments, Maud would turn her head, thinking she'd heard a snatch of the song about the rainbow, only to realize it was nothing but a passing car horn or the wind in the camellia bushes outside her windows. Perhaps she could have a few minutes to speak with Judy, to get to know her a little better, to give her some hints about Dorothy. From the little she'd seen of her, she suspected that Judy might be more open-minded to her suggestions than any of the men were.

This time when Maud arrived at the studio property, she was allowed to drive past the crowd of autograph seekers thronging outside the gates. Her name had been added to the list of approved visitors for Production #1060, and the guard directed her to Sound Stage 27.

Outside the sound stage, a different guard gestured toward a red light spinning above the door, the signal that entry was prohibited because the cameras were rolling. Maud leaned up against the stucco wall to wait. The bright California sunshine reflected off the white walls of the alley, and a fringe of palm trees, visible above the rooftops, looked like a row of shaggy poodles against the clear blue sky. Maud had not been waiting long when a large group of costumed people—at least twenty—rounded the corner, chattering excitedly. Each one of them was tiny—the tallest reaching only as high as Maud's waist. Three gents wearing lederhosen, striped tights, and elf shoes with curled-up toes pulled cigarettes from their pockets and lit them up. A tiny woman in green tights with a papier-mâché flowerpot affixed to her head kept popping up on her tiptoes, trying to see over the others' heads. And an older gentleman dressed in a floor-length purple robe repeatedly bumped into the others with his especially broad-brimmed purple hat. It took a moment for Maud to realize that most of these people were chattering to each other in German.

Maud was startled by this improbable congregation, but the guard's implacable expression did not change. He pointed to the spinning light, and the group clustered around Maud, preparing to wait. She smiled down at the people around her, but no one was looking at her, distracted as they were by the fanciful sight of two gleaming black ponies in white harnesses trotting up the alley, pulling a tiny carriage behind them.

Was this a dream? She peered into the glaring light of the alleyway, convinced that surely Frank himself would be bringing up the rear of this startling parade, a twinkle in his eye and a pipe clamped between his teeth, waving his unmistakable fingers in the air and telling her that he had conjured up all of this specially to delight her. Maud remembered the day in Chicago when she'd been waiting to meet him near the gate of the Columbian Exhibition and had then caught sight of him, marching and waving majestically in the middle of a parade of courtiers accompanying the king of Spain. He had smiled at her and tipped his hat as he passed. Later, he'd explained that he'd been mistaken for part of the king's coterie and had decided to play along. That was Frank. Today, behind the black ponies, there was nothing but an empty alleyway, flooded with sunshine.

A moment later, the red light blinked off and the guard pushed the door open. Maud waited for all of the costumed Munchkins to enter before she slipped in. As her eyes adjusted to the dim light, an entire new world began to materialize. The giant warehouse-like interior had been transformed into a brightly hued paradise of blooming flowers. A miniature village stood beside a bright blue lake spanned by an elegant arched footbridge.

Maud spun slowly in a circle, taking it all in. Her first impression was that it was beautiful, like California, with its blooming flowers and blue skies; only here everything was heightened, the artificial colors more brilliant than real life.

"What do you think? Impressive, ain't it?" Maud turned to see the producer, Mervyn LeRoy, standing next to her with a big smile on his face. "Come on in and take a look," he said, gesturing grandly. "Everything is built to scale."

"Well, it's . . ." Maud looked around. She was at a loss for words. Everything was exquisitely rendered; even the graying wooden house, plopped in the middle, slightly askew, looked startlingly real. Yet unreal. A fantasy, built from the things of this world.

But now Maud's attention was drawn to an unexpected sight. Sticking out from under the crooked gray house was a pair of legs, with sequined red shoes attached to the feet.

"Oh my!" Maud's hand flew up to her mouth.

"Not a thing to worry about," LeRoy laughed. "Nobody at the end of those legs. That's the Wicked Witch of the East. She's wearing the magical slippers."

"Magical slippers?" Maud said, inching closer. "But those are red. They're supposed to be silver."

"We tried silver, but it didn't show up well in Technicolor. You wouldn't want the magic slippers to look as gray as old galoshes, now would you? Not just red slippers—they're *ruby* slippers!"

"Ruby slippers," Maud said slowly, processing this unexpected bit of news. Frank had been fascinated with color photography, experimenting with hand-colored magic lantern slides long before Technicolor had been invented. Certainly, Frank would prefer sparkling ruby slippers to magic slippers of washed-out gray.

"I suppose it's a sound decision. As long as you don't go changing the color of the Yellow Brick Road."

Leroy tipped his head back and burst out laughing. "We're building Oz from the ground up," he said. "And nobody knows how to do any of it. We're making it up as we go along. Everybody is talking about the Disney animation of *Snow White*—biggest hit picture last year, and it was a fairy tale about a bunch of dwarfs. But you know what I say? I say that if Disney can make imaginary characters seem real, then, by golly, we can make real people seem like they are imaginary. Don'tcha think, Mrs. Baum?"

Maud didn't answer.

"Mrs. Baum?"

Maud, transfixed, was staring down at her feet, which were standing on the tip of a large curlicue of yellow paint. It looped around, then straightened out, stretched for about a hundred feet on the ground, then climbed up a painted wall of scenery. For the barest moment, she felt as if Frank were standing beside her, but as she turned toward the apparition, she saw LeRoy looking at her expectantly.

"Not bad, eh? Matte painting. Looks even better on camera."

As they'd stood there, a large group of costumed Munchkins had swarmed around them, and over the tops of their heads, Maud caught sight of Judy, skipping along behind them, wearing her blue gingham Dorothy costume.

"Mrs. Baum!" she called out cheerfully. "Did you come to watch us dance?"

LeRoy looked over at Judy. "No dancing now, doll." He glanced at his watch. "You can break for lunch. We won't need you for an hour or so."

Maud saw her chance. "Judy?" She waved the girl over. "Would you let me take you to lunch?"

"Oh, I'd love to, but . . . I have to eat in the commissary."

"I can join you in the commissary," Maud said.

The girl smiled. "Sure, that would be swell!"

As Maud emerged from the dim sound stage, the sun was so

bright that the world outside looked like a wash of white. Maud followed Judy's bright blue gingham down several alleys and around a couple of corners until they emerged in front of the commissary.

Inside, tables covered with white tablecloths were crowded into a large, noisy room, filled with the sound of conversation, laughter, and the tinkling of glasses and silverware. Some of the diners appeared to be in costume—a motley crew of evening dress, cowboy wear, and military uniforms. Others wore dapper linen jackets with colorful silk handkerchiefs in their pockets and well-shined loafers, their slicked-back hair and jowly faces marking them as money men.

"That's Clark Gable," Judy said in a stage whisper. Across the room, Maud picked out Gable's familiar face. He was holding court at a table near the center of the crowded dining room, next to a voluptuous brunette in red silk. The rest of their party, a group of men in dark suits, leaned in and appeared to hang on his every word.

Being accustomed to seeing his face nine feet high, Maud was surprised by how small he looked in person. She noted a few more movie stars—Carole Lombard was sipping from a goblet, her platinum blond hair impeccably waved. Myrna Loy, dressed in a pale blue sheath, tilted her pretty face as a man in a dinner jacket whispered something in her ear. Maud would have loved to linger, but Judy led her to a secluded table near the kitchen's swinging doors that was partially hidden from the dining room by a couple of large potted palms. It was likely the worst seat in the house for stargazing, but it did afford a bit of privacy.

A uniformed busboy appeared at the table, poured out ice-cold water from a sweating silver jug into their glasses, and then silently slid away.

"You must be hungry after all that work!" Maud said brightly.

"I'm ravenous!" But then Judy's smile collapsed again. "Except I'm not supposed to eat, because this dress is too tight. They had to let it out with a safety pin today, and so now I'm in big trouble." She smiled again, and Maud marveled at the way her face was as changeable as a spring day in Dakota: sunshine, dark clouds, and sunshine again, all in the space of a minute.

"Every other day, I'm not allowed to eat a single thing," she said. "Or I won't fit into the dress. I'm positively starving. They want me to look like a little girl, not a young lady. Did you know they wanted Shirley Temple instead of me—desperately! She's not even eleven yet."

Maud frowned. "Oh dear no. Shirley Temple would have been all wrong for Dorothy."

Judy looked relieved.

Of course, Maud thought, but would never had said aloud, Judy Garland was also all wrong. She was much too old to play the part. The book's Dorothy was just a girl—maybe six or seven—though her exact age was never stated. Maud sympathized with the way Judy had tried to tame her developing figure into a girlish dress that was much too young for her. She recalled her own schoolgirl days when she had tried to hide her emerging breasts. It was disheartening to think that with all of the things that had changed for women, in-cluding education and the vote—privileges her mother had fought for but never seen come to pass—some perceptions had still not changed for girls, like the simple fact that the growth of one's own body could be seen as an act of treason.

"Not allowed to eat?" Maud said. "That sounds quite dramatic."

"They give me pills," she said. "They're supposed to make me less hungry, but they don't.

"Two grilled cheese sandwiches," Judy said to the waiter, uni-formed in black and white. He raised a single eyebrow at her but said nothing. A few minutes later, he placed a green salad with a scoop of cottage cheese on it in front of Judy, and a grilled cheese sandwich in front of Maud.

When Judy saw the salad, her mouth tightened into a furious little bow. "No matter what I order, if Mr. Mayer sees me, he tells them to bring me this horrid salad with cottage cheese—which I hate."

Without saying a word, Maud pulled the salad in front of her own place, pushing the nicely toasted grilled cheese in front of Judy. "I'm so fond of salad," Maud said. "I hope you don't mind!"

Judy shot her a grateful look, grabbed the sandwich, and took a big bite.

"So, have you read the book?" Maud asked.

"Oh, no, ma'am. I'm not much of a reader." On the set, Maud thought, Judy had appeared so confident, so effervescent, too grown-up to be Dorothy really, but one-on-one this way, she seemed young and eager to please.

"Well, that's all right. Did you know that my husband, Frank, always said that once moving pictures were perfected, people would probably not read much anymore?"

Judy seemed more interested in her sandwich than anything Maud was saying.

Maud tried again: "Did you know that there are more than three million copies of *The Wonderful Wizard of Oz* in print right now?"

"You don't say." Judy looked past Maud, fidgeting with her paper straw.

"And Mr. Baum could imagine moving pictures, ever since he saw Mr. Thomas Edison's Kinetoscope at the Columbian Exposition—probably even before he saw it. He was fascinated with photography."

Judy's hand covered her mouth. Her nostrils flared. Maud realized she was trying to suppress a yawn. This was not going well. What could Maud do to get this young girl's attention?

"I would almost say that when he sat down to write *The Wonderful Wizard of Oz*, he was writing it for the year 1939 and for somebody named Judy Garland to come along and be ready to play Dorothy. It might seem crazy to you—"

"Do you really think so?" Now Judy leaned forward, resting her chin on her clasped hands. She looked intently at Maud. "I bet every girl in the country wishes she could be the one to play Dorothy. I bet any number of them could do it better."

"Not true. They've chosen you, and for good reason. I just know you'll do a wonderful job." Maud's voice rang with conviction, even though, inside, she still did not think this young lady looked like pigtailed, skinned-kneed Dorothy. But she did look like a girl in need of encouragement, and that was something Maud could offer.

"What was he like?" Judy said suddenly. "Mr. L. Frank Baum. Was he a good man? And what did the *L* stand for? Was that his real name?"

"His first name was Lyman, but he always went by Frank. He was a very good man." Maud paused, smoothing her cotton napkin in her lap, trying to think of how to convey the essence of Frank to this young girl. "When I first met him, he was an actor in a theater company."

Maud noticed a glimmer of interest. "My father's real name was Francis, but he always went by Frank," Judy said. "He was in vaudeville. He's the one who taught me how to sing." A pained look washed across the girl's face and then retreated as fast as a foam-crested wave on Santa Monica Beach.

"That must have been lovely," Maud said.

"Well, it *was* lovely . . . when he was still around." Judy trailed off and looked searchingly at Maud. "My father is dead."

"Oh," Maud said, reaching out and placing her hand over Judy's. "I'm so sorry."

The girl's expression closed up, but Maud suspected that she wanted to talk about him, so she persisted. "I've told you about my Frank—can you tell me about yours? What was he like?"

For a moment, Judy's brown eyes seemed to be looking inward, but then she brightened. "My daddy loved to sing—and he had a terrific sense of humor. He wasn't like most stuffy old grown-ups. He could make some fun out of anything. He used to write the grocery list in rhyme, and make up a tune to go with it, and then, if he forgot what we needed, he'd sing it right there in the store." Judy giggled and dropped her voice. "Once a mean old lady with blue hair told him to stop singing because we were in a public place. I was so embarrassed I wanted to fall through the floor, but he just smiled, and said, 'May I have the pleasure?' and before long she was dancing right there among the canned peas."

"What a delightful man. You must miss him very much."

Judy took a sip of water and looked away.

"I know I miss my Frank, and he sounds just like your father. He was always making things up and making people laugh."

"When did Mr. Baum die? Was it a long time ago?" Judy looked back at Maud, her brown eyes damp.

"Oh yes, my dear, Frank has been gone for almost twenty years. I certainly never expected to live so much longer than he did, but life never seems to go as one expects, does it?"

"Do you think it was magic that brought the coat back?"

The girl was staring at the tablecloth, her brow furrowed in concentration, as if a lot was riding on Maud's reply.

"Well, I don't really know," Maud said. "What we deem magical depends a lot on our own point of view."

Judy said nothing, didn't even look up, just picked at a tiny speck on the tablecloth.

"When did you lose your father?" Maud asked.

"When I was thirteen. But I still miss him all the time. I still can't believe he's gone. Sometimes I try to talk to him. I suppose that makes me crazy."

"Oh my dear, no. That most certainly doesn't make you crazy. By the time you reach my age, you've lost all kinds of important people, and talking to those who are gone comes to seem quite in the ordinary course of things. What is it that you want to talk to him about?"

Judy fiddled with her fork, turning the tines down and raking them lightly across the cloth.

"I keep wishing . . ." She looked up. "I really can't tell you. It's, well, it's kind of a secret . . ."

"The kind of secret you can't share with anyone or the kind that might feel a little better if you had someone to share it with?"

"I'm not sure I know. How would I know if it's better to keep it to myself or to share?"

"I suppose it depends how heavy it feels. If it feels very heavy, sometimes sharing it can lighten the load."

Judy rubbed her right shoulder and frowned. "Well, it is very heavy . . ."

"Then why don't you tell me?"

"Because, I'm afraid I'll sound silly . . . or maybe—" Judy broke off. She rubbed her palm against her forearm, her eyes downcast. "Maybe I'm afraid that if I say it out loud, it will seem more likely never to happen."

"Your secret is safe with me," Maud said firmly. "I've accepted many secrets for safekeeping over the years, and I'm a most unmagical person. I think I can hold on to secrets without affecting them in the slightest."

"Well, all right," Judy said. "What I wish is . . ." She laced her fingers together, turning her palms upward.

"I wish he would give me . . . some kind of sign." Judy stared down at the crumbs on her plate.

Maud chose her words carefully.

"My husband believed very deeply in signs, and messages coming from other worlds, and all kinds of mystical and spiritual things."

"But was your husband's coat—a sign?" Judy asked.

"I think," Maud said, "that when people imagine things, such as Oz, those things take on their own life, and something seems to happen, and those things seem to have meaning . . ." If Frank were here, he would have said, *Of course it's a sign!* To him, the work of serendipity was at play all around them, never questioned, always believed in. But as much as she'd loved Frank, Maud had remained a shopkeeper's daughter, firmly anchored in the palpable things of this earth—things that could be observed and touched, measured and weighed.

Judy's voice trembled. "I was in the studio," she said. "I was singing on the NBC radio show, and my mother told me it was my big break and I couldn't miss it for anything. They turned on the radio for him in his hospital room, so that he could hear me singing, and I sang it for him . . ."

"Oh my dear child!"

"But I don't know if he heard me," she said. "What if he was asleep or, I don't know, too sick to listen? It was the only thing I could give him, so I tried to sing it as well as I could. I thought it would help him get better. But he died before I ever got to ask him.

The next day he was gone. And I keep hoping and wishing and praying that he'll give me some kind of sign, just so I'll know that he was listening. But all I hear is silence . . ."

Maud struggled to think of what she might say to console the girl, but death was hard, and sometimes no words could truly provide consolation. Instead, she reached out her hand again to clasp Judy's.

"And your mother?"

The girl's lower lip quivered. "Mother says being a star will make me happy—and of course she's right—"

"A star," Maud said.

"Even though I'm not glamorous . . ."

"Let me tell you something about stars. I once lived in Dakota, where the stars shone like bright diamonds, so close you truly believed you could reach up and pluck one from the sky. Some people are just born like that, glowing so bright. My Frank was. I don't believe that's something you can become. You're either born that way—or you're not. Just be yourself, Judy. I promise you that what you already are is good enough."

Judy wiped her mouth with her napkin, leaving a smear of bright red on the cloth. Her brown eyes glowed like wet stones in a clear stream. "You know what? That's exactly what my daddy told me. Mother always says, 'Work harder, give 'em what they want. You're going to be a star someday,' but Daddy always said, 'Judy's not *going* to be a star. She already is.' "

Just then, Maud saw the waiter approaching. She deftly switched their plates so that Judy's empty plate was in front of her and Maud's half-eaten salad rested in front of the girl.

"Dessert?" he asked.

"Black coffee," Judy said.

"Chocolate cake and a glass of milk for me," Maud said. As he retreated, she leaned toward Judy. "Hope you like chocolate cake," she whispered.

The presence of a fat slice of cake and a tall glass of milk turned the mood cheerful. Maud gave the girl a moment to let her get a head start on her cake.

"Can I ask you a question?" Judy asked through a mouthful.

"Of course! Ask me anything."

"Who was Dorothy? Was she your daughter?"

The question startled Maud, but she tried to keep her face composed. A vision of unkempt braids and faded gingham flashed before her eyes.

"No," she said, her voice tight.

Maud noticed that the clinking of silverware and glasses seemed to have stopped, and the murmur of conversation lulled. She looked up to see Clark Gable, dapper in a hound's-tooth jacket and black silk cravat, making his way across the crowded dining room, weaving among the tables with the occasional wave of his hand or nod of his head.

Maud leaned forward and whispered conspiratorially, "He's just as good-looking in person. Maybe even better!"

Judy washed down the last trace of her cake with the dregs of her milk, then wiped her face with the back of her hand.

"He's dreamy," she said.

"I've always been partial to a man with a moustache," Maud said. "But make no mistake, he's much too old for you!"

Clark Gable was about halfway across the commissary now, and as he reached their secluded corner, he popped his head behind the potted plant, winked at Judy, and gave a jaunty half salute to Maud before continuing on his way.

"I wish he were playing the Wizard," Maud said.

Judy laughed. "Me, too. . . . But I heard he got loaned out to David O. Selznick to play in *Gone with the Wind*." She polished off the cake, and Maud again switched the plates back.

Half a second later, Judy's mother appeared next to their table. Without saying hello, she tapped on her watch. "Judy, you're needed on the set. Everyone is waiting. You haven't been eating too much?"

Judy's jaw clenched and her eyes flashed black at her mother. She jumped up rapidly, dropping her napkin on the floor.

"Absolutely not!" Maud said, flashing a charming smile at Ethel. "Diet plates for both of us. I need to keep my figure trim."

Ethel did not acknowledge Maud at all. She tugged on Judy's

skirt, brushed a few imaginary crumbs from it, and hurried her out the door.

Maud could plainly see the truth of the matter. Judy Garland didn't need to lose weight—she needed to stop growing up, and *that* was something that all the cottage cheese and lettuce leaves in the world could not change.

ITHACA, NEW YORK

1881

SIX WEEKS AFTER MAUD'S RETURN TO CORNELL, WINTER had settled over Ithaca like a block of ice. Bodies hurried past each other so wrapped up in overcoats and scarves that it was often difficult to tell people apart. Maud found this an improvement over the warmer weather of fall, when walking across campus had made her feel so conspicuous.

That evening, a thin, gray sleet was falling as she picked her way across the campus from Sage. Maud was hoping that the dispiriting weather would keep most students in tonight. The fewer classmates who attended this lecture, the less unwanted attention would accrue to herself in the following days. Loyal Josie had promised to accompany her, but she was coming down with a cold, and Maud had insisted that she stay in. The other girls, Maud knew, did not want to attract attention to themselves by attending a lecture on such a radical topic as women's suffrage. While some young women participated in the scholarly clubs, only a few of the most resolute older girls showed interest in the controversial subject of the vote for women.

Inside Association Hall, a small knot of people, professors in their dark suits and vests, some seated next to their wives, were clustered in the first few rows, talking in low murmurs. About an equal number of male students were scattered in groups of four or five, islands in a sea of empty seats. Maud estimated the total number of attendees in the hall to be under thirty.

Making her way into one of the back rows, she slid into a seat, shivering. She pulled her shawl tighter around herself. Each time the doors opened, a blast of cold air sent a chill down her back.

The auditorium was still mostly empty when the soft murmur of conversation hushed as a small group of people mounted the stairs next to the auditorium stage. Maud recognized Henry Sage, the benefactor of Sage College, two faculty members, and a Unitarian pastor.

Mr. Henry Sage gave a lengthy speech about the coeducational experiment and the civilizing influence of education for women, before at last he announced, "Please welcome our distinguished speaker, Mrs. Matilda Joslyn Gage."

Her mother was not tall. Only her head and shoulders appeared over the large oak podium, her elegant face framed by soft waves of silver hair. Maud remembered the story, oft retold, of the time her mother, just twenty-one years old, asked permission to address the women's conference in Seneca Falls. Struck by stage fright, she spoke so softly that some of the women demanded that she leave the stage. But Mother wouldn't be deterred.

Maud saw none of that shy twenty-one-year-old now. At fifty-four, her mother was formidable in manner and address, her voice clear and true, her manner confident. That she believed entirely in her cause was evident, and coming from a woman of petite stature and calm, feminine ways, this resoluteness carried especial force.

Although the audience seemed generally respectful, Maud did not let down her guard. Her mother was no stranger to heckling, but Maud herself had never grown used to it. She was fiercely proud of her mother, who could stand before men and women and speak without fear. If she had been given the chance to study at Cornell, Maud didn't doubt she'd have made a brilliant career of it. But Maud's surge of filial love was tempered, as always, with a wish that she could have gone about her business on campus without her mother's notoriety following her everywhere.

She began to lose interest in her mother's speech—as much as she believed in the cause, all of this was as familiar to her as her own face in the looking glass—and soon drifted off into her own thoughts. The Navy Ball, the winter's biggest social event, was to take place in just three days and the girls had all been swept up with fittings for their gowns. Maud was thinking about her dress—white dotted Swiss with a demi-train and pink sash—but while she was looking forward to the dance, she still felt a sense of unease about it. All of her friends were now sweet on someone, except for Catherine Reid, who was interested in nothing but the study of the natural sciences and showed an innate disinclination to any sort of merriment. Maud had dreamed twice now that she was at the ball—once she awoke with a start after imagining herself waltzing in the arms of Teddy Swain, but the second time, she dreamed that she was dancing with a tall stranger with bright gray eyes.

Maud had not had a word of communication with Mr. Baum since she'd last seen him in the foyer of Josie's home on Christmas Eve. Returning to school, Josie had been all aquiver, wanting to hear news, and wondering why they had not asked Frank to come and call. She even read aloud parts of Frank's letter saying how much he had enjoyed meeting her. Maud had wanted to die inside. She was not accustomed to keeping secrets from Josie—her dearest friend—but she could think of no suitable way to address the subject. If Maud explained that Matilda would not even consider a call from the young gentleman due to his line of employment, it would seem insulting to Josie's entire family. So, instead, Maud pretended that she was not interested in suitors as she was wholly devoted to one thing, and one thing only: obtaining her diploma. Josie had taken to calling her "schoolmarm," as that is where they both knew Maud would be headed if she obtained a diploma but no husband. In dedicating Sage College, Henry Sage himself had specified that his goal in facilitating female education was to create a fallback position in case a woman found herself in a circumstance of want. A widow with a diploma could teach school, but nobody thought teaching school would be better for a woman than having her own household.

Maud was so deep in her reverie that she scarcely noticed when another cold blast of air blew down her back. She pulled her shawl tighter, unaware that someone had just opened the doors and entered the hall. But as she heard footsteps coming down the aisle behind her, she turned her head, wondering who would be arriving so late.

A figure in a dark overcoat with flecks of sleet still clinging to it was shuffling sideways into the row of seats behind her. His face was obscured by a heavy wool muffler. Something about the gentleman struck her as familiar, but she couldn't place him, and not wanting to appear to be staring, Maud quickly averted her gaze. After a few minutes, however, she started to feel as if he was looking at her.

In the past, Maud would have simply spun around and looked again, but her months at Cornell had improved her in the matter of self-regulation, and so she sat with the uncomfortable, prickly feeling, while restraining herself from further investigation. A moment later, a loud bang sounded from the back of the hall, along with a freezing gust of wind as the double doors swung open.

Into the hall and down the aisle strode a group of six Cornell men. Each had a colorful lady's skirt tied around his waist, and each had his face powdered and lips rouged. To make matters worse, each carried a broom. Matilda, seemingly unfazed, paused, and then continued. But her mother's words were soon drowned out by the loud chanting of the men, who now held their brooms aloft and began to chant in unison, *"In hoc signo vinces"*—in this sign, we conquer. The group made the circuit of the room, down the left aisle, across in front of the rostrum, and back up the right aisle. Maud, her face flaming, turned to watch, and as she spun in her seat, she turned far enough around to catch sight of the figure who had come in late. Now that he had unwrapped his muffler and removed his cap, she could see his gray eyes clearly. She was staring directly into the face of Mr. Frank Baum, who seemed to have found the embarrassing spectacle most amusing, as there was a giant grin on his face.

Matilda, without missing a beat, looked up at the departing riot-ers and said, "I suppose you all believe that all witches are wicked, and that they are long since dead, but that is simply not true. Wise women have long been accused of witchcraft! To be called a witch is a high form of compliment." And then she continued with the speech, as if the intruders were nothing but recalcitrant children who had failed to provoke their mother.

Maud sat frozen, her jaw locked. How could it be that the men had imitated her own speech and actions with the broom so precisely? Could it be that one of her own dear friends had been gossiping about her behind her back? As an insult to her mother, this was bad enough, but that it should seem to point so directly to Maud's own private mischief was troubling in the extreme. And of all the disarray that now entered Maud's mind, the worst of it was the appearance of Mr. Frank Baum in the middle of this. Maud, so startled to see him under such appalling circumstances, had whirled around to face forward without so much as acknowledging him, though she knew that he still sat almost directly behind her.

Now, overcome with emotion, Maud did the one thing that was most likely to call attention to herself: she jumped up and ran up the aisle to the back doors, from which the broom-wielding boys had so recently exited.

She swung one open and slipped into the blasting cold of the anteroom, taking care not to slam the door behind her, then looked around nervously. The costumed pranksters had already made their exit; one of the outer doors stood open, as if left ajar in haste. Maud pulled it closed and tried to compose herself. Through the hall's inner doors, she could still hear her mother's voice, now muffled.

Maud smoothed her skirts, patted her hair. But her mind's eye was still spinning in a crazy circle, one minute seeing the dressed-up boys holding the brooms, the next minute imagining the gray eyes of Frank Baum and the giant grin of mockery upon his face. Why on earth was he here in Ithaca and not on the road with his theater company in Pennsylvania? Maud could simply not think of what to do next. If she reentered the hall, she'd have to pass him; if she did not reenter, she'd have to tell her mother that she'd been overtaken by nerves and had to leave, not a story for which her mother would show much sympathy.

But before Maud had even managed to stop her mind from spinning, her speculation was cut off by the emergence of Mr. Frank Baum himself through the doorway. She found herself face-to-face with the man who had preoccupied her thoughts for so many weeks. Now in the flesh, he was so much more vividly real than the way she had imagined, that it was all she could do not to reach out and touch his cheek.

"Come with me," he whispered, nodding toward the cloakroom door.

Maud knew that the correct response to this suggestion was to refuse, but instead she allowed him to take her arm and usher her into the confined space of the cloakroom. Inside, in the semidarkness, the scent of damp wool filled her nostrils.

"What are you doing here?" she whispered.

"I came to hear Mrs. Gage's speech," he answered. His manner was easy and friendly, as if they weren't standing close to each other in a cloakroom—as if they weren't near strangers. "I'm most interested in the topic of women's suffrage."

Maud, rarely at a loss for words, felt as if her tongue were stuck to the roof of her mouth, and her heart was pounding so furiously that she was sure he must be able to hear it.

"If you are so interested in women's suffrage, perhaps you should still be inside, listening to my mother, rather than here in the cloakroom with me!" Maud burst out, in spite of herself.

But Frank only smiled, and Maud's breathing slowed. There was something about this man's presence that she found calming, even in the current unnerving circumstances.

"Miss Gage, why didn't you ask me to call? I waited and waited. Even cousin Josie couldn't get a word out of you. If you truly detest me, just say so, and I promise I'll molest you no further."

"Tell me why you are here!"

Frank looked around the cloakroom as if seeing it for the first time. "I could have stormed the podium and demanded that you listen to me, but I was afraid that would not make a favorable first impression on your mother." He said this so intently that Maud couldn't tell if he was serious or joking, and she had to cover her mouth with her hand to repress a smile.

"No, I mean, why are you in Ithaca? I thought you were touring with your play in the oil country. I was so startled when I saw you, I couldn't think straight. You gave me such a fright, I thought I would faint—except I'm not the fainting sort. I'm blessed—or cursed—with a strong constitution. Mother would say it's a blessing, but sometimes I feel as if it's a curse, because it's quite difficult to get out of things when you are never ever ill . . ." Maud clapped her hand over her mouth again. "I'm babbling, aren't I? See how flustered you've made me?"

Frank smiled even more broadly. "I should think that you would be more flustered by the spectacle of all the powdered and bewigged men brandishing broomsticks. Now, that was a sight to behold! Is that what Cornell gentlemen learn at college? If so, I feel quite relieved that I've not undertaken any further study." Frank's tone was light, but Maud's eyebrows pinched together. Was he mocking her? Had Josie confided the story of their Society of the Broom? Did he know that their protest had surely been directed squarely toward Maud herself?

She tried to wrench her mind back into the present moment. From where they stood she could no longer hear her mother speaking, and she was unsure how much longer her speech would continue; and when the speech ended and the crowd was released, a horde of coat-seeking people would storm in upon them and find her alone with a gentleman.

"You must stop talking in circles and tell me why you have come," Maud said, aware that her tone sounded severe.

"Miss Gage," he said, leaning in close to her and speaking in an urgent whisper, "I could not stay away. I've thought of nothing but you since our meeting at Christmas. I waited in vain for a message before I had to depart to rejoin my troupe. Josie said you mention me not at all. But I most desperately wanted to see you. When she wrote to me that your mother was going to speak tonight, I hazarded a guess that you might attend, and I hoped I might catch a glimpse of you, but I dare not approach you until your mother has given me permission to call."

"Mother said no!" Maud whispered, blurting out the truth. "She said it was because your profession was unstable, but I know the truth—she wants nothing to distract me from my pursuit of a diploma."

"A diploma," Frank repeated, as if bewildered. "But what need have you of a diploma—isn't it possible to learn in any setting, and does the possession of a testimonial bearing a signature and seal make a man (or a woman, I should say) any better equipped with common sense?"

"I would say no, but that is immaterial," Maud said. "I can't disappoint Mother—she has sacrificed much for me to be here."

Frank leaned even closer to her and again spoke in an urgent whisper: "But does it delight your heart?"

Maud looked straight into his gray eyes, bright even in the dim light. Did this man, almost a stranger, truly concern himself with her heart's delight?

"What delights my heart is of little consequence," Maud said. "I must return to the hall before the crowd lets out. I don't want Mother to know I went missing. Nor do I wish that our presence here be discovered. It would be disastrous for my reputation, as I'm sure you can well imagine."

"Can you leave me with no hope?" Frank asked. He was standing so close to her that she could catch his scent, a mix of wet wool, and clean soap, and something underneath that made her feel as if she were floating several inches above the ground. "Do you not wish to see me? Just say the word, and I'll go away as quickly as I came."

Maud took a deep breath, trying to memorize his scent. She gazed up into his eyes. "I do wish to see you," she said. "I do, most emphatically, I do. I will try to convince Mother."

His eyes danced. "Tell her that her daughter has got me bewitched."

Maud's mouth flew open. Her cheeks flamed. "How dare you!" For a half second she was angry, but then she laughed.

He placed his hand on her forearm. "Seriously, do you think there is a chance to persuade her?"

"I'll try. But I can't promise anything. . . . I must go immediately."

Frank reached out as if to caress her cheek; at the same moment, Maud ducked away. She knew that her mother's speech must be almost over.

She hurried out of the cloakroom, relieved that the anteroom was still empty. Frank emerged just behind her. He stood still, watching her, then stretched an arm toward her as if he wanted to detain her and uttered a single word in a hoarse whisper: *"Please!"*

"And don't ever spring yourself on me again," Maud whispered after him, though she suspected he hadn't heard, as he was already disappearing into the night, leaving nothing but a blast of frigid air behind him.

Maud composed herself, reentered the auditorium, and slipped back into her seat. When Matilda's speech concluded, Maud waited until most of the crowd had departed before walking to the front of the hall to take leave of Mother. But her mother, always perceptive to subtle changes in Maud's mood, pressed her about what was bothering her. When Maud was not forthcoming, Matilda assumed that it was the interruption of the hecklers that had flustered Maud.

"Witches are wise women. There is no greater compliment than to have a broom brandished at you. Now, study hard, my dear. Every day gets you one step closer to your diploma."

Maud embraced her mother and listened as the well-wishers gathered around her and spoke to her about the fineness of her speech, then kissed her on the cheek and said goodbye.

Outside, Maud picked her way over the icy paths toward Sage, where warm lights beckoned in the distance. She could not stop thinking about what had happened, and wondering how she was going to convince her mother to change her mind.

But as she pushed the doors open to enter Sage College, she felt a new sense of uneasiness. Someone among her small group of friends must have spread their intimate activities as gossip—and now, it seemed, Maud had been branded a witch. A *good* witch, her mother would say, not that the distinction would help any. Maud had watched her mother spend a lifetime trying to secure votes for women, to no avail. How much less likely was it that Matilda Gage would ever convince anyone that witches could be forces for good?

IN THE AFTERMATH OF Matilda's visit, Maud felt constantly on her guard. She knew that the campus was chattering about the escapades of the men during Matilda's speech, and in Sage, she tried to suppress the suspicion that girls' whispered conversations would fall silent as she passed. Josie was ever loyal, but Maud had clammed up even to her—afraid that she would be tempted to blurt out the news of her secret visit from Frank. No place seemed safe. To shelter herself from the gossip, she spent most of her time at one of the long mahogany tables in Sage Library, her *Bain's Composition Grammar,* Lounsbury's *English Language,* and *Select Poems of Tennyson* beside her. In whispers, she memorized Titania's speech to Oberon from *A Midsummer Night's Dream.*

Maud had always loved books. She had read and reread her copies of *Little Women* and *Rose in Bloom* until the spines were broken and the pages were soft. As a girl, she had enjoyed nothing more than curling up in front of the fire and listening to Matilda read aloud from Sir Walter Scott—*Rob Roy* or *The Bride of Lammermoor.* Yet, sitting in the library in silence, working out the scansion of Keats's "Ode on a Grecian Urn" with neat rows of pencil marks, Maud felt alone. In the parlor at home, reading invoked lively discussion, with Matilda pontificating, Maud arguing, and even Julia surprisingly opinionated when it came to bookish romance. Maud had imagined that her life as a coed would be full of light and life and discussion. Instead, she sat alone, aloof, her nose buried in a book, trying to rise above the gossip that seemed to follow her everywhere except the library. When not focused on her work, her mind was consistently drawn back to Christmas, to the merry dancing eyes of Frank Baum, to his insouciant and evident disregard for formal education.

One day, staring out a beveled window at fat snowflakes drifting down, she remembered Frank's odd tale about Jim the Cab Horse—how cab horses had interesting stories to tell because they went so many places. Where was Frank Baum right now on this wintry day? What was it like to be in a traveling theater? Perhaps a person could learn more from being out in the world and seeing new things every day than from being shut up in a library? Was it only six months ago that Maud had been certain that her life at Cornell would be full of adventure? And couldn't she be reading these poems anywhere? Maud imagined herself somewhere, on a train, Frank by her side, reading her Tennyson as fantastic, unfamiliar landscapes whirred by. But out the window of Sage, there was nothing moving except the snow, against a background of dark trees. The more Maud thought about Frank, the more she longed to see him again, but the winter just dragged on. February turned to March, then March to April, yet the shadows in the library and the gray skies out the window never seemed to change.

At last, small signs of spring appeared on campus, bald patches of brown grass appearing from under the snow and a few crocuses poking bravely through the sodden ground. The girls shed their heavy woolens and tied flat straw boaters on their heads. And then it was time to return home for Easter. Maud had decided. She would speak to her mother about Frank.

MATILDA WAS WRITING FURIOUSLY when Maud popped her head into her mother's small office. Two days ago, Maud had arrived home from Cornell for her spring recess.

"May I have a word with you?"

Her mother looked up, her expression conveying not so much irritation as bewilderment. Maud was most familiar with this look, the one that her mother bore when interrupted in her writing, as if beckoned from a great distance.

"Come in," Matilda said.

Maud sat on the wooden chair in the corner of the room, a familiar spot from which to have an audience with her mother.

"There is a matter I wish to discuss with you," Maud said.

Matilda nodded. "Certainly."

"You may recall that at Christmas I was introduced to Josie Baum's cousin, a gentleman by the name of Mr. Frank Baum."

Maud watched her mother's face for clues to her mood, but her mother appeared calm and attentive, giving no hints of her disposition.

"I do recall," Matilda said. "You are speaking of the young man who travels with a troupe of actors and has no steady line of employment?"

Maud sighed. "Mother, what difference does it make if you don't approve of the line of work he's in? It seems to me that you would give my own opinion more consideration . . ."

Matilda removed her glasses and rubbed the bridge of her nose, then looked out the window, where a bright spray of forsythia was visible at the back edge of the garden.

"You are surrounded by young men at college, yet your interest is being held by one who is not a student at all. You might as well go next door and marry Mr. Crouse's scarecrow, whose head is stuffed with straw."

"Mother! The very idea! Surely you don't believe that unless a man has a diploma, he has no brains at all? By that logic, every woman who has been deprived of an education, through no fault of her own, is no better than a man of straw."

Matilda smiled in spite of herself, appreciating Maud's verve in fighting back.

"Duly noted," Matilda said. Laughter bubbled up in her eyes. "What is it that you like about him?"

Maud was surprised by her mother's question. What did she like about him? She'd only met him twice. The first time, he had struck her as fanciful and unusual, and the second time the circumstances had been impromptu and, more than anything, quite unsuitable. But whenever she thought of him, she imagined his eyes, and his smile.

"I like his eyes," Maud finally said. Then, realizing that this was

most likely exactly the wrong thing to say, she sat back and waited
for her mother's retort.

To Maud's amazement, Matilda smiled. "Well, then," she said.
"That is a genuine reason—so I know you are sincere. I shall invite
him to come call. I see no harm in it, as long as you remember that
your diploma is an armamentarium against all of the poor out-
comes of women. Your father is a fine man, and so is your brother,
but don't forget that whether he be a drunk or a fool, a pauper or a
bully, a husband can drive his wife any way he wishes, just as a rag-
man drives his hack—and, Maud, you know that you do not fancy
being harnessed at all."

Maud nodded her assent, reluctantly. Her mother was certainly
right about this.

"And you know what gives a woman her freedom?" Matilda
asked.

"A diploma," Maud answered dutifully.

"Indeed," Matilda said. "Yet the heart cannot be denied. You will
have your visit from the minstrel with the beautiful eyes. Happy
now?"

Maud jumped up and threw her arms around her mother, but
Matilda was already settling her glasses on her nose and picking up
her pen, her mind back in her writing. Maud knew that her mother
was so immediately absorbed that she didn't even hear her leave
the room.

HOLLYWOOD

1939

AFTER THEIR LUNCH TOGETHER IN THE M-G-M COMMISSARY, Judy and Maud said goodbye. Judy was headed back to the new dressing room, a trailer on wheels. It had been presented to her with great fanfare, propelled onto the sound stage with a giant ribbon tied around it, for her sixteenth birthday, a sign that the studio believed that her role as Dorothy would make her a bona fide star.

Outside the commissary, Maud turned in the opposite direction, back toward the sound stages, mulling over what she'd learned about the young actress. The thought of a thirteen-year-old Judy singing her heart out, hoping that her voice would cross the airwaves to find her sick father, only to find out that he had died, pierced Maud's heart. Was she wrong to allow the girl to believe that there was some kind of magic afoot with the jacket, that Maud was somehow connected to something greater? Certainly, a bit of hope to connect with her father's spirit couldn't be a bad thing. Maybe this girl could do the part of Dorothy justice, assuming her role had been written properly. If only Maud could have a chance to read the script while there might still be time to make suggestions.

Lost in her thoughts, she rounded the corner of the alleyway leading to the sound stage at a fast clip and almost jumped out of her skin.

A scarecrow was leaning up against the wall next to the studio door, smoking a cigarette.

"Oh!" She jumped back a step.

"Beg pardon, ma'am," the Scarecrow said, nodding his head at her. "Didn't mean to frighten you."

"I didn't mean to scream. I was just surprised."

The Scarecrow eyed her reflectively as he took a slow drag on his cigarette. He was wearing a face mask made of thick rubber, leaving only a circle around his mouth and two around his eyes exposed. Real straw protruded from the edges of his costume, and wisps were scattered around his feet.

"Gotta say, your costume looks more comfortable than mine."

"It's not a costume," Maud said icily. "I'm Maud Baum. Mrs. L. Frank Baum."

"Sorry about that. Thought you might be an actress. L. Frank Baum? Isn't that the fella who wrote the book?" An ember that had been teetering on the end of his cigarette broke off and floated downward, igniting a piece of straw. In a rapid, loose-limbed motion, the fellow quickly stomped it out with the sole of his boot.

"Doesn't it make you jumpy, smoking a cigarette while you're wearing all that?" Maud asked.

"If I only had a brain, I probably wouldn't do it." He chuckled, much taken with his own wit.

"It's extraordinary . . ." Maud leaned a bit closer to inspect his rubberized face.

"A talking scarecrow? I daresay."

"No, it's your costume. It looks just like the illustrations in the book."

"I'm so glad you noticed," said a voice behind Maud. She turned to see a small man dressed in a dapper gray suit. He was holding a long cigarette holder in the V of his slender, nicotine-stained fingers. "Adrian. Costume designer." He took a puff, then blew a series of smoke rings. "I must have worn that book out poring over those illustrations. Wanted him to look as if he'd just jumped off the page. We're not finished yet. Still putting on the finishing touches."

"I think you've done a great job," Maud said, turning back to the Scarecrow. "And good luck to you, Mr. . . . Bolger, is it?"

"In the flesh," the Scarecrow said. "It's a pleasure to meet you, Mrs. Baum. I've been a fan of the Scarecrow ever since I saw the Broadway show. Can't believe I was lucky enough to land this part."

"You've got your work cut out for you. You'll be hard-pressed to equal Mr. Fred Stone's performance."

"Oh, don't I know it," Bolger said. "Did you know they asked me to play the Tin Man? I begged and pleaded to be cast as the Scarecrow. I never wanted anything as much as I wanted to play Fred Stone's role." Bolger mimed as if he were stuck on a pole, did a shuffling two-step, then straightened up, the motions so perfectly executed, down to the wisps of straw that trailed him, that Maud burst into applause.

"Thank you kindly," he said, bowing to her.

"There was only one problem with Stone," she confided. "He was such a terrific dancer, he completely upstaged Dorothy. I trust you'll take care not to do that."

"Oh sure." He winked. "Would never try to upstage a little girl. Wouldn't want one single clap of applause more than I deserve."

Maud found this fellow engaging—a bit of a wag, for sure, but she sensed that his kindness was genuine. He'd be kind enough, she hoped, to look out for his young costar. Maud thought of Judy's difficult mother, of Mr. Freed pulling the girl a bit too close. "Tell me, Mr. Bolger, have you ever read the book? *The Wonderful Wizard of Oz*?"

"Beg pardon, ma'am?" He pointed his straw-filled glove toward his ear. "Speak up. It's hard to hear through all this rubber."

Maud leaned in. She could smell the rubber, dusty straw, and perspiration. The dust tickled her nose, and she almost sneezed. "I was wondering if you'd ever read the book."

A smile lit up his face. "I have indeed. Read all of 'em. Loved those books when I was a kid. Scarecrow, Tin Woodman, Lion."

"Well, then, if you've read the book, you know that the Scarecrow looks after Dorothy. I'm hoping you'll remember that as you develop your character."

Bolger laughed. "I saw you sitting with Judy in the commissary. She's a real charmer, ain't she?"

"She's a young girl. Can you look out for her?" Maud tried to read the Scarecrow's expression, hoping for a favorable reaction. "As a favor to me."

"Don't worry about the girl," Bolger said. "She's a real pro."

"Yeah," added Adrian, elegantly flicking ash onto the ground. "And I wouldn't want to cross that mother of hers."

Maud watched the ash drift close to the Scarecrow's feet. "I know Judy's a pro, but she's still just a girl."

"Set your mind at ease, Mrs. Baum," Adrian said. "Everybody loves Judy."

The Scarecrow fell silent, finger on chin, as if he were deep in thought. "You mind if I ask you something, Mrs. Baum?"

"Anything you like."

"Seems like the Scarecrow's a pretty smart fella—head full of straw or not. So why, in the last scene, does the Wizard decide to present him with a diploma? Seems like a person can do all the thinking he wants to do without ever earning a diploma. Was your husband a university man?"

"A diploma?" Maud asked, a bit bewildered as to where this talk of diplomas was coming from. "There's no talk of diplomas in Frank's book. My husband didn't give much stock to formal education. He hardly attended school at all. It was my mother who was so concerned with earning a diploma."

"Well, that's good to know," Bolger said. "I never finished school myself. Dropped out to make my living as a song-and-dance man. Started when I was only seventeen. But I consider myself a bit of a thinker. I've got the whole *Encyclopaedia Britannica* lined up in my dressing room. I pull one down off the shelf and read it any chance I get. Why, just this morning—"

"Careful now!" Maud lunged forward to brush off a glowing ember that had fallen onto his straw-stuffed shoe.

"Ouch!" he said, then winked at her. "Just playin'."

"Please don't burn yourself up, Bolger," Adrian advised in a languid voice. "I'd hate to have to make that costume again."

Bolger flicked the cigarette away, gave Maud a jaunty salute, and almost fell, then staggered forward. Maud reached out to grab him before she realized he was just acting.

He chuckled. "There's more where that came from," he said. "But I can't spend it all out here. Gotta save something for the cameras. Nice meeting you, Mrs. Baum." He whirled around and gave her a final straw-strewn salute, then followed Adrian through a door marked COSTUMES.

Maud watched them go with a pinch of irritation, worried that she had failed to get her point across. Bolger, with his slapstick and silliness, seemed perfect to play his role, but ever since lunch she had been thinking about something Frank wrote in the book: "Neither the Woodman nor the Scarecrow ever ate anything, but she was not made of tin nor straw, and could not live unless she was fed." There was no helping the little girl he'd been thinking of then. But what about the girl they were trying to squeeze into Dorothy's costume now? And she knew that Frank didn't just mean that children needed food, but love and care as well.

Back in the studio parking lot, light was glinting off the shiny chrome on the Bentleys and Duesenbergs, sparking up like heat lightning in a Dakota sky. Maud had read in *Variety* that *The Wizard of Oz* was slated to be M-G-M's biggest-budget motion picture of 1939. As she made her way through the lines of parked cars, as elegant as a row of tuxedoed gents in a dance number, she was struck by the sheer amount of wealth contained in this studio parking lot. She thought of the dark-suited men who clustered around the stars in the commissary just as marsh wrens flocked to the Dakota sloughs. She remembered how people had swarmed around Frank—from the fans, to the publishers, to the newspaper hacks looking for a story. They had been happy to splash his great successes across the headlines. Each one of these elegant motorcars belonged to someone trying to earn a living on the backs of the few among them who possessed the inborn artist's gift. It had been hard enough for Frank to bear, and he had been a grown man. What must the weight of so much expectation—of men, and their ambitions and desires—feel like on the shoulders of a lonely teenage girl?

SYRACUSE, NEW YORK

1881

ON THE NIGHT OF *THE MAID OF ARRAN*'S DEBUT, MAUD FUSSED with her hair in front of the looking glass. What would it be like to see Frank Baum up on a stage with everyone looking at him? She chided herself for being so nervous—not just her own sentiment in seeing him again, but also a worry about what Mother and Papa would think of him. Frank's play was appearing at the Syracuse Grand Opera House, and he had given them four tickets so that the entire family could attend. Even Papa was healthy enough to come.

Maud's father seemed at least neutral toward Frank Baum, but her mother was not yet won over to the young man's charms. She had made several pointed remarks to Maud about his lack of education, his dubious career path, and her hopes that Maud would choose a college graduate. The main point in his favor was that he had declared his full support for women's suffrage. That would have been enough for most men to obtain Matilda's good graces, but in the case of a suitor for her Cornell daughter, even that was not enough to convince her of his merits.

On the spring evening when they set out to see Mr. Frank Baum's play at the Syracuse Grand Opera House, the sun was shining, the trees were blooming, and Maud's spirits were high.

In no time, they had entered the outskirts of Syracuse, and soon were arriving in the elegant district of Clinton Square. A sharp tang from the Erie Canal wafted over South Salina Street. Barges crowded up along the street's edge, and the shouts and clanging from the docks vibrated in the air. Flanking the square on the other side was the towering turret of the Syracuse Savings Bank, topped with a flag that rippled in the light spring breeze.

Just adjacent was the Syracuse Grand Opera House, where snippets of excited conversation floated up from a crowd of well-dressed patrons debarking from carriages.

Mr. Baum had graciously provided a complimentary ticket to each member of the family, and Papa was suitably impressed when he learned that the price of a ticket was five dollars and fifty cents. His shopkeeper's brain was always toting up numbers, and when he multiplied the ticket price by the more than three hundred seats in the Syracuse Grand Opera House, his esteem for the young theater man increased. Papa approved of any endeavor that turned a neat profit—especially those in which a man was his own master.

The usher led them down the aisle to the best seats in the house, in the center of the third row, just behind the orchestra pit.

The caterwauling of tuning violins filled the grand chamber, and the crowd fell silent in anticipation. The light man fired down the gas table, dimming the theater, as the orchestra struck up a lively Irish tune. The heavy velvet curtain parted. Up on the stage stood Frank Baum—or "Louis Baum," since he was going by his stage name. He was dressed in velvet leggings and a fitted brocade jacket that accentuated his slim form and height. Bathed in the silvery light of the carbon arc spotlight, he appeared ethereal. Even at this distance, his lightness and his wit were evident. Maud's heart swelled each time the grand hall erupted with laughter or sounded with applause. When he bent down upon one knee to sing a plaintive love song, she was certain that he caught her eye.

For the duration of the show, Maud was completely transported. She knew that Frank had built this marvel from the ground up. He was not just an actor, looming large on the stage. He had written the play, composed the music, created the lyrics, imagined the costumes, and engineered the elaborate and technically complex set.

As she watched him, she realized that up until now, she had seen only bits and pieces of this remarkable person. Tonight, she was seeing the man in full. And she was enchanted. Never once since starting at Cornell had she been able to so fully escape the world and her place in it. It was as if the actors upon the stage had pulled back the curtain and revealed that there was another world on the other side of it—a world brighter, more colorful, more vivid, and more intense than the quotidian one in which she passed her days. It felt as if her humdrum heart soared and lifted out of her body and hung somewhere under the rafters—levitating as surely as the wooden table had refused to do when Maud had acted as the medium last Hallowe'en. For a few hours, Maud tasted a bit of the sublime. One thing she knew: she wanted more.

THE FINAL CURTAIN SWEPT SHUT. The audience exploded into applause. Then the curtain swept open again as the actors took their bows. Maud glanced at her companions' expressions and saw their unmitigated delight.

In the foyer, a porter presented himself to Papa with a bow. He said that the Gage family was formally invited to visit the backstage area at the request of Louis F. Baum, and thus they were escorted away from the crowd, down a corridor that ran alongside the orchestra pit, up a flight of stairs, and onto a stage that surprised Maud with its size. From here, she could see that the set, a giant ship, which had appeared so real from their seats in the audience, was nothing more than a false-fronted wooden structure controlled by a complicated set of pulley ropes and guy lines.

From the shadowy recesses of the backstage emerged Frank himself, still wearing his costume, as well as a layer of makeup so thick upon his face that Maud was startled at the sight of him. Frank looked so odd in his costume—not bad, mind you, she thought, as he was tall and svelte, but the makeup was so garish up close that he seemed like a parody of himself, and something made her think of the neighbor's scarecrow that had terrorized her childhood.

Maud's mother began clapping, and Papa as well. Julia, usually reticent, proclaimed, "Magnificent!" Only Maud, tongue-tied, remained silent.

"Thank you for coming. Did you truly enjoy it?" Frank, who was half a head taller than Papa, bent over and spoke in an urgent tone, as if the Gage family's pleasure was a matter of capital importance.

"The finest entertainment we have seen in Syracuse," Papa said heartily.

"We all found it most enjoyable!" Mother chimed in with an enthusiasm she usually reserved for the finer points of law.

"Indeed we did!" Julia hastened to add.

"Why, up close you look like Captain McNally Jackson Blair," Maud exclaimed, then immediately clapped her gloved hand over her mouth, mortified that she had blurted out the very first thought that came into her mind.

Frank only smiled. "And who might this captain be?"

Maud wanted to drop through the floor and she earnestly considered making up a story on the spot, but she did not get a chance as Matilda chimed in, "I certainly can see the resemblance . . . !" At the exact same moment, Papa said, "Like Bob Crouse's old scarecrow? Why, not in the least."

Julia cast a sympathetic glance toward Maud.

"Only in the sense that the makeup changes the aspect of your face," Maud added, mortified that she could feel her face flushing red.

"The songs were lovely," Julia said, deftly changing the subject. "I should think it would take much courage to sing in front of such a large audience."

"Courage—no! Foolhardiness, rather," Frank said.

"Not foolhardy at all," Mother said. "You have a pleasing singing voice."

All this while, Maud found herself inexplicably mute after her outburst about the scarecrow. Since when did she find herself so witless? Maud, who always had something to say, Maud, who spoke even when it was more advisable to stay silent, suddenly found herself as silent as an aspidistra. Frank was standing close enough to her that she could catch his scent—sweat and greasepaint and wool—but still her tongue lay thick and useless in her mouth.

"Mr. Baum!" A short bald man, stuffed into a grubby tweed suit like a sausage into its casing, gestured to Frank from behind the scenery. "We need your assistance!"

"I'm terribly sorry!" Frank said to the Gages. "Please excuse me, but I want you to know that I'm deeply grateful that you came."

Before he left, he said, "Good evening," extending his hand to Papa, who grasped it and pumped it several times.

"It has been our pleasure. Seems like you've got a good business going here," Papa said.

Maud watched her mother attentively. Mother appeared pleasant, as always; her cheeks had a hint of pink flush, making her look younger; and her manners, also as always, were cordial and kind. That she had enjoyed the play, Maud had no doubt; but whether this had swayed her in the young man's favor was impossible to tell.

He gallantly held out his hand to Matilda and said, "I hope to see you all again soon."

The stagehand gestured again urgently, and Frank's eyes darted toward him as he started to back away. In a moment, he would disappear behind the black curtains that formed the backdrop of the stage.

But just as he was about to duck behind the curtains and disappear, Matilda called out, "You must come visit us at our home in Fayetteville."

"I would not stay away," Frank said as he bounded away from them backward, waving his hand merrily as he went, until he tripped over a guy line bolted to the floor, sending the wooden set into a paroxysm of shuddering above them. He managed to right himself in such a comical manner that Maud burst out laughing, and at last regaining her composure, which had fled her at the first sight of him, she called out after him, "Goodbye!"

In a moment, he was gone, and Maud came down to earth, where she noticed that Julia had raised an eyebrow and was staring at her with a merry look on her face. Maud could read her sister's expression well enough to know that Julia had divined the true state of her emotions.

All the way back to Fayetteville, Maud was silent, but she felt immersed in a glow, as if a trailing fire of limelight had come along, flickering along behind them, leaving a bright tail of sparkles in the darkness.

In a matter of days, Frank would pack up the costumes and sets and take to the road. The tour was winding down, but the show had garnered such success that he was going to spend a week in New York City—on Broadway itself! It was as if Frank Baum had flung open a door and allowed Maud to peer through it, and what was on the other side was a magical land, all heightened colors and remarkable illusions, and that pathway led to something that, Maud suddenly realized, she wanted more than anything: freedom. It dawned on her that she and Julia shared the same deep yearning. Like convicts in adjoining cells who whispered feverishly through the bars to each other about their impending jailbreak, they were both longing to escape.

IT WAS LATE MAY, and Maud was packing her trunk, preparing to leave Sage College for the long summer break. The window to her dorm room was flung open, and a spring-scented breeze floated in. Outside, Cayuga Lake glittered, a jeweled blue, ringed by trees crowned by minty fluttering wreaths of new leaves. Maud folded up the yellow dress she had worn on her first night, a tightness aching at her throat. What high hopes she had had back then, as she'd descended Sage's broad staircase in her elegant frock, her new friend Josie at her side. But that memory had been irreparably colored by what had followed—the high-spirited dancing that had been just the beginning of her troubles here. Maud had carried a heavy mantle upon arriving—the hopes and dreams of Mother and her friends, their lifelong fight for women's equality, of which Maud's diploma was to be a shining symbol.

Maud had nursed her own secret dreams, however: of bursting out of the confines of other people's expectations, of finding her own strengths and her own ambitions. Being mothered by one of America's most outspoken women made it hard for Maud to find a voice all her own. Yet she had to admit to herself that in this respect, her first year away from home had been a failure. Her academic marks were excellent. She was progressing toward her mother's cherished diploma. But somehow Sage College had ended up feeling even more cloistered and stuffy than her life at home. Even worse, Maud had yet to discover her own passion—something that burned from inside her, not the handed-down deferred dreams of the previous generation. If she asked herself what this quest for a diploma was for, she could give herself no answer.

Room emptied, goodbyes given, trunk loaded onto the train, Maud once more watched the quilt of towns and fields pass, and the closer to Fayetteville she got, the more she realized that she was shrinking, smaller and smaller, until soon she would fit in the palm of her mother's hand.

AND INDEED, WITHIN A week of Maud's arrival back home, the walls of the Gage house seemed to be closing in on her. She received letters from school friends reporting on vacations filled with boating parties, picnics, and travel, but Maud had no time for fun. Papa's health had declined rapidly over the past few months, and Julia, who was no doubt worn out from nursing him, promptly fell ill with a prolonged sick headache, leaving the running of the household to Maud. Mother was distracted and cranky—with Papa no longer able to run the store, she worked feverishly on her writing, hoping to bring money into the household from royalties. Maud heard the sound of her mother's fountain pen scratching until late into the evening. Money was short, and it pained Maud to realize how much the family had been sacrificing to make her studies possible—and how little she was able to appreciate it.

But then, in late June, Maud received a letter from Josie with an interesting piece of news. Frank Baum's play on Broadway had closed after just a few days. He was returning to Syracuse and planned to remain for the rest of the summer before heading back

out on the road. Josie hinted that his decision might have had
something to do with his desire to see Maud again. The hope of
spending time with Frank made the household drudgery more
bearable, until at last a date was set for him to call at the Gage home,
on the second Sunday of July. Maud took pains to hide her excitement from Mother—fearing that if Matilda sensed the true state of
Maud's emotions, she'd do more to discourage his visits—but there
was no hiding from Julia, who watched and clucked as Maud tried
and discarded different dresses and fussed with her hair. Maud remembered her awkwardness during their encounter at the theater,
and the oddity of their conversation in the cloakroom at Cornell.
This time, she was determined to show herself as cool and collected.

Maud was waiting for Frank to arrive when she was distracted by
a soft vibration, like a finely plucked string, that sounded as if it
was coming from upstairs. In the front-facing bedroom, the sound
grew louder. Now it sounded like a strangled cry. She looked around
the bedroom, even peering under the bed, but the room was empty.
Maud realized that it was coming from outside the open window.
She leaned out and saw a calico kitten, swaying on a spindly branch
of the dogwood tree, mewling pitifully.

"Poor kitty," Maud purred, stretching an arm out the window.
The kitten, which looked to be only a few months old—just barely
weaned—was almost within her grasp. Leaning as far as she dared
out the second-story window, she could touch the tip of the branch
where the kitten was clinging for dear life. Maud angled herself a
bit more and grabbed hold of the foliage that was within reach, but
the twigs snapped, leaving her with a handful of green leaves.

Maud hastily stuck her now-mussed hair back into her combs
and straightened her blouse as she ran down the stairs and burst
out the front door. The kitten peered down at her wide-eyed. The
tree trunk was studded with familiar footholds from her younger,
short-pants-wearing, tree-climbing days. Now she was all hemmed
in with heavy skirts, petticoats, and a corset, just when she needed
to be limber. But the kitten's pitiful cries were too much for Maud.
Without further thought, she hitched up her skirts and shinnied

up the tree, then slowly inched forward along a bending branch, trying to get close enough to the kitten to reach out and grab it. But before she got there, a loud crack sounded and the branch swayed, boomeranging the kitten into the air. At that exact moment, Frank Baum strolled up the front walk. Maud watched in silent horror as the ball of calico fur tumbled down, knocked Frank's hat askew, then somehow gained purchase on his shoulder, where it clung for dear life.

"Now, what in the name of all that is holy!" Frank exclaimed. One hand flew up to retrieve his hat, while the other grabbed at his shoulder. When he realized that a live kitten was fastened to his wool morning coat, he reached up and ever so gently coaxed the terrified animal into unhooking from his jacket, then cradled it against his chest, crooning.

Maud held tight to the tree branch just over Frank's head. How could she possibly have found herself up in a tree, hair all in a muss, white blouse streaked with tree sap, just as Frank Baum arrived? Desperate to think of a solution, she determined to hide silently there, hoping that he would knock on the door and enter the Gage house so that she could escape the tree, slip into the house through the back door, and pull herself together. For a moment, she held steady while Frank stroked the kitten and murmured softly, but she felt her hands tiring. Slowly, she loosened her grip and tried to adjust her position, but no sooner had she done so than Frank, hearing the rustling leaves, looked up and spotted her.

"Well, hello there, Miss Gage! Will you be the next creature to fall from the sky? I've already received this precious kitten."

The jig being up, Maud climbed down from her perch. A moment later, she stood face-to-face with Frank.

"The kitten was stuck," Maud said.

Frank beamed. "A kitten rescue! Well done, well done."

"But I'm all a mess!" Maud blurted out in spite of herself.

Frank only smiled and reached out to brush a few leaves from her hair.

Smoothing her skirt and patting down her hair, Maud showed Frank up the front steps and ushered him through the door. The wayward kitten was now contentedly asleep in Frank's arms. Standing in the foyer as they entered, frowning, her mother looked Maud up and down, taking in her state of disarray.

"Good heavens," Matilda said. "What happened to your clothes?"

"Mrs. Gage. What a delight to see you again!" Frank interrupted, extending his right hand in greeting while continuing to cradle the now-purring kitten with the other. "Do you suppose you might have a bit of milk for this poor puss?"

Matilda was trying to keep a stern face, but she had a soft spot for all furry creatures. She opened her mouth as if to say something critical, then shut it again, and led Frank into the kitchen. There she unlatched the icebox and poured out a generous saucer of cream.

"I think she likes you," Maud whispered to Frank as they headed back to the parlor, leaving Matilda in the kitchen fussing over her newfound pet.

"The kitten?" Frank smiled. "I thought she was quite forward, leaping into my arms like that." He winked.

"No!" Maud whispered. "Mother! She's trying to dislike you, but she just can't help herself."

After that first visit, Frank began to make a weekly buggy trip from his home in Chittenango, eight miles away, to Fayetteville. Mother made no further protest, but Maud feared that this was more because Matilda was occupied with her work than because she'd altered her overall opinion on the matter. The kitten slept in a basket at Matilda's feet in her study while she worked. Her mother had grown quite fond of her foundling pet. Maud could only hope she would have as much affection for Frank. But as much as Maud looked forward to seeing him, often their conversations felt stilted and awkward. Frank was charming and affable, always ready with an amusing tale, but neither of them could relax knowing that Mother was always seated within earshot. Maud understood how deeply her mother concentrated on her writing, but it was still hard to believe that she didn't occasionally eavesdrop.

One afternoon in early August, Frank and Maud were seated in the front parlor and Mother was working in her study, so close that the feverish *scritch-scratch* of her fountain pen was audible, punctuated now and again by pauses while she stopped for reflection. Each time the sound of writing stopped, Frank stopped, too, cocking his ear, and would not speak again until he could tell that Matilda's writing was once again under way. Maud noticed his affliction with bemusement until, unable to resist the impulse, she raised her voice and said loudly, "Why, I do believe that the house is afire— we'd best get out!" Frank looked around the quiet parlor, the grate empty in midsummer.

"What on earth, Maud?"

Instead of answering, she jumped up, grabbed Frank by the hand, and pulled him out the front door, shutting it loudly behind them.

Once outside, Maud started to giggle as she watched a mystified expression cross Frank's face.

"There is clearly no fire. Do you wish to explain what you are doing, Miss Gage?"

Maud kept giggling and pointed at the window where her mother's head, bent intently over her writing, was visible. "Just as I suspected! Mother has not budged from her writing desk. You see? Not even a cry that the house is on fire would disturb Mother from her work. We could do almost anything and she would never notice!"

"Well, in that case, let's go for a ride!"

Maud looked at him—a wicked smile on her face.

"Hurry up, then. I'll bring round the horses," he said encouragingly.

Maud hesitated, but just for a moment. "Let's go!" she whispered. "But we can't stay out too long. Mother always breaks for tea around four."

Moments later, Maud was seated next to Frank in a jarring buggy headed west, out of town. At first, Maud worried that people would see them—Maud alone, unchaperoned, in a buggy with a man—but then she thought, *Well, really, what difference does it make?* She was the coed, the Cornell girl, the suffragist's daughter. Wasn't this exactly the kind of behavior her closed-minded neighbors would expect? Maud was certain that if any gossip came Matilda's way, she would staunchly defend her daughter, as a matter of principle. But as it happened, in the quiet midday torpor, houses were shut up tight with the blinds drawn, and they encountered no one in the street as they clattered swiftly out of town.

For the first few minutes, Frank wouldn't tell her where he was heading, but soon they were bouncing along a wooden road, its planks rattling under the buggy's wheels, until they had entered the nearby town of Mattydale. Just outside of town, on the crest of a high hill, was a large brick house, fronted by an ornate wrought-iron gate. It was prettily situated among formal gardens. Frank pulled up in front of the house, descended from their buggy to tie up the horses, then helped Maud down.

"This is where I grew up—our home, Rose Lawn. I wanted you to see it."

Paths traced around the garden, bordered by a profusion of pink, red, and yellow roses that delicately scented the air. He pushed open the iron gate, and once inside, Maud could see that the elegant garden was neglected, the house shuttered, paint peeling from its shiny black shutters and sturdy front door.

Maud looked at him, wondering.

"When my father and oldest brother died, my mother couldn't keep it up anymore. She decided to sell it. It was once the grandest estate in these parts, but by the time she sold it, it wasn't worth much. The man who bought it lives in New York City and has never set foot on the property, as far as I know." Maud heard an unfamiliar note of melancholy enter his voice.

"That must be hard!" she said.

A momentary frown crossed Frank's face, though it soon passed. "But today, it is ours!" he said.

She linked her arm through his, and they walked up a leaf-littered path toward the crest of the hill. Dried leaves also littered the wide front porch.

Frank led her behind the big house, where the view took in a shallow valley, dotted with gracious oaks and maple trees, an apple orchard, and a stream meandering at the far end of a pasture. Turning around, Frank pointed up to a pair of windows on the south end of the second story. "That was my room," he said.

"What a lovely view you must have had."

"I used to imagine that I was a prince and that these were my realms," Frank said. "Every piece of this place had an imaginary name, and the whole of it was a kingdom. I called it Roselandia . . ."

"Realms," Maud said, teasing. "That is quite a big imagination for a small boy."

"Too big," Frank said. "It was quite distracting."

They continued to stroll around the estate's large, overgrown grounds. Dark clouds had gathered on the horizon, and to Maud it seemed that the air had an electric tinge, though she was unsure if what she sensed was the result of a storm being imminent or simply that the gravity of what she had done was beginning to sink in. She was alone with a man, with no one else around as far as the eye could see. In the sultry air, Maud could feel perspiration forming at the nape of her neck and on her upper lip. Frank led her up another path; it meandered across a meadow and brought them to a spot under the spreading branches of a stand of pines, where a small marble bench had been placed in the shade, overlooking the fields and the distant stream. He bowed low to Maud. "My captive princess, please sit down."

"Oh, so I'm a captive, am I?" Maud said, arching her eyebrows to show that she believed no such thing, and yet, she was a captive in a sense. If she wanted to flee, there would be nowhere for her to go. But she felt no desire to leave. Instead, here, beside Frank, seemed like the safest place in the world. She took a seat on the bench, and Frank sat down beside her.

"When I was a child," Frank said, "I was often alone, and I amused myself by making up stories—the grounds of our house seemed a world apart." He pointed out some of the special places he remembered from his imaginary world: the apple orchard where trees could reach down and grab with their branches, a shabby outbuilding that was the dwelling of a magical woodsman. Maud marveled as she listened, amazed at his vivid imagination.

His father had sent him away to school when he was twelve, he explained, but he'd lasted barely a year before he begged to return home, lonely for his imaginary world and its population.

Maud listened sympathetically. Since she was so much younger than her elder sister, her own childhood had often been lonely.

"So, now you see what drew me to the theater," Frank said. "It's the closest I can come to creating my very own world."

"For me," Maud said, "books are like that. I've never visited a Scottish moor, and yet I believe that I could step out onto one and feel quite at home."

Frank beamed at Maud. "So would you like to write one some-day?"

"No," Maud said decisively. "There's no appeal in that for me. I grew up watching Mother's head bent over a writing tablet—so ab-sentminded and absorbed. I like to enjoy what's happening right now, in the moment—like this moment," she added, looking into Frank's gray eyes for a second, but then quickly looking away. He was gazing at her, and she felt an unfamiliar swooping sensation, suddenly acutely aware, once again, that they were alone. "Though I so appreciate that there are those who have the writing bent."

Frank smiled, and Maud noticed how the corners of his eyes crinkled up, his pink lips parting to reveal even white teeth. "So, you don't find me odd and strange, with so many particularities of the imaginary sort crowding up my mind?"

"Oh, no, Frank, I do find you odd and strange—" Maud stopped abruptly, embarrassed that she had said such a thing aloud. "I mean, you are strange in a good way—you seem unlike other men. Which is not a bad thing, as other young men have not given me cause to admire them much!"

"And you are utterly unlike other women," Frank said, now looking at her earnestly and leaning in closer, so close that Maud could feel the heat of his breath on her face. She looked up, and his soft lips met hers—for a moment she was flying through space, the world as she knew it tilting and tipping and disappearing, replaced by a white-hot light.

When the kiss ended, it took a moment for Maud to come back

to earth. As she settled, she had a sinking feeling, and her cheeks grew hot. She liked this man, truly she did, and now what had she done? Jumping up from the bench, she retreated several feet away from him, avoiding his gaze, wondering how she had managed to let all this happen, fearful of what would come next.

Every young gentleman she had fancied had turned out the same—a disappointment. They might say, she reflected, that they wanted a modern young woman, an educated woman, a woman with spirit, but in the end, they all seemed to accept a world in which they retained all of the freedoms—to travel where they wanted, to associate with whom they pleased—while voicing no regret whatsoever at the constrained nature of a young woman's life. They might pretend to embrace the principles of equality, but not when asked to put them into practice. Now she had not only hopped into a buggy alone with Frank, she had consented to his kiss—and what a kiss it had been, one she wouldn't mind repeating—and yet, she was convinced that she could spend a lifetime looking for a man who would accept her the way she was, who was looking not for a potted plant but a person with her own voice and spirit and vision.

She had dared to hope that Frank could be such a person—now, suddenly, she feared it was time to find out that she was wrong. It was one thing to go out with him unchaperoned, but Maud knew the grave consequences of being perceived as having loose morals. One of her friends at Cornell had been found talking to a male student in one of the side parlors in Sage, the two of them alone, with no chaperone present, and she had faced such censure that she had been forced to leave school. None of the girls had dared voice support for her, except in whispers, and later Maud had overheard the girl's former beau talking of his ex-sweetheart in the most cruel and denigrating terms. *He* had not been forced to leave school—only the girl. *So unfair!* And yet, every young woman understood the rules. Now Maud had been reckless. And she feared that she was about to discover that Frank was no different from other men.

Maud voiced none of these jumbled thoughts aloud, but after a few minutes of silence, she turned and stared mutely at Frank, waiting to see something, some change in his demeanor. His eyes remained steady on hers, unwavering, gentle, kind.

"We'd best get back," Maud said in a rush. "Before anyone notices I'm missing. You know I shouldn't have come out here with you?"

Frank's expression was serious, hard to read, and he said nothing.

"But I did it because I wanted to. I make up my own mind about things."

She looked at him quizzically, trying not to focus on his lips, which now monopolized her attention. "Mother always told me to be myself," she said, tipping up her chin, her eyes now flashing, challenging him to contradict her. "And this is who I am."

Just then, a bright flash of lightning crackled, swiftly followed by a rumble of thunder. A hard rain started pouring down. Making no response to her torrent of words, Frank grasped Maud's hand and they ran down the hill, pushing through the squeaky wrought-iron gate and clambering back into the cab. Frank hurriedly snapped up the rain cover, and they trotted back toward Fayetteville. The downpour made so much noise on the canvas top that they scarcely exchanged a word. When they arrived in front of the house, Maud could see her mother's head, still bent over her writing. She did not appear to have moved since they left.

Frank helped Maud down from the buggy, bowed low, and clasped her hand for a long moment, as if he were reluctant to let go. He made a hurried excuse about needing to head home before the roads flooded, then sprang back into his buggy and was gone. He did not even see her to the door.

When Maud entered the silent parlor, Mother poked her head through the door and said, "Oh, you've been so quiet I entirely forgot you were here! Has Mr. Baum gone?" Maud could see the edge of her own reflection in the hall mirror, drops of moisture clinging to the tendrils of her hair, her clothing soggy, but Mother did not appear to notice.

"Yes," Maud said, her voice glum. "He's gone."

———

THE DAYS THAT FOLLOWED were agonizing—a confusing mixture of distress and joy. Giddily she reimagined the kiss—a sensation so sweet that she'd never before been able to imagine its full flavor. But each recall was swiftly followed by remorse as she remembered how cavalier she had been—consenting to ride alone with him, allowing his caress—and wondered what he now thought about her. She read in his hasty departure an indication that he would most likely shun her now, but then she remembered the way he'd lingered over their last hand clasp, as if he had been reluctant to go. By the week's end, Maud had convinced herself: he would turn out to be just like other men, interested in Maud only as long as her free spirit was not revealed, no longer interested now that he'd understood what she was really like. And yet, in spite of all that, she had no regrets.

But the following Sunday, Frank's jaunty knock sounded on the door at the usual hour, and this time, he invited both Maud and Julia to go for a ride. The following Sunday, he arrived with a home-baked cherry pie and enticed Mother to join them in the parlor, where he actually got her laughing with his stories. After their secret jaunt and stolen kiss, his manner toward Maud had certainly not grown colder. And for her own part, Maud found that her longing to see him had only grown stronger, the days between his visits dragging past. She had begun to count with dread the number of Sundays between now and the day she would have to return to Cornell. Frank never raised the subject of her imminent departure; nor did she, unwilling to even touch upon the painful prospect of their upcoming separation.

One Sunday in the middle of August, just two weeks before her fall semester was to start, Frank began telling Maud a long, complicated story about one of the actors, who had gotten into a scrape and ended up fleeing his boardinghouse in nothing but his underwear. The story bordered on inappropriate, but Maud was listening without blushing when out of the blue, he leaned in very close, appeared to pause to monitor the sound of her mother's active pen, and whispered to Maud, "We're going to be married. Don't say no, as I will simply protest until you accept."

"I'll do as I please," Maud snapped, almost as a reflex.

Frank brushed his moustache with his thumb and forefinger, eyes twinkling. "Of that, I've no doubt."

Maud forged on bravely: "I won't let you or anyone else order me about or tell me what to do!" She watched him uncertainly, wondering how he would react to her sharp words. Would he withdraw his proposal immediately? At that exact moment, Maud realized just how much she didn't want him to. But to her relief, he just laughed softly, reached out, and squeezed her hand.

"I wouldn't dare order you about," Frank said. "And I don't want you to quit Cornell. We'll wait until you graduate—I would be very lucky to have an educated wife."

"That's what everyone wants." Maud pouted. "For me to be educated."

Frank was studying her anxiously, leaning closer.

"If I have to," Frank said, "I'll give up the theater. I'll settle down and find a more respectable line of work."

"No, Frank! You can't give up the theater," Maud said in a rush. "It's the love of your heart!"

"I do love the theater! But *you* are the love of my heart. I don't want to choose, but if I have to, I'll choose you. I know, you don't have to tell me that your mother does not want her daughter to marry a man with nothing but sawdust and pins and needles in his head."

"Pins and needles?"

He leaned closer again. "To prove that I'm sharp."

Maud giggled. "I know lots of fellows at Cornell. They may be chasing diplomas, but many of them are fools. They are not clever enough to invent whole new worlds, as you do. Don't quit the theater—that would be like chopping off one of your hands! Why couldn't I come with you?"

"My life is just a series of departures," he said. "We pack up and leave, a new town every few days. It's a wonderful routine, but not for a typical woman. No one knows you. You live your life among strangers."

"You think I'm a typical woman?" Maud asked seriously. "My notoriety trails me as stubbornly as a severe case of lice."

Frank laughed aloud. "I'm open about the time frame, but not about the answer," he said.

"And how exactly do you intend to compel me?" Maud said archly.

"Not by force," Frank answered. "By power of persuasion."

Maud thought of a million words of protest, but instead she blurted out, "I'm persuaded, Mr. Frank Baum. In spite of my best intentions, I'm persuaded."

MATILDA WAS, AS USUAL, so intent on her writing that when Maud stepped through the doorway to her study, at first she didn't even look up. When she did at last, for a moment her gaze was miles away.

"What is it, dear?" Matilda said absentmindedly, turning back to her notebook and jotting down a few more words. Maud waited for her mother to finish, knowing that she needed Matilda's full attention.

"Do you need something?" Matilda asked a full minute later, when she looked up from her writing again. Outside the window, Maud could see her mother's daylilies blooming in the garden.

"Mother, I have something I need to tell you. Frank has proposed marriage, and I've accepted. We'd like to be married as soon as possible."

Matilda flew to her feet so quickly that she knocked over her chair. Trying to stay calm, Maud bent over to right it.

"What ever can you mean? You can't give up on your education—I will not have my daughter be a darned fool and marry an actor!"

Maud had pictured that she might someday need to have this conversation with her mother. She had imagined so many words of protest from her mother—she had imagined the various ways her mother might admonish or cajole her to finish her degree—and, even worse, she had imagined the look of crushing disappointment that might come over her mother's features. But she had not imagined that her mother would take this aggressive tone with her—nor that she would attack Frank, the love of her life.

"Well then, Mother, I suppose you won't be seeing me anymore!"

Matilda stared, her expression severe. "What are you saying, Maud?"

"Well, I intend to marry Frank, and I'm sure you wouldn't want a darned fool around the house, so I guess you won't be seeing me anymore."

Maud kept her eyes fixed directly on her mother's. Matilda stared back, brows knit together in a tight line, until, slowly, Maud started to see signs of laughter playing around her mouth and eyes.

"Well, I guess I taught you to be independent!" she said.

Maud threw her arms around her mother so vigorously that Matilda lost her balance and landed back in her desk chair, Maud almost collapsing on top of her.

"No diploma?"

Maud shook her head. "I'm sorry, Mother. It's just not what I want."

A single crease appeared between Matilda's brows and her eyes clouded, but to her credit, she smiled, stood up, and grasped Maud's hands in hers. "Well, you won't obey me, so don't go obeying him, either . . ."

She cupped her hand under Maud's chin. "Marriage is serious business. A woman submits herself to a million indignities when she marries, and only a man's own rectitude can protect her. She has so few protections under the law."

"Mother, Frank is a good man, and I'm no fool. Please don't worry about us—just give us your blessing if you're so inclined."

"I'm not inclined," Matilda said. "But I can see you've set your mind to it, so consider yourself blessed."

———

A FEW DAYS BEFORE the wedding, Maud's mother came into her bedroom carrying a parcel wrapped in brown paper. She shut the door.

"It's time for us to have a small discussion," Matilda said, settling herself on the edge of the bed.

Maud unwrapped the paper and found a small book entitled *A Woman's Companion*. She looked up at her mother. "What is this?"

"I'm not surprised you've never seen it before. Mr. Anthony Comstock, the United States postal director and, I might add, a vehement anti-suffragist, has outlawed this useful book, and others like it. He's made it a crime to send this kind of information through the mail. But within its pages you will find the secret of how to limit your family size."

From her skirt pocket, she extracted a small lacquered box. Inside was a round sponge, about two inches in diameter. Attached was a piece of silken thread.

"Soak it in carbolic acid," Matilda said. "Enter it inside your womanhood and push it all the way against the mouth of the womb. When you are finished, you can extract it by pulling on the thread."

Maud stared at the small sponge with a mixture of queasiness and fascination.

"Will it work?"

"Applied diligently, it may delay—but nothing prevents," Matilda said, "except abstaining from a man's embrace."

"But, Mother . . . !"

Matilda held a finger up to her lips. "Say no more. Children are a blessing, but God has given us a brain, and we are not prevented from using it to help us organize our lives."

ON THE EVENING OF November 9, 1881, Maud stood at the top of the stairs and looked down at the bright faces of the guests assembled there. All of Matilda's friends from the suffrage society were there. Mrs. Stanton was turned out in yards of tiered lace that made her look like a wedding cake. Skinny Auntie Susan wore a plain black dress, and her hair was pulled back so tightly that it seemed to draw her eyebrows farther apart. The string band tucked into one of the upstairs rooms started to play the wedding processional, and all eyes turned upon Maud as she slowly descended the staircase. When she reached the bottom, Papa, thin and pale, but out of bed for the occasion, slipped his arm through hers. Maud steadied herself against him before she took the few steps necessary to reach the parlor.

Frank, in his gray morning coat, stood regal and tall.

She faced him, her heart all atremble.

"Do you take this man, to love and to cherish and to honor . . . ?"

Maud and Frank proudly spoke their identical vows (omitting the word "obey," as they had agreed), and Frank eased the ring over her finger. In that simple exchange, Maud realized, she had slipped out of the person she had been and turned into another person altogether.

ON TOUR

1881–82

TWO WEEKS LATER, AFTER A BRIEF HONEYMOON IN SARA-
toga Springs, Maud had already started to get the rhythm of traveling with the company of *The Maid of Arran*. Each day, another train,
a ruckus of hammers and nails, the loud chatter as the actors applied their face paint and the musicians tuned their instruments
and the stage crew fiddled with the sets. Every evening, the thrill of
sitting in the back of the theater, watching the curtain rise. Every
night, the cast gathering together, drinking coffee or whiskey, and
hashing out the finer points of the night's performance, and even
later, Frank and Maud locking themselves into another hotel room,
stripped bare with no shame, and finding each other's embrace.

Late one night, they lay close in an uncomfortable hotel bed that
sagged in the middle. Frank's steady breathing comforted Maud,
the moonlight whitening the expanse of his chest, bare under an
unbuttoned nightshirt. Through the windows, Maud could see the
stars glittering in the sky, and she marveled that these were the
same stars she had seen through her window at Cornell and yet now
she saw them from such a different place. She rolled back toward
her beloved, burying her face in the hollow of his neck as his arms
encircled her. If these were the bonds of marriage, then she was
happily bound, and happy to throw away the key.

In Tuscaloosa, Frank and Maud awoke before dawn, realizing that they were covered with itchy red spots. They had been so eager to find each other after a long night that Maud had neglected to check the mattress for bedbugs, and now every inch of their skin was welted with bites. Fortunately, Matilda had sent Maud on her journey with a small kit filled with her natural remedies, among them a soothing Vaseline-and-lavender salve. Maud lovingly stroked it all over Frank's bare body, and then he did the same to hers. For the next three days, they were so itchy they could barely sleep, and by the time they reached St. Paul, Minnesota, they both had dark rings under their eyes and kept dropping off to sleep whenever they sat down.

Their stage director, Carson McCall, a ruddy Scot, poked fun at them as they fell asleep over coffee in a diner near the Prestige Theater in St. Cloud, Minnesota.

"Not getting much sleep at night, are ya, ya two lovebirds?"

Maud blushed to the roots of her hair, but Frank just smiled smooth as could be, placed one hand over Maud's, and said, "I would certainly say we are not!"

SEVERAL MONTHS INTO THEIR life on the road, Maud had grown so used to traveling that she could hardly remember what it felt like to stay in one place. Early one morning, she and Frank sat, knees bumping, across from each other in the dining room of a cheap hotel in Peoria, Illinois, where the Baum Theatre Company was currently settled for a few days. Between them was a small table covered with a dingy cloth. The window was pushed open and the pleasant early spring sunshine brightened the dreary surroundings, but Maud had hardly touched her coffee, and the bun on the plate was uneaten. The sight of its shiny surface made her feel queasy.

Maud had received a letter from Julia, who'd written from her new homestead in Dakota. Her account seemed fantastical—she described swarms of mosquitoes as dense as fog, a vast treeless landscape buffeted by high winds and hail the size of goose eggs, a one-room shanty so spare that when she'd arrived it had no windows and no roof. When Maud tried to conjure an image of her sister in those circumstances, all she could come up with was the sight of Julia with a sick headache, lying in her four-poster bed with a mustard plaster over her forehead, groggy from her medicine.

Frank's long legs barely fit under the table, and each time he moved, he jostled it, sloshing their coffee into the saucers. Maud was reading Julia's letter aloud. The contents were making Frank chuckle. " 'With all of the pain I've suffered, I've never suffered such agony as I did that night. My dear James, not always so patient, was almost WILD and he prayed aloud, "Oh Lord, give us hail, give us rain, give us snow, give us anything but take away these mosquitoes." ' " Maud kept glancing up at him, and as she read she could feel irritation bubbling up inside her, until finally she flung the letter down on the table between them.

"What's so funny?" she demanded.

"Well, now, the thought of your sister dressed in her fine city clothes, moving at a mule's pace across the wild prairie, with a black swarm of mosquitoes buzzing around her head. It's a right colorful image, if I do say so myself."

"Frank Baum! How can you say such a thing? She's describing the most painful night of her entire life, and it makes you laugh?"

"Vivid language! Brings it all alive!"

"She's miserable!" Maud said.

"She's having an adventure. *You* like adventures, Maud." He gestured at the tawdry dining room, where a drunk was slumped in one corner, emitting a faint snore.

"Is absolutely everything a lark to you? She's my sister. I worry about her. Her situation sounds perfectly dreadful to me."

"And if you were to write her a letter right now," Frank said, his tone still mild, "it would begin, 'My dearest Julia . . . I'm sitting at a table the size of a postage stamp, drinking three-day-old coffee in the presence of an actor, a tabby cat, a stale breakfast roll, and a flatulent drunk . . . !' "

Maud let out a snort, and her hand flew up to cover her mouth.

"You see," Frank said. "It's all in the telling."

"It's not in the telling," Maud objected, stamping her foot under the table. "I'm worried about her! You don't understand!" Hot tears sprung to her eyes. "Stop teasing me!"

She jumped up from the table, causing the cups to overflow, the saucers to slide, and a large stain to soak into the dingy tablecloth.

Frank reached out to touch her arm, but she pulled it away and ran from the room, bursting through the dining room doors, where she almost ran smack into Carson McCall, all red-eyed and wild-haired, as if he had been up all night.

"Well now, lassie, where are you headed in such a big hurry?"

Where *was* she headed in such a hurry? She realized that she and Frank had just had their first fight.

"To the theater!" Maud said. She ducked past the director and ran up the street until she reached the theater's back door.

Picking up her mending basket, she set to working on a frayed cuff and sewed until the rhythm of her needle started to calm her.

A moment later, a square of light appeared at the doorway and Frank tentatively poked his head in, looking thoroughly abashed.

Maud glanced up from her mending.

"Oh!" She had stuck herself in the finger with the needle. "Oh, for heaven's sake," she said. "I'm so clumsy."

Frank grasped her hand and held her finger tight until the smarting subsided. "I'm sorry, Maud, I didn't mean to offend you."

"I know."

"Believe in Julia. She's having an adventure. Don't you think that's what she wanted when she hitched up with a gentleman ten years her junior and moved to Dakota?"

"I suppose," Maud said. "At least she's gotten out from under Mother's thumb!"

"Julia will be fine. Why, I'd love to see Dakota myself. I hope that we'll be able to visit her someday."

"Wouldn't that be something?" Maud said. "We've traveled all over kingdom come—why not Dakota?"

"Why ever not?"

But looking at Frank's joyful face only reminded Maud of her secret worry. She had a feeling that their adventuring days might be
numbered.

BY MID-MAY THE WEATHER was humid and stifling. Inside a
run-down theater in a small town near Akron, the cool of the
morning had turned to a suffocating torpor by midday. They were
getting set to start performing a new play, called *Matches*. Frank was
convinced that it would be an even bigger hit than *The Maid of Arran*.
Maud watched as he rehearsed the scenes and signaled the piano
player to start and restart, start and restart. Frank never quit. He
was as eager to try a line the fortieth time as the first.

Inside the close theater, Maud was starting to feel dizzy, so she
went outside, hoping to find cooler air. Out front stood an
exhausted-looking pair of black geldings hitched to a jitney.

Maud looked at the poor beasts with sympathy. There was not a
hint of shade on the street. Just then, one of the nags lifted his tail,
and the sharp scent of manure waved over her. The street turned
first white, then fuzzy, then gray.

She felt a cool cloth on her forehead and looked up to see Frank's
anxious face peering down at her.

"What happened?"

"Don't you remember?"

"I went outside to get a breath of fresh air, and then . . ."

"Ya keeled right over like an oak struck by lightning," a dusty-
looking fellow wearing a livery driver's uniform said. "I was standing by my horses, when I seen you come out. Went white as a sheet,
and toppled."

"I fainted?"

"It was so hot in the theater . . ." Frank said.

Maud sat up. "Thank goodness Mother wasn't here to see that!
She has no patience with fainters."

"Here, darling. Take some cool water."

Maud took a sip, and then a long draft. "I guess it was the heat."

That night was the debut of *Matches*. After sunset, the heat hardly abated, and inside, the theater was a hot box. The house was only half full, and the laughs were sparse. Some of the people walked out in the middle of the first act, but Maud assured Frank that it was only due to the temperature. Back in their hotel room later, Frank continued to fret about the poor reception.

"Did you think people liked it?"

"Oh yes," Maud said. "It was splendid. Everyone loved it!"

"We're going to take it on the road, maybe all the way back to Broadway!"

Maud knew it was time to tell him the truth. In spite of following Matilda's instructions with the lacquered box to the letter, every morning for the past month, she had awoken queasy and could scarcely nibble at her food. She reached out and pulled his hands into hers, rubbing her thumbs across their bony ridges, but not meeting his eyes.

Releasing one hand from her grasp, he tipped her chin up gently with his thumb. "What is it, darling?"

"We're going to have a child."

She watched as his face drained of color, then turned bright red, and he flung his arms around her, almost knocking her over.

"Are you sure? Are you quite sure?" Frank leapt out of his chair.

"I'm sure."

"This is the happiest day of my life!"

"We will have another mouth to feed."

"And feed him we shall!" Frank said. "Fresh oranges and marbled cuts of meat, seven-layer cakes and pumpkin puddings—"

Maud put her hand over her mouth as she felt her stomach heave. "Please, no more," she whispered.

"All right then," Frank said, putting one arm around Maud and gently easing her to sit on the edge of the bed. "Our child shall have milk toast and chamomile tea. . . . Is that better?" he asked worriedly.

Maud smiled weakly. "A cup of tea would be nice," she said.

THE SKY WAS LOW and close, and a heavy rain poured down outside the train station in Dayton, Ohio. The train had disgorged
them into an empty street where not a single cabby and pair awaited.

Maud had already let out her traveling dress three times, and still
it felt tight across her midsection. She was shivering from the cold
and faint with hunger—she'd had nothing to eat but a cup of tea and
stale cake at the depot in Columbus. A problem on the tracks had delayed their train for several hours. They had expected to arrive before
sunset; now it was close to midnight, and the street outside the depot
was deserted and dark. The rest of the troupe had stayed behind to
pack up the sets and would meet them the following day. Frank held
a folded newspaper over their heads to shelter them from the rain,
but the paper was already sodden, and the cold rain was soaking
through her cloth coat and running down the back of her neck.

"Go back and wait inside the depot," Frank said. "I'll walk up the
street a bit and see if I can find a place to lodge."

"No, darling, I'll come with you." She had noticed the collection
of drunks and ne'er-do-wells clustered on the benches inside. She
preferred that they stick together. The streetlights had already
been extinguished, and there was no obvious clue which way to
turn—Frank looked up and down the street before he picked a direction, seemingly at random, and headed that way, carrying their
two suitcases, at a fast clip. Maud held up her skirts, but her feet
were soon soaked through. Her back ached from sitting so long in
the train, and her bladder was so full she knew she needed to find a
water closet soon.

"Well, here it is!" Frank said, in a tone of utter delight. Maud
saw that he was pointing to a theater marquee; the sign said, MAJES-
TIC THEATER.

Though it was dark, Maud could make out the letters. She saw
the name of an acting troupe and a play spelled out, and it was not
their own.

"Let's duck inside," Frank said. "Someone will be able to tell us
where to find lodgings."

The front doors were bolted shut, so they passed into a back alley, where a black cat startled Maud as it leapt out from behind a stack of wooden crates. The narrow way was putrid with the scent of rotting garbage and effluent, and there was no way to avoid the puddles. Bile rose up in her throat.

Now, thoroughly soaked, she stood beside Frank, shivering, feeling the life inside her kicking up a fuss, as if to say, *Get out of this cold rain!*

Frank tried the stage door. Finding it locked, he first knocked, then rapped loudly, then finally located the string that allowed him to pull the bell. After a long time, the sound of locks turning was audible and the door opened a crack before the chain stopped it from swinging farther. The pale face of a wizened old man peered through the gap, his face illuminated by the light of a single candle.

"Whatcha want?"

"Please, kind sir," Frank said, his voice friendly, "can you open up so that we can conduct this conversation out of the rain?"

"State your business," he said. "I'm not opening the door to no vagrants, no matter if cats and dogs is raining down from the heavens. This here is a cutthroat environ, and I prefer to keep my throat uncut."

"Oh no, dear sir, we are not throat cutters, we are actors! I'm Frank Baum, and this is my wife, Maud. We are here for our run of *Matches,* but our train was delayed and we arrived at the train station so late that all of the hacks were departed. If you'll just let us inside for a moment, we'll explain ourselves further."

"Matches," the man said suspiciously. "That's the one that wasn't selling tickets. Your run was canceled. Did you get the letter? You'd best get back on that train. We've got nothing for you here."

"Open the door and let us in," Maud said. "I am the manager, and I need to speak to the theater director. We will sit here until morning if necessary." Maud spoke confidently, hiding the tremor in her voice.

"Skedaddle!" the man said. "You're not wanted here!" With that, the door clicked shut in their faces, and Frank and Maud found themselves alone again in the dark alley.

"Oh!" Maud cried out. She felt something under her skirt, wrapping itself around her leg. She jumped, flinging her sodden skirts up and down, and the black cat emerged from under her petticoat and sped off down the alley, disappearing from sight.

Frank wrapped his arms around her for a brief second before picking up the suitcases and leading the way back out of the fetid alley, onto the wet, lonely street.

For the next three days, Maud shivered with fever, tossing and turning in gray sheets, inside a run-down boardinghouse a few blocks past the theater. Frank left her side only twice: once to confirm that the show had indeed been canceled, and the next time to bring in a doctor. The doctor offered only a foul-smelling purple patent medicine, but she was unable to swallow it. He advised her to rest until she felt better, then went on his way.

Frank brought her tea and soup, and though she had no appetite, she tried to choke it down for the baby's sake. She dozed on and off, forgetting her surroundings, and each time she awakened to the sight of the one soot-caked window and the peeling floral wallpaper covered with water stains. She held a clean embroidered handkerchief over her mouth to keep away the stench of faded cigar smoke and tried to imagine that she was home, at the house in Fayetteville, in a clean bed with ironed sheets, and that Mother was periodically coming into the room, laying a cool hand on her forehead. But each time she fell asleep, she had terrible nightmares of being cast adrift on a stormy sea, holding a lifeless baby in her arms, and in some of the dreams, she could see her own dead body, lying blue and pale in a puddle of blood, and she would awake with her heart pounding and her mouth dry. Each time this happened, she saw Frank sitting beside her, gently offering her a sip of cool water.

On the fourth morning, she awoke to find the fever gone. They took all of their belongings from the horrible lodging house and settled themselves in a tea shop, where Maud, her appetite restored, ate enough for three men.

"More sugar in your tea? Let me butter your bread. Do have a bite of this egg and the strawberry jam . . ." Frank had a pucker of worry between his eyebrows as he fussed over her.

"Frank! Enough!" Maud snapped. "I am perfectly able to feed myself. I'm feeling better."

Frank's shoulders relaxed a bit. "I was just so worried," he said. "I am dreadfully sorry that you got caught in the rain."

"It's not your fault, Frank. These things happen."

He took both of her smaller hands in his, rubbing one finger distractedly along the tip of her left index finger, which was callused and pricked from mending costumes.

"You needn't worry," Maud said, slipping her hands from his grasp, then giving his hands a squeeze. "I wired ahead to our next stop. Our run is confirmed. There's no possibility we'll face the same situation again."

"Maud," Frank said, reaching out and tilting her head up with the tip of his finger. "Look at me, please. We can't keep traveling. I'm no nursemaid, and I'll be frantic every time you catch a draft."

"Don't be ridiculous. I'm with child, not ill. I'm as sturdy as a horse."

"Sturdy as a horse," Frank said. "Normally, yes, but these last few days . . ." He spread his hands helplessly before her.

"Besides," Maud continued, ignoring his comment, "we're booked solid for the next month. You know as well as I do that we can't back out of our commitments. At best, we'll have to pay them back, and at worst—they'll never have us back again. The name of the Baum Theatre Company will be ruined."

"I said nothing about backing out of our commitments," Frank said. He stroked his moustache and swallowed hard. "The company will tour without us."

"But you're the lead actor," Maud said.

"And so I was. But now, we have other responsibilities."

Maud saw a light cloud, like a thin mist of fog, cross her beloved's expression and settle around his eyes. "The troupe will still be here. We'll rejoin it later."

Maud dug into her satchel and consulted a small notebook filled with neat lines of script. "You know we are already booked in Vermilion, Parma, Mentor, Ashtabula, and Erie," Maud said. "We need those ticket sales to pay off our debts."

Frank reached out and brushed his finger along the curve of her cheek. "You are a stern taskmaster, my darling. But I insist that after we finish the run in Erie, we'll head north to be closer to home. Surely we can find a suitable rental in Syracuse."

"We'll see," Maud said, sensing that she might lose this battle. "Let's see how it goes."

By the time they got to Erie, even Maud's deft needlework couldn't find a way to let out her clothes, and every day when she unlaced her boots, she saw creases in her skin where her ankles had swelled. Frank had begun to talk cheerfully about returning to Syracuse for the winter. He wanted to send the troupe on without them, promising Maud that the two of them would do nothing but clip coupons and live in the lap of luxury on their proceeds. But in the end, it wasn't his words that persuaded her. She added up the figures and saw that the troupe wasn't making enough—not to support them in Syracuse, nor to support them on the road. So Maud agreed to Frank's proposal. The troupe would head south toward Clarion and Brookville to finish out their last two engagements, then continue on to the Baum Theatre in Richburg, New York, where they would pack away the sets and costumes and go their separate ways. Maud and Frank said their goodbyes and boarded the Lackawanna toward Syracuse.

As the train headed east, Maud sat next to the window, the swaying motion of the compartment helping to soothe her sadness. She looked out over the fields and woodlands, now showing the faded browns and yellows of late November. Their train car was empty except for a single man who had pulled his overcoat up over his face and gone to sleep. The dim late autumn light was melancholic. She felt as if the world had cleared out and stilled, leaving a void between the ending of one thing and the beginning of something else.

She snuggled down next to Frank, laying her head on his shoulder. "We won't make this the end, will we, Frank? We won't become one of those dull old couples who trade stories of the few adventuresome days of their youth while sitting dumb as doorposts in front of a fire, knees wrapped in blankets, mouths full of old stories?"

"Dear Maudie," Frank said. "Why ever would you think such a thing?"

"You know I've come to love it as much as you do—it's just that the numbers don't add up. For the last six months we weren't breaking even. I'm not sure how to make that change."

Frank let her remark pass without responding. Maud knew that he didn't have a head for numbers. He had an optimistic streak that included a firm belief that pennies would fall from heaven, in the nick of time, to save the day.

"Frank?"

"We'll return to the theater the moment our little girl is born. We'll have her playing Shakespeare before she can walk. I'm picturing her dressed as Ariel, with flowers threaded through her hair."

"Our *girl*?" Maud said, grinning impishly. "And what makes you so sure?"

Frank smiled. "I'm just convinced that the mighty spirit of the Gage women will certainly prevail."

Boy or girl, right now it was kicking Maud in the ribs. She sucked in her breath and shifted on the bench. Her gloom over their goodbyes had passed. She wasn't sure what the future would hold, but at least they would face it as a family.

WHEN MAUD'S LABOR PAINS set in, one day in early December, she looked around her trim and tidy home. Her linens were starched and ironed; her layette was neatly folded and smelled sweetly of lavender sachet. Chicken stew simmered on the back of the cookstove, a neat supply of kindling and firewood was stacked by the fireplace, and fire burned in the grate. Out the window, gentle flakes of snow drifted down from a white sky. Turning from the window, she surveyed the order and harmony she had created in their small rented home in Syracuse. As she felt a band of pressure tightening across her belly, and her breath sucked in, then steadied and slowed, she knew it was time, and she prepared to face it well.

Eight hours later, a healthy baby boy, Frank Joslyn Baum, was born.

ON CHRISTMAS EVE, FRANK, Maud, and little Frank, affectionately known as Bunting, stood near the large evergreen festooned with candles and red ribbons in the parlor of her mother's home in Fayetteville. Maud's color was high as she shared hugs and kisses with friends and relatives who had come from far and near. But there was a melancholy tinge in the big old house. It would be her first Christmas without Papa, who had succumbed to his fevers earlier that year.

T.C. had arrived from Aberdeen, Dakota Territory, bringing tales of business opportunities in the recently founded western railroad hub. But Julia and her husband could not afford to make an eastern visit this year.

When Maud noticed that her mother and Frank were deep in conversation, she worked her way across the crowded room to see what they were talking about.

"And what kind of work do you plan to do now?" Matilda was asking.

"I haven't quite decided," Frank said. "I have an interest in a great many things—so many that it can be hard to pin myself down. I've always liked publishing, and the breeding of fancy poultry, and, of course, the theater . . . and . . ." Frank was meandering through this speech in a way that Maud found quite charming, but she could see the corners of her mother's mouth drawing in.

Frank and Maud were still nursing a plan to return to the theater, only without ready cash to mount another production, they'd had to leave the exact date up in the air. All of the assets of the company were stored in the Baum Theatre—the sets, the scripts, the costumes—but the theater itself was shuttered for now and was unlikely to open again. Frank's father had built it during the oil boom, when men with money in their pockets had crowded the town of

Richburg, New York. Once those heady days passed, there weren't enough townspeople left to support a theater. Nowadays it was serving only as a warehouse for their deferred dreams.

In truth, it was clear that Frank needed to find another line of work to sustain them, at least for now. Loyally, Maud believed that he would be successful in whatever he tried, but she also did her best to steer him in a practical direction.

She laid a hand on Frank's arm, gave him an encouraging smile, and then interrupted him: "Frank is taking up the family enterprise. The Baum family oil business. He is working with his elder brother Benjamin."

Matilda smiled approvingly. "Wonderful! I had hoped you'd soon tire of that acting business. This sounds like an excellent prospect."

"Baum's Castorine," Frank said affably. "A perfect greaser for buggies, wagons, carts . . ."

"Sounds perfectly sensible," Matilda said. "Everyone needs axle grease. My husband always said that it's wise to center your business around things that people can't do without."

"Of course, we're not finished with the theater," Frank said. "As soon as we can get up another company, we plan to take it back on the road."

MAUD WAS IN THE KITCHEN, chopping carrots, when she heard Frank at the piano, plinking out a sprightly melody. She had sent him to put Bunting down for his nap a few minutes ago. Was he going to put the baby to bed only to wake him up again?

"Baby Bunting, pudding pie, take a flight, across the sky . . ." Frank's light tenor floated through the kitchen door.

Maud peeked out into the parlor and saw that Frank was holding the baby with one arm and using Bunting's feet to tap out the melody with the other.

"Frank!" Maud laughed at the comical sight.

"I'm teaching him to play piano—and sing!" Frank said. "Listen!"

Maud glanced at the clock. "He's supposed to be napping! Please don't get him too excited—he'll never want to fall asleep."

"I asked him if he wanted to sleep and he said no—didn't you, Bunting?" Frank tickled the boy's cheek, making him giggle. "He said he wanted to dance. He's helping me write a song." Frank again started tapping out a melody with Bunting's feet, and the baby, obviously delighted, cooed along with the music, which Frank was clearly improvising as he went along.

"Little boy beauty, soldier, clown. Turn the baby—UPSIDE DOWN!" Frank did exactly that, which only made Bunting giggle louder.

"Frank!"

"He likes it!"

Maud reached out her arms. "You go ahead and write your song. I'll put Bunting to bed."

"You're not cross, are you? It's just that I've had a spark of inspiration, and I want to get it down. Before I lose it. Sometimes a tune worms its way into my ear and then crawls right out the other side . . ."

"I'm not cross," Maud said. "I just want the baby to get some rest." She frowned without meaning to.

"I'm sorry, darling—I feel like I have so little time now. I'm trying to get this new play written, and it's hard to do it when I'm traveling all the time. I try to come up with words, and all that comes out is *'Baum's Castorine, best buggy grease you've ever seen . . .'"* He looked dejected.

Maud was patting Bunting on the back and rocking him, and his eyes were already drifting shut.

Frank tapped out a few notes and the baby's eyes flew wide open, then scrunched up as his mouth opened wide and he started to wail.

"Can you just not play right this minute, Frank? Maybe after his nap?"

Frank looked as if he was about to protest, but then his shoulders slumped a little. "Of course, darling."

As Maud carried the baby upstairs, she realized that they'd been having these kinds of exchanges more often. She knew full well that

Frank was still pining for the theater. He scribbled new play notes, sketched out sets, and noodled new songs on the piano whenever he had a free moment. The bright notes filled their house, and then Frank, a pencil in hand, muttered to himself while he paced across the living room.

But most of the time, his hours were taken up by business. Throughout the winter, Frank traveled across the depth and breadth of New York State. In the morning, as he buttoned his frock coat and waxed his moustache, she could see in his eyes the look of a chained-up dog that whimpered when you passed. After a long sales trip, it always took a day or two before he brightened; but always, soon enough, the house would fill up with his lightheartedness—he was always whistling a tune or glancing up from a pad of paper with an amused expression on his face. At the end of each week, Maud looked over the household accounts and tried to set a bit aside for Frank's theater projects, though at the rate their meager savings were accumulating, she knew it would take years, not months, for them to save up enough to put up a new production—and what would they live on even if he could manage to debut a new play? Frank's wages paid their bills. The Baum Theatre Company had never been more than a break-even operation, started with an infusion of capital from his then-flush father.

For her own part, Maud had grown absorbed in her new life, full of caring for the baby, visits with family, and reading in the evenings. During the lonely spells when Frank was traveling, she had even returned to her childhood hobbies of fine embroidery and tatting lace, skills learned from her father's mother. She was proud of the beautiful gifts she made. As the months passed, Maud began to notice that Frank, too, seemed less preoccupied with the theater. The piano in the parlor fell silent. In the evenings, he read the newspaper or chatted about his sales trips. Maud started to hope that he'd made peace with his new life, as she had. They had lived their adventure, hadn't they? Which was more than most people ever did, and as Maud had learned at her father's knee, when the numbers didn't add up, wishing and hoping wouldn't change anything, so you might as well be content with what you had. And who was to say that sometime in the future there wouldn't be more adventures in store for them? After all, they were still young.

"Let me hear one of your songs," Maud said one Saturday afternoon when she and Frank were sitting in the parlor, with Bunting sprawled on the rug near the hearth, amusing himself with blocks. "I never hear you singing anymore."

Normally, Frank was quick to take a seat at the piano, but now he gazed at her balefully. "Not today, Maudie dear."

"Why not today?" Maud said. "I miss hearing you play. The house seems so quiet. Don't you need to work on your play?"

Frank's gray eyes turned stormy; he stood up—so suddenly that his chair's legs scraped on the parlor floor—and crossed to the window, where he paced in place, rubbing his hands together.

Maud looked at her husband with surprise. Why had her simple request for him to play music upset him so? Sometimes this business of marriage still confused her. He had never reacted this way before.

Frank whirled around, facing Maud. "You don't understand, do you?"

Maud gazed at him, bewildered.

"To you, it's just music . . ."

"Frank dear, what ever are you talking about? I've upset you. I'm sorry. I just thought it would be nice to hear you play."

"See . . ." Frank said, now pacing across the parlor. "That's not how it is. I'm not playing the piano just for fun. When I'm writing songs and lyrics, I want them to have some purpose—to be part of a play. I want that play to be real—not just spinning around in my mind, but actually created, staged, out in front of people. Lights, applause."

"But, dear, I know," Maud said.

"You don't know!" Frank said, his voice now growing louder. "You don't know how I feel."

"But, Frank—"

Maud stood up and walked toward him, but as she tried to put her hand on his arm, he jerked it away.

"You know, Maud, I try," Frank said.

"I know you try. You work so hard—"

"Hear me out! I try *not* to have flights of fancy. I try to do as other men do. I watch them and see how they concern themselves with the mundane matters of this world. They think about train schedules and dinner menus, bank accounts and calendars, and their minds seem to settle contentedly on these things—like yours does, Maud—but it doesn't work like that for me. These ideas come to me, they crowd up my brain, and they want to go somewhere—they want to be expressed!"

"Of course, darling," Maud said. "I *do* understand. I know who you are." Tears welled up in her eyes. Did Frank really believe that she wanted him to be as dull as other men?

"That's why I fell in love with you," she went on. "You bring light and color. You lift us up, the rest of us, whose lives are just a million shades of gray without you."

Frank turned to Maud. Resting both hands on her hips and drawing her close, he looked her straight in the eye.

"Tell me now, Maud, honestly, do you think I'm going to succeed in putting on another play?"

Maud nodded, but her eyes darted briefly away from his gaze.

He let go of her and returned to the window, where he stared out at the empty street, now gray from a cold drizzle that had been falling all day, his shoulders hunched in a dejected slump.

"It's just the money," Maud said. "I set a few pennies aside every week, but to mount a play—it's hard to see where we'd get that kind of cash. You'd need to find a sponsor . . ."

"Oh, it makes no difference," Frank said. Without looking at Maud, he picked up his overcoat and umbrella. "I'm going to go for a walk now," he said.

Maud watched at the window as he retreated up the street, rain dripping off his black umbrella.

THAT NIGHT, UNABLE TO SLEEP, she watched the moon rising in the cloudy sky. She sensed that Frank was still awake, and she rolled back toward him. "You can go," she said.

She could feel him suddenly become alert beside her. "What do you mean?"

"Back to Richburg. I know you won't sleep right until you see *Matches* back on the stage."

"Maudie dear, you know I can't do that. I've got my sales schedule all set. We've no money to put on another show. I'm not even sure we can find an audience."

"We'll manage somehow," Maud said. "But you need to do it or you just won't be *you.*"

"Oh, Maudie!" Frank said, his voice thick. "You won't be sorry! And we'll figure out how to make it not so rough for you and the boy on the road."

"Oh no, Frank. Bunting and I can't go. We would just be in the way, and it would be too expensive. We'll move in with Mother to save money. You know she's lonely in the big old house all alone."

Frank rolled over and studied Maud's face. She could see his shadowed features in the moonlight. "Would you really do that?"

Instead of answering, she placed her lips on his.

The next morning, Frank was already out of bed before Maud awoke. From the landing, she saw him alone in the parlor, dancing to some melody only he could hear. His eyes were closed, and he looked almost as if he were waltzing in a dream.

Maud didn't say a word. She descended the stairs and reached out her hand, and without missing a beat, he felt her presence, slipping his arm around her waist and drawing her close in a two-step. As they spun around the narrow parlor, the room, silent but for the shuffling and gliding of their feet, was filled with music.

FOR THE NEXT FEW WEEKS, whenever Frank was home he was in a fever of creation—playing songs, scribbling on his notepad, sketching out costumes and sets. But the evening prior to his departure, as soon as the door pushed open, she saw the look on his face, and she knew something was terribly wrong. He plopped heavily into one of the parlor armchairs, and stared up at her, his eyes so red that she thought he must have been crying.

"Frank, tell me at once! What is it? Is someone sick? Has someone died?"

"Yes," he said mournfully. "Someone died. The actor Louis
Baum died today."

"Frank!" She narrowed her eyes. "Have you been drinking?"
She sniffed the air but smelled no whiskey, just his familiar tweedy
scent.

"It's the Baum Theatre in Richburg. It caught fire and burned to
the ground."

"No!" Maud said.

"They salvaged nothing. It's all gone."

"The whole theater?"

"Everything!"

"But surely the costumes, the scripts, the scenery . . . some of it
was saved?"

Frank shook his head, then sobbed aloud, burying his face in
her bosom.

A week later, Frank returned from a trip to Richburg with his
worst fears confirmed. Every bit of property belonging to the Baum
Theatre Company was gone. Every single copy of the script for
Matches had disappeared in flames. All of the costumes and the
elaborate sets for *The Maid of Arran* had turned to ash.

A melancholy silence fell over their home as her husband
stopped tapping out melodies on the piano. Week after week, Frank
hit the road with his horse and buggy, loaded up with his tin-can
samples. He tried desperately to make the dull business of axle
grease seem more amusing, composing little songs and ditties
about it and always remembering to bring Maud back an amusing
tale from the road.

Four months later, Maud realized that she was expecting her
second child, and Frank rented a larger house in Syracuse for their
growing family to live in. Their life was settling in. Their days on
the road were clearly now behind them, and Maud was beginning
to convince herself that Frank had adjusted to their new life.

One day, some of Matilda's relations came to visit, bringing with
them several young children. Maud heard excited laughter coming

from the parlor. She slipped quietly through the doorway to find that Frank had rigged up a curtain and was performing a one-man show. He had invented a character, a man made of tin who was left out in the woods and couldn't move until all of his joints were greased up with Baum's Castorine Oil.

"But why is he made of tin?" one of the children piped up, eyes wide.

Frank turned to the boy in utter seriousness. "Oh, he wasn't always made of tin," he said. "Once he was flesh and blood, like you and me."

"What happened?" another small boy cried out.

"Well, you see, he was a woodcutter by trade, but unfortunately, he was clumsy. He kept accidentally cutting off parts of his body." Frank mimed the hacking off of a leg, followed by an arm. "And each time he cut off a part, he went to the tinsmith, who made him a new arm or a leg out of tin. Until there was nothing left. He was entirely made of metal."

"What about his head?" one of the children asked.

"His head, too!" Frank said. "Head, body, arms, legs—entirely made out of tin, just like a tin can. Was quite inconvenient when it rained, as he would start to rust. And the only thing that would save him was . . ."

"Baum's Castorine Oil!" they all cried together as Frank held one of the cans aloft.

The oldest of the four children, however, looked skeptical and spoke up. "But if his entire body was made out of tin just like a tin can, then he was empty."

"That's right," Frank said. "As hollow as an old tree trunk that's been struck by lightning."

"But that's not possible," she insisted.

Frank bent down on one knee in front of the girl. "Not possible?" He mimed extreme surprise.

"Because if he were hollow, he would have no heart!"

"Indeed," Frank said. "He had no heart. And, you know, a man who gives up his heart is little better than a tin can . . . and all the Baum's Castorine in the world couldn't make him better. That's why he was so determined to find one. Sometimes, when the tin woodman leaves home, when he goes on the road, leaving his family to sell his chopped wood, he feels so hollow he bangs on his chest, just to hear the echo inside. That's what it's like to be a man of tin. It's very lonely."

At that moment, Frank caught sight of Maud, and his face flushed crimson. He leapt to his feet, smoothing back a lock of hair that had fallen onto his face.

"Well, there you are, Maud! We're just having a bit of fun here."

Maud smiled, but right then she knew *she* had a heart, because she could feel it breaking. She remembered the image of Frank standing on the stage in Syracuse, bathed in luminous light, when he had seemed to be ten feet tall. The work of a traveling salesman was honorable and it kept a roof over their heads, but she knew it did not delight his heart.

HOLLYWOOD

1939

I T HAD BEEN WEEKS SINCE THE APPEARANCE OF THE MYSTERIOUS coat, and Maud could say for certain that it had conjured no magic, at least for her. The long process of filming was well underway, and she had yet to get her hands on a script, or even get a peek at one, so she was no closer to knowing whether she had succeeded in protecting the Dorothy of Frank's creation.

She continued to show up on the M-G-M set day after day, in the hope that something would occur to her, or perhaps that she would find some elusive sign that could point her in the right direction.

A few weeks after her lunch with Judy, Maud was waiting outside Sound Stage 27 for the red light to go off when a lanky form darted around the corner. *Langley!* He was about to disappear down another of M-G-M's labyrinthine alleys when she called out to him.

He turned in surprise, then bounded back toward her.

"Why, hello there—Mrs. Baum, isn't it?"

"How nice to see you again." As she had hoped, a copy of the paperbound script was tucked under his elbow. "How is the script coming along? All finished now?"

"Hardly," he said. "It's a work in progress." He flipped it open, revealing a page crisscrossed with strike-throughs in blue pencil.

"Mind if I take a look? I might have some insights—coming from the book, you know." Maud reached toward it.

Just then, the red light flickered off, and the stage door burst open. Out came Jack Haley, the Tin Man, in full uniform—his silver makeup blinding in the sunny alley.

Maud took her eyes momentarily from the script, only to find that Langley was slipping it into his valise.

"Afraid not, Mrs. Baum. Script is embargoed. Short list of people outside the cast are allowed to see it—and that list comes straight from the top. But do let me know if you think of something important. I'd be happy to take it under consideration." Langley nodded to the Tin Man, spun on his heel, and bounded away. Maud stood, arms akimbo, wishing like all hellfire that she weren't old, that she were wearing short pants and could tear off after him and steal the script, as she would have done as a young girl. Alas, Maud was attired in a floral A-line dress, stockings, and sturdy pumps, and Langley had a good head start. Going after him would be futile.

It took a moment for Maud to notice that the costumed Tin Man was looking at her with interest.

"Hello there," the silver fellow said affably. He flicked his head in the direction Langley had disappeared, then stuck a cigarette between black-painted lips. "Writers. They're all one-eyed sons-of-bitches—beg pardon, ma'am." He stretched out a silver-gloved hand. "Jack Haley."

"Mr. Haley. You must be the fellow who replaced Buddy Ebsen? How's he doing, do you know?"

"Poor guy. Got an allergic reaction to the makeup and ended up in an iron lung. Now, that's what *I'd* call a tin man."

"Oh dear. I hope you don't have a similar problem."

"Makeup mixed up the aluminum powder with grease so I don't breathe it in. Maybe I'll end up in the hospital, too. Who knows? Wouldn't mind," he said, taking a long, satisfied drag on his cigarette. "I get so hot in this costume. Fella wouldn't mind ending up in the hospital, some days."

"Well, I'm pleased to meet you, Mr. Haley. I'm Maud Baum. My late husband—"

"Wrote the book?" he said. "Yeah, I know. I've seen you around."

"Is your costume really made out of tin?"

"See for yourself. Bang on my chest if you want."

Maud tentatively stuck out a finger and tapped. Not metal.

"Leather," the tin man said. "It's buckram covered with leather and spray-painted. Looks real though, don't it?"

The stage door pushed open, and a young man with a clipboard appeared. "Back to work, Haley."

"Aww, my heart is breaking. Except, of course, that I don't have one," he laughed. He flicked the black-smudged cigarette onto the asphalt and ground it out with his giant silver, rivet-covered foot, pulled open the door, and gallantly held it until Maud had passed.

Maud found her way to the rear of the dimly lit sound stage and took a seat on the viewing platform. Transformed again since her last visit, the set was now crowded with lifelike trees studded with artificial bright red apples. A segment of painted yellow road ran along a post-and-rail fence. Behind it was a rough brown façade that Maud recognized as the woodcutter's house. With dismay, she realized that this scene corresponded to chapter 6 in the book. Chapter 6! With each dancing step the characters took along the road to Oz, more of the spooling roll of film was in the can. For all of these visits to the set, what had Maud accomplished?

The Tin Man took his place as the set decorators draped him with ivy and adjusted his stance just so. After some time, Judy emerged from the shadows. Two women in pink smocks trailed her, one brandishing a comb and the other holding a makeup sponge. At last, the director signaled and the camera clicked into action. Maud watched Judy get down on her hands and knees, find two bright red plaster apples at the Tin Man's feet, and rap on one foot before she looked up and realized she was beholding a man made of tin.

"You've got to be more surprised," the director scolded. "It's not every day that you run into a tin man. The characters are imaginary, but you're a real girl. Act astonished, Judy!"

This kind of direction went on through several takes. From what Maud could tell, this part of the script hewed pretty closely to the original scene in the book. She watched anxiously as Judy tried again and again to get it right. No one let up on the girl just because she was young. The director and producers bossed her about, the male actors constantly tried to upstage her, and her mother sometimes darted onto the set to tug at her daughter's dress or make some whispered judgment. But Judy remained at all times professional, unflappable, calm.

After a while, the men stopped to solve a camera problem and the action ground to a halt. The actors lounged about while a makeup artist fiddled with the Tin Man's face. Blue-covered scripts were scattered here and there on the stage, some splayed open. Maud's yearning to hold one in her hands, to leaf through it at her leisure, was so intense that she could hardly concentrate as the director adjusted tiny aspects of the lighting and the camera's angle. Maud had been trying to catch Judy's eye, but the girl was not looking her way.

A young man hurried through the back door and straight up to the director.

Fleming turned to the actors and said, "I've got to take a telephone call. Ten-minute break."

Judy seemed to have disappeared somewhere into the set. The rest of the actors were streaming toward the exits, no doubt for smoke breaks. The door swung open and shut several times, and then stayed shut, leaving Maud alone on the viewing platform. The sound stage, bustling just a moment earlier, was now empty and silent.

Maud looked again at the empty stage—the painted Yellow Brick Road, the trees made of chicken wire and foam rubber, the façade of the woodcutter's house. She reached into her purse to pluck out the paperback she was reading, but then, on second thought, put it back as she realized what was right in front of her. Scattered on makeshift tree stumps and abandoned on director's chairs were several copies of the script. Maud drew a sharp breath inward and stood up slowly.

Would she?

She pictured her own mother, Matilda Gage, in 1876 when she and Auntie Susan and the rest of the officers of the National Woman Suffrage Association had stormed the dais at the nation's centennial celebration to present a Declaration of the Rights of Woman directly into the hands of the vice president of the United States. Certainly, her mother had not raised her to shy from a challenge.

Maud slipped her purse over the crook of her elbow.

The heels of her pumps sounded like a cannon fusillade in the silent room as she hurried across the wooden floor, her eyes fixed on the director's chair. Swooping in, she grabbed the closest copy of the script and tucked it under her arm. None too soon. A crack of light had appeared at the back door. Without thinking, she rushed away from the light—hoping there was a back door somewhere so that she could duck out unseen.

The first possible route of escape was a door marked WARDROBE. She tried the doorknob, found it unlocked, and slowly pushed it open.

"Oh!" Maud said.

"Oh!" Judy replied.

The young actress was swamped inside a giant black cloth garment—the Wizard's coat.

"What are you doing?" The girl looked alarmed.

"What are *you* doing?" Maud said. She held the script tucked under her arm, but Judy, whose face was beet red with embarrassment, wasn't paying attention to that.

"You must think I'm an old fool!" Judy said.

"I don't think you're a fool—and certainly not old," Maud answered, turning her body at an angle to hide the pilfered script. "But what are you doing? Isn't that the Wizard's jacket?"

Judy was already wriggling out of it, her face still crimson.

"Don't tell anyone! Don't you dare!"

"I won't breathe a word," Maud said. "But I have a funny feeling I know what you were up to."

Judy raised a single eyebrow.

"You were hoping for a little bit of magic?" Maud asked gently. "A sign from your father?"

Judy shook her head and wiped a tear from her now-brimming eyes. "I just thought . . . I miss him. He used to stick up for me. Now nobody does."

"You don't have to explain. We all need a little bit of magic from time to time."

Maud reached out to embrace the girl, forgetting that she was trying to conceal the script. At the same moment, someone called out, "Judy! You're needed on set!"

Judy scooped up the heavy cloth coat, looking around nervously, and shoved it onto its hanger. Meanwhile, Maud slipped the stolen script onto the table, planning to retrieve it as soon as Judy exited the room.

"Judy!" The voice was getting closer.

"Not a word!" Judy said. "Promise?" She then picked up her basket, scooped up the script, apparently thinking it was hers, and rushed out of the cramped room. As the door slammed behind her, Maud stood in astonished silence. She had lost the script! All that trouble for nothing, and now she was going to have to find a way to sneak out without attracting notice.

Maud waited a few minutes before emerging. She looked this way and that, then realized that her presence was concealed from the set by several large crates and boxes stacked outside. She glanced around, hoping for an escape route, and her eyes alighted on a door marked LAVATORY.

Inside, Maud was suddenly confronted with her own reflection in the mirror. She saw a face furrowed and lined, imprinted by decades of worry, thinned lips pressed together in determination, eyes sharp from her wariness of soft dreams and illusions. And if Frank had been standing beside her? She pictured her husband as she had first known him: his soft lips, so quick to smile; his twinkling eyes, the first to see the humor in any situation. He had tempered her toughness, stayed her worst instincts, teased out the kindness she'd inherited from Papa, and toned down the grit her mother had taught her. What would he think if he could see her right now?

In her heart, Maud knew. Frank wouldn't have been focusing on stealing a script when something more important—the welfare of a child—was at stake.

Her worn face in the mirror was telling her something. Reminding her that of all the roles she had played in her life—tomboy, student, wife, mother, widow, and steward of Frank's legacy—the most important of these had been mother. Was she really so old that she had grown blind to the plain truth in front of her? No doubt that Judy's talent, her almost preternatural gift, made her seem older and wiser than her years. Nevertheless, she was still a lonely young girl who missed her father and was looking for someone to take care of her. It was almost eerie, now that Maud thought about it, how terribly fitting it was that Judy was playing the role of Dorothy. Like another young girl long ago, Judy needed someone to help her.

After several more minutes had elapsed, Maud pushed her way out of the bathroom and crossed toward the set. Mercifully, the actors were standing around while the director fussed over some bit of minutiae with the Tin Man's ax, and no one heeded her as she picked her way over the camera cables taped to the floor and slunk toward the sound stage exit.

As Maud drove home, she sorted through her thoughts about this confusing day. Judy and Dorothy, Dorothy and Judy. She now understood that they were one and the same. You couldn't love the character and look past the girl who was pinned into that gingham dress. Maud's instinct told her to take the girl—to carry her away—to find a different life for her somewhere where predatory agents and fat men with cigars weren't all looking to take advantage of her gifts.

But Maud had learned some bitter lessons in her life—and perhaps one of the hardest was that you can't always rescue people, no matter how much you want to.

SYRACUSE, NEW YORK

1886

MAUD STAGGERED DOWN A LONG HALL, FLANKED BY DOORS on each side. She flung each one open with a bang, but each revealed only an empty room. Far off in the distance, a baby was crying, as faint as the chirping of a tiny bird. The hallway telescoped out in front of her.

Frank! Maud cried out, but his name, instead of coming out fully formed, wafted out of her mouth like a puffy cloud. *Frank!!* The words seemed to float above her, a line of vaporous puffs. Suddenly, she was seized by fear. She couldn't move; she was paralyzed. She twisted and turned, but she was caught up in something. It wrapped around her torso like a vise, so tight, so tight, that she shrieked out in pain.

"There, there, dear Maud." Maud opened her eyes and saw Julia leaning over her, wiping her forehead with a cool cloth.

"You've had quite a fever," Julia said. "I think it's coming down now."

Maud closed her eyes, but again she saw the long hallway, the empty rooms. She opened her eyes, and this time, she saw not just her sister's face but Frank's, peering at her with concern.

"Maud," Frank said, in the gentlest voice. "Have you come back to us?"

"But where have I been?" Maud said. Why was she here, in this upstairs bedroom? She was . . .

Maud's hands flew to her belly, but she drew them away quickly—her stomach was hot and painful.

She closed her eyes again and willed herself to concentrate, but her head was so thick and fuzzy, she couldn't think straight. Bits and pieces came back to her. She remembered her pains coming in waves; she was standing by the window, looking at the garden.

Frank's face was so close she could reach out and touch it, but her arm was too heavy to lift. She could see tears blackening his long lashes.

"Don't leave us again, my dearest. I can't lose you."

Through the fog in her mind, through the confusion of the image of the long corridor, she remembered. She remembered that she had given birth. She could remember the lusty cry and the ruddy body slick with the white grease of birth.

Where is the baby?

Julia's face hovered above her.

"Maud, Maudie dear? Don't try to talk, just rest . . ."

Where is the baby?

Now a man with whiskers stood over her. She recognized Dr. Winchell. He murmured, "You need to rest." She felt the sharp stick of a hypodermic, and then everything receded.

MAUD AWOKE TO A bright sun shining in the window. She blinked her eyes and tried to roll to her side, but she felt a sharp pain in her belly and then a gentle hand on her arm.

"Maud? Are you awake? How are you feeling?"

Frank had placed a hand on her forehead.

"You feel cooler."

"Frank." Maud was trying to speak clearly, but her breath came out in a whisper.

"What is it, dear?"

"The baby? Where is the baby?"

"Oh, Maudie dear, don't trouble yourself about the baby. He's beautiful, and I'm taking good care of him. You just take care of yourself."

"The baby—is okay?" Maud tried to smile, but she felt herself slipping away again.

MATILDA APPLIED A CAMPHOR plaster to Maud's tender, swollen midsection. Maud's teeth were chattering, and she shook so violently that the bedstead shuddered against the wall.

"I've brewed you some willow-bark tea to bring your fever down." Matilda lifted Maud's head and spooned the tea into her daughter's mouth.

Maud heard babies crying. The sound seemed to echo and multiply. How many babies? Why were they crying? Was one of the wails coming from her own child?

Mother disappeared and Julia arrived. Julia left and the doctor came in. The doctor left and Frank came to rest by her side. And still, the babies cried.

At one point, Frank said, "I'd like to bring Bunting to see you. Just for a moment. It would cheer him up."

At the mention of her son's name, she felt her face grow wet with tears, even though she didn't know she was crying.

Bunting stood in the doorway, one foot crossed over the other, dressed in his nightshirt, his golden hair tousled. He looked like an angel. Maud tried to sit up, only to collapse with a sharp stitch in her side.

"Hello there, darling," she whispered, but her voice was so soft he couldn't hear. She reached down inside herself, pulling up all her strength. "Come in, sweet Bunting, don't be afraid. It's just your mama." She tried to smile.

The boy darted back down the hallway. Frank disappeared after him.

Maud closed her eyes. She floated on a dark wave of pain.

Sometimes when she opened her eyes, she could see the tree outside her window. Bare of leaves, it looked like a giant hand reaching up to a white sky. Maud saw black crows perching on the branches, and she counted them, rhyming in her head: *One for sorrow, two for joy, three for a girl, four for a boy* . . . But then they disappeared, and she wondered if they had ever been there at all.

JULIA KISSED HER CHEEK, smoothed her brow, and told her that she was leaving, going back to Dakota.

"No, you can't go!" Maud tried to sit up, but she couldn't. In the next moment, Julia was gone.

Songbirds sang outside the window, and the tree was suddenly green, dusted with tiny buds. The sky was bright blue, and scattered across the blue, white fluffy clouds floated like balls of cotton.

"It is a testament to your youth and fortitude, and to your family's devoted care, that you are still alive," Dr. Winchell said. "I've seen few women recover from such a severe puerperal sepsis. But make no mistake, you are not yet fully recovered. The slightest strain or draft of cold can still kill you."

Maud was only now beginning to understand what had happened to her. On the third day after childbirth, she had developed the dreaded fever. That she was still alive was nothing short of a miracle. But she could not see for what purpose she had been spared. Five times a day, her nurse placed a folded length of cotton between her legs, and each time, the pad was soaked with the devil's brew—green and yellow, foul-odored. Her cheeks were sunken and gray, her hip bones stuck out, her arms were useless twigs, and below her umbilicus, where she had once been strong, her belly remained swollen and sore to the touch. Nevertheless, Maud had begun to refuse the morphine injections, determined to uncloud her mind.

She could see what had happened from the faces of them all—from her frightened little Bunting, who hovered at the sickroom door but refused to come in, from the weary faces of her caretakers, from the softly repeated rosary of the Irish nurse, from the grave way the doctor addressed her—and she understood that she was no longer Maud. She had become that most dreaded household figure: the female invalid.

"We've done everything we can do for you here," the doctor said. "The only hope is to put you in a sanitarium."

Maud lay in the bed, almost too tired to speak. Perhaps Frank expected her to protest, but . . . but instead, she felt nothing, except for a dark, gray, blank relief that she would no longer be a burden.

DR. VANDER WENK'S SANITARIUM was clean, bright, and quiet. Maud was relieved that her family was spared the sight of the hideous tube that stuck into her belly, draining foul-smelling pus, the same pus that still dripped from between her legs. But here, there was nothing for her to do—no words to say, no loved ones to worry about, no children to cry, no weary face of her husband, no kindness and pity of her mother, no dutiful face of the private nurse.

When, at last, the tube came out and the wound slowly healed over, leaving nothing but a shiny pink divot, Maud spent her days sitting in a rocking chair near the big windows, sun streaming onto her face. The staff brought her nourishing broth and then fresh food. At first, she was allowed to walk down the halls, and then a nurse wheeled her out into the gardens. She sat in the dappling sunshine pining for home—for Frank and Bunting, and the baby, Robert, whom they were calling Robin. How she missed them! But she was determined to set aside her impatience and focus on regaining her strength. When at last she was able to circle the garden once on her own two feet, she was ready to go home.

The first time Frank carried her new baby to her and placed him in her arms, Maud looked down at him in confusion. This pink, healthy, strapping six-month-old was completely unfamiliar to her, and as soon as she held him, he set to fussing. Maud looked up at Frank, tears filling her eyes. Frank, for his part, handled the infant expertly, jiggling him on a hip to send him to sleep, pulling silly faces to make him laugh. Maud scarcely recognized the child.

She could hardly believe that he was her own—he had never suckled. Never fallen asleep in her arms. He might as well have been a beautiful changeling dropped off on her doorstep.

And Bunting! When had he gotten so tall and full of words? When Maud reached out her arms to her beloved firstborn, he was too shy to run to her. He hung back, peering between his father's long legs. Her heart cracked. Her eldest son had become a stranger.

IT TOOK MAUD MORE than a year to fully recover, but finally she was able to care for the household and the boys again, and she started to feel like herself. The memory of the first day home, when the boys had seemed like strangers, had long since faded, and they no longer remembered that she had ever been absent. But one thing between herself and Frank had permanently changed. Each night Maud lay alone, curled up on the far side of the mattress when Frank crawled into bed. She wanted more than anything to roll toward him, to bury her face in his chest and allow him to wrap her in his embrace, but her doctor had given her firm instructions: she must not conceive another child. The sponge in the lacquer box was not enough protection. Another parturition would put her life in immediate peril.

Frank had agreed to the restriction. He treated her with the utmost kindness and concern, but Maud no longer felt like herself. She was a dainty piece of china, a teapot with a mended spout. She had no doubt of his love for her, but she longed constantly for his embrace, and treated him coldly for fear that she would have a moment of weakness.

One night, Frank rolled toward her in the dark and placed his chin on her shoulder. She could feel the scratch of his moustache through her gown.

"Maudie, darling?"

"Yes, dear?"

"I feel like I'm suffocating here in New York. So much competition. So many people fighting for the same dime. It sounds like out in Dakota, a man can really be somebody. What if we head out there? Take our chances? Try to make our fortune?"

Maud felt a slight stirring somewhere deep inside her, like the wings of a baby bird cupped in her hands.

"I know you miss Julia and T.C.," Frank continued. "Tell me, darling, what do you think?"

Maud could have ticked off a million reasons why it was a bad idea, such an uncertain venture, with the children so young. But they had left the theater company to keep Maud well, and look what had happened: she had gotten sick. Safety, certainty—whose choices in life gave them that kind of guarantee?

"Well, all right then," Frank said, mistaking her silence for unwillingness.

Maud lay her head against his chest and felt his heart thumping in her ear—Frank, so good, so kind, so generous, so bighearted. He had been such a hollow man of late. Maud was stronger now. Why shouldn't they adventure once again?

HOLLYWOOD

1939

MAUD SAT IN HER PERCH AT THE STUDIO WATCHING JUDY play a scene with Bert Lahr, the Cowardly Lion. Maud had heard that Lahr arrived at the studio at six-thirty in the morning to allow for the two hours it took to apply his rubberized mask. The poor man must have been stifling under the hot studio lights in such a thick costume. None of this, however, seemed to affect him in the least. He was carrying on with a high dose of histrionics that never seemed to flag, no matter how many times they repeated a scene. He was funny to the core. Filming required strict silence on the set, but when Bert Lahr was giving his lines, sometimes Maud had to cover her mouth with her hand or pinch the inside of her arm to keep from laughing out loud.

Evidently, Judy was having the same problem. In this scene, holding Toto, she had to tell the lion that he was nothing but a coward, only each time she tried, she burst out laughing. The poor girl was seized by the giggles, and there was nothing she could do to stop them. Watching Judy trying to suppress her laughter, Maud remembered how Bunting used to torture his little brother Robin, making faces at him during Sunday dinner. He would squirm in his seat and bite his knuckles trying not to laugh, but Bunting got him every time. This was what was happening to poor Judy now. They shot the scene four or five times, and each time, the girl's mouth would start to twitch, and before the segment was finished, she'd be doubled over with laughter.

At first, it was amusing, but soon the director's tone grew sharp.

"We don't have all day to do this," Fleming said. "You need to get ahold of yourself."

Ethel Gumm, who had been sitting quietly near Maud, listening, now jumped up and bustled down to the stage, her heels rat-a-tat-tatting on the wooden floor. She leaned in and whispered something in Judy's ear. The actress's expression grew momentarily stormy, but she quickly turned her attention back to the director, a serious look on her face. Nevertheless, halfway through the next take, Judy dissolved into giggles so intense that tears were running down her cheeks. Lahr appeared to be enjoying his power to make the girl laugh, but Fleming looked agitated.

Ethel Gumm now approached the director and whispered something to him.

"Take it from the top," the director said. "Take thirteen. Judy, get ahold of yourself."

This time, Judy almost made it through her lines. Her lips quivered, her eyes creased up, her nostrils flared. Maud crossed her fingers in her lap. The girl was trying. But it was no use.

As soon as she began to say the line "Why, you're nothing but a great big coward," she burst out laughing.

Fleming, his jaw taut, streaked across the stage toward her. With a loud smack, he slapped her in the face. Judy staggered backward and then, startled, started crying and rushed off the set.

Maud gasped. She looked over at Judy's mother, who still stood near the director, expecting her to say something or rush to her daughter's side. Ethel, however, did neither. She was smiling.

Maud stood up, marched down the stairs from the viewing platform, and pushed her way past the cameraman until she stood directly in front of Victor Fleming.

"Shame on you! How dare you slap her? You're a grown man, and she's just a little girl."

Fleming spun, glowering. "Excuse me? Mrs. Baum. You need to leave the set immediately. We're trying to work here."

"She's not a little girl," Judy's mother interrupted. "She's a professional actress, and she's expected to act like one. I gave him my permission to slap her, if that's what it takes to keep her in line."

Maud could feel anger welling inside her. Speaking in a low voice, she shook a finger at Fleming. "Don't you ever strike that girl again, or I promise you I will make you regret it."

To Maud's added fury, Fleming seemed amused. "And what are you going to do to me exactly?" He turned away from her. "Who let her on the set?"

"Now, now there." Mervyn LeRoy had appeared out of nowhere. "Mrs. Baum," he said, nodding Maud's way, "what seems to be the problem?"

"He struck that poor child. Since when does a grown man hit a child?"

"Now, Victor," LeRoy said, slipping his arm around Fleming's shoulder. "You can't hit the girl."

"I didn't mean to hurt her," Fleming said. "I was just trying to get her attention. It was her mother's idea."

Maud looked around for Ethel, but Judy's mother had chased after her daughter and was nowhere in sight.

"If you ever lay a finger on the girl again," Maud said, "I'll contact every newspaper in the country and I'll tell them that you've ruined The Wizard of Oz."

"Well now, Mrs. Baum, I don't think you'd do that," LeRoy said soothingly. "That'd be cutting off your nose to spite your own face, wouldn't it? If this picture does half as well as we think it's going to, you're going to sell a million more copies of that book."

"You think it's money I'm after? A man does not lay a hand on a woman in my presence," Maud said. "I'm not speaking as a businesswoman here. I'm speaking as a mother and a human being."

A moment later, Judy came back, dabbing her eyes with a tissue, accompanied by the assistant producer, Arthur Freed, who had his hand on her arm and was speaking to her softly.

"All right. All right," Fleming said. "I shouldn't have hit the girl.

Judy, come on over here and give me a big old punch. That will teach me a lesson."

"I won't hit you," Judy said, sniffling. "But I'll give you a kiss." She stood up on her tiptoes, leaned forward, and kissed him on the tip of his nose.

"Truce?" Fleming said, sticking out his hand. Judy shook his hand, but Maud noted that the girl did not meet his eye.

The makeup crew rushed in and touched up her makeup, chalking out the reddish splotch on her cheek.

"Now, let's get on with it."

As Maud watched warily, the film started rolling again. This time, Judy made it all the way through without cracking a smile.

"MRS. BAUM!" AS SHE was heading home for the day, Maud turned to see Arthur Freed trying to catch up with her.

"I just want to thank you for what you did in there. We get so heated up, so involved, we forget sometimes that our actress is just a child. I'll personally make sure that no one lays a hand on her. I don't think Fleming meant anything by it—"

"Someone needs to look out for her. She's just a girl."

"I couldn't agree more," he said affably. "I've seen you hanging around the set, Mrs. Baum. I'm a great fan of Oz, you know. Grew up reading those books. I'm the one who wanted to bring the book to the studio."

"That's nice to hear. But the success of your picture depends on the role of Dorothy, so I suggest you treat her well."

"You have my word, Mrs. Baum." He reached into his breast pocket and pulled out a card.

"We want to get this right." He handed her the card. "If you think of anything, just let me know."

Maud studied the man, trying to gauge how sincere he really was. "If you truly want to get this right, there *is* something you can do." She paused, to give him a chance to understand the seriousness of her request. "I made a promise to my husband, Mr. Freed. Long before this film got started, I vowed to protect Frank's story, to ensure that Oz stayed true to Oz. You just said yourself how much you loved the books as a child, so you of all people should understand. Oz must be Oz. Dorothy must be Dorothy. I understand Oz better than anyone. Yet I've not even had a chance to read the script."

Freed looked quizzically at Maud. "Read the script? It's not even finished yet. It's a work in progress. I don't think a layman would get much out of it."

"I know the book backwards and forwards. I just want to make sure you stick to the facts."

Freed laughed. "Facts? But Oz is a fantasy!"

Maud squinted at him as if he were a slow-learning child. "Of course Oz is a fantasy. But it's true to itself." She took a deep breath before continuing. "Just remember, there are millions of children out there who believe that Oz is a real place. Who *need* to believe that Oz is a real place. Because Oz is hope, and children can find themselves in dark places."

Freed rubbed his chin. "When I was a kid, I had all of the Oz books lined up on a shelf in my room. That first one was always my favorite."

Maud nodded.

"Listen," he said. "This is Hollywood, and Hollywood works on one rule and one rule alone. Do you know what that rule is?"

Maud shook her head.

"Never promise anything!" He chuckled, then mock-punched her arm. "Talk about a fantasyland."

"You'll get me a copy of the script?" Maud said, not laughing.

"No promises," he said, then winked. "But I'll see what I can do."

THE FOLLOWING DAY, Maud presented herself to Freed's secretary.

"Mr. Freed has promised me a copy of the script for *The Wizard of Oz*."

The secretary looked at her skeptically.

"I spoke to him yesterday," Maud said, extracting the card he had given her as proof.

The ginger-curled secretary took her time, languidly regarding the card.

"Mr. Freed is not in," she said. "You'll need to come back another time."

"I'll wait until he returns," Maud said.

The secretary cast a nervous glance at the closed door that bore a plaque with Freed's name on it.

Maud distinctly heard rustling from beyond the door.

"Perhaps you should just call him, in case he happened to return and you didn't notice."

A loud scrape followed by a bump was clearly audible behind the closed door.

The secretary's eyes darted back and forth between Maud, Freed's door, and her phone. Eventually, she pressed her intercom's button with a reluctant jab.

Maud heard a tinny voice through the speaker: "I told you I was taking no calls!"

"Sorry, sir, it's just that a Mrs. . . . ?"

"Baum," Maud supplied.

"Baum is here. She said you 'promised' her a copy of *The Wizard of Oz* script?"

The tinny voice sounded again through the intercom: "Tell Mrs. Baum to come back in a couple of weeks. Script's still being polished right now."

"Come back in a couple of weeks," she parroted.

Maud did not even answer. She darted around the desk, grabbed the doorknob, and flung open the door to Freed's inner sanctum. Freed sat behind his desk. A shapely brunette ingénue, not a day over seventeen, was seated on his lap.

Freed stood up so quickly that the girl almost tumbled to the floor. His face was a mottled purple, his eyes flashing. Under his suit jacket, his shirttails were untucked.

"Mrs. Baum, I'm in the middle of a meeting," he said, his voice

tight. "If you could excuse us please. *Hazel?*" he called to his secretary.

She popped her head through the doorway. "Mrs. Baum?"

"Meeting!" Maud muttered to herself as she strode out the door.
And this was the man she'd trusted to stand up in the teenager's
defense!

A FEW DAYS LATER, Maud ran into Judy just outside the sound
stage door, where she was lighting a fresh cigarette from the end of
another.

Leaning back against the door, Judy pulled from the cigarette
with alarming ease. "Good morning, Mrs. Baum," she said, exhal-
ing.

"You really shouldn't smoke," Maud said.

"The studio doctor wants me to smoke eighty cigs a day."

"Eighty?" Maud said, unable to believe she had heard correctly.

Judy nodded, taking a puff. "It helps me lose weight. But it's
hard to get enough time when we're filming all day."

Judy took one last drag and pulled the door open for Maud,
blowing twin streams of smoke out of her upturned nose.

Inside the studio, Maud saw that the day's scenes were set in the
interior of the Witch's castle. Margaret Hamilton, the actress playing the Wicked Witch of the West, was in full costume. The thick
green-tinted makeup that covered her skin made her teeth and the
whites of her eyes appear yellow.

Whenever they were dealing with the Witches, Maud thought,
the story veered too far from Frank's conception. He had never
meant for his story to be frightening. This set was creepy—all dark
grays and menacing ironwork, a crystal ball, and a large hourglass
filled with red sand. A piano was pushed near the edge of the set.
Maud recognized the fellow with the pencil behind his ear—the
lyricist, Yip Harburg, whom she'd seen a number of times—and the
cranky piano player, Harold Arlen. Maud also spotted Arthur Freed,
who gave her a wary glance. Maud had given up hoping she'd get the
script from him. At least she now knew he wasn't one to trust.

Judy was engaged in a friendly conversation with the Witch, with whom she seemed to have a warm rapport, but she almost jumped when Fleming walked onto the set, her smile replaced by a watchful expression. The scene being filmed today involved only Dorothy and the Wicked Witch. None of the other actors were present. In the scene, Judy was locked in the Witch's tower. Maud watched as the glowering green-faced character turned over the giant red hourglass and threatened the girl with her screeching voice and long-pointed fingernails. Maud squirmed in her seat as the Witch reduced Judy to tears. Of course she was acting, but there was something about her anguish that seemed too real, as if the girl's heart was constantly poised on the cusp of breaking, so that just the slightest provocation brought her sorrow to the surface.

Since her first day visiting the set, Maud had not heard the song about the rainbow again. So her ears perked up when Arlen struck a few chords that she recognized immediately. She waited to hear the girl launch into that beautiful song she remembered, but she soon realized that this time it was not quite the same. It was only a reprise, a short snippet of the longer song, which Maud presumed must come elsewhere in the film. In this scene, the reprise started just as Judy was reaching a fever pitch of despair. The Witch flipped over the giant hourglass filled with the blood-red sand, telling Dorothy that she had only that much time to live, and it was at this moment that the piano player started up with the chords. Each time the filming reached this point in the scene, take after take, the actress, usually so poised, appeared visibly shaken. Gone was the big voice, the confidence, the sheer joy of singing. In its place was the tremulous sound of a young girl, frightened, alone, trapped in a place where the woman looking after her was not a loving aunt but the terrifying, green-faced Wicked Witch. As she sang, the piano player, who'd been improvising an accompaniment to go with her uncertain tempo, suddenly fell silent, leaving nothing but the sound of Judy's voice quavering, then cracking, until she was too choked up to continue.

"I'm frightened, Auntie Em! I'm frightened!"

The stage, the set, the room fell away, and Maud was kneeling on a barren plain, next to a violet-eyed girl with messy braids, dabbing tears from her smudged face with a clean white handkerchief.

I'm frightened, Auntie Em! I'm frightened!

"Judy?"

Arthur Freed hurried over to the young actress, who was sobbing quietly.

"I'm sorry," she said, rubbing her nose with her fist. "I'm so sorry. Let's do it again. I'll do better."

Maud sat rigidly, fearful that there might be a replay of the director's heartless slap from the day before. But the director didn't say anything, and Freed was all honey.

"Let's take a break, sweetie. You've worked hard enough for now." He slipped his arm through Judy's, and Maud watched warily as he led her away.

Fleming held a hand up. "Okay, everyone. Let's call it quits for now."

As people started to shuffle away, Harburg, who had been scribbling notes on his pad of paper, looked up and gave Maud a friendly smile. "Hello there," he said, approaching her. "You're Mrs. Baum, aren't you? I'm wondering if you would be willing to let me ask you a few questions?" Harburg was holding a copy of the script, which he folded shut.

"Certainly," Maud said. "I'd be delighted." Her eyes narrowed. "Is that the latest copy of the script?"

"For now," Harburg said. "It's a—"

"—work in progress, it changes every day. Yes, I know. I'd love to take a look at it," Maud said.

The fellow cocked his head. The stage lights reflected on his eyeglasses, hiding his expression.

"Fair enough," he said. "Maybe we could get a bite to eat? You ever been to Musso & Frank's?"

"Of course," Maud said. It was one of Hollywood's most popular writers' hangouts. "I live just around the corner."

" 'Round five?" he said.

"Five it is."

As Maud was leaving, she looked around for Judy, hoping to see that the girl had recovered from her harrowing day's performance, but the alley outside the sound stage was empty.

AS MAUD WAS CUTTING behind the Thalberg Building, on the way to the parking lot, a back door pushed open, and Judy all but tumbled out right in front of Maud. Her hair was mussed, and she was frantically trying to rebutton her blouse. She was crying. When she caught sight of Maud, her face flooded with relief.

"Mrs. Baum?"

"Judy?" Maud gasped. "What happened? Can I help you?"

Judy reached into her handbag, took out a bottle full of pills, shook one out, and swallowed it without any water to wash it down. She sobbed, then balled up her fists in her eye sockets, as if forcing her tears into retreat.

"He told me he was taking me to see Mr. Mayer," Judy said. "But when we got there, Mr. Mayer wasn't in . . ."

"Who?" Maud asked.

"Freed. Mr. Freed." Now all the tears and the fluster were gone. Judy seemed kind of wooden.

"Go on."

"I can't tell you."

"Do you see how old I am? There is *nothing* I haven't heard before—or experienced myself."

Judy smoothed her skirt and straightened her blouse.

"Mayer has his own elevator that goes out the back," Judy said. "Freed said we'd go out that way. As soon as we got in and the door shut . . ." She didn't finish. She didn't need to.

Maud was furious.

"Listen to me," Maud said, placing her hand on the girl's arm. "Don't ever be alone with him again."

"I thought he was being nice to me." Judy peered at Maud. "You probably think I encouraged him."

"I think no such thing! It's not easy being a young woman. It wasn't when I was young, and it isn't now. But I have a solution for you." She rummaged around in her purse until she found what she was looking for: the small sewing kit she carried everywhere. She extracted a long straight pin with a pearl on the end.

"If a fellow gets too close and you don't want him to, poke him with this pin. It'll teach him."

"My mother told me to be nice to the studio men so that they'll like me."

"Now, listen to me, Judy Garland. Being nice means saying 'Good morning' and 'How do you do?' But if a man tries to touch you and you don't want him to, you say no, and if that doesn't work, you step on his foot as hard as you can, and if that doesn't work, you poke him with the pin. He'll squeal—and that will give away his bad intentions."

Just then, Ida Koverman, Louis B. Mayer's secretary, out of breath, rounded the corner of the building. Her glasses, hanging on a beaded chain, were banging against her ample chest.

"Oh!" she said, slowing to a walk when she saw them. "There you are . . ."

"Ida!" Judy said, running over to the stern-looking matron and giving her a big hug.

"I didn't realize that you were with Mrs. Baum," she said, still huffing a little bit. "I saw you go in with Mr. Freed, and when you didn't come out, I thought . . ."

"That he had used the back elevator?" Maud said.

"It wouldn't be the first time," Ida said. "I watch this one every day. I'm not blind. I know what goes on."

"Don't get on an elevator alone with a man!" Maud and Ida said in unison, then looked at each other in surprise.

"It's not easy for these girls," Ida said.

"It's not easy for *any* girls," Maud replied.

Judy held up the hatpin Maud had handed her.

"Good!" Ida said. "And don't be afraid to use it."

MAUD SLIPPED INTO A booth in the clubby, wood-paneled interior of Musso & Frank's at five minutes before five. A moment later, she saw Harburg coming through the door. He sat down and placed the script on the table between them.

"Not sure how much it's going to help you—it's very much a work in progress. Langley wrote it up one way, then Ryerson and Woolf changed it all around, Langley came back and tried to put it right, and now it's my job to try to stitch the whole thing together."

"But aren't you the lyricist?"

"Lyricist, wordsmith, jack-of-all-trades. Lots of writers arguing with each other, but the songs are going to drive the story." A red-coated waiter materialized next to the table. "Pastrami on rye," Harburg said. "And for the lady?"

"Just a bowl of tomato soup," she said.

"So, Mrs. Baum, you don't mind if I ask you a question?"

"Of course not," Maud said.

"It was something you said the first day I met you," Harburg said. "About the rainbow song."

At the mention of the song, Maud became alert.

"You said there wasn't enough wanting in it. . . . I've spent a long time thinking that over. I'm trying to get it just right."

"It's quite extraordinary," Maud said, "that of all of the ideas, that's the one you would choose—the rainbow, I mean. After all, there is no mention of rainbows in the book."

"Why so extraordinary?" Harburg asked.

Maud fell silent. The story of the rainbow was one she had never told anyone. The bleak prairie, the wooden wagon jouncing along on a road baked by relentless sun, the worst day of Maud's life—even with Frank at her side.

"It's just an extraordinary coincidence—and Frank was a great believer in signs."

"The song is the bit that holds the whole thing together, in my opinion," Harburg said. "If we can just manage to get it exactly right."

"May I?" she asked, nodding at the closed script that lay between them. Her heart was racing. She could hear a roaring sound in her ears, but she tried to appear calm.

Harburg nodded. "Don't see why not."

"Don't see why not? Let me tell you something: you're the first person who hasn't objected. Everyone else is keeping it as locked down as Fort Knox."

Harburg tipped his head back and laughed, so that she could see several gold crowns on his teeth.

"Capitalists."

"Capitalists?"

"They're just worried it's not good enough yet. Word leaks out that M-G-M's big new fantasy has a rotten script. That would be a killer for the studio. You know how much money they're pouring into the project? A lot more than they should. L.B. has got a soft spot for the picture, thinks it's 'magical.' It's going to be big trouble if it turns into a flop."

"L.B.?"

"Louis B. Mayer—that's what everyone calls him."

"Well, then L.B. is right. Oz is magical. And it will most certainly not be a flop," Maud said. "Not if you do your job properly."

"The script's okay—better than most, but they're just afraid to let any rumors get started. Always worrying about the bottom line."

Maud shivered as she turned back the first page and began to read. She looked up at Harburg, blinking in alarm. "But who are all these characters? Hickory? Hunk? Zeke?"

"Oh that's Haley, Bolger, and Lahr."

"I beg your pardon?"

"You know: Tin Man, Scarecrow, and Lion."

"But then why do they have different names?"

"Because that's in Kansas," he said. "That's the conceit. Dorothy already knows all these guys. And then they show up again as characters in the Land of Oz. Like it's a mirror of Kansas. Clever, isn't it?"

"But that can't be!" Maud said, louder than she expected. Blood was rushing through her ears. "Absolutely not! That's not how the story works. There is no one in Kansas but Uncle Henry and Aunt Em." Maud's voice quavered. "Oz isn't just a mirror. It's a real place. My husband was absolutely adamant about that. It was a place you could visit, and then return from. It's here right now—or at least Frank would say it was—it's just that we can't push aside the curtain to see it."

"But of course it's a real place, way I see it," Harburg said. "I'm familiar with that place—a place where fat cats don't take all the money but share it with the poor, a place where women get treated with the equal rights that they deserve—"

"You take an interest in the rights of women?" Maud asked.

Harburg had a crooked smile that revealed just a few of his teeth. His eyes were twinkling. "I should say I do," Harburg said. "Along with the rights of workers, and support of unions, and . . . I know your mother was a great supporter of those things as well."

Maud flushed with pleasure. "You are familiar with Matilda Joslyn Gage?"

"Of course I am," Harburg said. "I've got a show I've been working on called *Bloomer Girl,* about an abolitionist who dons Amelia Bloomer's daring pantaloons. Hoping we'll get it up on Broadway one of these days."

"Well, then," Maud said, "I consider you an ally."

"No sides here," Harburg said. "We're all on the same team. We want to make a great picture—something memorable."

"You know, my husband never wanted his stories to be frightening. He said he wrote fairy tales with the sad parts left out. It was hard to watch those scenes today. I worry about Judy . . ."

Harburg removed his glasses and rubbed the bridge of his nose. "A studio lot is not an easy place to grow up," he said. "But that girl was born for the stage—and she knows it. She'll do all right."

"She should be more than just 'all right,'" Maud murmured. She returned her attention to the script. The pages were riddled with pencil marks.

Harburg tapped the page she was reading. "Keep in mind, this could all change before the picture's in the can—sometimes you've got to switch things around. What makes sense in a book doesn't always make sense in the picture. What you're trying to capture is its essence. Think of it like the melody, if you will."

Harburg returned his attention to his sandwich, allowing Maud to focus on the script. There were so many corrections and scribbled notes that it was hard for her to tell what she was reading, and she felt no closer to understanding how the film would come out than the first day she'd arrived on the set.

She flipped to the last page, scanning the text until she came to the final line. Without realizing it, she shook her head vehemently, mouthing the word *No*.

Harburg looked at her quizzically. "What is it? You don't like the ending? It's just like the book." He reached out and spun the script around so that it was facing him.

" 'She claps her heels together three times. "Take me home to Aunt Em," ' " he read aloud. "What's wrong with that? It's straight from the book."

"Oh no," Maud said. "You must change this line."

"Change it? But why?"

"Just don't let Dorothy say she wants to go back to Aunt Em. Please! Can you just have her say that she wants to go home?"

"I suppose that would work well enough, but why?"

Maud could picture the faded gingham, the sunburnt face, the eyes, with their thick, dark lashes, squeezed tightly shut, and the girl murmuring under her breath.

"No reason," Maud said.

"No reason?" Harburg said. "Are you sure about that?"

Maud thought about telling him everything, pouring it out, right there at the table with this kindly man. But she couldn't. She pursed her lips firmly. She was not going to confide more than she intended. She had held on to the story's secrets for all these years. She was not going to change that now.

"Do I have your word, Mr. Harburg? You'll change the line?"

Harburg ran his hand over his slicked-back hair, leaned in, and opened his mouth, as if to persist, but Maud's fierce expression dissuaded him.

"All right, Mrs. Baum. I don't see that it makes any difference. Let me ask you something else, if you don't mind?"

"Go ahead."

"I never asked you my question. I'm working on the rainbow

song, trying to get it just right. Have you ever been to Kansas?" Harburg asked. "I wondered if there was some reason why the story starts out there."

Maud traced her finger along a ridge in the dark wooden table. In fact, the Baum Theatre Company had briefly passed through Kansas once, just a few months after her wedding. She remembered almost nothing about it except that she had received a heavy black-edged envelope; it had contained a note in her mother's hand letting her know that her father was at last in peace. When she pictured Kansas, all she could see was that letter, and her tears, and the way Frank had comforted her. Nothing else remained.

She realized that Harburg was waiting for an answer. "Frank and I went through Kansas once, not long after we were married. It was a long time ago."

"Must have made quite an impression on Mr. Baum?"

"Oh, Kansas isn't the state of Kansas," Maud said. "Kansas is just the place you're stuck in, wherever that might be."

CHAPTER
16

ABERDEEN, DAKOTA TERRITORY

1888

IN SEPTEMBER 1888, FRANK, MAUD, AND THE TWO BOYS
arrived in Aberdeen, Dakota Territory, on the Chicago, Milwaukee
& St. Paul Railway. The tracks had arrived in Aberdeen just five
years earlier, sparking the fast growth of the town. In this flat land,
set upon a plain that had once been a prehistoric lake, the horizon
was a distant line and the earth seemed swallowed by the sky. When
the railroad first arrived, Aberdeen had fewer than one hundred
residents. But Maud peered out the window at a town that had
grown to a population of three thousand settlers and an economy
that had burgeoned with the business the railroad brought, and
several years of bumper wheat crops.

It was a fine sunny day with wispy white clouds floating far over-
head as they climbed into T.C.'s rig. He settled their traps in back,
and soon they were passing along a crowded street.

"That's the Northwestern National Bank," T.C. said, pointing
out a large brick structure still under construction. "When it's finished, it will be the tallest building west of St. Paul."

Frank nodded approvingly.

"And as you can see, there are several empty storefronts along
Main Street for rent," T.C. went on. "I'm sure you'll find a good spot
to locate your dry-goods store."

"Bazaar," Frank said.

"I beg your pardon?" T.C. looked puzzled.

"Baum's *Bazaar,*" Frank said. "That's what I'm aiming to call it. And it will be no ordinary dry-goods concern. I'm planning much more of an emporium."

Maud smiled as she listened to her husband's good cheer. He'd borrowed from a few friends, scraped together some savings, and was going to enter the business of shopkeeping, but, as usual, Frank had a way of making the mundane sound spectacular.

The main street of Aberdeen surprised Maud, flanked with an improbable mix of weighty brick establishments and spindly frame-built storefronts that looked as if they might be about to blow away. With the train depot firmly anchoring one end, the commercial hub of the town was crowded with people and horse-drawn wagons, but just beyond the end of the busy thoroughfare lay a flat unbroken expanse of wavy grass extending as far as the eye could see. The sky, more prominent than any of the buildings, seemed to have a personality of its own—now blue, now gray, and now a startling pink and orange. From a distance, the prairie appeared to be a study in monochrome muted greens, but up close it burst with yucca flowers, blue sage, and butterflies. Something about this juxtaposition, this showboating rendered so tiny and insignificant by God's majesty, brought a smile to Maud's lips. Her first unguarded impression of Aberdeen, Dakota Territory, was that the town was nothing more than a vaunted practical joke—man's attempt to put his mark on something so vast, so untouchable, that his efforts were bound to come to nothing.

Frank had secured them a modest rental near downtown, and Maud set out to make it comfortable, unpacking her crates, ironing each crewel lace antimacassar, unwrapping the majolica, and lining up her volumes of Tennyson and Sir Walter Scott on a shelf. Each September sunrise turned the horizon into a vast expanse of fiery reds and yellows. In the morning, outside the window, she could hear the song sparrow's trill, and sometimes she could almost imagine that she was still home in New York. But as soon as she stepped outside, she was faced with an unfamiliar world. When

she and the boys ventured two blocks to the south, the small neighborhood of houses gave way to the limitless expanse of switchgrass,
blue grama, and needle-and-thread, where red-winged blackbirds
sang out their sounds of *conk-luh-ree, conk-luh-ree,* and where,
apart from the birds warbling and the rustling prairie grass, the
stillness was so profound that silence almost seemed to carry its
own tune.

MAUD HAD ARRIVED IN Dakota Territory anxious to see her sister, but she had not fully understood just how vast Dakota was—and
how difficult it was to get to anyplace that wasn't on the railroad
line. The closest town to Julia's homestead was almost eighty miles
north of Aberdeen, a good ten miles from the nearest train depot.
To her frustration, Maud realized that it was no easier to see Julia
now than it had been when she was back in Syracuse. Maud had
received several worrisome letters about how her sister's new baby,
James, was not feeding well. Maud wrote back, urging her to come
to Aberdeen, where it would be easier to procure medical treatment, but Julia's answers were always noncommittal.

By the end of the first week, Maud's new house was all set up.
She was sweeping the kitchen floor when peals of laughter brought
her outside to their rough patch of prairie grass, where she saw
both boys and Frank lying flat on their backs staring up at the sky,
which was studded with fluffy white and gray clouds that were sail-
ing fast across the wide blue expanse like barks on a heavenly river.

"Choo-choo train!" Bunting called out, pointing to a cloud for-
mation as it skidded past.

"Elephant!" Robin cried.

"Lion!" roared Frank. "And that there is none other than a
bear—" Seeing her, he broke off. "Come on down, Maud," he called
out, reaching up to tug on her hand.

"Those aren't mythical beasts, Frank Baum, those are rain
clouds! Get up off that damp ground and bring the boys inside before the three of you catch cold!"

"Nonsense!" Frank cried. "We are not lying on the damp ground. Why, we're watching a parade, aren't we, boys?"

"A circus parade!" Robin lisped.

"With elephants and lions," Bunting said.

"And don't forget the bears!"

Frank tugged harder on Maud's hand. A million things flitted through her mind: the heap of potatoes that was only half-peeled, the fire she needed to light in the stove now that the cool September evening was beginning to close in, the dinner to cook and the dishes to wash and the mending she wouldn't get to until both of the boys were in bed.

"Hurry up! Maud dear, a seventy-six-piece brass band playing the 'Sons of Temperance March' will be coming by soon. You don't want to miss it!"

"Yes, come on, Mama!"

Off in the distance, a bell jangled on the harness of a passing dray horse.

"That's it," Frank called out. "I can hear it starting up already."

In spite of herself, Maud clambered down, arranged her skirts, and lay on the spiky grass next to the three boys staring up at the sky. As if the heavens wanted to prove her instinct right, she immediately felt a fat raindrop fall on her forehead.

But there was no stopping the irrepressible Frank. He had started to hum, whistle, and thigh-slap a fair approximation of a marching band, and the four Baums lay on the grass, watching the clouds skidding by on the giant prairie sky, calling out one after another, "I see the fife!" "There's the trombone!" "Lookee there—it's fourteen cornets!" until a loud thunderclap shook the ground and the boys and Maud jumped up, leaving Frank still lying on his back, grinning, shouting out, "Why, what's the hurry? That's nothing but the big bass drum!"

At that moment, the heavens unleashed a torrent of rain. Maud grabbed each of the boys by the hand and hurried them inside. First she peeled off their wet shirts and then hurried to get the fire started in their Oakland stove. She made the boys sit near the fire until each had drunk a cup of warm milk from the back of the stove, while the storm grew more furious, lashing the windows and rattling the panes.

"We shouldn't have let them out in the cold like that," Maud said, wrapping a shawl around each boy's shoulders.

Frank came up behind Maud, pulling her close and resting his head on hers.

"Don't worry so much, Maudie. The boys are healthy. A little cold won't hurt them. They're thriving in this healthful country air."

As Maud turned around and gazed into his large gray eyes, a feeling rose up in her, a heat like melting silver that ran down the sides of her face, along her arms, and down her belly.

The family settled in quickly, and Maud could tell that Frank and the boys were thriving in their new home. Only her concern about Julia weighed upon her. Since writing to say that the baby was sick, Julia had sent no more letters. Maud feared this was a bad sign—if the baby was doing poorly, she might have no time to write.

Then, a few weeks after their arrival in Aberdeen, Frank came home from town with a telegram.

ARRIVING SATURDAY STOP BABY SICK STOP

"I wonder how she got the money for the tickets," Maud said. "She wrote several times that she hadn't enough."

"How indeed," Frank said, then whistled a happy tune.

"You bought the tickets?"

Frank smiled. Maud flung her arms around her husband. "Thank you, thank you!" she said.

MAUD WAITED IMPATIENTLY AT the depot. Julia's train was delayed. When at last she saw the signalman illuminate the green lantern, she scanned the flat horizon for the first sight of an approaching train. The last time she had seen her sister, Maud had been too weak to sit up to say goodbye. How peculiar, how unpredictable that she now waited for her sister on the platform of this distant town—Maud healthy and hale, and Julia nursing a sick child.

At last, Maud spotted a faint smudge of black against the blue sky. A few minutes later the train pulled into the station, and soon Maud saw a woman who resembled her sister—and yet, could that worn-looking woman truly be Julia?

But yes, she had raised her hand in greeting.

Julia had never been tall, but now her figure was stooped, her face sunburnt and lined, her clothing faded. One of her arms gripped an infant swaddled in grayish flannel, while her other hand held the small hand of a wan-looking girl of about seven. The girl's face was thin, framed in a halo of golden strands that had pulled from her messy plaits. Her eyes, a dark violet, sunk deep in their sockets, seemed to mirror the stormy Dakota sky, and her chin was small and pointed. In her arms, she held a cheap, naked doll of porcelain bisque, a Frozen Charlotte, who stared with unblinking painted eyes.

"I'm Magdalena," the girl said gravely. She curtsied stiffly, then coughed, her chest rattling as she held a grimy handkerchief to her mouth and whispered, "How do you do, Aunt Maud?"

Maud leaned down, smiling brightly at the awkward little girl, hoping to put her at ease, then turned to her sister, who was fussing with the swaddled baby, her thin lips puckered.

Maud reached out her arms—and without a word, Julia handed over the baby. Maud's heart tugged at the familiar weight of a babe in arms. The baby looked like a little old man with a pale face punctuated by two rheumy blue eyes. He felt limp in her arms.

Maud looked up and met her sister's glance.

"Darling, darling Maudie. You look ever so much yourself. The last time I saw you . . ." Maud held up her hand, but Julia continued: "I wasn't sure I'd ever see you again."

"This poor little one . . ." Maud said.

"He's not holding anything down," Julia said.

"We'll nurse him back," Maud said. "Just like you did for me. That's a promise."

"Oh, Maudie," Julia said. "It is so good to see you!"

———

BY THE TIME THE doctor arrived, a few hours later, Maud had stoked up the fire in the sheet-iron stove so high that the room was uncomfortably warm. Julia stripped baby Jamie's layers of clothing, removing his long white dress, his flannels, his binder, and two diapers. Maud floated a soft shawl onto the wicker weighing basket, and Julia held the baby close, covered by a flannel blanket, while the doctor fiddled with the scales, adjusting the weight to zero. Only when all was ready did Julia reluctantly remove the blanket from Jamie's body and place him in the scale's basket. Laid out naked on Dr. Coyine's scale, his layers of swaddling gone, baby Jamie's condition was visible to Maud for the first time: his sunken body, his bloated belly, the sticklike legs and scrawny arms. His skin had a grayish cast. The doctor fiddled with the brass weights and made some marks with his pencil in a small notebook, then hooked his stethoscope in his ears, lay the bell against the baby's distended midsection, and listened intently. At last, he gently palpated each quadrant of the abdomen, then placed his two forefingers on the belly, tapping with the other two, to elicit a hollow percussive sound, turning his head to listen to it carefully.

Jamie was strangely passive throughout. Maud knew that most infants would be crying by now, but he appeared to be sleeping, his translucent eyelids fluttering open only to fall shut. At last, the doctor nodded to Julia that he was finished. She quickly threw a thick flannel over the infant, picking him up and holding him against her breast.

"Let's start with his weight. Eleven and a half pounds," the doctor said. His voice was gruff and gravelly but betrayed no emotion. "He should weigh at least fifteen by now. He is suffering from catarrh of the bowel. You must follow my feeding instructions precisely."

Tears glistened in Julia's eyes as she listened to the doctor's instructions. Maud gently began to wrap the baby back up: one diaper, then a second, then his binder, then his leggings, until the tiny, shriveled infant was fully swaddled again. Awake now, the baby bleated with little strength. Julia picked him up and rocked him gently, humming softly while tucking the tails of his blanket around his spindly legs. At last he gave up fussing and quieted.

AFTER THE DOCTOR HAD GONE, Maud stood at the stove. Into a clean quart jar, she emptied the contents of one Fairchild's pepto-nizing tube, a yellow powder that promised to partially digest the baby's milk. The smell of the peptonizing powder reminded her of the sanitarium. She poured in a gill of cold water, stirred for a min-ute, and added a pint of fresh, sweet milk, then screwed on the lid and placed the jar into a bath of warm water. She noted the time on the clock. The doctor had ordered that the baby's milk be pepto-nized for fifteen full minutes.

When that had passed, Maud filled the glass bottle and affixed the India-rubber nipple. She scooped the baby up from his cradle and carried him to Julia, who sat slumped over with her eyes closed. Julia looked as if she'd aged a decade in the last three years. Her face was creased from too much sun, her hair had lost its lustrous sheen and was now a faded tawny color flecked with gray, and her body, once gently curved, was now hard and wiry. But it was her sister's hands that had changed the most—her fingers thickened, her palms callused, her forearms crisscrossed with scars and bruises from fieldwork. On the table next to her, the lamplight shining through its amber glass, was a bottle of Godfrey's Cordial, a patent medi-cine.

Maud hadn't the heart to awaken her sister, so she settled her-self into the rocker to feed the baby. She tested the milk on the inside of her wrist, then licked it up. Peptonizing the milk gave it a bitter taste, and the flavor almost gagged Maud as it brought vividly to mind her own long illness and convalescence. She wondered that a baby would take such a strong flavor, but this was what the doctor had ordered.

Baby Jamie would not drink the milk from the bottle. His small body felt limp in her arms, and he kept drifting off to sleep. She

tickled his cheek, but he took only a halfhearted suck before turning his head away, the milk dripping down his cheek.

At first, Maud was so intent on the baby that she scarcely noticed
Julia's daughter, Magdalena, who was hovering near the hearth,
playing with her doll. She seemed used to being ignored and played
quietly, careful not to disturb her sleeping mother. But now and
again, she would look up with her deep-set eyes, a watchful expression on her face.

Maud coaxed the infant into swallowing some of the milk. She
worried the corner of his mouth with the tip of the nipple, hoping
to encourage him to suckle, but it only seemed to irritate him, and
after a few attempts, he started to cry. Julia's eyes fluttered open.

"I must have dozed off for a moment. Oh, now listen to my poor
dear thing."

"Mama!" Magdalena said, but Julia was looking only at the baby,
a worried frown on her face, so Magdalena returned her attention
to her doll.

Julia reached over and picked up the bottle of medicine from the
table beside her.

"Give him a few drops of this," Julia said. "They call it 'mother's
friend.' It always seems to soothe him."

Maud looked at the medicine skeptically. Matilda had always
held patent medicines in great suspicion. "Perhaps we should con-
sult the doctor first."

Julia shrugged, then uncorked the bottle and poured herself a
dose. Maud watched with concern.

"For my sick headaches," Julia said.

"Come with me, Magdalena," Maud said. "Let's go into the
kitchen. I'm making a pie, and you can help me crimp the edges."
The little girl's eyes widened, but the hint of a smile lightened her
expression. She quickly gathered up her doll and scampered after
her aunt.

"Let me see your hands, dear," Maud said, filling a washbasin
with warm water from the stove.

Looking at the floorboards, the girl jammed her hands into her
skirt pockets.

Maud knelt down so that she could look her niece straight in the eye.

"You don't want to show me your hands?"

Magdalena shook her head, her eyes downcast, a single pucker creasing the center of her chin.

"You can't help me with the pie unless your hands are clean. You don't want to help me with the pie?"

A round circle of pale skin showed that the girl had washed her face before setting out, but closer to her hairline was a rim of smudged dirt. Maud held out her own hands.

"Show me your hands, sweet pea."

Shyly, Magdalena pulled her hands from the folds of her skirt. Maud noted the black crescents of her fingernails. The girl blinked at Maud, her mouth puckering. "I tried to get them clean," she said. "But we didn't have any more soap. Mama said she was going to make more but the baby was too sick."

Setting aside the pie-making project, Maud washed the girl's hands; intertwining Magdalena's small fingers with her own, she worked up suds with a bit of lye soap. Then Maud laid out a slice of bread with butter and fresh chokeberry jam and put a kettle on the stove to heat the bathwater. When the girl had finished eating, Maud set to work on her matted braids. Magdalena submitted stoically to Maud's comb, grimacing only when Maud tugged on the knots, but when the big kettle started singing, Maud picked up the shears.

She considered asking Julia's leave, but she didn't want to disturb her, and there was no choice in the matter. Maud guessed the girl's hair had not been fully combed out in months.

Magdalena looked at the scissors, white-eyed as a spooked colt.

"I'm sorry, sweet pea, it's just that your hair is too tangled to comb out. I'm going to cut your braids off. If you don't like it, it will grow out in no time."

Five minutes later, Magdalena's hair hung below her chin, and the comb slipped through without resistance.

As Maud poured the hot water into the large washbasin, the room filled with steam. She stripped the girl down next to the warm stove. The girl's tiny frame was knobby and unsubstantial. Dark tan lines ran across her forearms and lower legs and the back of her neck. Maud tested the water, added a bit of cold, swirled it, then picked up her spindly niece and placed her into the warm water. Magdalena sat quietly in the bath, allowing Maud to scrub her until her skin was rosy and her hair was clean.

Throughout, Magdalena clutched her doll, who was now colored a streaky gray from the bathwater.

"Can I wash your dolly for you?" Maud asked. She didn't care for these cheap Frozen Charlotte dolls. Naked, chalky white with painted features and immovable joints, they were sold in boxes that looked like little coffins. "I think she'd like to have a bath, too."

Reluctantly, Magdalena stretched out her arms and let her take the doll. Maud rinsed the naked porcelain figure carefully and dried her with a clean dishtowel.

"What's your dolly's name?" Maud said. "Would you like me to make some clothes for her?"

"Her name is Dorothy," Magdalena said softly. "I think she would like some clothes. She gets very cold when the wind blows."

Maud wrapped her niece in a towel she had set out to warm near the stove, then swiftly plaited her hair, the braids so short now that they stuck out from the sides of her face. When Maud had the girl completely clean and re-dressed, her face pink, her hair smooth, the pair reentered the parlor, where Maud found Julia once again asleep, this time with the baby in her arms. The bottle of pepto-nized milk was still almost full. Julia's eyes opened, and she looked at Magdalena, now nicely combed and scrubbed clean, but she hardly reacted. She had a glazed expression on her face, and a yellowish pallor showed through her cheek's wind-whipped suntan.

"Julia, I'll take the baby now. You go on up and get some rest."

Julia retrieved the medicine bottle before she crossed the room and trudged slowly up the stairs. As the hours passed, Julia did not make a reappearance, and Maud, hoping to let her sister rest, sat with the baby in her arms, trying to coax him into feeding while Magdalena hovered nearby. Robin and Bunting, happily amusing themselves, zipped through the room from time to time, full of laughter, carrying toys, a ball, and, once, a stray calico cat, and then ran outside again.

"Run along and play with the boys, Magdalena," Maud said. But the girl shook her head and stayed near Maud, whispering imagined conversations with her doll. Though Maud longed to follow the boys outside into the brisk prairie air, she stayed at her post, abandoning the bottle and using a teaspoon to dribble milk into the baby's mouth, most of which appeared to drain back out without being swallowed. In spite of four straight hours of feeding, he had taken in just a few ounces. Maud longed for her mother, always so competent in the sickroom. Surely, she would know what to do.

As if in answer to Maud's wish, the following day, the post arrived with a letter from Mother, who had heard the news of baby Jamie's illness. A great believer in healthful remedies, like Maud she was a skeptic about many of the popular pharmaceuticals, dubious concoctions that, she believed, sometimes made people sicker. Mother treated people with natural tinctures and soothing balms—using the old-fashioned treatments she had learned from her father, a doctor.

In her letter, her advice was firm:

> You must find a wet nurse for the baby. Not a single one
> of the medical concoctions will bring a baby to health
> like a mother's milk.

As Julia read Matilda's letter, she looked forlorn. She said that the nurse who had attended her on the homestead had encouraged her to dry up her milk because the hard life she led would spoil her milk, and so Julia had dutifully bound her breasts. But the baby could not keep any of the substitutes down—not the lactated powder, not the bitter peptonized milk, not even the teaspoons of brandy the doctor had prescribed to stimulate his appetite. Maud had given the baby no further drops of the Godfrey's Cordial, convinced that it made him too sleepy to eat, but little Jamie remained frail and sluggish in spite of Maud's constant ministrations.

Within a day of receiving Matilda's letter, Maud had found a stout Bohemian woman who sat in the corner holding Jamie all day long, putting him at the breast, and if he wouldn't suck, she would simply let the milk drip into his mouth from her swollen brown nipple. After several days, he started to rally. At night, the nurse went home, and Maud made herself a cot so that she could sleep beside him in the warm kitchen, where she fed him condensed milk from a bottle, insisting that her sister needed to rest. But Julia still seemed exhausted and continued to drop off at odd moments throughout the day. Maud watched worriedly as her sister kept her amber dram of Godfrey's Cordial always at her side.

The sisters were consumed with caring for the children and the sick infant and rarely left the house, so more than ever Maud craved Frank's good cheer, which burst like rays of sunshine whenever he was home. In the mornings, he got up early, dressed, and headed downtown, where he was working on his new variety store. His cheerful manner, friendly voice, and jaunty step on the stairs always set Maud's heart soaring. The children ran to him, and Frank regaled them with stories of the goings-on downtown. He described his new store, Baum's Bazaar, and all of the splendors that would be sold within. Half the time, Frank came home from downtown with something in his pocket—a can of oysters, a stuffed clown, a box of chocolates. Even Julia seemed to perk up when Frank was home, listening to his tales with an unfocused gaze.

Only Magdalena didn't join in at story time. Since the day of the bath, she had attached herself to her Auntie Maud, playing at housekeeping as Maud swept and cooked and made beds and served and cleared the table and ironed. She had arrived in Aberdeen looking as raggedy as a beggar girl, but now, with Maud's attention, she was clean and tidy, with an angular face and giant watchful eyes. The girl had taken to bringing Maud little gifts—a single bluebird feather, a bunch of bee balm, a smooth round stone—offering these small tokens on the palm of her outstretched hand. Her deep-set eyes, fringed with dark lashes, calmly regarded Maud. She rarely smiled or spoke above a whisper. Again and again, Maud marveled at how different her niece was from her own two boys, a rough-

and-tumble mess of torn britches and scabbed knees, and both of them mile-a-minute talkers, full of wild stories—clearly cut from their father's cloth. Maud adored her happy-go-lucky sons. Yet she had never imagined that she would be a mother to only boys. She wanted a girl to complete their family, and to carry on the Gage tradition. Nevertheless, Maud had accepted that she would never have another child. The doctor had made it clear: another pregnancy would endanger her life.

One evening, as Maud sat carefully mending and patching one of Magdalena's worn dresses, she asked Frank if there was a little bit of spare fabric at the store that she might use to make Magdalena a new one. The following evening, Frank showed up with a bolt of cotton cloth.

Maud stood on her tippy-toes and kissed him on the lips, feeling the tickle of his moustache. "Blue gingham!" Maud exclaimed. "It's perfect. It will set off the blue-violet in her eyes."

After supper one night, Frank sat in his usual spot at the table with a pen and ink, writing up advertisements for his store's grand opening. Maud sat across from him, her sewing basket out, working on Magdalena's new dress. All of the children were asleep, even baby Jamie, and Julia had retired early. Maud's deft fingers moved steadily as she enjoyed the peaceful house—just the sound of the wood crackling in the stove and the scratching of Frank's pen on the pad of paper. Frank sometimes mouthed the words as he wrote, his expression amused. He seemed to enjoy writing—so different from her mother, who had always looked fierce at her desk, and woe upon anyone who interrupted her. Frank appeared just the opposite, as if he were reading a book that he just happened to be writing. She knew that he wasn't thinking up any new plays at the moment, just jingles and advertisements for the store, but still, he seemed to be having fun.

"You're hard at work," Maud said.

Frank glanced up at her with a smile. "Work? Not at all . . . I've invented a poetry grinder. You turn the crank, and out pop clever advertising rhymes."

Maud smiled. "Fancy that! And perhaps you could also invent a prose grinder for Mother—you turn the crank and out pour important women's suffrage tracts!"

"Why, I imagine that I could! Give it a whirl."

Maud laughed, setting aside the blue-and-white-checked sleeve. She held her hand up to his ear and pretended to turn a crank.

Frank straightened up, cleared his throat. "Women are granted natural and inalienable rights . . ." Maud tried not to laugh. Her husband could do a wicked impression of Matilda. She cranked again. "Votes for the women of Dakota!"

"All right," Maud said, picking up her sewing again, "let's leave dear Mother alone. And let's see what you've come up with for the store."

He began to read, cranking his arm alongside his ear:

> *"At Baum's Bazaar you'll find by far,*
> *the finest goods in town,*
> *the cheapest, too, as you'll find true,*
> *if you just step around . . .*

"Much easier than making it up myself, don't you think, dear?" Frank asked, then read on a bit, all the while cranking, as if he needed to operate the crank in order to turn the gears in his head:

> *"And then the toys for girls and boys*
> *are surely—"*

He stopped, pretending that the crank was stuck, and jerked his head back and forth and up and down with the most theatrical motions, as if he were a marionette and someone was pulling his strings.

"Oh, dear!" Maud laughed. "What happened?"

"The machine broke," Frank said.

"Broke?"

"Too much fun jammed up inside!"

"You do love toys, Frank Baum! You're as bad as the children."

"Did you know that on opening day, we'll have one hundred and ninety-six different toys? Why shouldn't the children of Aberdeen be visited by the same Santa Claus that visits Syracuse?"

"Why not indeed?"

Nothing—not sickness, nor bad weather, nor the trials of life—could dampen Frank's love of children, and more than ever she felt the burning deep within her, the desire to have another child. In the cold light of day, she knew the facts. If she died in childbirth, her boys would be left behind, motherless. To Maud, this was an unacceptable risk. But slowly, over these last few weeks, as she'd watched little Magdalena start to blossom, she knew it would be hard to let her niece go when the time came.

JULIA HELD A LETTER in one hand, baby Jamie, asleep on her shoulder, in the other. She was frowning.

"What is it?" Maud asked.

"It's James. He wants to know when I'm coming home. Says he hasn't eaten a decent meal or had time to do a washing since I left."

"But you can't go back now!" Maud said. "The baby is on the mend, and the cold weather is settling in. You and the children need to stay through the winter. What if the baby takes sick again—what if there is a big blizzard? You'll be stranded with no access to help."

"He says to come now as the weather may turn and we'll be stranded."

"Julia, be sensible. Better that you be stranded here than there!"

She shook her head. "He's right. We need to head back north before we get snowed in here. The weather has been pretty mild the last few days, but you know it won't last." She peered down at the baby. "He's doing better now. Dr. Coyine said so. I'm going to wean him from the wet nurse and keep him on the concentrated milk day and night."

Maud tried to hide her frustration. She knew that if Frank were in the same situation, he would put the children's safety over his laundry and cooking. Already, just caring for the baby was exhausting Julia. How could she cope with the baby and the work of the farm, not to mention looking after Magdalena?

"Tell him no!" Maud said. "Explain yourself. Surely he'll understand."

Julia's face clouded as Maud spoke.

"It's not like that," Julia said. "He's not like Frank. You wouldn't understand."

"Wouldn't understand what?" Maud said, putting down her sewing and looking her sister in the eye. "It would be crazy to leave Aberdeen now. What is there to understand?"

"James doesn't like to be challenged."

"Challenged? You are not challenging him. You are looking out for your family, as any woman would do."

"It's different for you." Julia sounded peeved. "Frank is so good-hearted. James doesn't like it when I act too independent. He thinks Mother encouraged me to speak my mind too much."

Maud's mouth fell open. "He wanted a potted plant and got a sentient human being instead? Julia, that's nonsense!"

Julia's face turned sheet white. She raised her voice: "Don't tell me that's nonsense! Tell me nothing unless you've walked a mile in my shoes. What do you know about anything, Maud Gage? Everyone has always indulged you. Beautiful Maud! You think my life has been as easy?"

"Dear sister, please don't get vexed with me." Maud's voice was placating. "Forgive me if I've offended you. But surely James would understand that the baby is sick—that you need to think of the children first."

Julia's pallor had taken on a yellowish cast, the color the Dakota sky turned when storms were brewing. "James expects me to obey. I didn't drop that pledge from my wedding vows, as you did."

Maud folded her hands in her lap and regarded her sister with dismay. How many times had she heard her mother repeat that a married woman was at the mercy of her husband, whether he be drunkard or sober, wise man or fool? And despite all of Mother's protesting and speechifying, here was her own daughter yoked to a man who seemed to think of nothing but himself and his own self-ish interests, with Julia lacking the backbone to stand up for her-self. She was blind to her own situation, just as blind as the day James had chased Maud into the storeroom and had then had the audacity to present her sister with a ring!

Maud gave up her hope of convincing Julia. Instead, she nursed a quiet plan. Magdalena needed a mother, and whatever mothering instincts Julia possessed seemed to be used up by caring for the baby. When it came time to leave, Maud would insist that she leave the girl in Maud's care.

AT LAST IT WAS opening day for Baum's Bazaar. Maud had not seen Frank so buoyant since his theater days. Julia insisted on staying home to look after Jamie, so Maud decided to bring Magdalena along. She had finished her blue gingham dress, shined her shoes, and tied her hair up in rags the night before so that it fell in curls that framed her face. Even Magdalena's doll, Dorothy, had a new dress, sewn from the leftover gingham scraps. Maud made each of the children line up so she could put a last bit of spit and polish on them, and last of all she checked her own hair in the looking glass.

It was mid-October and the sky was bright, but a cold wind whipped across the prairie, carrying a crisp scent of clean air and drying grass. Maud and the children settled into the back of T.C.'s wagon and trotted the short distance into town. As they approached, Maud saw a gay crowd of well-dressed men and women, so large that it spilled right out the front door of Frank's shop. Men carried silver-tipped walking sticks and sported bowler hats. Women wore dresses sewn in the latest eastern styles. Frank was constantly bringing home snippets of information about the citizens of the boomtown of Aberdeen—the young town now had seven newspa-pers, three hundred pianos and organs, seventy lawyers, seventeen doctors. Today, all that boomtown prosperity was on display.

Maud's heart leapt as she caught sight of Frank. Tall and gra-cious, he was greeting his patrons at the doorway, shaking each gentleman's hand and passing a free gift box of Gunther's candies to each lady. When a child entered, Frank squatted down, engaged in a brief conversation, and pressed a piece of penny candy into each palm.

Inside, the store looked like a colored plate of Aladdin's Cave in a children's book. Everyone was commenting about the artful way the merchandise was displayed. It reminded Maud of the theater. The store was a stage, the wares were the set, and Frank was the star of the show, dressed in his immaculate long-tailed coat, starched white collar, and bow tie. Maud thought about her own father: his apron, his eyeshade, his neat rows of numbers stenciled on a pad. Baum's Bazaar was not even a close cousin to that enterprise. Up in the rafters, Japanese paper lanterns twinkled in shades of rose, blue, yellow, and orange. Piles of crockery and cut-glass vases sparkled. Fancy silver tea sets and sugar tongs glittered like jewels.

Maud could scarcely contain the children's excitement as they took in the vast array of toys. There were monkeys, horses, rabbits, cats and pug dogs made from fur; there was a miniature tin kitchen with a full set of pots and pans; there were lead soldiers and toy villages to delight the boys, all manner of toy guns—pop guns, BB guns—and swords, plus steam engines and magic lanterns. Magdalena held tight to Maud's hand as she looked with wonder at the dolls. There were dressed dolls and waxed dolls, patent dolls and bisque dolls. Dolls that cried when you lifted them, and dolls that said "Mama." There were carriages and cradles, doll high chairs, and doll swings. Hobbyhorses with long manes and tails made of real horsehair were poised to gallop to imaginary lands. Shiny sleds with bright red runners would surely delight the children back home, but she wondered where a child could sled on such a pancake-flat landscape. Maud soon lost track of the boys, who had crowded around a brand-new bicycle.

Magdalena was gazing at the doll display, Dorothy clutched tight to her chest. When Frank joined them, he reached into the display, picking out the largest and most elaborate doll. It had jointed limbs, real hair, blue eyes that opened and closed, and a trunk full of elegant clothes.

Frank knelt down beside Magdalena. "What do you think about this one?" he said. "She's mighty fine-looking, isn't she?"

Magdalena stayed mute, gripping her porcelain doll.

"Would you like a new Dorothy?" Frank asked. He touched the doll's hair and pointed out her fancy wardrobe, stroking the real fur of the doll's muff with the tip of his finger. But Magdalena just shook her head and stared back at the floor.

Frank patted her on the shoulder. "You needn't worry, little one. I think I know how you feel. You love your very own Dorothy better than any of these dolls. Why, now that I look at her, I can see why. Look at her beautiful black hair," Frank said, pretending that the penny doll had real hair, instead of painted-on black that was already half rubbed off. "And see how she smiles? Why, you know what?"

Magdalena looked up.

"I think I know what Dorothy wants! A high chair!" he said, pointing to the doll furniture.

Magdalena shook her head. Her eyes furtively darted toward a miniature china tea set, nested in a small wicker suitcase.

Frank saw where her eyes were resting. "You like that, don't you?" He gently tapped her on the tip of her nose. Magdalena nodded, eyes wide.

"Dorothy likes it," she whispered.

"And don't you both look as pretty as buttons in your new blue dresses," he said.

A smile washed across Magdalena's usually somber face, bright as a prairie sunrise, and to Maud's surprise, she dropped into a curtsy and then, holding her doll at arm's length, twirled so that her skirt and curled locks billowed out around her, a beatific smile lighting up her face.

Then, just as suddenly, she resumed her watchful, puckered expression. Maud's face was serene, but inside, she wanted to shout for joy. Like a little crocus poking through the snow, Magdalena was starting to come to life.

The next morning, when Maud came downstairs, she saw the little tea set sitting on the table. A moment later, she heard Frank's jaunty steps skipping down the stairs.

"Oh, Frank," Maud said, throwing her arms around him. "You remembered! She will be so delighted!"

"JULIA!" MAUD TRIED TO get her sister to listen to reason. "You mustn't leave! Can't you just stay through the winter with us? What's the hurry?"

Julia was upstairs, packing.

"Maud, please, don't ask," Julia said. "You already know where I stand."

"Then, sister, let me ask you something else. You know I can't have any more children—or, rather, I think that perhaps I *could*, but I know that I must not. Frank and I have both grown to love Magdalena dearly. Why don't you let her stay with us? You can give more attention to the baby, and it's one less mouth to feed."

Julia paled. She looked away.

Maud reached for her sister's hand. "Julia, there's no shame in it. I know you've been through hard times."

"Maud, my dear little Maudie. You don't know the half of it. A single summer hailstorm ruined most of our wheat." She lowered her voice to a whisper. "James had to mortgage the claim to make up the difference. If we lose it, we'll have nothing—and James, he . . ." Julia clapped her hand over her mouth, as if she realized she was about to say something she would regret. "Sister, you can never imagine the loneliness I feel out there. Sometimes, James has to go away for days at a time. The view out my window is utterly devoid of life and seems to stretch to the ends of the universe, and at night, the only company is the sound of the wolves howling. It plays on a person. It can make your thoughts turn dark and confused. I can't leave Magdalena here. The girl is my only company. Without my little girl, I fear that I would lose my mind!"

"But, Julia"—Frank had just come into the room and had overheard the tail end of the conversation—"surely you can put the girl's welfare above your own loneliness? Your daughter would be in the safest and most loving hands with Maud," he said. "We would treat her as our own daughter. We'll give her the best of everything."

Julia's eyes flashed.

"I see what you do! New dresses and toys! How can I compete for my own daughter's affections when I can offer nothing of the kind?"

"Julia, please," Maud said, stunned by her sister's bitter tone. "We are not competing for Magdalena's affection. We are trying to help you—and her!"

"I've accepted your charity, and now Jamie is on the mend. From here on in, we will take care of ourselves. I'm selfish, I suppose," Julia said. "But I can't bear being alone."

Maud's temper rose to a flash point. She opened her mouth, ready to leap to the defense of her plan, but Frank caught on to Maud's torrent of emotion, and he placed a staying hand upon her arm, cocking a single eyebrow as if to say, *Not now.*

"You are her mother," Frank told Julia. "You must do as you see fit. But please know that our door is always open—for Magdalena, for baby Jamie, and for you as well. If you change your mind, just say the word and we'll come and fetch her."

That night, Frank stroked Maud's back and wiped away her tears.

"We should have insisted," Maud said. "If anything happens to Magdalena, I'll never forgive myself."

"No, Maud. I'm afraid if you demanded, that would only set Julia's mind more firmly against it. Let her return to the homestead, and perhaps she'll begin to reconsider."

Maud flipped over and buried her face in his chest. "I hope you're right."

Maud shivered on the platform as the northbound train toward Ellendale pulled away, with Magdalena's pale, narrow face pressed up against the window. Maud did not stop waving until the train was gone and all that was visible was a faint gray smudge of steam on the horizon.

A WEEK AFTER JULIA'S DEPARTURE, Maud was stirring a stew on the stove when she heard Frank push open the front door. As he entered the kitchen, she was surprised that he looked so dejected.

"What is it, darling?" Maud said.

"I'm afraid we've had a spot of bad news. Nothing to trouble you much . . . it's just a business matter."

Maud turned around and took in his pinched brow and tightened mouth.

"But you must tell me, Frank. Perhaps I can help you with it."

"It's just that there has been a big storm on Lake Huron. The *Susquehanna* has gone down."

"The ship?" Maud was puzzled. "Oh, dear. Were people drowned?"

"No, thankfully, the crew was rescued, but it's not so good for us," Frank said. "It was carrying my entire Christmas order. All of the goods that I needed to stock the store . . . I'll have to reorder everything, and nothing will arrive before the twenty-fifth."

Maud could feel a furrow forming between her eyebrows. She rubbed it away with her finger, determined to appear calm.

"Wasn't that the inventory you purchased on credit?" Maud asked.

"I'm afraid so." Frank sank into a chair, looking utterly defeated. "I'm going to have to pay the bank back. It wasn't insured."

Maud laid a hand upon his shoulder, absorbing the weight of his news. "Never mind, Frank. I'm sure we can recover."

Frank turned to Maud, looking mournfully at her with his wide gray eyes.

"It's not the money," he said.

"Of course it's the money," Maud said. "What else would it be?"

"Maud, darling, do you really not understand? I've made a solemn promise that Baum's Bazaar would bring Christmas to every child in this part of Dakota Territory—we don't have near enough merchandise on hand to fulfill the need."

Even now, after seven years of marriage, sometimes Frank deeply surprised her. Maud had quickly taken stock of the parameters of this disaster: Frank had overextended and gone into debt in order to have plenty of goods on hand for the Christmas season. The 1888 harvest had produced Dakota's third straight bumper crop of wheat. While some of the small individual farmers, like Julia's husband, were struggling, the townsfolk in Aberdeen were feeling prosperous, with extra money to let them indulge in Frank's luxuries. But the Dakota people were a practical lot—they might gratify themselves at Christmastime, but they would not consider doing so all the year round. Frank had been counting on a big holiday season to put his enterprise firmly into the black; instead they would miss the Christmas season and have to go deeper into debt. Yet sales had been brisk so far. Frank would need to be careful, but with good management, they would come out all right. But to Frank, kind, good-hearted Frank, none of this was what mattered. He was worried about children not getting their favorite toys for Christmas.

"It's nothing more than a minor setback." Frank's tone had an edge of forced cheer. "There are still quite a few nice toys in the store, and if we don't have the sales we were hoping for, it will all even out over time."

ON CHRISTMAS EVE, there was not a fir tree to be found anywhere within a hundred-mile radius of Aberdeen, but Frank came home from downtown dragging a fine balsam fir that had been shipped in from St. Paul and surely had cost more than Maud would think wise. He stood it up in the parlor, filling the room with the crisp scent of Maud's childhood. They decorated the tree with candles and popcorn that Maud cooked on the back of the stove, and silvery tinsel and red glass balls that Frank had brought home from the store.

In the morning, when Maud came downstairs, she found Frank standing beside the tree with a look of unmitigated delight.

"But, Frank!" Maud opened her mouth to protest, only just then Bunting and Robin, clad in their red woolen long johns, appeared at the top of the stairs, their faces slack with astonishment.

Under the tree, Frank had constructed a city of blocks the likes of which Maud had never seen. It had tall buildings and turrets, roadways and rivers lined with shiny blue paper, and even tiny flags that fluttered from its ramparts. There were miniature trees, and tiny people, and a mechanical train that surrounded all of it. Maud knew that all of these toys must have come from the store, but only Frank could have so artfully constructed it.

"With all of these oohs and ahs, I think we must christen it the Land of Aahs," Frank said, clearly pleased at the boys' reaction. They had already crept forward, eyes bright, and knelt down to inspect their magical city up close. Now they looked at their father with wonder.

"Tell us about it, Father!" Bunting and Robin said together. "Tell us the story!"

"Well, it's a fairy kingdom," Frank said, "and of course that means it's inhabited by fairies . . ." The boys sat rapt, each on one of his knees while Frank spun a tale about his imaginary kingdom that he conjured seemingly from thin air.

For Maud, there was a delicate Japanese paper fan, and in a small square box, Maud was astonished to find a ring with a sparkling emerald.

"Frank?" Maud looked at him, puzzled. It was one thing to buy toys, and another thing entirely to buy jewels.

Frank bowed low. "I'm afraid, my darling, that it's nothing but paste, made up to look like an emerald for a queen."

Maud's face relaxed. "Oh, thank goodness!"

Christmas Day of 1888 was full of cheer and happiness, of delighted children and laughter, of carols and cakes, and, of course, the enchanted fairy kingdom Frank had built for the boys, which kept them occupied, wrapped up in make-believe, for the rest of the day. But in spite of her delight in the boys' happiness, Maud felt a niggling undercurrent of concern, and she couldn't help but add up in her mind how much all this must have cost. Like the paste jewel Frank had given her, everything was sparkling and bright, and yet she felt as if a single tear in the shiny fabric would expose the flimsy garment underneath.

Two days before New Year's, Maud was washing dishes when she realized she'd forgotten to take off the ring. She pulled her hand from the scalding water only to realize that the paste stone had faded to a dingy gray and the gold finish had stripped off, revealing the tin underneath.

Maud showed Frank the ring. "I'm so sorry! I should have taken it off. Look what I've done."

Frank whirled her around and planted a kiss on her forehead.

"No, darling! I'm the one who's sorry. You deserve a genuine emerald. I promise I'll get you one someday."

Maud wanted to tell Frank that it was not an emerald she craved as much as stability—a home, her family, and some money in the bank for a rainy day—but how could she fault Frank now? She remembered the first time she'd seen Frank on the stage, in the theater, how she had fallen in love with his magical world. She had seen that expression on the boys' faces as they stood at the top of the banister, looking down at the world of wonders Frank had created. Wasn't that the gift she had married?

AFTER HIS DEPARTURE FROM Aberdeen, Jamie lived only a few more months. On March 15, 1889, Maud received a telegram. The baby had passed that morning, and the burial was planned for that afternoon. But the northbound train was delayed, and so by the time Maud arrived in the tiny town of Edgeley it was late afternoon, and they still needed to make the journey by wagon to Julia's claim, about eight miles to the west. Reverend Langue, a Presbyterian minister, made the journey with her. A wooden box, covered in a dark cloth, rested at their feet.

Baby Jamie was laid out on the kitchen table in the main room of Julia's shanty. His shriveled body still smelled faintly of the brandy from the bath Julia had given him to try to revive him after she'd found him not breathing. Maud helped her sister dress him, inserting his stiff little legs into woolen stockings, then threading his rigid arms through the sleeves of a fine white dress that Maud had hand-embroidered.

Julia placed her son into the small pine coffin lined in white cloth. Affixed to the box was an engraved silver plaque: SUFFER LIT-

TLE CHILDREN TO COME UNTO ME. Maud had brought Kenilworth ivy, rose geranium leaves, and smilax vines from Aberdeen, and they draped these over the rough pine box.

Outside, the ground was covered with a thin crust of frozen snow. The men had worked up a sweat digging Jamie's narrow grave in the expanse north of the house. At half past five, the March sun hung low like a flat disk. The long, straight horizon was colored a faint orange and shrouded in haze as the small group of people gathered next to the open grave, also lined with pristine white cloth. James Carpenter stood, shoulders hunched, staring into the grave without expression.

Magdalena's eyes were dry, and she held herself stiffly. She was dressed in a faded black frock, with a wool shawl wrapped tightly around her thin shoulders. Now and again she shivered, but otherwise she was completely still. Maud held tight to one of her hands. With her other hand, the girl grasped her doll. As the first spadeful of dirt hit the coffin, Magdalena flinched. With a sudden jerk, she wrung her ice-cold hand free from Maud's grasp and rushed forward to the edge of the open grave. Violently, she hurled her doll into the pit. The porcelain doll hit the edge of the pine box and shattered. Its head, sheared from its body, settled on the newly spaded dirt, its painted blue eyes staring up unblinking into the heavens.

"Magdalena!" Julia shrieked. "What have you done?" She yanked her daughter's thin arm, pulling her away from the edge of the open grave. "Why did you do that?" she screamed.

Magdalena stared silently at her mother, her violet eyes shimmering in the fading purple light.

"Dorothy wanted to go with Jamie," she answered quietly.

Into the silence, the reverend struck up singing "Thou Art Gone to the Grave," and one by one the assembled joined in, their voices so frail against the giant landscape that the small knot of them seemed to make scarcely more sound than the eternal rustling whisper of the wind through the prairie grass. Magdalena didn't blink or make another sound as she watched the remains of her doll and her baby brother disappear under the unforgiving earth. The sun had plunged below the horizon, and the temperature plummeted. When they crowded inside Julia's tiny house, everyone was shivering. Magdalena clutched her now empty hands to her chest.

Neighbors from adjacent claims had brought food, so the small group quietly broke bread and ate soup, warming by the fire as a sharp wind beat across the flat land outside.

Maud sent her sister to bed, noting that Julia took a generous dose of Godfrey's Cordial before she retired, insisting that it would help her sleep. Next, Maud put Magdalena to bed in her narrow cot next to her parents' bed, staying with her niece until she was sure she had fallen asleep. All the while James Carpenter, who had said almost nothing all day, stayed near the stove with a jug of spirits, staring morosely out the window.

By the time the kitchen was straightened, Maud wanted to faint with fatigue. She had planned to make a cot for herself near the fire, but she didn't want to stay alone with Julia's husband, who had not moved from his spot by the window. Eventually she pushed open the door to the back room and crawled into bed next to Julia. Her sister's medicine had evidently not worked. Maud found her sister wide-eyed, and no sooner had Maud joined her than wolves started howling outside. It was clear that their lonesome cries came from the north side of the house, where the baby had just been buried. Maud stroked her sister's forehead and said nothing. For a long while, Julia lay perfectly still in the bed. The wolves finally ceased their howling and Maud listened to her sister's breathing, hoping that at last she had fallen asleep. But after a few moments of blissful silence, the wolves started up again. Julia flung herself upright, threw back the bedclothes, and leapt out of bed so quickly that her white nightdress swirled around her like a wraith. She began pounding on the wall of the house with both fists.

"Quiet now!" she cried out. "Quiet now!"

Maud leapt out of bed to follow her, shivering as the frigid air cut through her nightdress.

"Come now, Julia," Maud whispered. "You'll wake Magdalena. Come back to bed."

"I don't care!" Julia said. "I don't care who I wake. Don't you know what that sound is? That's the sound of my dead baby, crying in the cold, cold ground."

The wolves kept howling. Maud pulled Julia toward her, trying to muffle her screams. From the front room, Maud heard rustling, the scrape of the dead bolt, then a door slamming.

Out the window, the yard was lit up by a full moon shining on the snow. The fresh mound of dirt over Jamie's grave was the only dark spot. It lay like a splotch of dried blood on the brittle crust of snow. James, rifle in hand, was staggering across the icy ground. He tripped over the fresh dirt, then continued unsteadily. He stopped abruptly, visibly swaying, pulled the rifle up to his shoulder, and fired a shot. Its sound was so loud that for a moment, Julia was stunned into silence, and the wolves' infernal cry ceased. James lurched a bit, staring off into the darkness, but after a moment, the wolves started up again, wailing like inmates of Bedlam when the moon was full. James shot again—but his arm was too unsteady to allow him to take aim. Still holding up the rifle, he took a couple of steps back toward the dwelling. Julia pushed the bedroom door open and lunged into the front room, her nightdress billowing up behind her. The door was wide open and banging in the frigid wind.

"Julia, no!" Maud tried to grab her sister's arm to prevent her from going outside. James was now pointing his rifle in the direction of the room where Magdalena was sleeping. James held the rifle up to his shoulder, preparing to fire again.

"James!" Plunging outdoors, Julia immediately slipped on the ice, letting out a loud scream. James turned to look at her. Maud rushed forward, careful not to slip herself, and picked Julia up from the ground.

Maud all but shoved her sister back into the house. She jammed her feet into a pair of Julia's boots that stood by the door, grabbed a folded blanket from the settee, and ran out into the frigid night, heading straight toward the man who was holding the rifle, now pointed directly at her heart.

"Drop that gun right now, James Carpenter, before you hurt yourself or somebody else!" Maud's voice sounded firm and steady, but her knees were trembling so hard she thought she might collapse.

The night had gone silent again. The wolves, no doubt scared off by the ruckus, had stopped howling.

"I'm not going to stop!" James said, his words slurred. "Got to chase those wolves away from my son!"

Maud tried to think fast. "But listen, James," she said, her voice now much more gentle. "You are such a good shot. You've killed them! See, it's quiet now."

James kept the rifle cocked, its muzzle swinging unsteadily.

"Now, you come on back inside the house," Maud said. "It's cold out here, and we need to get you warmed up."

James swayed, rifle still cocked. Maud's teeth were chattering so hard it sounded like gunfire inside her head. She could see the black shaft of the rifle as it meandered back and forth, now aiming at the house where Magdalena slept, now yawing point-blank at Maud.

"James? Come now." Slowly, Maud stretched out her hand, palm up as if approaching a frightened dog.

The whites of James's eyes reflected against the snow.

For a moment, neither of them moved. Maud looked back and forth from James's wild eyes to the gun's muzzle, afraid to breathe. At last, James dropped the rifle to his side and shuffled back to the house. Maud, shivering as if gripped by a mortal fever, followed behind. Inside, James propped the rifle up in the corner and flung himself down on the settee, still wearing his boots. Maud took the blanket from her own shoulders and laid it over him.

"Go to sleep now," she said. "We've all had a long day."

Maud looked up to see little Magdalena standing in the bedroom doorway, her hand on the doorjamb, shivering in her nightdress, her eyes dark and wide.

"What happened, Auntie Maud?"

"Nothing, sweet pea. Let's get you back into bed."

When Maud at last climbed back into bed next to her sister, Julia was still awake.

"Julia! He could have killed us all with that rifle!"

"It's the drink that does it," Julia whispered to her sister. "He's a good man, but he goes to the devil with drink."

Maud pulled her sister around to face her. "Julia! A good man does not go to the devil with drink. A man who goes to the devil with drink is not a good man!"

"There's nothing to do about it," Julia said. "Whenever I tell him to stop, he says he'll leave me here and not come back. Where would I be alone out here with the children?"

"You do not have to stay out here alone! Come to Aberdeen and let him do as he will. We will look after you. You can stay with us. Don't you remember what Frank said? Our door is always open."

There was such a long silence from the other side of the bed that Maud thought Julia had fallen asleep, until she said, "Maudie, you just don't understand."

"A drunken husband firing his rifle. You lost a child today. Do you want to lose another one? Did Mother teach you nothing at all about standing your ground?"

Julia did not respond, but her body was shaking and tears shone on her cheeks in the moonlight. Again, she whispered, "You don't understand."

"It's been such a long day," Maud said. "Let's rest. We can think about this tomorrow. Here now . . ." Maud pulled a handkerchief from the pocket of her nightdress and dabbed her sister's tears.

Maud lay like a board until Julia's sobbing subsided. At last all was still, just the quiet breathing sounds of Julia and Magdalena.

Then the wolves started up their howling again.

THE NEXT MORNING, while James snored on the settee, deep in a stupor, Maud implored her sister to gather up her things and leave. But Julia acted as if the events of the previous night had not even happened and insisted that she needed to stay near her newly buried child.

Maud boiled strong coffee and plied James with several cups of it, until he was ready to drive her back to the Edgeley depot so she could catch the train back to Aberdeen.

As she was getting ready to leave, Magdalena tugged on Maud's hand and looked up at her plaintively. Her hair had grown out a bit, and her braids now hung below her shoulders again. She tilted her face upward, her chin pointing like a prow through stormy waters.

"Do you have to go, Auntie Maud?"

"I'm afraid I do, sweet pea. But I won't stop thinking about you when I'm gone."

"Can I come with you?"

Inside, it seemed as if a poisonous snake had wrapped around Maud's innards, slowly squeezing them until she longed to gasp aloud. But on the outside, her expression was serene, as she knew that any sign of sadness would just make the poor child feel worse.

"Not this time," Maud said.

Somber little Magdalena, stiff as a Sunday school teacher, didn't even utter a word of protest. She nodded solemnly and squeezed her Auntie Maud's hand until finally she dropped it, and clasped both hands behind her back, looking even more solitary without her beloved Dorothy in her arms.

Riding away on the wagon, Maud watched all of it—the dreary, isolated shack, the fresh grave, her pale, weathered sister, and the brave little girl—retreating and retracting, until they dwindled down to a single dot and disappeared.

That night, after Maud returned to Aberdeen, Frank didn't ask her for details about the trip, the funeral, or her sister; nor did he ask her what was making her so sad. Once they were in bed, he just enfolded her in a soft embrace and stroked her hair. It seemed as if she were shrinking, until her entire fiery heart and soul and all of her sadness had joined to form a round, bright ball of fire encircled by heat. She lifted her head and looked into Frank's eyes for a long time, and a certainty overtook her. Baby Jamie had not been meant to live, but Maud was young and strong—strong enough.

Maud reached down with her hand, guiding her husband toward

his sacred and loving duty. He paused, looking at her searchingly. He breathed so softly, "But, Maudie, are you sure?"

Maud averted her gaze from him but nodded. He cupped his hand around her chin and brushed her hair up from her forehead until he was looking her straight in the eye.

"No, I won't do it, unless you tell me with words. I would never ever hurt you."

Maud stared straight at her husband.

"Frank, I'm sure."

HOLLYWOOD

1939

MAUD FELT A PRICKLE OF COLD AIR AND HEARD THE sound—like an old man wheezing—as she entered the Thalberg Building. A day had passed since she had found Judy sobbing in the alleyway, but she could not get the thought out of her mind. She was determined to find a way to help her.

In the lobby, Maud noticed a new girl seated in the receptionist's chair. The young redhead frowned slightly when she saw Maud. "Mrs. Baum?"

Maud squinted in confusion. How did this stranger know her name? But with a closer look, she realized that this was the same young woman she had met on her first visit to the studio, only now her hair, which had been platinum blond, was dyed a fiery shade of red.

Maud smiled. "I'm sorry, I didn't recognize you. It's the hair."

The girl touched her bob and colored slightly. "Casting was looking for redheads," she said. "I'm an actress. Aspiring actress. Just haven't landed a part yet."

"Be patient," Maud said. "I'm sure your turn will come soon. Now, if you please——"

"I'm sorry, Mrs. Baum. Mr. Mayer is not in today. And neither is

Mr. Freed." The girl spoke a bit hastily, as if to preempt any further inquiry.

"That's not a problem. I'm looking for Mrs. Koverman."

"I'm sorry." She chewed her lip. "You're not on the schedule." Maud noted that she had not even glanced at the appointment book that lay open on her desk. "I was told—" She stopped short, and her eyebrows shot upward like the wings of a gull taking flight.

"That's all right." Maud smiled sweetly. "Don't worry about it, dear. I'm not going to make a fuss." The girl looked relieved as Maud turned away, but instead of moving toward the outside door, Maud pivoted the other way, dashing across the lobby to the elevator and punching the button. The doors slid open immediately. Relieved, she stepped into the waiting car. "Tell her I'm on my way up," Maud called through the closing doors.

When Mrs. Koverman saw Maud stepping out of the elevator, she jumped up, grabbed her pocketbook, and signaled that Maud should follow her down a short hallway, away from Mayer's office. She stopped in front of a door marked LADIES.

"Welcome to my office," she said with a wry smile. Ida ushered Maud into a well-appointed ladies' room consisting of a large anteroom furnished with floral couches and large mirrors. An open door led to a row of toilet stalls arrayed behind.

Maud looked around in surprise. "Quite a palace," she said.

"Not bad, eh? This is where I hold all of my most important meetings," Mrs. Koverman said with a laugh. "No one is ever in here besides me. It's the quietest place I know. Please . . ." Mrs. Koverman seated herself and gestured for Maud to follow suit.

Maud sat stiffly on the edge of a floral upholstered divan, her handbag balanced on her knees, trying to project a businesslike manner. "Mrs. Koverman."

"Please, call me Ida."

Maud collected her thoughts. "After the unpleasant spectacle that we witnessed yesterday . . ."

Ida nodded.

". . . I feel it incumbent upon me to speak up on Judy's behalf. My husband, Frank, was a great advocate for the rights of women.

He would have found it most intolerable to see the girl who was cast to play Dorothy be treated in such a heartless manner."

Ida clucked sympathetically, adjusting her bulk on the uphol-stered chaise. "Freed is a pig," Ida said. "But if it ever leaves this room that I said so, I'll lose my job, and I need this job. I've got a family to support."

"And what can be done?" Maud said. "I came to you first because I believed I could enlist your sympathy, but I'm unafraid to speak to anyone—from Louis B. Mayer on down. I thought you might be able to advise me in developing a strategy."

Ida sighed. She reached into her pocketbook, pulled out a com-pact, and proceeded to freshen her bright red lipstick. "I want you to know something. I love that girl as if she were one of my own. That voice . . ." Ida sighed again, kissed her fingertips, and looked heavenward. "Straight from on high. She could melt an iceberg with that voice."

"It certainly is something," Maud agreed. "I was quite struck from the moment I heard it."

Maud watched as Ida pressed her lips together, blotting her fresh coat of lipstick, then dropped her compact and the shiny metal lipstick tube back into her purse. Next, unfazed by Maud's presence, she reached under her dress to fiddle with her garter, then hiked up one silk stocking. Maud tried to hide her surprise at Mrs. Koverman's nonchalant handling of her undergarments, but her expression must have shown her discomfiture. Straightening her skirt, Ida chuckled. "Sorry, Mrs. Baum. I don't spiff up when the gents are present, but I figured in the ladies' room, it's anything goes."

"As for Judy . . ." Maud paused, wishing her voice didn't sound quite so stiff. She considered herself a modern woman, but per-haps not quite as modern as Ida Koverman!

"Let me tell you something, Mrs. Baum. Most people don't know this, but I'm the one who discovered her. I heard her singing at a nightclub in town, she was just a wee thing, not even thirteen, and I knew right away that she was something special. But I couldn't get anyone to listen to me. You know how men are. They'll chase after a

paste jewel but miss a real-life diamond if it's got a little dirt on it."
She reached under her skirt again, tugged on her other garter, then
slipped off one shoe and began to massage her stockinged big toe.

"So how did you do it?" Maud asked.

"I got her to sing 'Eli, Eli' to Mayer. It's a Yiddish song, so beautiful. Reminded him of his childhood. By the time she stopped
singing, he had tears running down his face." Ida let go of her
stockinged foot. "And he signed her. Just like that. But Mayer, bless
his heart, and he's a good man deep down, he just couldn't see it,
couldn't see past the funny-looking package that big voice came in.
You have no idea what they've done to the poor child since then—
they've straightened her teeth, they've fixed her nose, they've fed
her cottage cheese and diet pills and stuffed her into corsets, and
all the while, you and I both know, as women, that the light that
shines from that dear girl has nothing to do with the shape of her
nose or the straightness of her teeth. It's that inner beauty." Ida
slipped her foot back into her pump and groaned softly. "These
gosh-darned shoes make my bunions flare up. I put on slippers the
second I get home."

"What about her mother?" Maud said. "Doesn't she protect her
from—from people who don't have her best interests in mind?"

"Ethel?" Ida snorted. "She sees that girl as the First Bank of
Hollywood. Worst kind of stage mother. Now, her father—he was
cut from a different cloth."

Ida was leaning back comfortably on the upholstered chaise, but
Maud still sat stiffly upright, ankles crossed. "She seemed to be
very fond of him."

"Frank Gumm was a lovely man—pretty to look at, and sweet as
they come. 'Course, being the way he was didn't make it any easier
for them." She dropped her voice and leaned forward as she said
this, even though they were quite alone in the room.

"The way he was?"

She adopted a dramatic whisper. "The way I heard it, that family
got chased out of town more than once. Frank Gumm owned several movie theaters, but he seemed to get on too well with the young
male ushers."

Maud took this in.

"Now, don't get me wrong—nothing wrong with it, far as I can see. Just between you and me, a lot of our fans would be pretty disappointed to find out how many of our leading men prefer the gents to the ladies. Best-kept secret in Hollywood. But in Judy's case, I think that family went through hard times—and she was so fond of that daddy of hers. She misses him, and it makes her come on too friendly to these older men. She's looking for another daddy, but they'd rather be sugar daddies, if you catch my drift."

Maud nodded. "I'm afraid I do."

Ida slid her wristwatch around on its silver chain. "I better not stay in here too long. Somebody will be looking for me. Now, how is it that I can help you, Maud?"

"What can be done?" Maud said. "To protect that girl? Who should I speak to? What can I do?"

"I can sense you're a good woman. But that's not really how it works around here. There are thousands of girls who would trade places with Judy Garland in a heartbeat, right now, in spite of everything she endures. And there's an army of mothers out there who would kill to have that chance for their daughters, even knowing the price it comes with. You know what I mean?"

"I certainly do."

"I'm not a big fan of Ethel Gumm, but in a way you have to give her some credit. And you've got to give Judy credit, too. I don't suppose they'd be better off dragging from one two-bit nightclub to the next trying to keep body and soul together."

"My husband and I got our start in the theater. I have an idea of what that life is like. Quite a bit different when you're trying to feed yourself than when you're doing it for a lark."

"That's exactly my point. If Judy Garland succeeds as a star, she'll have a lot of money, and with that money she can make her own decisions. She won't need her mother anymore, and she won't even need Louis B. Mayer. If you're a star, you call the shots. Nobody made them sign that studio contract. They *wanted* it—even if they're not deaf, dumb, and blind to the price they have to pay to keep it."

Maud was warming up to Ida Koverman, starting to understand why she had been given the job of sitting, like a three-headed Cerberus, to guard the studio's innermost sanctum. Maud could imagine Ida, in another era, fitting right in with Matilda and Susan B. Anthony, fighting for the day when women could vote, a day so far distant that it wouldn't even come to pass in their lifetimes. Maud could almost picture a day when Ida would be seated at the studio head's desk, and Mayer would be typing and answering phones outside. Surely the kind of treatment Judy had to endure could not continue if a woman were in charge?

"If those men harness one-tenth of the power of the Oz magic, then Judy will be a bigger star than anyone right now imagines," Maud said. "They just need to do the story justice."

Ida stood up, straightened her skirt, fiddled again with her garters, and took a peek in the mirror. "I'm sure you're right. Now, if you'll excuse me, I need to take a tinkle before I get back to my desk. I give you my solemn promise that as long as I'm here, I'll try to look out for her as best I can. And I want you to know that it's real nice of you to take an interest in the girl's welfare, and I hope that this picture is all that you hope it will be, because I get the feeling you loved your husband very much or you wouldn't be here fighting for him so hard." Ida glanced toward the row of stalls.

Slipping her purse over her arm, Maud stood up. "Thank you, Ida. It makes me feel better to know that we are both watching out for her. If anything else comes up, may I call on you?"

"Don't mind me," Ida said, ducking behind a toilet stall door. "And yes, come around anytime," she called through the closed door. "My office is always open."

Maud rode the elevator back down to the lobby, smiling at the nervous-looking redheaded receptionist as she passed. Outside, the day was bright and the walkway was bordered with bright orange birds-of-paradise. Even more brilliant than the flowers was a group of women, each more beautiful than the next. They hurried past, clad in acres of taffeta and lace, spangled in costume jewelry, adorned by shining coils of hair elaborately arranged upon their heads like crowns. From their lithe forms and graceful movements,

Maud suspected they were all dancers, most likely headed off to perform one of M-G-M's big dance numbers. Judy Garland was not elegant in the same manner as these women—and yet, Maud was certain, if she could just manage to capture the essence of Dorothy, her star would burn brighter than any of theirs.

ABERDEEN, DAKOTA TERRITORY

1889

BY MAY 1889, MAUD WAS CERTAIN SHE WAS EXPECTING ANOTHER child, and as if the entire world wanted to follow suit, the last of the snow melted, leaving behind muddy shoes, daffodils outside her doorway, and a riot of prairie flowers blooming in the grasslands. The Christmas sales at Baum's Bazaar had been a disappointment but not a fatal one—the store was still generating just enough income to keep them afloat.

After being cooped up inside with the children all winter, Maud loved being out-of-doors again. In the afternoon, when her chores were finished, she wandered along the lane until it petered out, and gathered bunches of bluebells, delicate white yarrow, and purple prairie fleabane. She took the house apart, beating every rug, mattress, and pillow, scrubbing every lintel and baseboard until the house gleamed and smelled of floor wax and Fairbank's Gold Dust Washing Powder.

When Frank came home from downtown in the evenings, he regarded their sparkling home with bemusement, asking if she could not spend the afternoons with her feet up, but Maud was convinced, no matter what any doctor might tell her, that she had best stay strong, take long walks, and breathe fresh air, as only her strength would get her through the danger she faced in childbirth. If she sat still too long, her mind and hands idle, she had flashes of fear: What would happen to her children if she did not live through this lying-in?

One night, as they lay in bed, Frank's hands cupped around her swelling belly, she whispered to him:

"If I don't live, please find someone else, Frank. And be sure to choose someone kind."

"You mustn't say such things," Frank said. "Nothing will happen to you. You are strong."

Maud gripped his hands hard and whispered fiercely: "No, promise me right now, Frank Baum. I can't bear the thought of my children growing up without a mother."

"Maud, no!"

"Say it!" Maud said. "Say it now! And don't choose pretty—choose kind!"

Maud lay perfectly still, listening to the sound of Frank's measured breathing.

"I can't do it, Maud. I fear that it might bring us cursed luck. It's not natural."

Maud sat up, threw back the covers, and walked to the window.

"You'll say it now, or I'll not sleep in this bed again until you do."

Frank sighed and sat up, his long, skinny legs, in woolen underwear, illuminated by the moonlight shining in the window.

"Come back to bed, darling, please. I will honor your wish. Just don't make me repeat such a thing aloud."

"Frank, you're superstitious, aren't you?" Maud said. "Just shake my hand and tell me that you swear. It will set my mind so much at ease."

Maud came back and sat down on the bed next to him. Frank put out his hand, and he solemnly shook her hand as he said, "I solemnly swear that I will abide by your wishes." Maud flung both arms around him, and the pair sat in an unmoving embrace until Maud realized that Frank was crying—his silent tears had drenched her shoulder.

Gently, she wiped away his tears.

"Courage, dear," Maud said.

"I love you, darling," Frank said, his voice clotted.

She squeezed his hand and looked up into his gentle eyes. "It's worth it," she said.

"I have faith in you," Frank replied.

A DRY SPRING HAD started to cause chatter among the Dakotans about the fearful possibility of a damaged wheat crop, but as May ended with little rain Frank continued to feel bullish about the prospects for Baum's Bazaar. Maud could not fail to notice how very differently he conceived of his business than anything her father had ever done at the Gage General Store. Her father's motto had always been to make sure that you have what folks are looking for—and not much more; it was important to keep a tight watch on the books, as every penny could be the difference between failure and profit. Frank's idea was different. More modern, he insisted. He brought the razzle-dazzle of the former theater man, with the lollapalooza of a man who had once written advertisements to entice people to buy his axle grease.

"You see, Maud dear," Frank said, feet up on the footstool, a cigar stuck in his mouth, one night after their supper, "people don't know what they want. You have to show them. Don't expect people to just walk into your shop and know exactly what they're looking for—no sirree. You've got to prime the pump—you create the desire, and once people want something, they'll stop at nothing to get it."

Maud was tatting a lace handkerchief. She needed to keep count in her head as she listened, so she let Frank talk on without paying him too much mind. Maud enjoyed a happy Frank—his enthusiasm was infectious, buoying her past her worries; he always had one foot already into some sparkling, imaginary future. The particular future that had enamored him of late was America's game. Baseball.

"Bats, balls, uniforms," Frank said. "Ticket sales. Why, the Hub City Nine will need to be fitted out, and can you imagine how many small boys all over town will drag their mothers and fathers into the store to buy official Spalding balls for them? That's what I'm saying, Maud. They didn't even know how much they missed America's game—but they're going to know soon. We're going to remind them."

Maud kept counting under her breath as she weaved the tiny stitches. She smiled and nodded.

"But the Hub City Nine is more than just baseball—it's civic pride, it's something to put our town on the map. When the vote goes up for statehood, and we get to choose our capital, do you reckon Huron and Pierre will be able to compete with Aberdeen? I don't think so. By the time our team wins the Dakota Territory Championship, it will seem like only common sense that the capital of the new state of Dakota will have to be located right here—Hub City, home of the Hub City Nine. And when Aberdeen is as big as Chicago, we can triple, maybe even quadruple the size of our store—we won't even have to mind it anymore, we'll have a full-time staff of paid clerks. Won't it be something? We'll leave it to the boys—oh, and our little girl of course," Frank added, looking toward Maud's belly with a smile.

Maud placed her hand over her stomach and frowned a bit. "Let's not get ahead of ourselves, Frank dear."

ABERDEEN'S BASEBALL DIAMOND SAT between the edge of the town and the railroad tracks. From the bleachers, you could see over the fence and to the great expanse of bright grassland beyond. On the roof of the Ives House Hotel, about a half block behind the fence line, a crowd of people had gathered—young boys with their legs dangling off the roof and old men who had brought along their own wooden chairs. Frank frowned up at the gaggle on the roof.

"Hard to make a living if half the folks in Aberdeen won't buy a ten-cent ticket," he said, but there was no real malice in his voice.

When the nine men ran out onto the field, a shout of joy went up from the gathered people—those inside the baseball field and those up on the roof.

"Those uniforms are terrific," Bunting said, craning forward on his seat and shading his eyes with his hand. Maud had to admit that the uniforms, in gray and maroon, with each player's name and number and the words HUB CITY NINE embroidered on them, were a sight to behold. Frank had not only set up the team, he had fronted the money for the uniforms and all the equipment, expecting to earn back the cost from ticket sales. Maud felt a familiar twinge of worry as she saw the half-filled stands and the crowds of people peering through the slats in the fence, but today was opening day, and all of Aberdeen appeared to be in attendance—ticket holders or not. Maybe Frank was right about baseball.

Maud had filled a basket with fried chicken, hard-boiled eggs, and lemon cake. The morning sickness that had been plaguing her had at last abated, and the entire afternoon seemed enchanted. Frank held Maud's hand and talked excitedly about how the Hub City Nine was going to play for the territorial title and win at the state fair. The sunny weather held for most of the afternoon, but during the ninth inning, a cold wind picked up and black clouds, which had appeared distant on the horizon, now scudded in, casting the ball field in shadows.

"Oh, I think it's going to rain," Maud said, quickly packing up their basket and pulling on the boys' woolen jerseys. Sure enough, a few fat raindrops splashed their faces, but in a moment the black clouds sailed past, and the sky was a tranquil blue again.

"What a relief!" Maud said. "I thought we were in for a downpour."

"I guess you're not a farmer, ma'am!" A fellow seated on the bleachers in front of her turned around and looked at Maud with a frown. "It's past Independence Day. We're already way behind on the spring rain—I've got my wheat crop in. We need it."

Maud was gathering her wits to respond—and it would have been sharply—but Frank jumped to her defense. "No need to speak that way to the lady. We're all hoping for rain as much as the next person." Frank reached into his front pocket and pulled out his card: L. FRANK BAUM, PROPRIETOR, BAUM'S BAZAAR.

"Frank Baum," Frank said, extending his hand in a friendly manner. He pumped the farmer's callused hand in greeting while clasping his left hand around the man's arm. "You're right as right," he said. "Right as rain, you might say!" Frank was smiling broadly. "And I'm sure that those rain clouds that just blew past will come back and stick around."

"I 'preciate you saying that," the fellow said, a touch more warmly than he had spoken to Maud. "We're already far behind in rainfall right now. If we go another week, the first crop will be stunted."

Maud only half-listened to Frank's optimistic predictions about the weather. She considered it a personal failing that she couldn't muster very much interest in farming. There was a capriciousness in it that went monumentally at odds with everything Maud cherished: order, predictability, and calm. But here in Dakota, it seemed as if God himself had designed a way to torture people. Blizzards so sudden and severe that a body could get lost on his own property, hailstones the size of hen's eggs, a relentless sun beating down upon you and not a spot of shade in which to escape it, rains so heavy that a flash flood could carry you away—and the most dreaded of all, the tornadoes, with their ungodly black funnel clouds.

Personally, she had been enjoying the long streak of sunny days without rain. Maud tuned out the men's chatter and turned her attention back to packing up their day's belongings. She folded up their blankets, dusting off the crumbs, tucked the rest of the jar of strawberry preserves back in the basket, wrapped a clean linen cloth around the half loaf of bread, and returned her attention to the game, which was now at the bottom of the ninth inning.

Frank was promising the farmer that rain was imminent, as if Frank Baum controlled the weather himself.

"I'll tell you what," Frank said. "I'm so sure it's going to rain, I'll make you a wager. If it hasn't rained by next Sunday, you can step right into Baum's Bazaar and I'll give you a dollar's worth of merchandise on credit. You can pay me back out of your fine harvest next fall."

"Frank, I—" Maud tried to interrupt Frank before he shook on this crazy promise, but it was too late. The farmer, now smiling broadly, was pumping Frank's proffered hand.

"Mr. Baum, you have got yourself a deal."

After the man had turned his attention back to the game, Maud whispered to Frank: "Darling, do you think that is such a good idea?" Already, not five minutes had passed since those few raindrops had spattered down, and the sky was a blue as bright as a piece of china, with not a single cloud in sight.

"Don't worry, Maud. The almanacs are certain on the point that we'll have rain early this week. Those rain clouds were just the harbinger. Farmers do get themselves all in a tizzy about rain, understandable, but you know as well as I do that this climate suits the wheat crop perfectly. We've had three straight years of bumper crops. 'Rain follows the plow,' as they say. And you know what? Even if, for some reason, I'm wrong, and it doesn't rain, that fellow will come into Baum's Bazaar to collect, and I'll have created something much more valuable than the dollar I spent. I'll have created a customer! For that one dollar, I'll probably sell him another ten dollars to boot!" Frank, so impassioned about what he was saying, had raised his voice, and the farmer turned around again with a smirk on his face and said, "Nope, betcha won't!"

Frank just smiled sunnily and tipped his hat, and just at that moment, a Hub City Niner hit the ball with a crisp *thwack* and the ball sailed up into the bright blue sky and then clear over the ball field fence. The crowd jumped to their feet, crying out in delight as the player jogged around the bases, capturing the game for Aberdeen's home team.

As they walked home from the ball field, little Robin grew tired, and Frank hoisted him up onto his shoulders. As they strolled along together, Maud was struck by how their little family felt peaceful, as if they belonged here in Aberdeen. To cap it all off, for the first time, Maud sensed a glimmer of movement, just tingling bubbles tickling her under her navel. She said nothing, but a small smile lit up her face. It was the end of a beautiful day.

A week later, on Sunday, it had not yet rained.

A BASEBALL CRANK. That's what Frank had turned into. As the secretary and chief booster of the Hub City Nine, he threw his efforts into promoting his team. It certainly lent an air of gaiety to Aberdeen, which, as a dry July turned into a parched August, was otherwise teetering on the brink of a bad year. The ticket sales at the first game had exceeded one thousand, and all of the town's newspapers could talk of little else. For the team's first out-of-town trip, Frank organized a marching band, and more than five hundred townspeople accompanied the players as they boarded the special train that would carry them to their next match in the neighboring town of Webster.

At home, Frank and the boys seemed to breathe the game. Bunting and Robin spent all their time playing catch with a genuine Spalding ball that Frank had brought home from the store for them (replacing the first two, which the boys had lost in the tall prairie grass). Maud was only passingly interested in the ins and outs of baseball, and she gently remonstrated with Frank when she thought he was taking too much time away from the store—worried that he was focused on too many things at once.

But Maud was relieved in one way. Frank's baseball fascination kept him occupied and out of the house—she'd seen no more of the melancholy fear related to her upcoming parturition. Maud had learned to live, for the most part, with the shadowy fear of childbirth that was every woman's lot. She managed to keep it distant and boiled down to the essence of a pinpoint, barely perceptible in her field of vision, although with the slightest encouragement, her fear could swell, billowing up like a menacing black cloud settling over her home, her life, her future.

To lose a child, as Julia had, was a terrible thing, but nothing haunted a woman like the bright faces of her children. Their gentle, obdurate patience when she combed a tangle from their hair or helped them put on their nightdresses. Trust. Children believed that their mother would rise and set as reliably as the sun, having no idea that danger lurked nearby, that each subsequent child might try to snatch away his mother's life as he made his way into the world. These were the terrified thoughts that could occupy Maud's mind if she let them. So, she didn't think. She cooked and cleaned and washed and scrubbed and tatted and mended and took

long walks and visited with the neighbors and brewed tea and said
her prayers. *Yea, though I walk through the valley of the shadow of
death, I will fear no evil,* Maud prayed under her breath as she
worked. She found the bubbly glimmers of life as intoxicating as
ever. And yet, the shadow remained.

AS AUGUST WORE ON, the weather continued hot and dry. Clouds
would mass only to depart without rain, leaving a big blue empty
sky. The pleasant warmth of early summer had turned to torpor.
Grass dried up. The afternoon winds carried a fine gray dust that
crept into every corner. Not a drop of rain fell.

Now, anywhere you went in Aberdeen, drought was all anyone
could talk about. The economy of Dakota was based on the price of
wheat, and already where there should have been acres of lush
growing fields, there were expanses of shriveled brown stalks. Everyone seemed to have an idea of what to do about it, from raising
funds to creating artesian wells to seeding the clouds—a good idea,
if anyone could invent a way to do it—but for the time being, they all
watched anxiously. Maud had quickly learned what Dakotans already knew: as the farmers went, so went the towns. And if the
townsfolk were suffering, then the farmers were hurting hard.
Maud worried how Julia was faring. She wrote to her sister constantly but received few letters in return, and those few had a somber tone that did nothing to ease her concerns. Finally, Maud
broached the question that had been plaguing her since baby Jamie's death. Had Julia reconsidered? Would she send Magdalena to
Aberdeen?

A week later, Maud received a brief reply.

My dearest Maud,

Thank you for your kind offer to let Magdalena live with
you. I'm afraid that I must decline. In light of your delicate condition, I fear that she should grow too attached

to you only to suffer a loss. I keep you in my prayers
daily, Maudie dear, and hope that you will pass safely
through the shadowy vale. God speed.

Your loving sister,
Julia

Maud's hand trembled violently as she beheld the letter. She
crumpled it and threw it into the fire. A moment later, Frank came
into the parlor.

He rushed up to Maud. "Darling? What is it? You are so pale! You
looked like you've seen a ghost."

Maud said nothing. She stared into the fire, watching the paper
curl, spark, and burn until the black ashes floated up the flue.

I've seen a ghost, Maud thought, *and it is mine.*

ABERDEEN, SOUTH DAKOTA

1889

MATILDA ARRIVED THE WEEK BEFORE THANKSGIVING with a plan to stay all the way through Maud's accouchement and recovery, to help with the household and the baby. But, as this was Matilda, she also brought a second mission: to help with the organizing effort to secure votes for women in the brand-new state of South Dakota. At the train station, Maud caught sight of her mother, framed in an open doorway of the passenger car. She was wearing a black silk dress, and her hair, now snow white, was coiled at her nape. Pausing at the top of the passenger car's iron steps, Matilda looked like a queen surveying her subjects. Maud was struck by how poised and confident she appeared, how unlike the other women milling around the depot. As Matilda descended the steps and alit on the platform, Maud couldn't help herself. She rushed forward and embraced her mother, not remembering how large her belly had become, the result being that Maud's belly landed first, before the kiss.

Matilda beamed at the sight of her younger daughter. She looked her up and down and then proclaimed her fit as a fiddle.

Back at the house, Maud installed her mother in Robin and Bunting's room. The boys would bunk with her and Frank while her mother was in town. T.C. had left several months earlier, traveling out west, hoping to find investment properties farther along the railroad line, and had to miss his mother's visit.

"I'm still worried about Julia," Maud confided to her mother as they sipped tea in the parlor. "She seems well enough in body, but fatigued in mind. She took the loss of the baby very hard, and the medicine she takes for her sick headaches makes her so subdued . . ."

"You know my feeling about patent medicines," Matilda said. "Your sister would be better off sticking with natural remedies. I sent her lavender oil and told her to put a drop on her handkerchief and inhale it slowly."

"Perhaps she does, Mother, but she seems to rely more on Godfrey's Cordial."

Matilda stared out the window, lost in thought. "You and your sister are so different—born of the same mother, suckled at the same breast, and yet . . ."

"And yet what, Mother?" Maud said impatiently. "We are two different people with different minds." Maud prickled defensively on her sister's behalf. She had never understood why her mother was so hard on Julia. But she was genuinely worried about Julia and needed her mother's advice, so she pushed down her irritation and tried again.

"I don't understand why we're different," Maud said, choosing her words carefully. "She's kind and caring, but she doesn't seem to know how to take her own part—the homesteading life is so hard. I hear stories all the time of women growing 'shacky-wacky,' terrible stories. I try to help her, but sometimes, Mother, it's as if she resents my help. In the end, she does as she pleases."

"So much suffering falls upon women," Matilda said. "Imagine how much work we could do for the cause if we were not constantly being tossed like a ship during a storm. A woman's life is punctuated by these squalls that push her from her right course. A mother's health, her child's health. It is hard to imagine a greater right than the right to the health of your own body. It's why I fight."

"And how could the vote help us with any of that?" Maud asked.

"I don't exactly know what women will do with the power of the vote, but I'm sure it will be something to behold. Imagine an army of women doctors—don't you think they might hurry up and find a cure for childbed fever? Don't you think they might look for a way to ease our labor pains? I don't know how the vote will help, but I'm sure that it will."

"And before we arrive at that glorious future? What about Julia?"

Matilda stood up, smoothing her skirt, and crossed to the window, staring out through the gap between the houses to the vast expanse of parched brown prairie grass beyond.

"Julia lacks strength."

Maud continued to be haunted by the scene in the cabin the night of Jamie's death, but she could not betray her sister's confidence by sharing it with her mother.

"Julia needs to take her child and move into town," Maud said. "She can leave James to tend to the claim."

"And what's stopping her?" Matilda said.

"Nothing but money. They will lose everything if they let the claim go. I've asked her to let Magdalena stay with me."

"That is very kind of you. Why would she not agree? One less mouth to feed for her."

"Because," Maud said, "she doesn't trust me not to die."

Maud saw a look of utter seriousness cross her mother's face. "Never fear, my dear Maud. I have not arrived unarmed." Matilda lifted the lid of her traveling trunk, wedged into a corner of the parlor, and dug around until she extracted what she was looking for. She laid it on the table in front of Maud with a thump.

Maud read the title aloud: "*The Science and Art of Midwifery,* by William Thompson Lusk."

"Your dear grandfather tutored me in anatomy, physiology, and the natural sciences," she said. "I may not have achieved a medical diploma, but I've not lost my brain. There have been significant advances in the science of midwifery, especially as it pertains to childbed fever."

Matilda opened the heavy book and began to read: " 'When summoned to a patient, the physician should go armed to meet the sudden emergencies of obstetrical practice. He should go provided with chloroform, Magendie's solution of morphia, ergot, the per-chloride of persulphate of iron, and a small vial of sulphuric ether—' "

Maud, suddenly dizzy, leaned back in her chair.

"You're pale," Matilda said. Reaching into her trunk once again, she extracted a bottle of brandy, poured some into a glass, and handed it to Maud.

"Revive yourself. I don't mean to upset you, but I want you to know that I've made a study of it. You will not suffer from puerperal fever again."

Maud smiled weakly at her mother and sipped the brandy.

" 'Ergot for flooding,' " Matilda continued to read, " 'scrupulous cleanliness of the environment and careful cleansing of the perineum with a carbolic solution—' "

"Mother, please," Maud said faintly.

"You will be fine!" Matilda said. "I promise you, Maud, that I will do everything in my power. And that includes making sure that you are treated with chloroform. The idea that a woman's labor pains are God's punishment for the original sin . . . !"

She fell silent, then went back to her trunk, where she dug again, and this time produced a second thick tome.

Maud read the title: "*The Key to Theosophy,* by H. P. Blavatsky?"

"I've made quite a study of this one as well." She flipped the book open.

"Isn't that just occult and superstition?" Maud asked.

"Just the opposite. It is an inquiry into the philosophical realm. Strictly scientific."

"Scientific?" Maud said. Her skepticism was evident in her voice.

"Madame Blavatsky believes in the Astral Plane—when people die, they are not really gone. They pass into a different dimension. That makes sense to me."

Maud listened in silence. She was not devout, but she and Frank attended the local Episcopal church, where she found comfort in the familiar hymns and prayers of her childhood. She had no de-sire to look for newfangled theories about other worlds and Astral

Planes. Although she decided now to tolerate her mother's beliefs, she had lost all interest in spiritualist practices that night at Cornell when she had summoned the spirits by whacking her knee on the underside of a table.

"So, Mother. If I understand correctly, you're doubly prepared. You've come up with scientific methods to keep me safe in childbirth, and if they fail, you've got a brand-new religion that promises that if I die, I won't really *die*, I'll just pass to an Astral Plane?" Maud's tone was light, but she was vexed. Her mother had become disenchanted with organized religion, convinced that the church's patriarchy was setting back the cause of women's rights and women's suffrage. She had begun to look for spiritual truths elsewhere— lately becoming fascinated with Native American beliefs and with spiritualist practices.

"I'm not speaking lightly. I will keep you safe," Matilda said firmly. "I am giving you my solemn promise."

Just then, Frank waltzed into the room with a big smile on his face.

He spotted the book on the table, picked it up, and started perusing it.

"Theosophy," he said. "I hear that's the latest thing."

HARRY NEAL BAUM WAS born without incident on December 17, 1889. Matilda's iron fist ensured the strictest adherence to modern hygiene, and so the third, fourth, and fifth days passed without a sign of fever. By the time the New Year had passed, with mother and baby both thriving, Maud realized that the dark cloud that had haunted her constantly for the last nine months had finally lifted.

She was seated in her immaculate room, dressed in a nightgown, her hair freshly brushed and pinned. Baby Harry was asleep in a wicker bassinet next to the bed, and sun was flooding in the windows, which were framed with white lace tie-backs, casting a gentle light on the sleeping baby and picking up the golden highlights in Maud's hair.

The door pushed gently open, and Frank stood at the threshold.

Maud looked up, smiling, but when she saw Frank's face, she said, "Frank? What is it?"

Frank's lower jaw quivered, then clenched, and she saw tears filling his eyes.

"Frank! For the love of God. Is it one of the boys? What is it?"

Frank crossed the room and sank wearily onto the edge of the bed.

"No, of course not. The boys are downstairs, playing with their iron train. It's nothing like that . . ."

"What then?"

"Northwestern National Bank."

"What about them?"

"They've taken our store for failure to pay the mortgage."

ABERDEEN, SOUTH DAKOTA

1890

MATILDA WOULDN'T LET MAUD GET UP UNTIL A FULL
fourteen days of convalescence had passed, so day after day, Maud
lay in the front upstairs bedroom with stacks of inventories, IOUs,
and bills of sale surrounding her on the covers. Frank had brought
them to her, all jumbled up in a crate, asking if she wouldn't mind
taking a look. As she pieced them together, Maud started to see
what had happened. As times had gotten harder, Frank had extended credit to cash-strapped farmers and had collected on fewer
IOUs. Finally, it had caught up with him, and there was no money
left to pay the bank.

After Maud spent a while poring over these sad records of the
store's declining income, her neat rows of figures revealed the
truth: Baum's Bazaar was doomed. Selling all of the inventory would
settle their bank loan and leave them a bit of money to spare.
Enough, Maud hoped, for Frank to figure out another line of work—
although what this would be was not evident. Frank's business was
not the only casualty of the hard times. The local economy was in a
tailspin after the failed wheat harvest. People were selling their belongings at cut rates and leaving town. Aberdeen's booming prosperity of the previous year was over.

"You are adept with a printing press," Matilda told her son-in-law one evening when they were all in the parlor. "I've seen how you hand-printed those advertisements, and many of them were clever."

"But what good is a printing press if I've no goods to advertise?" Frank said.

"I've heard that John Drake is giving up and returning to Syracuse. He is looking to sell off his newspaper at a bargain price."

"A newspaper?" Frank said, lowering the paper he was currently reading, unlit pipe stuck between his teeth, legs draped over the arms of the upholstered chair. "There are seven daily newspapers in Aberdeen right now. Two Democrat, one Republican-leaning," he went on, tapping the paper he held with his finger. "One staunch Republican, one for the Farmers' Alliance, one for the Knights of Labor, and one that seems to have no purpose for existing whatsoever. If there's anything Aberdeen has too many of right now, it's newspapers. I'm full up on hobbies. I'm looking for a moneymaking concern."

Even as down-spirited as he was, Frank managed to make this long speech sound halfway cheerful. Matilda was not deterred by his pessimism.

"Nobody writes anything of interest to ladies," Matilda said. "You need to write about education and the health of children, and the suffrage cause."

"And parties and social gatherings," Maud added. "You'll have the wives asking to subscribe."

TWO WEEKS LATER, Frank put out the first issue of his new newspaper, which he had christened *The Aberdeen Saturday Pioneer*. Eager to redeem himself, Frank had dived into his new business with a fervor. He was out the door early every morning and didn't come back until late into the evening. The work seemed to suit him; after several months, however, the emerging financial picture was less rosy. From the first day, Frank had struggled to keep up subscriptions, but Maud remained optimistic. Everyone said that once the spring came and the rains started up, a single wheat crop would put everyone in the black again.

But the summer of 1890 showed no change in the weather, and a curse seemed to have fallen upon the new state of South Dakota. Rapacious bankers foreclosed on farms and businesses. A steady stream of Aberdonians were giving up and leaving town. With each family that departed, a part of the economy departed with them. The baseball team disbanded when most of the players left town to look for work. Frank kept up a steady drumbeat of positive booster-ism for the town in his editorials. Still, everyone knew that one more failed harvest would drive the town to the brink of extinction.

Maud received few letters from Julia, but she knew that if times were hard in town, they would be doubly so on the homestead. Al-though she thought of Magdalena constantly, her pride prevented her from approaching her sister again about sending the girl to Ab-erdeen. She had not gotten over the shock of learning that her sis-ter had expected her to die in childbirth. Still, she waited, and hoped that in such hard times, Julia might at last relent.

The Baum family could not control the weather, so they threw their energy into the upcoming vote for women's suffrage. The big day—November 4, 1890—was when the voters of South Dakota would decide whether or not they should strike the word "male" from the suffrage plank, giving women the right to vote. Maud had stuffed envelopes, embroidered banners, baked cookies for so-cials, and donated her fine lace to the white elephant sales. Frank penned pro-suffrage editorials and served as secretary of Aber-deen's Women's Suffrage Club. Enough was enough. Women needed to win the vote!

By now, Matilda was traveling all over the state to canvass in tiny towns and on lonely farms. As the vote approached, Frank worked himself into a fever pitch of excitement, convinced that this one thing, this one single thing, could turn the tide of misfortune that had beset Aberdeen. The South Dakotans were going to embrace women's suffrage, and then, magically unfolding from this one great event, the rains would come and the town would bounce back, and all would be well.

Maud waited up on the nights when he came back late from the printing press, now smeared with ink, as he'd been forced to let the typesetter go to save money. With fewer subscriptions, Frank worked just as hard for a third less money. Maud had been scrimping on everything.

She guarded these quiet evening hours when the children were in bed and Frank was not yet home. With the three children, Maud felt as if she never got a moment's peace. This day had been particularly trying—baby Harry was teething, and Robin and Bunting had done nothing but squabble all day. When at last all three boys were settled, the dishes washed and put away, and she had finished sweeping up, Maud collapsed gratefully into an armchair and picked up a novel. Soon she was carried away to the Scottish Highlands, forgetting her cares for a moment.

Unfortunately, the blissful interlude was short-lived. As soon as Frank burst in the door, his words came out in a torrent. Although Maud loved Frank dearly, right now she wanted to steal a few more quiet moments before heading up to bed, and she hoped that more conversation could wait until the morning. She had never expected to miss those long, peaceful hours she had once spent in the Sage Library, her books lined up next to her, lost in a Shakespeare play or an epic poem, but now she sometimes wished she had a place like that to slip away to, where no one would interrupt her while she read.

"Hello, darling," she murmured as he stooped down to kiss her on the cheek. She smiled, tapped on her book, and said, "I'm just going to read for a few more minutes." Frank, however, seemed to have been storing up speeches all day, and, undeterred, he prattled nonstop as he took off his hat and scarf.

"You see, Maud," he went on, "people just need to have a little bit of imagination. The problem of rain seems insurmountable now, but there is enough water in the James River to irrigate a hundred thousand acres, and the technology already exists to do it—

artesian wells. And it's not just wells. The world is changing so quickly. We're just ten years away from the twentieth century, and the pace of technology is moving along so fast—faster than the speed of our imaginations. See what the iron horse did to this part of the world? Imagine that soon the iron horse might fly through the air like a mighty iron Pegasus! Machines will till the fields! Farmers can just stroll down Main Street, stop for a shave, and return home to find a silo full to the top. You remember why we came here, Maud? It was promise. It was a blank slate. It was a town to build the right way from the ground up, where men and women are equal citizens, so there's double the energy to get things done."

"Perhaps we don't need to solve all this tonight?" Maud kept her eyes on her book.

"This is the turning point, my dear!" Frank exclaimed, so dramatically that Maud looked up and studied him. What was agitating him so? He was making a rapid whirling motion with his hands, as if he were responsible for the spinning of the world itself. His gray eyes were almost black, and the whites of his eyes flashed in the dim room. He ran his fingers through his hair, making it stand up like a lion's mane. The heels of his shoes tapped furiously as he paced the floor.

"The vote will save us! Mark my words, darling! In three years, we'll most likely be up to ten thousand subscriptions and wondering why we don't have more. All we've got to do is have a little imagination. Why can't the citizens of this one-horse town do as I do? Why can't they push the curtain aside and peer just a little bit into the future?"

Maud tried to quiet her growing feeling of impatience. She had snapped at the boys several times today, and she feared that soon she would snap at Frank, too. Reluctantly, she placed a bookmark between the pages and looked up at him. His eyes were feverishly bright. He paced back and forth in the small parlor, gesticulating wildly. There was a dark ink smudge on his left cheek.

"I don't know, Frank dear," Maud said soothingly, hoping to calm him so that she could return to her book. "Why don't you sit here by the fire for a moment. I'm sure we will not solve all of Aberdeen's problems, nor secure the vote for women, this very night."

"November 4, 1890," Frank said, ignoring her suggestion. "Once women have the vote, they will vote sensibly, my dear Maud, as you would do, and Aberdeen will be set on a right path to the future."

"Frank." Maud was growing exasperated. "We all hope to see women win the vote, but the success of the movement is far from certain. This is your first time dabbling in these waters. Just think of it: Mother and her friends have been working for this all their lives and have yet to see it come to pass. You have to be patient."

Although Maud was familiar with Frank's flights of fancy, she worried to see him so keyed up, so certain that this one thing would change the tide of fortune. The lesson she had learned from her mother's activism was that votes for women were astonishingly hard to obtain, for the simple reason that not a single member of the fairer sex could vote her own enfranchisement into law.

"Patient! Maud, tell me you are not suggesting that we be patient! Patient while the crops burn and the banks fail and farms are foreclosed and people leave town and the dream—the great American dream—the great promise that a person can make his own way—or *her* own way—unencumbered—burns along with it? How can we be patient?"

"You want to talk to me about patience, Lyman Frank Baum? How about you come home and spend a day in my shoes? You want to cook and clean and sweep and mend and count out pennies to every merchant? You want to make peace among the children and put salves on their sore gums and rock the baby on your hip all day? Don't talk to me about patience! How long do you think we mothers will have to wait to get our fair share of 'the dream,' as you call it? Why, we can't even vote!"

Frank suddenly looked weary, his face gray, dark bags puffed under his eyes, where once his skin had been youthfully smooth. He sank into a chair near the fire.

"Please, let's not fight, Maudie."

"This is not a fight, Frank. This is me stating my opinion about something I know a great deal about."

Maud picked up her book, opened it pointedly, and scanned a few words. But the mood was now broken.

"When I was at Cornell, I had nothing to do but read books all day," Maud said. "I chose a different life, and you don't hear me complaining about it, do you?" She snapped her book shut, stood up, walked across the room, pulled back the hearth screen, and dropped the novel into the flames. Frank stood up, his eyes wide in horror.

"Maud? What on earth? You're burning a *book*?"

She spun around and looked at him furiously. "I'm a woman. Why should I read? I might be happier if I couldn't! At least then I wouldn't be able to read the newspapers when they report that men have once again refused to give women the vote!"

Frank stared into the grate as the book's leaves separated and their edges lit up orange with flames, then looked back at Maud, dumbfounded.

Maud glared back at him, put her finger over her lips, and said, "Don't you dare say a word!" She turned and marched up the stairs, leaving Frank alone in the middle of the room as the odor of the burning leather binding filled the air. She heard his voice, calling halfheartedly up the stairs behind her, "Don't be ridiculous, Maud. Of course women will win the vote."

SUFFRAGE FOR THE WOMEN of South Dakota lost by a landslide, garnering only twenty-two thousand brave men's votes in favor, with forty-six thousand opposed. When the final tallies came in, the mood in the Baum household was bleak. For her own part, Maud was disappointed but not surprised. She had watched this cycle of hope and disappointment play out so many times in her life. Frank and her mother, however, were devastated. Matilda had stayed in the capital, Pierre, while the vote was counted. When she returned, she was uncharacteristically quiet. She sat all day with her *Key to Theosophy* book in her lap, reading meditatively, and

Frank seemed deeply depressed. The agitation, the feverish energy, the flights of fancy that had propelled him through the last few months, were gone. He ducked into the house late in the evening, strangely quiet. He was gaunt, and the bags under his eyes had become a permanent feature. At night in bed, he turned his back to her. For the first time since their marriage started, she felt him pulling away.

"Frank, darling," she whispered to him late one night. "Where have you gone?"

There was no answer.

Frank began sleeping in, and he didn't go into the newspaper office until midday. At night, he hunched over a pad of paper until late, filling reams of pages with his writings. As she tried to fall asleep, Maud could hear the furious scratching of his pen, but she dared not interrupt him, as he would simply look up at her with a dazed expression and then go on with his writing.

In the mornings, he took to lounging about in his dressing gown, drinking coffee and reading the Chicago newspapers, quoting snippets aloud to Maud, bothering her as she tried to keep up with her daily housework. Her mother, meanwhile, did nothing but read and correspond with members of the National Woman Suffrage Association. Every day, the post brought dozens of letters—some from women who were leaders in the movement, others from the group's rank and file. Matilda speared each letter with her silver letter opener, sat reading and clucking in dismay, and then carefully penned her responses. With Mother and Frank underfoot, it was even harder for Maud to get her work done, and she wished that one of them, either of them, would find some occupation outside of the house.

One morning, she was in the kitchen kneading bread when Frank called through the doorway: "The Columbian Exhibition is going to bring the future right to our doorstep. They are planning the biggest electrical exhibition in history. Pretty soon, you'll be loafing off and a machine will knead that bread for you. Do you realize how much all of this will change the world? But the people in Aberdeen just don't care."

Maud noted the new, bitter tone to his voice.

Frank kept writing, more and more feverishly, burning the kerosene lamp until the wick went low and the light sputtered out.
Maud had stopped reading his editorials, but she sensed that he
was using the newspaper now, more and more, as a place to express
his feelings, his strong views about everything: about the coming of
technology, the fate of the town. She missed the tender moments
they had shared while she was waiting for Harry's birth. Now Frank
seemed to scarcely think of her.

While Frank was on a tear, Matilda had remained uncharacteristically quiet. One day Maud came upon her mother sitting in the
parlor, an abandoned half-sewn christening gown for Jamie folded
in her lap. She was murmuring something under her breath.

"What are you doing, Mother?"

Startled, Matilda dropped the dress. "Connecting to my spirit
guide," she said. "Trying to speak to baby Jamie."

The next day, Maud found a seam ripper and tore the little dress
apart. She took the blue satin ribbon, rolled it up, and replaced it in
her sewing basket; a few minutes later, she picked up the ribbon
and threw it into the stove.

Matilda's fascination with theosophy was increasingly drawing
Frank in. While Maud tended to the household, her mother and her
husband spent hours immersed in conversation about the possi-
bilities that alternate worlds existed, just next to our own, and that
people could learn to sense them and even cross from one to the
next and back again. Maud despaired of getting Frank to pay attention to the world they lived in now—the one where there were
mouths to feed and bills to pay, laundry to wash and fold, and children to tuck into bed.

Frank brought a copy of *The Aberdeen Saturday Pioneer* home
each week. At first, the newspaper had been fun to read. The first
several pages were standard boilerplate—copy he purchased to fill
the pages—but he had also written amusing accounts of Aberdeen's
social goings-on and some opinion pieces about the affairs of the
day, and most of it had been quite fun and lively. Now, though, the
pages were filled with fantastic stories of flying machines and me-

chanical people and electric contraptions that did the work of people and wells that pumped themselves and irrigated the fields.
Frank kept saying that folks in Aberdeen lacked imagination, that
there was a fantastic future and it was right around the corner. But
Maud knew that the people of Aberdeen were too occupied with the
present to concern themselves with a fantastical future. Every day
another merchant closed his doors; every week she saw another
family piling their belongings on a wagon and leaving town.

Frank's readers surely wanted a solid weather forecast, an as-
surance that the bank was solvent, and a loan to buy wheat seed, not
stories of talking machines, just as Maud wanted money to buy gro-
ceries, shoes for the children, and to keep a roof over their heads,
not her mother's stories about a golden path that led to enlighten-
ment.

At last, Matilda boarded the train to return to Syracuse. Maud
found that she was relieved to see her go.

By February, their income had slowed to a trickle. Frank had
gone around making inquiries about securing more funds to get
him through this slow spot, but the local businessmen had given
him discouraging news. There were rumors that Aberdeen's biggest bank, the Northwestern National Bank—whose half-finished
brick structure had so impressed Maud their first day in town—
might not be solvent for long. Everyone was jittery. If the bank
failed, most of the people in Aberdeen and the surrounding county
would be wiped out. Frank's hopes of finding more investors for
his failing newspaper were dashed. The locals' advice to Frank was
candid: leave town.

It was then that Frank, who was normally full of energy, came
down with an ague and took to bed, shivering with fevers. A few
days later, both boys took sick, and soon the baby was fretful and
could no longer sleep through the night. Maud herself began to feel
feverish, but she ignored her symptoms, fueling herself on coffee
and sugar to save more food for Frank and the boys. Soon, she was
lightheaded and exhausted. Standing over the stove, stirring a pot
of thin soup with just some flour mixed in to thicken it, she felt
woozy. When she opened her eyes, she was lying on the floor with

the soup ladle next to her head and Bunting squatting down, crying "Mama," his eyes wide in fear as he shook her shoulder. The Baum household was in crisis.

In the midst of all this, Maud received a letter from Julia. Times were hard on the homestead. Julia had changed her mind. She wanted to send Magdalena to Aberdeen, after all.

Feverish and exhausted, Maud stared at the letter as if from a great distance. She had begged her sister so many times to send her, and yet now she had barely the strength to take care of her own family. She longed to bring Magdalena home, but Frank was too sick to get out of bed, their pantry was nearly empty, and they had no prospects for how to fill it. The small sum of money Mother had left them—all she could afford—was all gone, and T.C. was still out west, with no immediate plans to return to Aberdeen. What if Maud took the child from Julia only to realize that she could not provide for her? There was no work to be had in Aberdeen. Frank would need to hit the road and look for employment elsewhere—until then, Maud knew, the meager stores in the pantry were not sufficient to tide them over. Still, she'd have to make do somehow.

The next day, her fever abated, leaving her weak and exhausted, but still she held off for a few days, reading and rereading her sister's letter, tossing and turning at night, barely able to sleep. On the third day, she wrote a letter to her sister and, without showing it to Frank, sent it by afternoon post.

As soon as he was strong enough, Frank took their last few dollars to buy a one-way ticket to Chicago. Their dream—Frank's dream—that a man could find a place for himself if he just set out and looked for the right place to do it was dead.

And Maud realized the truth: that even after almost a decade of marriage, and three births, her family still had no real place in the world.

A MONTH AFTER FRANK departed for Chicago, he wired that he had found a job and was returning to help them pack up and move with him to the city. He warned Maud that the money to pay for their journey would have to be found by selling off most of their personal possessions. Maud looked around their small home, at their simple furniture and their few wedding gifts, remembering the high hopes she had felt two and a half years earlier when they had arrived here. Those dreams would soon be erased, torn asunder as if a prairie cyclone had come through and blown them all away. But no one could take her memories. She surveyed the comfortable rooms, determined to imprint on her mind the joyful times her family had spent there.

After Frank returned, Maud traveled to Ellendale, switched trains, and debarked at Edgeley. James Carpenter was waiting for her, but she was dismayed to see that Julia had not accompanied him to the station. At least he appeared sober. He greeted her courteously, if a bit distantly. Maud wasn't sure how much he remembered about their last encounter, although she remembered it all too vividly.

There wasn't much to the town of Edgeley, just some drab frame buildings, a short main street with a saloon on each end, and a few mean houses scattered around in a haphazard fashion. The road out of town led to their homestead, about eight miles to the west. Julia had few near neighbors, and most of them were German-speaking Hutterites from Bohemia who kept to themselves. At one point, Maud and James came upon a slough of water that reflected the sky with a deep slate color, its surface rippled in the breeze like furrows on a plowed field. A flock of Canada geese bobbed on the surface.

The sun was already falling when they reached the homestead. An unseasonable thaw the previous week had melted the snow, and the ground was boggy and barren-looking. Maud noticed that there were now a few scrawny trees Julia and James had planted for a windbreak, but still the setting was one of total isolation—the house looked as if a strong wind could blow it away.

James did not even come inside—he said he had to return to LaMoure, where he was helping a neighbor plant trees on his claim.

The wagon rattled away, leaving Maud with her small valise, stand-ing on the flat, empty plain.

"Auntie M!"

Ten-year-old Magdalena flew around the side of the house, braids whipping behind her, and threw her arms around Maud. She was wearing the blue gingham dress, now too short and so old that the blue checks had almost faded to white. A tear along the hem made it hang unevenly. Matilda's wool socks were bunched around her ankles, exposing the pale, bluish color of her thin legs.

"Slow down, Dorothy," Magdalena cried out as she slowed to a walk. Maud looked around but saw no one, not even a doll in Mag-dalena's arms. She could still vividly picture the shattered doll, its painted eyes staring blankly from inside the grave.

"Dorothy, mind your manners and say hello to Auntie M. And curtsy if you please."

After a moment's confusion, Maud caught on.

"Hello, there, Dorothy," Maud said, turning to face her niece's imaginary companion. "I'm very pleased to make your acquain-tance."

"And she's pleased to make yours," Magdalena said.

"Where's your mother?"

"Mama's sick."

"And who is looking after you?"

"Dorothy is."

Inside, the tiny house was neat, but the main room was freezing. The fire had gone out. Maud pushed the bedroom door open to a waft of fetid air.

Julia was turned away from her, and as Maud's eyes adjusted to the light, she realized that her bedding was stained with large crim-son splotches.

"Julia?" Maud whispered.

Her sister did not stir.

"Julia!" Maud placed her hand on her sister's cheek, alarmed to find it cold. She gave her a light shake, followed by a harder one.

Her sister opened her eyes slowly. "Maud?"

On the table next to her bed stood several empty bottles of Godfrey's Cordial. Next to the bed stood a bucket filled with bloody
rags. From the mess emerged the translucent curled-up fingers of
a tiny hand.

"Julia, you need a doctor! I'm going to call one at once!"

"Call no one, Maud. If I live, no one must know."

Maud leaned against the wall of the tiny room to steady herself.

"Julia, Julia . . . what have you done?"

"A Bohemian woman from the neighboring claim . . . James
said we couldn't support another mouth to feed . . ."

"Say no more!" Maud cried out. "Pray, Julia, say no more."

WHEN MAUD LEFT THE BEDROOM, Magdalena was perched on a
wooden chair, her heels on the chair rungs, her expression solemn. She had placed two cups from her miniature china set on the
table. "Dorothy and I are having some tea," she said. "Would you
like some?"

A locomotive was rushing full speed through Maud's head. Her
thoughts were garbled, her knees shaking, but she tried to force an
expression of calm upon her face so as not to alarm the child, who
was looking up at her with large, unblinking eyes.

"Auntie M?"

"Yes, sweet pea?"

"If Mama dies, please don't leave me alone here. Dorothy is
afraid of the wolves."

Maud turned her face to hide the tears that now flooded her
eyes. She squatted down and put her arm around the girl. "I will
never leave you alone," she whispered.

"Or Dorothy, either," Magdalena whispered. "Promise!"

"Or Dorothy, either," Maud said. "I promise."

THE EARLY SPRING NIGHT was moonless, and the heavens were
bedecked with a glittering expanse of stars. Alone, Maud wielded

the shovel, chipping away at the cold, hard ground. She sweated beneath her dress and wrap. When she paused to rest, her teeth chattered. Her hands were soon raw, her muscles aching.

Wolves howled in the distance. This only gave her more strength, as she was determined to bury what remained deep enough that the wolves wouldn't dig it up.

The torment from her hands, her neck, and her back engulfed her until the stars spun in the heavens and a faint dawn glow burned in the distant sky. The simple stone that marked baby Jamie's grave stood watch, taunting Maud not to give up before her work was finished.

At last the hole, though narrow, was as deep as the length of her arm. She upended the bucket and threw a spadeful of dirt on top of it.

Shivering in the predawn light, Maud tamped down the earth on top of her makeshift burial plot. " 'The Lord is near to the broken-hearted and saves the crushed in spirit,' " Maud whispered. "At least, I hope."

Dry-eyed but heavy-hearted, she returned to the little shanty. She was still seated on a kitchen chair, staring into the fireplace, when Magdalena awoke. In Maud's lap was Magdalena's dress, which Maud had mended while the girl slept.

A week later, Frank arrived, having found a neighbor to watch the boys and hitched a ride from Edgeley with a passing farmer. By then, Julia was able to sit up for most of the day. Maud said nothing of the condition in which she had found her sister, but she pulled him aside immediately and told him that there was trouble in the household, and that no matter the difficulty of their own financial situation, they needed to take responsibility for Magdalena's care. Frank quickly agreed.

Magdalena was happy to see her favorite uncle.

"Dorothy, this is your Uncle Frank!"

Without missing a beat, Frank dropped down on one knee and held out his hand in greeting. "Well, how do you do, Miss Dorothy? I'm pleased to meet you. And what a pretty red dress you are wearing."

"Her dress is blue gingham, Uncle Frank, just like mine."

Frank made an elaborate pantomime of rubbing his eyes. "Why, forgive me! It must be dust from the road that got in my eyes. Of course it is, blue gingham, and pretty at that."

"And she has black pigtails and a little pet dog that she carries around in a basket with her. And his name is Toto."

Frank fished around in his pocket and pretended to pull something out. "And look what I have here," Frank said. "Hair ribbons for a pigtailed girl and a nice meaty bone for her dog."

"Dorothy wants to take you out to see where the prairie dogs live."

"Well, then let's go see the prairie dogs. Come along, Toto." Frank whistled.

"He's going to ride in Dorothy's basket," Magdalena said. "You don't need to whistle."

They came back an hour later, Magdalena smiling as she recounted Uncle Frank's wild story about a city for the prairie dogs under the ground where they had streetcars and electric lights and could even talk!

After lunch, Frank and Maud sent Magdalena out to play, and Frank began to speak earnestly to Julia.

"We won't have much to offer," he said. "But pray let us take darling Magdalena with us. It will lighten your burden, and we will care for her as if she is our own."

Julia's face had been pale since Maud had arrived and found her ill, but now it turned a sickly yellow, with points of red flaming at the balls of her cheeks.

"How dare you, Maud?"

"I beg your pardon? I don't mean to offend you. We're offering to help because we understand that times are hard."

"But you said no!" Julia almost screamed. "I have it right here, the letter. Here!"

She pushed herself out of her chair like an old woman and began rummaging through a pile of opened letters that were stacked up on her chest of drawers.

"Here it is," she said, shaking it in Maud's direction. She began to read aloud in a wooden tone.

" 'My dear Julia, as much as we love our darling Magdalena as if she were our own daughter, our current state of family flux would make it difficult for us to accept Magdalena right now. As soon as our situation improves, we will bring her in with open arms. Love, your devoted sister, Maud.' "

"Maud?" Frank's brows rose over his eyes as he turned to look at her, eyes wide with surprise. He took the letter from Julia's hand and read it with disbelief, then turned back to Maud as if Julia were not even there.

"But darling! Why?"

Maud shook her head and avoided his eyes. Why, indeed? On the day she had received her sister's letter, she had felt so wrecked, so hopeless, yet this—this was so much worse.

"You see!" Julia said. She started pacing across the room. "You know how hard it is for me to let her go. She's my only companion, and the wolves, they do so howl at night, and James is away so often. One night, Magdalena awoke and said she saw a woman dressed all in white standing next to her bed, not saying anything. It gave both of us a terrible fright. So, I didn't want to let her go—away from me, my only solace—but James said we couldn't manage another mouth to feed. So I took matters into my own hands." She sounded half out of her mind. Frank glanced at Maud, who had not shared the intimate details of the past week.

"I'm dreadfully sorry," Maud said. "It is purely my own fault for not understanding that the situation was so dire. There were difficulties . . ." She looked at Frank imploringly. "I made a mistake. Now I understand, and I've changed my mind. We've changed our minds—right, Frank?"

"Let Magdalena go," Frank said, his voice firm. "You are not fit to take care of a child right now."

"Not fit! Not fit? How can you say that? I made the ultimate sacrifice." Julia's voice was shrill.

"Times are hard all around," Frank said mildly. "Just let us keep her for a while to ease your burden."

"That will never happen. I made my choice," Julia said. "I chose Magdalena. She will stay with me."

Maud glanced across the room, and to her chagrin, she saw that Magdalena was kneeling just beyond the slightly open front door, peeking in. She had been listening the whole time. Now she jumped up and, banging the door, ran outside. Through the window, Maud watched Magdalena run toward the horizon as fast as her feet would carry her, her skirt catching on sodden stalks of dead prairie grass, her braids flapping, her faded gingham dress billowing out behind her.

Frank and Maud found Magdalena seated next to her baby brother's headstone, knees drawn up, her face in her arms.

Frank touched her gently on her shoulder.

"I want to go with you," she said.

"Magdalena, you will always have a home at our house," Maud said.

"Always," Frank said. "As long as you live."

"But why can't I go now?" Magdalena said. Her face was streaked with tears, her manner serious.

Maud fished down into her pocket and pulled out a clean hand-kerchief, like a white flag of surrender, which she used to blot away the tears from her niece's smudged face.

"Your mother needs you here," Maud said. "You are a brave girl, and you will be all right without us."

Magdalena, however, was inconsolable. She lay on the damp ground next to her brother's grave and howled with a misery so profound that it seemed to expand to fill all the vast, bleak, flat, arid land around them, as if all of the sorrow of all of the people stuck out here trying to chip a living out of this vast, uncompromis-ing plain were contained in her small body.

While she lay there, black clouds massed, covering half the sky, and a few fat raindrops fell. The girl, clad only in her thin gingham dress and a shawl, began to shiver. Frank unbuttoned his wool jacket. He knelt down beside her and placed the heavy garment over her shoulders. They waited silently next to her.

Finally, Magdalena was all cried out. She sat up and wiped the rest of her tears off her cheeks with the back of her hand, and Frank brushed her straying hair up off her forehead. She appeared tiny, swamped in the oversize contours of Frank's jacket.

"Is Chicago very far away?"

"Just two days on the train," Maud said. "Not as far as you would think."

"Two whole days?"

"And we can write you letters, and you'll write to us as well. And as soon as we're settled, we'll invite you and your mother to come for a visit."

None of Maud's words seemed to mollify the girl in the least. The sky had grown menacing, but the sun shone through in places. Frank scooped up Magdalena, still wrapped in his jacket, to carry her back to the house.

Magdalena gasped, and Frank followed her gaze. "Well, will you look at that!" he cried out. He grinned and started spinning around with Magdalena in his arms. She leaned her head back to look at the expanse whirling above her. After he slowed, he set Magdalena gently back on the ground and knelt down beside her again, gesturing at the stormy sky. Fighting their way through the mass of clouds, bands of orange, yellow, blue, indigo, and violet shimmered in a short arc.

"Look right there, it's a bit of a rainbow, come to brighten our day. Make a wish!" Frank said quickly.

Magdalena closed her eyes and pressed them shut with her hands. She murmured, and Maud realized that she was repeating the word "Chicago" under her breath.

"Oh, but it's no use," Magdalena said, turning back to look at her homestead shanty, now turned the color of ash in the gloomy light. "I know I can't leave. Mama can't stay by herself. What if she gets sick and there is no one to take care of her? I'm responsible for my age. I can do the chores of a hired girl—Papa says so. It's just that sometimes—it's hard." Magdalena hiccuped, then choked back a sob, and then she was crying again.

Frank slipped his arm around his niece as he knelt beside her, pointing back to the rainbow, which was still visible, peeking through a break in the clouds.

"Look at that rainbow, and I want you to remember something."

Magdalena nodded. Her chin quivered.

"There's a man named the Rainbow King, and he lives in the heavens. In a beautiful castle. The sun always shines there, and there are so many good things to eat, and the beds are softer than a million feathers . . ."

Magdalena's eyes were wide.

"Sometimes he sends his daughter down to us. She walks right along the rainbow and comes down to earth to play. Sometimes her father pulls that rainbow up and she stays on earth for a long time, and she has lots of adventures. But when she really, really needs something, he puts it back down, and she skips right back to her daddy, right across that rainbow bridge."

Magdalena nodded solemnly.

"Now, I know your life seems hard sometimes, but I want you to remember that if you ever get very worried, just think about that rainbow—and if you use your imagination, you will be able to skip straight over the rainbow to play with the Rainbow King's daughter, in their beautiful land, and you won't feel so alone, and when you're ready to come home, you just have to tap your feet together three times, and he'll put the rainbow down, and you can come straight home."

Magdalena's face had brightened.

She stood up, raised her chin, straightened her braids, and smoothed down her skirt.

"You can do this," Frank said.

"I can," she said.

"Thank you," Maud breathed.

When it was time for them to leave, Maud held on to her little niece a bit longer than she should have, afraid that if she let go too soon, Magdalena would see her tears.

While they murmured their goodbyes, Frank pulled Julia aside. "The moment you don't feel safe here, Julia, you have a home with us. Promise you'll remember that?"

Julia and Magdalena stood side by side as Maud and Frank climbed into the hired wagon, the grizzled driver shifting in his seat, anxious to be off. When they were settled, he shook the reins and the pair started to trot. But just after they began to roll, Magdalena bolted toward them so fast that Frank leapt off, catching her so that she wouldn't get caught up in the wheels.

"Wait!" Magdalena cried, one arm outstretched. "I'm staying here, but Dorothy wants to go with you."

Maud looked at Frank and signaled him with an almost imperceptible shake of the head.

"I don't think so, Magdalena," Frank said gently. "Dorothy needs to stay to keep you company."

"No!" Magdalena's voice quavered, her chin all puckered. "She doesn't want to stay. She wants to go with you! She's very itty-bitty small. She won't take up any space at all."

"But, Magdalena—" Maud protested.

"Auntie M, please!"

"But Dorothy will keep you company. She would miss you, and the prairie dogs, and your house and the fields. She wants to stay with you," Frank said.

Magdalena stamped her foot and jutted out her chin, eyes flashing. "She says no. She says you're not listening. She wants to go to Chicago! She'll skip right back over the rainbow and tell me all about it, whenever she wants. Won't you, Dorothy?"

Julia stepped toward Magdalena and grasped her arm. "Come now, Magdalena. That's enough of your woolgathering. Your aunt and uncle need to leave—I'm sure it's about to rain."

Magdalena's face was wrinkled up like a furious prune, her brows knit together. She stamped her foot again. "She wants to go!"

Maud gave Frank a tiny nod. "Well, all right then, missy." Frank lowered the step and placed his foot on the running board. "Dorothy, say goodbye and then climb on up."

"And Toto, too!" Magdalena said firmly.

She clasped one hand over her stick-thin arm and watched, her large violet eyes unblinking, as Frank and Maud went through an elaborate pantomime, first making room on the spring seat for Dorothy, next tucking a robe around her imaginary legs, then pet-ting her pretend pup and setting its make-believe basket beside them.

As the wagon began to roll away, Magdalena lifted her hand and slowly began to wave, and Maud held her breath. Suddenly Frank jumped up, shaded his eyes with his hand, and cried out, "Oh, Toto! You naughty little pup! Where are you running so fast?"

Getting impatient, the driver raised his whip. His pair of horses picked up a faster trot; by now they were a good distance from the house. Balancing in the jarring wagon, Frank shouted, "I'm sorry, Magdalena, but that puppy wanted to stay with you. Here!" He scooped up something, a handful of air, and tossed it to the girl. "It's his basket!" he called out. "I think you might need it."

Magdalena teetered there for a moment longer, as if undecided, but at last Maud saw her grab the imaginary basket by its handle and disappear around the back of the house and out of sight.

They rode along in silence for a good long while, and they were almost back to the Edgeley depot when the rainbow reappeared, this time not just a piece of it but a semicircle, arching all the way across the big prairie sky, its vivid colors in sharp contrast to the gray landscape.

"You see that rainbow?"

Maud nodded miserably.

"You know where I'd like to live?" Frank said.

"Where, Frank?" Maud said.

"If one end of this rainbow lives on this bleak and soulless plain, then I'd like to be clear out at the far end of it. Somewhere, somewhere over there is a place that is better. I'm just sure of it, Maudie."

Maud scooched her way across the bare wooden bench until she was leaning up against him.

"Do you really think so?" she asked.

"I'm just sure of it," Frank said. "And another thing, Maudie, as hard as this may be for you—that godforsaken shack on the prairie, your cranky, bent-over sister, that field full of prairie dogs? That's home for Magdalena. Nothing can change that."

"We've let her down."

"No, we did the best we could," Frank said. "And you know what we'll do now?" he asked, miming that he was tucking a blanket around a child's legs. "We'll look after Dorothy. Together."

He regarded her, his eyes the same shade as the slate-colored sky. "Promise?"

Maud looked up at the rainbow. It appeared to start just over the cluster of lonely buildings that made up the town of Edgeley, but then it arched up and disappeared into the clouds. Was it possible? Was there really somewhere else—somewhere at the far end of the rainbow that was better than this place? She certainly hoped so.

"Maudie?"

She nodded morosely. "I promise."

HOLLYWOOD

1939

MAUD ENTERED THE SOUND STAGE AND SAW A PAINTED yellow road that ended at the feet of a giant plywood gate, and she realized with a start that this was it. The filming had literally reached the end of the Yellow Brick Road, the Emerald City. In yellow paint, she could read the truth. She was running out of time.

Maud saw no actors about—just a crew of workers. A fellow in paint-splattered coveralls had just pried open a can of paint and had left a broad swath of green across one of the white walls.

"Oh, no!" Maud cried out, forgetting herself. "What are you doing? Are you mad? The Emerald City is not supposed to be green!"

The painter looked up in surprise as Maud approached, handbag in the crook of her arm, a stern look on her face.

He stood up with the expression of a guilty schoolboy, tucked his paint rag in his back pocket, and stood at attention as if expecting a scolding. "Beg pardon, ma'am?"

"The Emerald City is not green!" Maud said.

The man doffed his cap, pulled a bandanna back out of his pocket, and wiped his brow.

"Not green, you say?"

Looking puzzled, he called over to his painter partner. "Hey,

Ray! The lady says it's not supposed to be green." He turned back to Maud. "Well, what color is it?"

"Well . . ." Maud said. "It's white."

"White, you say?" The painter's head was cocked as he squinted at Maud. "I've got orders for No. 2309. Emerald green."

"The spectacles are green. But the Emerald City is white."

The painter seemed to take it on Maud's authority. He shrugged, replaced the lid on the paint can, and prepared to leave. "Emerald City is white!" the fellow muttered. "It don't figure."

But at that moment, the director, Victor Fleming, strode onto the set.

"We'll need to see how that shade of green looks with the Technicolor. Just finish up that one wall and we'll give it a test."

"The lady said it's supposed to be white."

"What lady?"

The painter jerked his head in Maud's direction.

Fleming did not look amused. *"Mrs. Baum?"*

"Well, of course the Emerald City is white! Haven't you read the book? It's the Wizard who plays a trick on the inhabitants of Oz by making them all wear green spectacles."

"Green spectacles," Fleming said, frowning. "That's not in the script."

"That's the problem," Maud said. "It should be!"

Fleming all but rolled his eyes. "Right. Of course. Thank you, Mrs. Baum. I'll be sure to keep that in mind. Carry on there, fellows. I need that whole wall painted green, and get it done quick. Time's a-wasting."

Maud raised her hand to say more, but Fleming was already walking away. Undeterred, she chased after him.

"White!" she repeated. "The Emerald City was white."

Fleming ignored her.

"Mr. Fleming! I absolutely must speak to you about this!"

Fleming turned impatiently. "My good woman. We are on a tight schedule here. What is it that you want to say?"

"In *The Wonderful Wizard of Oz*, the Emerald City is white. The

Wizard is a humbug—a faker—and he creates the *illusion* that the city is green by making all of the inhabitants wear green spectacles, you see, because the Wizard isn't what he says he is. And that is the magic of Oz—the magic is that it isn't magic at all."

Fleming pressed his lips together, and his shoulders tensed. "This is a fascinating insight, but we've got a set to paint. How exactly do you propose that we get the audience to put on green spectacles?"

"But it's not the audience—it's . . . well, you see, the Emerald City was white because the White City was—"

"Right. Got it." Fleming turned his back to her. Maud realized that her audience was over.

"No, young man, you haven't got it. The Yellow Brick Road stops right here, at this gate." She pointed to the ground. "But what happens next is the heart of the story." Unfortunately, she realized that he was no longer listening.

As she turned to leave, she saw the painter rolling the bright green hue across the big expanse of white plywood flimflam they had constructed to serve as the Emerald City.

Maud was walking back to the parking lot when a voice called out to her.

"Mrs. Baum!"

Maud turned to see the young actress coming up behind her. "Judy!"

"Could I speak to you for a minute?"

Maud looked at her with concern. Her eyes were unusually bright, and she was chewing on her lower lip.

"Is everything all right? No more hat-pin trouble?"

Judy blushed. "No, it's nothing like that. I just wanted to thank you for helping me out the other day."

"Well, that's very kind of you, but I didn't do anything I wouldn't do for one of my own children."

Seeing Judy hesitate as if wanting to continue their conversation, Maud put her hand on the girl's arm. "Wait," she said. "Do you have time to go to lunch?"

"I'd love to, but not here," Judy said under her breath. "Everybody is watching every bite I eat."

Twenty minutes later, Maud and Judy sat in a wood-paneled booth inside the shadowy interior of Musso & Frank's. Maud noticed again the unusual brightness in Judy's eyes, and the way she fidgeted in her seat. Even her hand shook a little as she grasped her water glass. She tried to hide the tremor by steadying it with her other hand, but she saw that Maud had already spotted it.

"Are you sure you're all right?" Maud asked.

Judy frowned. "It's the diet pills. They make me shaky, and I can't sleep."

Maud peered at the girl. "You don't sleep?"

Judy sighed and traced a drop of water that had splashed on the scarred-up hardwood table. "If I can't sleep for a few days, they put me in the infirmary and give me pills to help. The studio doctors can do anything with pills—speed you up, slow you down." She sounded half-bored, as if all this pill taking were in the natural order of things.

Maud reached a hand out and placed it on the girl's arm. "Forgive me for prying, but does your mother know about this?"

"Ethel?" Judy said. "She's the one who told the studio doctors to do it. She calls them my bolts and jolts."

Maud thought of her own mother—her horror of patent medicines, her belief that they were a scourge for women. And she thought of Julia, and the medicine that had ruled her life.

"I would recommend that you be cautious," Maud said. "Medicines have a way of exerting a power that you would not expect."

Judy shrugged. "I really don't get that much choice in the matter."

"Let me tell you something right now. You may be young and you may be a girl, but I pray that you will remember that you *always* have a choice in any matter."

Judy sighed. "It sure doesn't feel like that."

A red-jacketed waiter stopped at their table. "Are you ready to order?"

Judy flipped open the menu.

"Everything is good," Maud said. "But I recommend the French dip sandwich. It comes with French fries. Two?"

"That sounds delicious!" Judy said.

The waiter nodded curtly and picked up their menus.

"Oh no," Judy said, ducking her head down a bit. "It's Yip Harburg, the lyricist. He's going to see me!"

A moment later, Harburg approached their table. "Why, if it isn't Miss Judy Garland. And Mrs. Baum."

"Why don't you join us?" Maud said. "I'm assuming you are not among those who are spying on what Judy eats for lunch."

"You kidding me?" Harburg said. "Half the writers in Hollywood who aren't supposed to be drinking are in the back room right now. Nobody's business what people want to do in their own free time, far as I'm concerned." He turned to Judy. "Don't worry, I'm not following you. I was browsing at the Stanley Rose bookstore when I saw you walk by." The bookshop next door was a popular gathering place for screenwriters.

"Well, it's perfect timing," Maud said. "Have a seat. I need to talk to you."

Harburg hung his fedora on the hook next to their booth. "May I?" He slipped into the spot next to Judy. "What can I help you with, Mrs. Baum?"

"It's the Emerald City," Maud said. "They are painting it *green*!"

One side of Harburg's mouth slanted upward. His eyes twinkled behind his horn-rimmed glasses. "The Emerald City *green*? You don't say!"

"You're laughing," Maud said, not amused. "But it's not funny. In the book, the Emerald City is white and people only think it's green. It's one of the Wizard's tricks."

"If it makes you feel any better, I do realize that. We talked about having the characters put on spectacles, but we decided to do it a different way. If you think of it differently, you might not mind as much."

"Differently?"

"What is Technicolor but a pair of green-tinted spectacles? Technicolor is more vibrant than the real world—it's a fever dream of color that someone could only invent in his mind's eye."

"You're suggesting that the Technicolor *is* the tinted spectacles?" Maud tried to grasp what he meant.

"That's right." Harburg grinned. "The wizardry begins when you sit down in the theater. There's magic in the whole crazy movie-making process. I don't know how it works, but it does. You start with cardboard, spray paint, chicken wire, and plywood, and you end up with—"

"The Land of Oz!" Judy said.

"Exactly!" Harburg said.

"Hmm," Maud said. "Sounds like Frank talking when you put it that way."

Harburg grinned and pushed his glasses up the bridge of his nose. "Wait until you watch the picture," Harburg said. "You'll see what I mean. I've gotta go."

He jumped up, grabbed his hat from the hook, and tipped it toward them.

"Nice talking to you ladies!" he said.

"Wait a minute," Maud said. "I've been wanting to ask you. What's going on with the rainbow song?"

"Judy." Harburg smiled. "That girl was born to sing that song."

"Judy? Yes, of course," Maud said, aware that he was avoiding her question. "But I mean the words. Have you finished them?"

"Don't worry about the words, Mrs. Baum. You said yourself it's in the manner. There just has to be enough wanting in it. Judy's got it just right. It's going to be a big hit." He tipped his hat to Judy again. "You're gonna knock 'em dead, kid."

When Harburg was gone, Maud noticed that Judy had left her plate of food half-finished.

"You didn't like it?"

"I'm just not that hungry. I guess the pills are working," she said with a brittle smile.

Even in the dim restaurant light, Judy's hair glinted with coppery highlights, her lips were plum-colored, her skin luminous and sun-kissed with a sprinkle of freckles, and her brown eyes, fringed with thick, dark lashes, reflected a wisdom greater than her years. By every measure, this girl was brushed with something special—and yet, Maud always sensed the vulnerability in her.

As they gathered up their things to leave, Judy turned to Maud.

"You know, I really don't like the Wizard," she said.

"You don't like the Wizard?"

"What kind of a man would send a little girl to kill a witch?" Judy said. "Why wouldn't he just help her?"

Maud thought of the day she and Frank had left Magdalena on Julia's homestead. It had been the hardest day of Maud's life.

"Sometimes," Maud said, "I was also angry at the Wizard. But the Wizard was right about one thing."

"What's that?"

"You always need to fix your own problems. Nobody else is going to fix them for you."

CHICAGO, ILLINOIS

1891

Maud gulped repeatedly and took deep breaths through her nose. She was *not* going to cry in front of the boys. Disembarking from the train in Chicago's dazzling new Grand Central Station had set the boys to chattering, as had the trolley through downtown. In every way—size, scope, people, number of buildings—everything here in the great city surpassed Aberdeen. Maud had marveled at the crowded streets, the giant edifices, the avenues of grand houses. It was all gleaming and modern and beautiful.

But eventually their hansom cab had clattered out of the new part of the city and reached the western neighborhoods, the part that had not been affected by the Great Chicago Fire of 1871. It was late March, but patches of sooty snow still clung in some of the alleyways, and a brisk wind cut through the curtains of the cab. Soon they were passing along an avenue lined with rows of narrow, shabby buildings that tilted against one another as if too exhausted to stand up on their own. The streets teemed with grubby children. Mothers gathered around communal water pumps, bundled up in bulky skirts with kerchiefs tied around their heads. When, at last, the cab pulled up in front of 34 Campbell Park, Frank announced in a cheerful voice, "We're home." And Maud, struggling not to let her true feelings show, took in the grubby clapboard-and-brick row house that was to be their new home.

The inside of the house was as dreary as the outside. The building had neither indoor plumbing nor a connection for gas. At night, the interior was dim and eerie, lit only by the flickering of kerosene. When Maud looked out the windows, she saw brick walls. But she did what she could to make it into a home. She scrubbed until the rooms were clean and smelled fresh. Frank hung a cheap reproduction of Millet's *The Angelus* over the water stain on the parlor wall.

At the end of the first week, Frank came home and spread the newspaper across the kitchen table. "Here it is, right here. My story about moving day has landed on the front page!"

Maud looked at the newspaper, searching for Frank's name.

"I'm afraid they didn't include a byline—but they will soon," Frank said.

"Where's your pay?" Maud asked, barely glancing at the newspaper.

Frank fished into his coat pocket and handed her some bills and coins. She looked at them in disbelief. Frank had secured employment with the *Chicago Evening Post,* one of the crop of new newspapers struggling to carve out a niche in the fast-growing city. He'd told her that he would be paid a salary of twenty dollars a week.

"This is seventeen dollars and fifty cents," Maud said, not even trying to keep the sharpness out of her voice. "Where is the rest of it? I can't pay the rent or the grocer or the fishmonger with seventeen dollars and fifty cents!"

"I'm so sorry, Maud. They promised me twenty dollars, but they didn't pay me as much as they said they would." He was apologizing, but his tone was light, as if this were an inconsequential matter.

"Do you understand," Maud replied icily, "that this is completely unacceptable?"

Frank looked taken aback. "But what am I supposed to do?"

"Tell them you are to be paid twenty dollars a week, as agreed upon. If they say no, then walk out the door. We are not in the business of providing charity to the *Evening Post*. You need to bring home twenty dollars a week. If they won't pay you properly, then find someone who will!"

"That's easy for you to say, Maud!" he said, his eyes flaming. "Do you really think it's so simple? Why don't you try it yourself! I'll stay home and look after the children and *you* find us a way to make ends meet!"

Maud's face flushed red, and her eyes flashed.

"Watch me!" She marched out the door, slamming it shut behind her.

WITHIN TWO WEEKS, Maud had drummed up enough fine embroidery work to close the gap. When Frank came home at night, he found the boys bathed and put to bed, the house spotless, and Maud hunched over her sewing basket, her eyes red from straining under the flickering kerosene lamp. Every night, Frank begged her to come to bed, but she shook her head angrily. The next day, she was up before dawn, starting again.

This was where life had led her—to this drafty, freezing, unpleasant house. She was taking care of the children, cooking all of the meals, toiling over tiny stitches of lace, while he spent the day downtown, looking dandy in his Prince Albert jacket. When Frank came in, later and later each evening, Maud didn't even glance up as he trudged past her silently with a hangdog look on his face. They had been married for nine and a half years, and through all of their ups and downs, the one thing that had held steady was their mutual affection—but now her goodwill was slipping away. Frank had let her down.

Maud fought a constant battle against the filth that surrounded them. As April turned to May and June, the chilly winds gave way to humidity and torpor. When the wind blew in from the west, it brought the scent of the stockyards; when it blew in from the east, it carried the reek of the sewage-filled river. Not surprisingly, there was a typhoid epidemic rampant among the city's children. Every few days, she saw the pair of black nags pulling the hearse stop in front of one of the neighboring tenements. She was afraid to let the boys out of her sight.

At night, when she lay in bed, she imagined the vast open west the way it had looked during their first spring in Dakota, before the drought, before all the troubles. She pictured the pale blue bowl of the sky and heard again the soft song of the wind in the prairie grass. Now outside her windows day and night she heard a constant chorus of horses' hooves and streetcars trundling by, of shouting peddlers and crying children. But the loudest noise of all was the one in her head. What if Frank was right? What if they should have waited it out in Aberdeen? Maybe Maud could have found embroidery jobs there, too—although she knew that was silly. No one had a spare dime for crewel and lace. She had agreed to come to this teeming, feculent city, but if one of the children succumbed to the fever, she would never forgive herself.

One evening, Frank came home and started up his usual fantasizing, regaling the children with stories about the coming scientific future that would be wrought by electricity.

"You boys need to see the financial district at night! Every building between LaSalle and Adams lit up like a tree at Christmastime, and every bit of it is electricity! Twice as bright as gas lights!"

"A house with gas lights would certainly serve us well enough." Maud looked up from her sewing. "Better than kerosene."

"And that is only the beginning of what electricity can do!" Frank continued, as if Maud hadn't spoken. "Mark my word, there will be electric trolleys and electric trains, electric staircases—"

"What's an electric staircase?" asked Bunting.

Frank leapt up and walked to the banister, where he leaned against the newel post. "You'll take a step onto the bottom stair, and the electricity will make the stairs do all the work. You'll just ride on up, pretty as you please."

"Can we have one like that in our house?" Robin piped up.

"Certainly," Frank said grandly. "No need for gas for your mama—we'll have electricity, and when she's tired and wants to go upstairs, why, the electric stairs will just carry her right up!"

Maud was studiously ignoring Frank's soliloquy, but as she heard him declaim all this nonsense to the boys, fury burned in her breast.

In her anger, she pricked herself with her needle. To her horror, she saw three drops of blood spill onto the white lace. She would never get the spots out! She'd have to start over, wasting the cost of the fabric and thread.

"See what you've made me do!" Maud cried out.

Her tone was so sharp that Bunting's lip quivered, Robin burst into tears, and Harry started wailing.

"What are you yelling at Daddy for?" Bunting said in an injured tone. "He's just trying to make things nice for you! Lights so your eyes won't get tired and electric stairs to carry you up to bed."

Maud stood up. Blood was rushing in her ears, and she couldn't even think straight.

"He will do no such thing!" she cried. "Don't listen to your father. The stories he tells you boys are just fairy tales. None of it is true! We live here on Campbell Park, in a shabby old house. Your mother is a seamstress, and your daddy writes newspaper articles for a few cents apiece. There is no shame in the truth. Let's accept our lot and make the best of it, shall we?"

Frank's expression was startled. Wounded. "Maudie darling, don't. Please don't. You'll just discourage the boys. We're in a temporary setback—nothing more. Why not a house with electric stairs? Can't a body dream?"

Maud set aside her ruined sewing, holding her pricked finger.

"Sure." Maud's voice shook. "We can dream of things that might come true. But when you stick your head in the clouds and tell the boys that you are going to give us things that don't even exist yet, instead of focusing on the here and now and figuring out the simple things like how to put food on the table, you know what that makes you?"

Frank did not answer. The boys were silent, witnessing the tornado of their mother's fury with terror.

"That makes you nothing but a humbug!" Maud said. "Plain and simple!"

Frank had no response. He stood there, staring at Maud as his face turned ashen, the tips of his ears bright red.

"Now," Maud continued, "you run along up to bed, boys—and don't expect any electric staircase to take you there. This is our life. Right here, in this house, in this city, and we are going to make the best of it."

No one moved. At last Frank said, "You heard your mother—it's time to go to bed!" He shooed the boys up the stairs and then turned to follow.

Maud said nothing, just threaded a new needle, preparing to re-start her sewing.

TWO WEEKS LATER, Frank came into the living room, knelt down, and clasped Maud's hands.

"I've let you down. I'm sorry."

Maud's eyes filled with tears.

"I'm going to make it up to you," he said. "I'm not sure how, but I promise."

Upstairs, the baby started to cry.

"I need to go tend to Harry." Maud jumped up and turned her back on Frank, not looking him in the eye.

"I know," Frank called to his wife's back as she ran up the stairs, "you think I'm nothing but a humbug! But I'll figure something out—something real. I promise."

THREE DAYS LATER, when Maud came home from delivering her finished embroidery to the home of a lady in a nicer neighborhood, she found Frank entertaining the three boys, a large trunk filled with samples of fine china open on the table before him.

"You see, madame," Frank said, holding a teacup to his lips and taking an imaginary sip. "For one as refined as you, only a fine tea-cup will do."

"Hey, that rhymes!" Bunting cried.

"Well, I can do better than that!" Frank said.

> *"A fine lady of Chicago*
> *must not sup*
> *with anything less*
> *than a china teacup.*
> *If the pattern of flowers*
> *is Pitkin & Brooks,*
> *the neighborhood ladies*
> *get admiring looks."*

Frank waggled his eyebrows. "Or perhaps it should be *will steal them like crooks . . .*"

While Frank rhymed, baby Harry was reaching out. He grabbed a saucer and almost managed to pull it over the edge of the table. Maud dashed forward and snatched it away just in the nick of time. Harry started to howl.

"Frank, what on earth?"

"Mr. L. Frank Baum, *salesman*, Pitkin & Brooks fine china," he said.

"You found another job?"

"Thirty dollars a week, plus commissions," he said. "You were right, Maud. This is a big city. All you have to do is knock on enough doors."

"Salesman?"

"Traveling salesman. My territory reaches as far east as Cincinnati. I leave tomorrow."

Maud sank into one of the kitchen chairs, unsure how to respond to this bit of news. Certainly, they needed the money. But she dreaded the thought of Frank hitting the road again, and Maud, expecting again, had an aching back and swollen ankles at the end of every day. At least when he came home, he helped out with the children. Sometimes by the end of the day, she had grown so weary that she snapped at them. Bunting was growing up, almost nine. She could barely keep track of him as he roamed the city streets after school—and she had trouble making him mind. It was easier when Frank was around.

Frank peered at Maud with concern. "Maud, I thought you'd

be happy. You told me to find another job, and I did it. I asked myself, Frank Baum, what's the one thing you've ever been any good at? Being a salesman, that's what. I figured that if I could sell something as dull as Baum's Castorine, then certainly I could sell something beautiful like floral-patterned china."

Frank was gazing at her with a look of utter helplessness, and Maud felt a stab of remorse. She could see what her husband was doing. He was giving up what he loved more than anything—writing—so that he could go out and make money for the family. He was returning to the very life he had tried so hard to shed. It was a puzzle to her. Why did the two things that mattered most to him have to conflict? Why must his love of writing and theater and art compete with his love for his family? She remembered Matilda telling her not to run away and marry an actor, but it was only now that Maud really understood: the part of Frank that made him an actor was the part that she had fallen in love with, but it was also the part that made him so ill-suited for the things of this world.

CHICAGO, ILLINOIS

1893

"PUT ON YOUR FINERY, MY DARLING MAUD, WE ARE GOING somewhere!" Frank had burst into the house one Saturday afternoon with an air of high excitement.

"Don't you even say hello, Frank?" Maud asked, crossing the room to kiss him in greeting. Frank had been away for two weeks, and she hadn't expected to see him until later in the day. He had sent a letter saying he'd be arriving on the six o'clock train, and now here he was, in the house at two in the afternoon.

"You're early," Maud said.

"I managed to reschedule my last sales call." Frank's eyes were twinkling.

By now, all four boys had gathered around, even toddler Kenneth, who had been born a few months after they'd arrived in Chicago.

"I've brought a little something for each of you," Frank said.

He fished deep in his pocket and pulled out four shiny copper pennies, and laid them out in a straight line on the table.

"Frank?" Maud was always wary of Frank's fits of generosity. Though their financial situation had improved over the last couple of years, she still budgeted Frank's earnings down to the last cent, then added the meager sum she earned from her own work. With her economies, she had set enough aside to purchase a lamp, and was just twenty cents short of the nice Persian rug she'd been saving up for.

"What did you bring for Mama?" Robin burbled.

"Emeralds!" Frank shouted.

"Emeralds. Frank! What on earth?"

Frank's eyes were merry. "Maud, get your coat. We're going out!"

"Frank. We can't just 'go out.' No one is here to watch the children."

Frank clapped his hands three times, and the doorbell jingled.

"What is that? Someone at the door?"

He made a big show of crossing to open it.

Outside stood one of the neighbors who sat with the children sometimes.

Maud tried to frown, tried to come up with a word of protest, but she could find none.

IN THE JUNE SUNSHINE, the blindingly bright, ornate buildings of the White City, erected for the Columbian Exhibition, stood out against the blue of Lake Michigan. They stood in line to buy the fifty-cent tickets, with Maud clucking all the while at Frank's spending habits. The family had already visited the fair once, and they'd had a wonderful time. Two visits struck her as extravagant.

"Maud, I've had a great couple of weeks. I earned a five-dollar commission. We've got to have some fun every once in a while. And there's something I've got to show you."

They made their way through the crowds and across the park so fast that Maud had no time to stop and look at anything until they arrived at the electric pavilion.

"It's in here," Frank said, pulling Maud into the phonograph display.

There was a line of people waiting to approach an upright wooden box shaped like a lectern. Frank explained that the device was called the Kinetoscope. The fellow at the front of the line was peering through what looked like binoculars into the interior of the

box. Maud saw over and over again that as each person looked inside, they pulled away, gasped, laughed, or exclaimed, and then
leaned toward the eyepiece again.

"What is it?" Maud asked.

"I'm not going to tell you. You have to see it for yourself."

Frank and Maud had waited in line for almost two hours when at
last it was Maud's turn. She stood next to the box, bent over, and
peeked inside. The operator pushed a button.

Maud gasped. Inside the box, there were three tiny men—
blacksmiths—hammering on an anvil. She drew her head away, and
there she was, standing in front of the box, with Frank by her side.
She put her head down again—it wasn't possible. It seemed that the
men were moving inside the box. Black-and-white photographs
that moved.

Frank took his turn next, and begged for a second turn, and then
a third, until the people standing in line behind them started to
clamor for him to move along.

Once outside, Frank couldn't stop talking about it. "That's the
future, Maud. Right there. The future."

"It's fascinating," Maud said. "No doubt about that, and yet, I
don't quite understand what it's for. Real moving people are all
around us. Why do we need to see them moving in a picture?"

"Because—oh, Maud. Do you really not see it? Everything it
touches becomes immortal!"

Maud shrugged. She liked the morning light shining through
the elms at home in Fayetteville; she loved the way the clouds skidded across an endless Dakota sky. She didn't need a photograph or
a moving picture to remember it. She did not understand what
Frank saw in this machine.

Maud wanted to linger and look at the displays, but Frank was
dragging her along at a rapid clip, as if he had a specific mission. In
the distance, the giant Chicago Wheel, studded with its thirty-six
swinging cars, loomed up against the sky. When they had brought
the boys to visit the fair, they had stood for hours, mesmerized,
watching the wheel lift the lucky riders high into the air, then
gracefully turn, each seat balancing so that the riders remained

level even as the world turned. Frank had explained, to the boys'
fascination, how the engineer, Ferris, had designed the wheel to
rival the grand Eiffel Tower in Paris. At first everyone had been
afraid to ride it. The spindly steel spokes didn't look as if they could
support the massive lacquered cars, fitted with grilles, that could
hold up to sixty people at a time. But Frank had read all about the
wheel in the newspapers, and he explained that the structure was
based on the most modern mechanical and electric techniques, including a double-sized Westinghouse air brake, just like those used
on trains, as a safety feature. The idea of soaring through the air
had intrigued the boys, but Maud had to put her foot down. They
had paid fifty cents each to gain admission to the park, and another
fifty cents each for five tickets to ride the Ferris Wheel was out of
the budget. They would have to watch from the ground.

This time, Frank hustled her along without stopping for a second look at anything, until they reached the base of the giant wheel.
The sun was hanging low over the lake now, the sky turning brilliant shades of purple and orange, and the fair's white buildings
tinged with pink. Then suddenly, in an explosion like fireworks or
a hundred shooting stars, the entire wheel burst into a confetti of
electric light that danced and shimmered as the wheel spun through
the air.

Frank pulled a shiny one-dollar coin from his pocket and laid it
in the palm of Maud's hands.

"We are going for a ride in the sky."

For once, Maud couldn't say no. She couldn't give another
speech about counting pennies. She held tight to Frank's arm as he
paid for their tickets and they clambered aboard the giant wheel
and settled into their seats.

Maud had never before felt so exhilarated as the wheel swung up
into the sky. Her stomach lurched, then settled into pleasant butterflies. The wheel climbed higher and higher, and when it reached
the pinnacle, they seemed to hang in the sky. The entire expanse of
the White City was laid out below them, glittering with thousands
of bright white electric lights. It was as if the night sky on the dark
Dakota prairie were now spread out below them in all its sequined

glory. As the cage hung there, rocking gently, Frank reached into his vest pocket and pulled out a pair of spectacles. "Quick, put these on," he said. He slid the spectacles into place, and Maud gasped. The entire dazzling White City was transformed into a bejeweled sparkling expanse of emerald green.

"You see it?" Frank said.

"Oh, Frank! It's beautiful!"

"Emeralds!" he said.

Frank cupped his hand around the back of her head and kissed her so passionately, right there, in front of everyone, that as the wheel dropped down again, she could no longer tell if the flying sensation came from the car's movement or from the stirrings of her heart, thawing, so slowly, from the ice that had encased it for the last three years.

AFTER DESCENDING FROM THE Ferris Wheel, Frank and Maud strolled along the crowded avenues of the White City, mostly silent. As she looked at her beloved husband's face, she felt as if she were twenty years old again, a Cornell coed, smitten with the most handsome young gentleman in the world. So much had happened between them, and yet, here they still were.

After a long stroll in companionable silence, Frank stopped and turned to Maud.

"The only thing I ever wanted in life was to be my own man, to have my own business, work for myself, earn my own fortune, and be beholden to no one. Your father kept his own shop, my father started his own business, my brother founded Baum's Castorine Company. But at last, my dear Maud, I've come to the conclusion that I am simply not fit for that life. I can sell other men's wares and make a decent living—or not so decent, I confess, but enough to keep a roof over our heads and the boys in shoes and clothing. And even if I'm chained down, my mind can still be free, can't it?"

"Of course it can, Frank."

"Maud, you are the kindest and most patient woman that God

ever put on the face of the earth, and I think I never would have proposed to you at all if I'd known it was my fate to take you out of your elegant home in Fayetteville and drag you hither and yon, and still find myself unable to keep you in the fashion that you so well deserve."

Maud reached out and placed her index finger gently upon his lips.

"Please don't," she said. "This day has been enchanted, this night magical. Please remember that I walked right out of my home with both eyes open because of one thing. I *wanted* to be with you. That has never changed."

"Then can I just ask one small thing? Just a tiny thing from you, Maud?"

Maud stiffened a little bit. Was he going to propose another wild plan for their future?

"In a place like Chicago, it's easy to feel like a tiny piece of a huge machine, as if a man is no more than a single rivet in a giant structure like the Ferris Wheel that spins on a motor that the rivet has no control over. We can shout and roar and try to make ourselves bigger than we are, but in the end, we are just rivets. Yet at the same time, we're part of something that is big and fancy that transports us to the future itself, and that is Chicago. Where men are small, but they are also part of one of the grandest experiments that mankind has ever known."

"And womankind," Maud added.

"Of course, womankind," Frank said.

"So, what do you want from me?" Maud asked. From their vantage point on the promenade, the lit-up White City resembled the magical block city Frank had constructed that first Dakota Christmas, as if the stuff of fairy stories had come to life. Frank's tall, slim frame was shadowed against it, his face dark except for the whites of his eyes.

"If you could just . . ." Frank paused. Maud could tell that he was searching for the right words.

"If I could just . . . ?"

"If you could just try to have faith in me," Frank said.

"But, Frank! How can you say that? Of course I have faith in you . . . it's just that . . ."

"Just what?"

"It's just that—well, you see, you are a good salesman, and you earn enough for us—we don't need so much. Anything extra, the little things, I can earn enough from my sewing to put something aside. You are too hard on yourself." Maud didn't mention that she also always set aside money to save for Julia, no matter how little.

Frank reached up and rubbed his thumb against Maud's cheekbone.

"No, Maud. I'll do what I have to do as long as I have to, but I promise you that somehow, someday, I'm going to do better for you. I may not have figured out how yet, but one day, I'm going to find a way. I want you to feel just the way you felt as we were sweeping upward on the Ferris Wheel, and teetering all the way at the top, where you could gaze out as far as the eye can see. I want you to see emeralds."

Maud opened her mouth to protest. To tell Frank once again that what he had given her was more than enough, even if his flights of fancy had sometimes led them down a difficult path. The hard times were not what she remembered about their life together. It was the moments, incandescent, transcendent—the silvery arc of a theater light, a marching band skidding across a Dakota sky, a rainbow against storm clouds, the nighttime expanse of the White City suddenly transformed into a kingdom of glittering jewels—when she could catch a glimpse of a world beyond. This vision, this second sight, was what Frank Baum had given to Maud. Without him, she trod along the pathways of the ordinary. A molten heat shivered down her sides, her knees went weak, and her cheeks grew hot. There was nothing she could do about it. This was the man she loved.

BY JUNE 1893, Maud had scraped up sufficient money from her sewing work to send enough to Julia for train fare so that she and

Magdalena could get out of the Dakota heat and spend the summer in Syracuse with Matilda. The plan was for them to stop and stay a couple of days in Chicago with the Baums en route. When Julia and Magdalena stepped off the train, Maud was surprised to see how much her niece had sprouted up. She was almost as tall as her petite mother, her long legs sticking out like skinny pokers. Maud noticed that she was wearing an unbecoming dress of faded blue serge. Maud frowned. Had she known, she would have sewn a new traveling frock for her niece.

At twelve, Magdalena had grown longer and thinner, as had her face, accentuating her eyes—still that startling violet, ringed with spidery black lashes. Her shiny golden hair had a straight part down the middle and was tightly plaited, her face and hands were clean, and but for her worn dress, she looked like an ordinary young girl, a far cry from the waif Maud had greeted at the Aberdeen depot five years earlier.

"Auntie M!" As soon as Magdalena caught sight of Maud, she bolted away from her mother and flung her arms around Maud. Then, letting go, she looked around. "Where's Uncle Frank?"

"Your Uncle Frank is away, traveling for business. He was so disappointed to miss seeing you! He sends his love."

Frank had been crushed to miss Magdalena's brief visit, but Maud knew that he was given his schedule and was expected to follow it without asking questions.

Magdalena looked temporarily crestfallen, then beamed. "That's all right. I'm so excited to see *you.*"

Maud turned anxiously to Julia, and saw that her eyes appeared free of the patent medicine fog. "Julia, darling. I'm so glad you were able to come!"

"It is a relief to get away," Julia confessed. "I've grown used to the life out there, but it will never feel like home."

Back at the house, Maud watched as her sister took in the Baums' reduced circumstances: the shabby neighborhood, her threadbare furniture, the pile of unfinished pieces of sewing.

"I'm surprised to find you living like this," Julia said with an air of disapproval.

"Living like what?" Maud said. "Frank is working hard, and so am I. Perhaps this is not the most elegant abode we've ever lived in, but I've tried to make it comfortable."

Where Julia was disapproving, Magdalena was enchanted by every novelty, from the cockroaches to the communal water pump to the rowdy street urchins who roamed outside.

"Edgeley is so tiny that if I stretch my hand out the window, I can reach all the way to the end of it. Chicago takes up the whole world!"

After the children were put to bed, Maud and Julia sat down together in front of the fire.

"How are you managing, Julia?" Maud asked.

"Not so bad, all things considered," Julia said. "It's much easier now that we've moved to town."

Unable to make a living at farming, they had lost their claim. James moved them into the tiny town of Edgeley, where he had secured a position delivering horses for a livery stable. The Carpenters still wanted for money, but life in town was not as isolated, and Magdalena was able to attend school. As Maud beheld her sister, she felt a melancholy ache under her breastbone. Ten years old when Maud was born, Julia had always seemed more like a second mother to her. She remembered her sister's funny face, framed with a frizz of tawny curls, always popping up when she needed something—ready with a bandage for her skinned knee or to match a lost mitten. That girl had been replaced by the woman before her. Worn out, arthritic, her hair now almost entirely silver. At least her eyes were clear. Ever since leaving Dakota, Maud's fear for Magdalena had sat like a black pit at the base of her heart. Seeing her sister appearing lucid again made her feel a little better.

"I'm glad to see you looking well."

Julia's hand shook slightly as she tucked a lock of hair behind her ear. "I've weaned myself from the patent medicines," she said. "I've been following the precepts of Mary Baker Eddy—Christian Science, are you familiar with it?" She continued without waiting for Maud to answer: "It teaches one to manage illness and pain without medicines."

Maud gazed into her sister's eyes and felt relief wash over her.

"And what about James. Is he . . . keeping steady?"

Julia looked away from her sister. "He travels quite a bit—for business—and sometimes we don't see him for weeks at a time. . . . I'm sure you know how that is now that Frank is on the road?" Julia glanced around as if to take in, once again, the modest house, the shabby furnishings, the street filled with peddlers and lurching horse-drawn carts.

Maud flushed crimson. A little voice in the back of her head told her to bite her tongue, but she couldn't. Her words came out in a furious rush: "Frank never drank to excess. He's never pointed a gun at my heart. He's never failed to treat me with kindness. You've made your choices, Julia Gage, but don't you ever equate them with mine!"

Julia colored, then studied her hands, suddenly meek. "Magdalena is a great comfort to me. She's an excellent student. The best student in our little school. I buy her books instead of dresses. She's clever like you and Mother, and just as determined." Julia paused, then continued. "I'm doing my best, Maudie. I'm trying to be strong for Magdalena."

"You see to it that she gets an education," Maud said, her eyes flashing. "Promise me right now that you'll keep her in school. If she ends up dropping out of school to be a farmer's wife, I swear I will never forgive you. I'll not have that girl assigned to a life of drudgery."

Julia looked reflectively at Maud. "You are speaking as a woman who dropped out of college to run away with a theater man? You are speaking as a woman who asked her family to scrimp and save to pay her tuition and then gave it all up—for what?"

"For what?" Maud said sharply. "For love! Which is a good reason. But I don't know what you'd know about that."

Julia sniffed. "You will never understand, Maud."

"You're right, Julia! I *don't* understand. But you take back what you said about Frank right now. He was brilliant at the theater, and he's a good, good man."

Julia opened her mouth as if determined to argue, then thought better of it.

"All right. I'll grant you that. Frank's a good man. He's good-hearted. I'm grateful that he paid for our tickets so we could take a break from that godforsaken place."

Maud picked up her embroidery basket.

"You think that Frank paid for those tickets?" she said. "Then you know *nothing* of the power of women. Now, you solemnly swear to me right now that come hell or high water, Magdalena Towers Carpenter will stay in school as long as her heart desires, and I'll get to work making that poor ragamuffin a new dress. I've enough scraps here to sew her a brand-new summer frock of pretty pink lawn."

At the sounds of the words "new dress," Magdalena's pixie face appeared between the rungs of the upstairs banister, scrubbed bright, with a big smile.

Julia stood up, creaking a bit as she raised herself from the chair.

"Magdalena! What are you doing up?"

"Nothing!" Magdalena said, and then she muttered, loud enough for Maud to hear, "Except that I'm going to go to school forever *and* get a brand-new pink dress!"

CHICAGO, ILLINOIS

1897

SEVEN YEARS AFTER THEIR MOVE TO CHICAGO, THE BAUMS
had left behind their dingy row house on Campbell Park and settled
into a modest home in a safe, middle-class neighborhood near
Humboldt Park. Even their youngest, little Kenneth, had started
school. As the boys grew, Maud continued to hope for a girl, but
month after month passed with no signs of another pregnancy. For
a long time, each monthly cycle brought fresh disappointment, and
then one morning, in the looking glass, she noticed afresh the silvery strands that now threaded through her hair, and she realized
that her time for creating new life had most likely passed.

Matilda arrived for her annual visit a few days before Thanksgiving. Her winter visit to the Baum family had turned into a tradition, but this year, she had almost canceled her trip, she'd recently
been so ill. So Maud was anxious to see her mother in person.

Maud waited impatiently for Frank, who had gone to pick up
Mother at the train station. She hated it when her roast chicken was
out of the oven too long before she served it—the skin got soft.

When the door pushed open, Maud rushed to greet her mother,
hugging her tightly. But as she stepped back to take a look at her,
Maud was shocked to find her normally robust mother looking unusually frail, and hoped she was just weary from the journey.

Maud tried to make the visit restful for her mother. She cooked the meals she liked best, made the boys stay quiet in the afternoon so her mother could nap, and attended to her every whim. Mother had always been the strongest person she knew—the one who never fatigued, who never complained, who always arrived ready to get the job done. So Maud was happy to have a chance to repay her in some small measure. Still, at odd moments, Maud realized that it had been eight years—*eight years*—since her mother had arrived in Aberdeen with her obstetric textbook and carbolic acid, determined that Maud would live through the birth of her third child.

How she had seemed like a giant to Maud then, looming over everyone and everything with her impassioned intellect, her fiery oratory, her encyclopedic knowledge, and, more than anything, her sheer confidence that the world would eventually bend to her bidding. Seeing her mother looking frail made Maud feel as if the natural order of things had been inverted, herself suddenly older than she had realized, needing to fill bigger shoes, and uncertain if she was ready.

One night, Matilda and Maud were seated in the parlor. Frank was traveling, and the boys were already in bed. Maud was sewing, and Matilda was reading; she set aside her book.

"If it's not too heavy a burden," Matilda said, "I would like to confide in you something that has weighed heavily upon me."

"Of course, Mother. What is it?"

"It's Julia."

"What about her?"

"I know you love your sister dearly, and I'm grateful for that."

"I'm not sure gratitude is called for. Of course I love her. She was always so kind to me when I was a girl. That is a debt I can never repay."

"She almost raised you. I was so busy with my work." Matilda stared off into the distance. "It seemed so close then, in the 1870s—we believed that we were just on the brink of securing the vote for women nationwide. I thought it was worth it, for your future, for the future of my daughters, and your daughters . . . and their daughters. And you were so spunky, so determined, I never needed to worry about you. You were born with the same iron stuff that I was made of . . ."

Maud smiled. She couldn't deny it. She had been born tough.

"But Julia—she was different. She was not as tough."

"Julia is strong in her own way," Maud countered.

"I didn't see it at the time. I was impatient with her physical frailty. I was angry at all that was the woman's lot—the housekeeping, the childbearing, the care for aging relatives . . ." She paused to snort out a laugh. "If you don't die in childbirth, then you might lose yourself to grief as you nurse an ailing child. If you and your child survive, then you face a lifetime of toil. And so many women are sickly—nervous disorders, female complaints, sick headaches, which leads to the imbibing of medicines that seem to do more harm than good. I was so impatient with all that. I thought if Julia were made of sterner stuff, she could simply will herself to health. That her headaches made her drop out of school was simply incomprehensible to me."

"Until one is ill, it is hard to fully understand the plight of the invalid," Maud said.

Matilda nodded. "Old age has taught me that."

Maud smiled, but then she noticed that her mother was crying.

"I blame myself for baby Jamie's death."

"But, Mother, how could that have been your fault? You weren't even there!"

"Julia wrote to me and asked me to send her money to return to Fayetteville for the delivery, as she had for Magdalena's birth. But, you see, she had sailed right through her delivery, while you had taken ill. And, Maud, I had no idea of the conditions she was living in. When I pictured her homestead in Dakota, I thought of a civilized town like Aberdeen. So, when she wrote to me, I said no. You remember, your father was gone, the store was closed, and money was tight."

"Of course, I understand."

Matilda held up her hand, dabbed her tears, and tried to compose herself.

"I wanted to attend the National Woman Suffrage conference in

Washington, D.C. I had enough money for my own fare. To send for Julia, I would have had to cancel my trip."

Maud nodded.

"I wasn't willing. I thought that the fate of all womankind was more important than the fate of one individual—my own daughter. I thought it was the duty of we women who were fighting the fight to stay strong." Now Matilda was openly sobbing. "I didn't understand that you can't always just 'stay strong,' that sometimes the conditions we are fighting are greater than our individual abilities. If that ignorant back-country nurse hadn't told Julia to dry up her milk, that baby might still be alive."

"Mother! You don't know that! You mustn't be so hard on yourself."

"No, Maud. I had to learn something that you always knew instinctively. The fight for all women has got to begin with the women closest to you."

"No mother is perfect," Maud said. "I've always been proud to be your daughter."

"But all that I've given up . . . and so little to show for it," Matilda said.

"So little to show for it, Mother? Not so! The day will come when you will be proven right. Your daughters, or at least your grandchildren, will be alive to see that day, and we will thank you."

Matilda was looking at Maud searchingly, as if hoping her daughter could answer her deepest fears. "And that will be enough?"

Maud stood and enfolded her mother's frail shoulders in her arms, catching her faint scent of mint and lavender. "Oh, Mother dear, of course it will be much more than enough."

ON CHRISTMAS EVE, the giant fir in the parlor of the Baum household reached all the way to the ceiling, and the entire thing was cordoned off behind a giant red curtain that Frank had fashioned to hide half of the room. At the agreed-upon moment, Maud pushed open the parlor door, and the boys tumbled in behind her, like a litter of puppies on their way out to play. The boys—Robin, twelve;

Harry, eight; Kenneth, six; and even fifteen-year-old Bunting—had not outgrown their excitement about Christmas. Every year, Frank spent weeks preparing an elaborate pantomime. In terms of gifts under the tree, no Christmas had ever equaled their first in Aberdeen, when a profligate Frank had brought half of their store home to place under the Christmas tree. Now Maud controlled the Christmas budget. She counted out just a few dollars for Frank to spend on gifts. But he more than made up for it in homegrown merriment.

"Well now, Santa." Frank's voice was audible behind the curtain. "Have I paid you enough? Will you be getting on your way?"

A deep hearty "Ho-ho-ho" followed.

"Open the curtain!" Kenneth piped up. "Open it!"

"Yes, open it!" the other boys called out. Even Bunting (who now insisted on being called Frank Jr.) had joined in the fun.

"Well now, don't leave just yet . . ." Frank's voice said behind the curtain. "There are some boys here who would really like to meet you!"

This was followed by some rustling of the curtain and the sounds of much shuffling.

"What? Don't leave! Please!" Bells jingled behind the curtain; then came the sound of hoofbeats. More bells.

Frank had rigged the red curtain on a rope pulley, and suddenly the curtain jerked aside to reveal the giant Christmas tree, trimmed with popcorn and cranberry strands, blue balls made of glass, delicate gingerbread men decorated by Maud, and shining candles that cast a warm flickering glow across the room. Underneath was a modest assortment of colorful packages tied up with bright satin ribbons.

A collective "Aaah" went up from all assembled.

Then little Kenneth said in a voice as clear as a silver bell, "But where's Santa?"

"Why, he's . . ." Frank feigned shock as he looked all around himself. "Why, I don't know. I swear he was just here a minute ago. I asked him to wait!"

Harry turned and pointed to the hearth.

"There he is!" everyone cried.

A pair of red pants and black rubber boots (that looked suspiciously like a pair of Frank's) were sticking out from the hearth. Only the legs and feet were visible.

"Santa! I thought you said you would wait!" Frank called.

The younger boys didn't notice when he grabbed a second rope, and with a flick of the wrist, suddenly the boots and pants disappeared, as if climbing up the chimney.

"He's gone!" Kenneth cried.

"Quick, everyone! Outside!" Frank called out. "We may just catch St. Nick's sleigh as he's flying away."

"Outside? Children, not without your jackets and boots!"

Ignoring Maud's entreaties, the entire group burst out the front door into the frigid night, where fat snowflakes were swirling, softening the city's edges and making the world look like a wonderland.

"Boys, come back inside! Frank, have you lost your mind? The children will catch their death!"

Matilda was already back in the house, but Maud had to scoop up the boys' coats and toss one to each of them. Frank was holding a lantern and telling them to scout for reindeer tracks in the snow.

"Daddy!" Kenneth called out. "Quick. Over here!"

"What have you got there, son?"

"Look, it's a bell! I think it fell off Santa's sleigh."

Kenneth held up a cheap penny bell. He shook it, making a muffled, tinny sound.

"Why, by golly!" Frank exclaimed. "I think you're right."

"Santa!" Kenneth cried out. "Come back! You lost your bell!"

Kenneth's teeth were chattering. Maud took his cold hand in hers and called to the rest of them: "Let's go in now. I've got hot chocolate warming on the stove for all of you!"

She shoveled more coal into the iron stove until it roared hot, then placed a cup of steaming cocoa in each boy's hands. Before bed, the children opened their packages, but none of their gifts—new woolen socks, and pencils and paper for school—could ever equal the special magic that Frank's imagination brought to the holiday.

That night, after the boys were all tucked into bed and Maud was resting in the rocking chair in front of the fire, Matilda placed her hand on her daughter's shoulder.

"You know, Maud, I was wrong about Frank in the beginning. I worried about you marrying an actor. But now I see it. He's been a good father and a good husband to you. You chose well."

Frank burst out from behind the giant fir tree, tinkling the glass ornaments and causing the candles to sway.

"Finally!" he crowed. "I've gotten the great Matilda Gage to admit she made a mistake!"

Matilda's eyes flew open in mock horror, and then all three of them dissolved into laughter.

MATILDA WAS SCHEDULED TO return home to Fayetteville just after Kenneth's birthday, in March. With Maud's nurturing, her mother had rallied and seemed much better, but then in late February, she came down with influenza. She had a high fever and a racking cough that persisted in spite of Maud's best efforts. Matilda protested, but at last she allowed Maud to call in the doctor. After examining her, he pronounced her to be weak and in need of fortification.

The doctor took out a small pad of paper and wrote down a prescription.

"There is a brand-new medicine that is working wonders for coughs. Please administer one injection daily."

Maud read the words on the piece of paper he handed her: BAYER HEROIN. 4 CCS Q.D.

FOR THE FIRST FEW DAYS, Maud was relieved that the heroin injections seemed to be working. The doctor had promised that Matilda would sleep easier and cough less, and indeed, that was the case. One day, Maud came into the bedroom to check on her mother and found her awake, propped up on her pillows, writing a letter.

"I'm so pleased to see you looking better," Maud said, sitting on the edge of the bed.

"There is something I need to tell you," Matilda said. "We need to have a private discussion. For when the time comes."

"Nothing is going to happen to you! You are doing much better with the new medicine."

"I am feeling better, but I can't live forever. I just want everything clear, in case something happens to me."

"All right," said Maud, settling on the rocker near the window. "What is it that I need to know?"

"My will divides my remaining fortune equally among my children," Matilda said. "It's not as much as I would have wished. You know that my book *Woman, Church and State* has been banned from libraries. Even with acclaim from all over the world, from Victoria Woodhull of London and Mr. Tolstoy in Russia, I still have not earned as much as I should have."

"You should have earned more," Maud said soothingly, "but your contribution to the world of ideas is more significant than money."

Matilda, mollified, continued: "Now, listen to me. I realize that your life is difficult. I see that your husband works hard but spins his wheels. You know the golden path?" Matilda was referring to her theosophical beliefs. Maud nodded.

"I have meditated upon this, and I feel that your journey is not yet over. So I ask you this. The money that I bequeath you is yours. Frank will think of uses for it. He will want to spend the money along the journey: newspapers, inventions—I don't know what it will be. Don't listen to him. A woman must never be without a home. You will know when the time is right. Use the money to buy a home for your family. But make that decision alone."

"But, Mother!"

"Do you promise?"

"But, Mother . . ."

"I shall not rest until you promise."

Maud promised.

MATILDA LAY ON A black leather couch, dressed in a dark blue tea gown. Her repose was restful, her hands crossed over her heart, left over right. Her shiny white hair was coiled behind her head, in death, as in life. Julia and T.C., along with Frank and Maud, were seated in Frank and Maud's parlor, along one side of the open casket. All day long, the post had brought letters and telegrams of condolence for the great woman.

T.C. read the will, which indicated that Matilda wished to be cremated, as she believed it was more salutary for the earth. Her casket and the entire parlor were filled with her favorite flower: the American Beauty rose. Frank had made the rounds of six different florists and bought out all of them.

When the undertakers placed Matilda in the coffin, she lay upon a thick bed of roses. Their delicate scent filled the room even after the coffin was closed.

Matilda's will specified that her ashes be scattered in the garden in Fayetteville. Frank was scheduled for a sales trip and, understanding that Maud wanted to make the journey, Julia kindly offered to stay in Chicago to look after the children, so Maud boarded a train for Syracuse alone.

It was late March, and the town was still locked tight in the grip of late winter. The trees were barren, and patches of old sooty snow remained on the ground. The train arrived late on a Thursday afternoon, and Maud rode in a hired hack, her mother's ashes in an urn, inside a box, on the seat beside her.

She had held herself together through her mother's illness and death and all of the obligatory ceremonies, but arriving at the family home, Maud could no longer contain her tears. She paused at the end of the front walk. The bare winter branches of the big dogwood tree she had once climbed to save a kitten still spread expansively over the front lawn. The house's exterior looked the same as ever, square and stately, its four white columns lined up across the front porch. But as she pushed the door open, she was greeted by chilly, stale air, and a strange stillness seemed to vibrate in her ears as she strained to hear the whispers of the pattering footsteps, swishing skirts, and excited conversation that had filled the home of her youth.

She made her way to her mother's parlor. A half-finished watercolor still sat on the easel. On the wall, in the place of pride, was a framed sampler embroidered with the words to "The Golden Stairs"; Maud had made it for her mother one Christmas. She had worked on it all winter, the year after they left South Dakota. Maud had copied the famous lines from her mother's favorite theosophist, H. P. Blavatsky.

Scanning the words now, she realized that she still had them memorized. The verse had grown so familiar to her as she'd slowly stitched the letters in golden thread. *A clean life, an open mind, / A pure heart, an eager intellect.* This was her mother. *An unveiled spiritual perception.* Mother had always been able to imagine the better future, a better world, as if she could divine things that others could not. *These are the golden stairs, / Up the steps of which the learner may climb / To the Temple of Divine Wisdom.*

She could remember hearing Frank and Matilda talking about this—the golden path—in those dark days in Dakota, the two of them sitting immersed in discussion about their theosophical theories while she busily went about her daily chores, a nugget of resentment in her breast. Yet now those times seemed dear to her, woven into the fabric of her life just as surely as her own nimble fingers had threaded the words of Helena Blavatsky into cloth. And wasn't there a golden path, after all? Looking back, she could see its traces, leading her out into the great big world and, wiser now, back to her old home.

The next day, Maud gathered her strength and walked to her mother's garden, behind the house. The towering fence that separated their property from the Crouse home next door was in fact only shoulder height. Beyond it, there was no sign of the old scarecrow that had once frightened her so much. Old Mr. Crouse had died many years ago. Leftover snow was still clumped in the shady corners. Her mother's lawn was brown, but a smattering of fresh green shoots had emerged.

Maud made her way to the back of the garden. She carried a small spade, which she used to clear away the snow. There, she found the flat rock where she had once buried her pet crow—her childish introduction to death.

Maud opened the silver urn and scattered the ashes over the place where she knew in the spring her mother's favorite peonies would bloom. She watched the ashes fall upon the cold ground, and brushed away the silvery gray grit that blew onto her black silk crepe de chine. Right now, on this cold March afternoon, she lacked the power to imagine that in June, this same barren patch of ground would bloom forth with the soft white and pink flowers, so heavy, so full of life, that the stalks would bend with the weight of their blossoms. Bees would buzz, butterflies would flit, and giant puffy clouds would float high in the sky. Now it was gray and cold, and that seemed fitting.

By the end of the week, Maud had sorted out and packed the house. When she left, she took just a few items with her. She took the embroidered message of the golden path, as well as a tin can labeled BAUM'S CASTORINE that she'd found in the back shed. And she took a handkerchief she had embroidered for her mother, on which she imagined she could still catch a whiff of Matilda's favorite homemade salve of dried lavender and mint mixed with Vaseline.

On her last morning, Maud made the rounds of each of the rooms, once full of a family, now populated by ghosts. She thought of her father, quiet and kind, always there with a word of encouragement, reaching into his pocket and pulling out an aggie or tiger marble and tossing it to her with a wink. She pictured Julia—the little mother, always running after Maud with a clean handkerchief or a warm scarf on a cold day. But most of all, Maud saw Mother: nurse and doctor, priest and witch, fighter and patient mender, brilliant mind and kindly heart.

As Maud locked the door behind herself, every home she had

lived in since leaving here flashed across her mind: the elegant
rooms in Sage College, the tawdry western boardinghouses where
she and Frank had happily spent their first married days, their
home in Dakota, where frigid winds had rattled the windows and
giant hailstones pelted the roof. She thought of Julia's square of
weathered wood perched on the landscape like a bird just alighted
and ready to fly away. She thought of the run-down row house on
Campbell Park, and of her present home on Humboldt Boulevard,
filled with the sounds of boisterous boys and joyful laughter each
time Frank came home from the road.

But unlike this house, each of those had a temporary quality. She
and Frank had never owned their own family home. As the heavy
lock clicked into place, Maud thought of her mother's instructions
for her small inheritance. Mother had been so certain that Maud
would know when the time was right to use it, but *how* would she
know? Maud whispered a prayer to her mother, asking her to always stay with her; then she turned her back and walked down the
sidewalk, away.

CHICAGO, ILLINOIS

1898

A S THE TRAIN RATTLED INTO CHICAGO, AIR FILLED WITH coal smoke hung yellow on the horizon, and the stench of the stock-yards seeped through the windows. Still, when she passed the murky effluents of the Chicago River, Maud saw the late afternoon sunlight winking on the tall buildings and caught a glimpse of the crisp blue of Chicago's Great Lake, and realized she couldn't wait to get back to Humboldt Boulevard. As she exited the train station, the crowd surged around her, and she spilled out, along with the press of humanity, into the city where she now belonged.

There was something else, too. Something that brought an extra bit of lightness to her step. Maud had realized while she was away that she was most likely with child. Deep in her heart, she imag-ined that she was nurturing a baby girl—a child to carry on her mother's legacy.

By the time she made it all the way back to Humboldt Boulevard it was past the boys' bedtime, so she pushed the front door open quietly and tiptoed inside. To her surprise, she found Frank sitting in an armchair in the parlor, his long legs propped over one arm, a pad of paper balanced on his knees, the stump of his pipe clenched between his teeth, and a pencil in his hand. When he noticed her, he jumped out of his chair, knocking aside the pad of paper and sending it skidding across the floor.

"You're home, dear heart! I didn't even hear you come in! Maudie darling, we've missed you. Was your trip all right?" He embraced her warmly.

"It's so good to be home," she said, resting her head against his chest. "How are the boys?"

"Oh, tip-top. We managed perfectly fine. Everyone made it through without a scratch."

"Without a scratch?" Maud said, smiling. "Well, that is rather a low bar."

Maud bent over to pick the pad up off the floor and saw that there were pages filled with his backhand scrawl. Frank reached out hastily, almost snatching it from her. He flipped the pad closed, as if he didn't want her to see what was written there.

"What is it, Frank?" she asked, now curious.

Frank tucked the pencil behind his ear and grinned in reply. "It's just the strangest thing. An idea for a story grabbed hold of me while you were gone. I'm writing it down as fast as I can."

"What's it about?" Maud said, taking off her coat.

Frank held out the pad so that she was able to read the title.

"It's called 'The Emerald City'? Really, Frank?" Maud still blushed at the memory of their ride on the Ferris Wheel. "Is it about us?"

"It's about the most beautiful place you can imagine. A land of Aahs."

Maud smiled. "You mean the story about the boys' block city?"

"Better!" Frank said. "An enchanted kingdom. A land I've called Oz. O-Z. Oz."

Maud put her arms around her husband's shoulders. "Oz may be beautiful, but I can't imagine anyplace more beautiful than right here in our very own home." She placed her hand over her lower belly and looked up at him through her lashes. "And soon we'll be adding to our blessings."

"Are we truly expecting another one?" Frank said joyfully.

Maud nodded shyly. "I think so, but it's early yet."

"Oh, Maudie," he said, drawing her close and kissing her long and deep. "This is such happy news! Another child! Perhaps a girl for our dotage."

Maud blushed with pleasure. "Perhaps."

IN THE FOLLOWING DAYS, Frank continued his frenzy of writing. She had never seen him so deeply absorbed, so absent. Day after day, Frank sat in the rocking chair in the front parlor, pencil in hand, a pad of lined paper in his lap, scribbling. And most days, he came home from work with pages to add to the pile. He wrote on any scrap of paper he could find: backs of envelopes, bills of sale, the blank flip sides of printed lists from Pitkin & Brooks with the inventory of china neatly printed on the front. At first, Maud tiptoed around him, careful not to disturb him, but soon she realized that he was so absorbed in his work that no amount of surrounding hubbub made the slightest dent in his concentration.

One afternoon, when Maud had been out delivering her finished sewing pieces, she heard what sounded like a riot going on in the parlor. Peering through the doorway, she saw Frank Jr. and Robin, diving and dodging, engaged in a lively game of catch, Harry pounding out "Chopsticks" on the piano, and little Kenneth entranced in running a small metal fire truck back and forth across one of Frank's long black shoes.

"Children!" Maud said, clapping her hands to get their attention. "Your father is trying to concentrate. And no playing ball in the house. You're going to break something!" All four boys froze at the sound of their mother's voice, and even their calico cat looked up languidly from its warm perch in Frank's lap, but Frank himself didn't seem to notice her presence. He held his pencil in midair, eyes focused out the window. With his other hand, he absentmindedly stroked the cat. A moment later, he scribbled a few more words, and then blinking, as if he suddenly remembered where he was, he looked up at Maud.

"Oh hello there, dear. Back so soon?"

"Oh, Frank, I've been gone all afternoon. How's the writing going?"

"Splendidly!" he said. "I'll be done with this story before you know it!"

"But what's it about?" Maud asked, wonderingly.

"Well, it's about a girl and her companions, and they're on the move. It's hard to explain, Maud, but it's all in there."

"*What's* all in there?"

"Why—everything!" he said, grasping her hands and gazing into her eyes. "Our whole life and everything we've ever endured and imagined, all wrapped up and turned into make-believe, and—oh, I can't explain it. But I promise you, by the time I'm done, it will *all* be in there."

In spite of Frank's unbridled enthusiasm, Maud watched the mounting pile of scraps of paper, of penciled jottings, with a growing sense of concern. At Frank's age, forty-two, it was a leap of faith, Maud knew, for him to try to return to the creative life. But, honestly, what would the book publishers think when her husband, a china salesman, showed up at their office, his briefcase filled with a manuscript scribbled on torn envelopes and the backs of shopping lists? Frank had been—well, not beaten down exactly, but certainly chastened by the ups and downs of their life together. And now, here they were—both of them—nurturing a small hope for something that had seemed too late to hope for. Just as she wanted to guard the small life blooming within her, Maud felt protective of her husband's kind heart.

MAUD LAY ON THE BED, staring at the ceiling. By turns she cried, then fell back to sleep. When Frank tried to console her, she turned her back to him; when he fetched the doctor, she told the man to go away. Maud had weathered it all—the hard days and the good ones, saying goodbye to Magdalena, the loss of her mother—but this loss, unimportant on the surface, just the barest promise of a new life, was the one she could not bear. Maud longed for her mother to come through the door, longed for the comfort of her snowy-white hair, her placid face. Matilda would have something to offer: a salve, a tincture, a soup, or a few words—something natural, something soothing. But now, the matriarch was gone and the flicker of hope for a girl to carry on her tradition had now been lost. Maud lay on her bed, her limbs heavy. The sunlight filtering through the curtains seemed insipid. Somewhere, in the back of her mind, she knew that she was no longer sick in body, just brokenhearted in spirit, but she could not bring herself to leave her bed. Frank brought her trays of food, looked after the children, and worried over her, but Maud did not yet have the heart to rejoin the land of the living.

After about ten days, Frank came upstairs and sat down on the bed. For a long time, he stayed there without moving or speaking. Maud didn't even turn to face him. He placed his warm, big hand gently on her shoulder.

"Maud, darling. Dearest Maudie. Can't you come back to us?"

Maud lay with her back to Frank, staring at the patterned wallpaper, and said nothing.

He kneaded her shoulder gently with his broad, strong thumb.

"There is something I want to say to you, Maud."

Maud didn't even look at him; she just made a soft sound to indicate that she was listening.

"I know I'm not perfect, but I've tried to be a good husband to you."

Maud continued to stare into space. Her body felt heavy, weighted down.

"I know you love the boys, but I wish I could have given you a daughter," Frank said.

Maud rolled over and looked at him. "A daughter was not yours to give."

"You Gage women, you are something else altogether, a force of nature. I feel so lucky that you came into my life. And I wanted to give you a daughter of your own, to carry on that legacy."

Maud pushed herself up and leaned against his shoulder. "Frank, you've given me everything I could hope for. And I had no right to pine for a daughter when I was given four beautiful, healthy sons—it's just that Mother . . ."

Frank waited as Maud struggled to find the right words.

"Mother was certain that her spirit would live on in a girl child . . . and now it feels like the end of the line."

Frank reached out and squeezed her hand.

"You remember how your mother always encouraged me to write? 'Write those stories down, Frank Baum!' You remember how she always used to say that?"

Maud nodded, barely, keeping her eyes fixed on a crack in the plaster shaped like a flower that ran along a seam of the ceiling.

"Well, I've named the girl in my story Dorothy."

Maud rolled over and stared at him. "*Our* Dorothy?"

"It's a story about hope. It's a story about knowing that there is always someplace out there that is better. Dorothy is a Gage girl, like you, like your mother, like Magdalena. Brave, tenacious, tough."

Tears leaked out of Maud's eyes and rolled down her cheeks. She made no move to brush them away.

"I'm sorry I never gave you a daughter, Maud. This is the best I could do."

Maud looked into her husband's gray eyes, noting the crow's-feet that now encircled them, the graying temples. She leaned forward until their foreheads touched.

"Our Dorothy is not made of flesh and blood," he said. "She's fashioned from words and paper, pencil and script. But she has one quality that no flesh-and-blood child has. She'll never grow up. She'll never grow old. She'll always be with us."

Maud buried her face in her husband's shoulder as he stroked her hair.

He whispered in her ear: "I did the best I could."

IT WAS LATE ON a Friday afternoon in October when Maud finished up in the kitchen and came out to the parlor to find Frank slumped back in his armchair, staring into space.

"Darling Frank, what is it?"

He held up the short stub of pencil in his hand.

"I've done it," he said.

"Done what?"

"I've finished."

Suddenly he jumped up and flung his pencil into the air. It hit the tin ceiling and ricocheted off the lamp before coming to rest at Maud's feet.

"By golly," Frank said. "I've done it. I've just written the words 'The End'!"

He was grinning like a small boy.

"Now," he said, "all I need to do is find a publisher, and what was just imaginary ramblings will sit proudly on our shelf. And if you want my opinion, I think we're sitting on a future best seller."

That night, Frank went to bed early and fell into a deep and satisfied slumber, as if finishing his story had taken a weight from his mind. But Maud had trouble sleeping. Her own loss still ached deep within her. She'd do anything to spare her husband a similar pain.

The next day, Maud stood at the parlor's threshold, looking around anxiously to make sure no one was about. But she was being silly. Frank was at work, and the boys were at school. It was only her guilty conscience that made her fretful. Resolutely, she walked across the room toward the shelf where the ungainly heap of pads and stray papers known as "the book" was piled up in a haphazard manner. She flipped one of the pads open to a random page and began to read.

> Even with eyes protected by the green spectacles
> Dorothy and her friends were at first dazzled by
> the brilliancy of the wonderful City. The streets
> were lined with beautiful houses all built of green
> marble and studded everywhere with sparkling
> emeralds.

Green-tinted spectacles? Sparkling emeralds? Vividly, she remembered the jeweled lights of the White City carpeting the ground beneath them as they swung aloft on the Ferris Wheel. Gathering up the rest of the pile, she settled herself on the sofa, bracing herself to start at the beginning and read straight through. She wasn't eager to find out what other parts of their lives she might recognize in the story, but she felt it was her duty. If what he had written wasn't good enough, she would let him down gently, save him from the struggle to find a publisher, and keep him from being embarrassed. She despised snooping on him and this wasn't her habit, but surely, this once, she could do it for his own good.

As she turned to the first page, she thought again of the view of the White City through green spectacles, and suddenly another memory came back to her from that night. After the Ferris Wheel ride, as they'd strolled along the promenade, what was it that Frank had said to her? She remembered now.

If you could just try to have faith in me.

The words came to her so clearly it was as if he were standing near her and spoke them aloud.

She looked at the pile of papers in her lap with shame and then placed it gently back on the shelf, unread.

FRANK SPENT THE NEXT COUPLE of weeks carefully recopying the jumbled manuscript, until at last he had a neat stack of pages. He tied it up with string and placed it in his briefcase. "Well, this is it. I start knocking on publishers' doors today!"

As the days passed, each time he pushed the door open in the evening, she studied his face, wondering what the day had brought. Every evening he said, "Not yet, dear heart. Not yet." Until one day, about two weeks later, he burst through the door carrying a bouquet of roses and swept Maud up into a warm embrace.

"I've done it!" Frank crowed. "I've found a publisher!"

"Oh, Frank! That's wonderful news!"

"We just have to invest a small sum of money," he said. "About two hundred dollars. To pay for the illustrations and printing, of course. You needn't worry—" Frank interrupted himself, his words tumbling over each other in excitement. "We don't have to come up with all of it. We can take out a small loan and ask the illustrator to pitch in half the money. We'll earn it back before you know it, and probably make money to boot! Oh, and Maud!" he said, embracing her and twirling her around until they dizzily collapsed in a heap on the sofa. "It's going to be a real, true book. With a cover, and pages, and my name on the spine!"

"You have to pay them?" Maud said. "But why? Shouldn't they pay you for all the work you've done?"

"Oh, not to worry, darling. They will! They will! Royalties on every copy we sell. The investment is just to help the publisher defray the cost of the printing. It's just a small company . . ." He stopped, and a flicker of worry crossed his face. "Tell me, darling? Do you think it's too much?"

In truth, when he'd said *two hundred dollars,* Maud had felt as if all the air had been sucked out of the room. The only money she'd set aside was intended for the boys' Christmas presents. But every argument she could marshal and every doubt she would normally have expressed died on her lips. It was her turn to believe in him. To take him and his story on faith.

AS CHRISTMAS 1899 APPROACHED, the last holiday of the century, Maud took an envelope out of the top drawer of her dresser and looked at its meager contents with dismay. Since emptying out her emergency fund to help Frank pay for the book, she had managed to pull together only three dollars and fifty-seven cents. Hardly enough to allow for a Christmas goose! Certainly not enough to purchase a single gift. Frank had told Maud repeatedly that initial orders for *The Wonderful Wizard of Oz* had been strong for the Christmas season. He was feeling hopeful. But that was his nature. And hope would not buy Christmas presents.

When she saw little Kenneth, forehead puckered in concentration, carefully writing out a list for Santa in his childish blocky print, she finally had to say something. Tentatively, she asked, "Frank, what if you went to the publisher and asked for a little something to tide us over? If the orders are so good, surely they could spare a bit to help us through Christmas . . . ? I remember my mother's publishers sometimes did that."

"But, Maud, I can't ask. They won't give me money before the book's even gone on sale. Once they've sold some copies, they'll pay me."

"But the money we spent . . ." Maud said softly. "I haven't been able to save much since. I just don't want to disappoint the boys . . ."

Frank looked so pained that Maud was sorry she had mentioned it. If they had no money for presents, they'd just have to find other ways to make the season festive. They'd done without plenty of times before.

"Never mind, Frank," she said, squeezing his arm. "We'll have a wonderful Christmas anyway."

Then, when Christmas was only a week away, Frank came in, holding one hand behind his back. Maud knew that look on his face. He was bringing her a surprise, a peace offering. She put down her iron and looked up into his eyes.

"Frank, what is that behind your back?"

"I asked for that advance, like you said, Maudie dear," Frank replied. A wide grin split his face from ear to ear.

"Oh, Frank, thank goodness! It's the last Christmas of the century, and I know we've had lean ones, but I was just hoping to have a little bit of extra money. Now that the boys are growing, they want more things."

With a flourish, Frank drew his hand from behind his back and laid a bank check on the ironing board.

Maud peered over to look at it, hoping against hope that the amount would be at least fifty dollars.

She read the words aloud: " 'Three thousand four hundred and eighty-two dollars?' " Her voice shook.

"Three thousand four hundred and eighty-two dollars!" Frank said.

He flung his arms around her and didn't let go until the scent of the scorching iron got their attention. For the first time in her life, Maud had burned a hole in a perfectly good shirt.

ON CHRISTMAS EVE 1899, Frank pulled out all the stops. Instead of the customary fir, he had set up four trees, one for each boy, in each corner of the parlor. The children opened their abundant presents with a joy that Maud had not seen since that first Christmas in Aberdeen—and she rested easy, because this time, she knew that those presents were not bought on credit but fully paid for, in cash, with plenty of cushion left in the bank.

At the very end of the evening, after the boys were upstairs and Maud and Frank were sipping eggnog and comparing notes on the evening's festivities, Frank reached deep into his pocket and produced a small box.

"This is for you, Maud, for all that you've endured with me."

The lid was embossed with the seal of a downtown jewelry shop. Inside was a sparkling green emerald ring.

"This one's not made of paste," he said. "This one will last. And one more thing." Frank handed Maud a brand-new copy of the book. It was bound in green cloth and stamped with a brilliant design of a red-maned lion and the words *The Wonderful Wizard of Oz*.

Maud opened the flyleaf and read:

THIS BOOK IS DEDICATED TO MY GOOD
FRIEND AND COMRADE. MY WIFE.

L.F.B.

HOLLYWOOD

1939

PERHAPS, MAUD THOUGHT, IN ORDER TO MAKE A TRULY GREAT
story, you've got to put an entire life into it—all the heartbreak, all
the glory.

Originally, Frank had never intended to write more than one
book about the Land of Oz, but words came easily to him, and readers had clamored for more. From Tik-Tok to the Patchwork Girl,
Princess Ozma to the Quadlings, the Land of Oz had taken on a life
of its own, as Frank penned fourteen sequels, including one that
had been taken from a safe-deposit box and published after his
death. Frank had tried to end the series after the sixth book. Even
as an author, he had the heart of a wanderer. He wanted to write
about new and different magical lands. He adopted pen names and
wrote more books about other characters and places, but none
equaled the stories about Oz or had the staying power. This beautiful, beloved place he had invented had grown to entrap him. At
times it had been painful for Maud to watch Frank realize, time and
again, that no matter what else he wrote, children still clamored for
more Oz! More Oz!

Maud was no writer, but she had always understood one thing:
the reason the first book was so beloved was that it started out in an

ordinary place and happened to an ordinary girl, and that unlike Frank Baum, most people wanted to visit the strange, the wonderful and beautiful, but for them a visit was enough, and after that, they were content to return home. Even if that place was gray and drab, it was still home.

It had been almost six months since *The Wizard of Oz* had started filming. Maud had seen so many different things that they blurred in her mind. Her son Robert had telephoned from his citrus farm in Claremont to ask her how the movie was turning out, and she hadn't known exactly what to say. She had seen the Haunted Forest and the Deadly Poppy Field; she'd seen the Yellow Brick Road and the Emerald City. She had seen the actors playing the different roles in their costumes and out of them. Even her frantic quest to read the script hadn't told her what she wanted to know. What would the finished picture be like? Would it have that ineffable, magical, whimsical, serious quality of her dear husband's book? She hoped, she prayed, but she still didn't know.

Today, when she entered the sound stage, Maud saw the front side of a wooden house. A chalkboard, propped up against it, identified it as "Uncle Henry and Auntie Em's Farm." In the scruffy yard outside, an animal handler was squatting by a large box, feeding corn to a couple of chickens from the palm of his hand. The dog trainer was sitting on a hay bale, holding Toto on his lap. After all this time, Maud was back in "Kansas." For technical reasons, they were filming the very first scene last.

A loud squawk sent one of the chickens hopping over the side of the cardboard box, almost landing at her feet, as the startled handler jumped up, saying, "Oh, sorry, ma'am!"

Maud burst out laughing. "Never mind. My late husband always said that a chicken can recognize a friend! He made a hobby of breeding fancy chickens. We used to keep a whole flock in our backyard." She reached down, picked up the errant fowl, and calmly handed it back to the fellow, who beamed in appreciation and surprise. "Welcome to Kansas," he said.

Maud immediately noticed that Victor Fleming was no longer

directing—he'd left to work on another picture, *Gone with the Wind*, which the trades were touting as the biggest movie of 1939. Maud was piqued that the director could be changed at such an important moment in the film—and why? Did Fleming truly believe that *Gone with the Wind* was more important? Maud sized up the new fellow, King Vidor, a slight man with light blue eyes and a round face who spoke with a soft Texan drawl. Maud thought there was a kindness to his expression. But she had no idea if he knew how important these Kansas scenes were. This last-minute substitution was disconcerting.

Maud saw Yip Harburg leaning up against the piano. The sourpuss pianist, Harold Arlen, was sitting on the piano bench.

Judy caught sight of Maud and waved. "We're singing the rainbow song today."

Maud closed her eyes, and suddenly, Frank's face appeared before her. Not Frank as he'd been in his last years, but young Frank, with his shiny brown hair and full moustache. Chicago Frank. His eyes were twinkling, and as if he were speaking aloud, Maud heard the words *It's all in there, everything.*

At that moment, Maud desperately wished she could cross over whatever it was that separated them and be with him. She wished that the world was as Mother and her theosophy had once imagined it—with nothing between them but a flimsy veil, so that with enough presence of mind, she could simply push that veil aside. But it was no use. Even now, the vivid image of her husband was fading. The piano player was running through some chords, and the director was blocking the shot for Judy, explaining where he wanted her to move as she sang.

Maud watched anxiously. She knew, she had always known, that for the film to contain the same essence that was captured in the book, the quality that had given the book its staying power, the audience would need to believe the girl—to understand that she was trapped, and genuinely miserable, but that somehow she looked beyond, harnessed her imagination, tapped into a deep wellspring of hope, and kept going.

———

MAUD WONDERED WHAT HER MOTHER would think of Judy Garland. For one thing, the girl had more liberties than her mother could have imagined. She could earn her keep with her acting and singing—a job that would have been impossible for a respectable young woman of Matilda's time. Yet in some ways she was enchained—afraid to push off the older men who surrounded her and tried to control her every move. The life of any girl was complicated—then as now.

Twenty-two years had passed between Matilda's death and the day when women at long last won the right to vote. August 18, 1920. Maud had thought of Matilda all that day, and each year after as she cast her ballot. Matilda had fought her entire life for something that had not come to pass until after she was gone. And Frank, too—Frank had grasped the promise of moving pictures long before sound, color, and technical wizardry could truly bring an imaginary world to life. Maud's job was to be present now, and to hope that somewhere out there, they understood.

When Maud heard the first chords of the rainbow song, she felt once again that strange notion that she already knew this song, that she had always known it, that in it there were notes of prairie sagebrush and yucca flowers, as well as city soot and torpid Chicago afternoons. She watched, her hands clutched tightly in her lap. Would the girl reach deep and give the song the rendition it deserved?

Judy spoke a few lines, then turned her eyes heavenward and leaned against a haystack. She opened her mouth, and out poured the slow, poignant notes, starting low and then sweeping upward. As Maud listened, eyes closed, she felt as if she were swept up out of her seat, out of the sound stage, up into the heavens where the stars danced, to the place where a rainbow would carry you. And suddenly, Frank, eyes twinkling, hands warm in hers, was twirling her around and around and they were waltzing through heavens as dazzling as a Dakota sky, as magical as the White City from atop the Ferris Wheel, as endless as the glittering lights of Los Angeles seen from the Hollywood Hills.

The song ended. Maud opened her eyes. Tears were running down her cheeks. She was back in the sound studio, and chickens were clucking, the dog handler was feeding treats to Toto, the director was standing nearby with his clipboard. At first, no one said anything, but then Harburg started clapping, and Arlen joined in, then the director and the chicken handler, and the dog trainer, the actors playing Uncle Henry and Auntie Em, Ray Bolger, Bert Lahr, Jack Haley, even the Wizard, wearing his Professor Marvel costume—everyone surrounded the girl, applauding her virtuoso performance.

Maud knew, right then, that Judy had done it. She had captured the magic Frank had put into his story, sucked it from the air and breathed it back out through her vocal cords. Maud felt in her heart that Frank must have been listening.

"Take a bow, my dear," the piano player said as the applause died down. "That was a knockout. You should have saved that for when we record it in the sound studio."

Judy looked bewildered. "I can do it again," she said. "As many times as you want."

Maud felt a pang of sympathy for the girl—maybe all true artists were like that deep down, filled up with a gift so intrinsic that they didn't even know where it came from.

"What do you think, Mrs. Baum?" Yip Harburg asked. "Did she put enough wanting into it?"

Maud pictured the stormy Dakota sky, the rainbow breaking through the clouds, her beloved Frank, the small stoic figure of Magdalena growing smaller, receding, as their wagon pulled away. "You know what I heard?" Maud said. "An anthem worthy of my husband's book."

HOLLYWOOD

1939

THEN SUDDENLY, IT SEEMED AS IF THE WORLD WAS AWASH in Oz. Every magazine Maud picked up, every newspaper, the radio, everywhere she looked there was publicity. There were Wizard of Oz cereal boxes and Wizard of Oz Jell-O. She saw the interior of Dorothy's house in Kansas as a "décor suggestion" in *House Beautiful* magazine. She heard interviews with all of the actors and snippets of the music on the radio, and even saw her own photograph: she was sitting with Judy on a sofa, the two of them looking at the book together.

The only thing left that Maud had never seen was the entire movie. She had begged and cajoled, but it was under complete embargo. The first sneak previews were scheduled for August 1939, a couple of weeks from now, and no one would be allowed to view the finished film until then. Just today, out doing some errands along Hollywood Boulevard, Maud had seen the lettering going up on the marquee of Grauman's Chinese Theatre. When she arrived home at Ozcot, the phone was ringing.

"Hello, Mrs. Baum? It's Yip, Yip Harburg."

Maud put on her hat and coat and hurried the two blocks to Musso & Frank's. Inside, as her eyes got adjusted to the dark, she caught sight of Harburg and was surprised to see that he was accompanied by Noel Langley and Mervyn LeRoy.

"Hello, gentlemen," Maud said, somewhat taken aback.

"Mrs. Baum, we've run into a bit of a sticky wicket," Langley said. "We thought you might be able to help."

"Harburg told me on the phone. There's a problem with the rainbow song?"

"The first sneak preview of the picture ran yesterday in San Bernardino," LeRoy said.

"Top secret. Nobody there except a few studio folk, and some of the Loew's people from New York."

"Loew's people?"

"Distributors," LeRoy said. "Money people."

"They think the film's running time is too long," Langley said. "They want to cut the rainbow song."

"We've all talked to Mayer. He won't listen to any of us. We thought he might listen to you."

"To me? Why would he listen to me? I haven't seen him in months. He wouldn't give me the time of day."

"He'll listen to you," LeRoy said.

"Why?"

"Because," Harburg said, "he believes in magic."

"Magic?" Maud said. "I know that's what you told me on the phone, but I'm afraid I've no talent in that direction."

"But Mayer doesn't know that," LeRoy said.

"It's the jacket," Langley said. "When your late husband's jacket showed up on the set, he was sure it was a sign. I mean, really, what are the chances?"

"It *was* strange," Maud admitted. "But truthfully, I'm not even sure it was his."

"It doesn't matter," Langley said. "Mayer believed in it."

"Can you go to him?" LeRoy asked.

"Remember when you told me that your husband used to talk about the rainbow, but it wasn't in the book anywhere, and then the idea for the song lyrics came to me, just like that . . . ?" Harburg said.

Maud nodded.

"We think that song makes the picture," LeRoy said. "I remember walking across San Francisco, right after the earthquake. It never seemed that the world would ever be made right."

"And when I was a kid," Harburg said, "some days, my pop came home without enough to feed our family, and the view from our tenement window was just more tenements, as far as the eye could see."

"My father was a headmaster at a school for boys in South Africa," Langley added. "The only thing the mates cared about was rugby. They were cruel. I was always getting beat up by the older boys, and my father hated me for being weak. How can you escape from a prison that is made by your own father? And somehow you hear all that when Judy sings . . ."

"All of it," Harburg said.

"Every bit," LeRoy said.

"It's all in there," Maud said.

"So, can you go to Mayer and ask him? We've been screaming at him and slamming doors—but it's not getting through to him."

BACK HOME, MAUD CALLED the studio and said that she needed an appointment to see Louis B. Mayer—and, as usual, she got nowhere. So she climbed into her Ford and drove to Culver City. But when she got to the front gate, a new guard was on duty, and he didn't recognize her.

"Name and business at the studio?" he asked in an officious tone.

"Mrs. Maud Baum."

He spent a long time perusing the paper in front of him.

"I'm sorry, ma'am. You're not on the list."

"Baum. *B-A-U-M*," Maud said impatiently.

"Ma'am," he said louder and more slowly, "I can't find your name on the list."

"What do you mean, you can't find my name? I've been coming here for months!" Maud said.

"On what business?" the guard asked, his tone making it clear that he could not imagine on what business this old woman could have been coming.

"Production 1060, *The Wizard of Oz*."

He leafed through his log, then smirked.

"That one's already in the can," he said. "Better luck next time. You need to get in line with the rest of them," he added, jerking his head toward the line of people that snaked down Washington Boulevard.

"I have a one o'clock with Mr. Louis B. Mayer." She might as well lie, she figured. She had nothing to lose.

"Nope," he said. "You're not coming in today, lady, not unless you get in line."

Maud wanted to cry. She had only twenty-four hours to fix this problem. The men had told her that the final cut of the movie was going to be on its way to theaters the next morning.

"I'm sorry, I misspoke. I have an appointment with Ida Koverman at one o'clock."

"Nope. You're not on her list. You need to leave or I'm gonna call over those fellas and tell them to make you leave." He jerked his head toward a couple of uniformed guards.

"Tell Mrs. Koverman I need to speak to her urgently about Miss Judy Garland."

Horns sounded up from cars behind Maud in line.

"You're blocking traffic," the guard said. "You need to move out of the way."

Maud realized she was stuck. There was nothing she could do. She put her car in reverse. But when she looked in her rearview mirror, she realized that the car behind her was a giant Rolls-Royce.

"Oh, dear me," Maud said, affecting a frail old-lady voice. "I don't want to back up. My husband never taught me how. I'm afraid I'm going to hit that lovely limousine right behind me."

The guard looked exasperated. The honking from behind started up again.

"Oh, all right. Pull forward and make a U-turn, then pull out the out gate."

As if to demonstrate her poor driving skills, Maud pushed down on the gas too fast, making the car lurch forward.

Maud glanced in the rearview mirror. The guard was looking at the next car. Now was her chance.

She gunned it, then careened around the corner to the back lot. Jumping out of the car, she ran across the parking lot as fast as her seventy-eight-year-old legs would carry her and turned onto the studio's main street, where she was immediately lost in the profusion of workers, costumed actors, folks carrying pieces of sets, and several grooms leading saddled horses.

She heard a commotion behind her—guards shouting—but she had reached the entrance to the Thalberg Building. She slowed her steps to a walk and tried to calm her breathing and the pounding of her heart as she entered the lobby.

Facing her was the same receptionist she'd encountered the first time she arrived at the Thalberg Building, almost nine months previously. She was blond again, and pretended not to recognize Maud.

"I've got an appointment with Mrs. Koverman," Maud said, still somewhat breathless from her sprint. "Maud Baum."

"Hmm," she said. "I don't see your name here."

"Call her!" Maud said. "Tell her it's Mrs. Maud Baum, here to speak to her about Judy."

"Have a seat."

"No! I'm not going to have a seat!" Maud said. "Call her now. Tell her it's an emergency."

But instead of waiting, Maud kept on walking. A moment later, she was on the elevator. She saw the studio guards entering the lobby just as the elevator doors slid shut.

Ida Koverman was sitting at her desk, guarding the entrance to Mayer's office like a German shepherd with a taste for red meat.

She barely looked up when Maud came in, but as Maud approached, she stood and jerked her head toward the ladies' room.

"We meet again," Ida said, as they stood in front of the mirrors in the bathroom. "What's going on? Is another one of the gents bothering our girl?"

"It's not that," Maud whispered.

"Well, that's a relief. I try to look after her—but, you know, she's badly outnumbered. The little-girl-to-creep ratio in this place does not work in her favor."

"It's actually something else," Maud said. She knew that Ida Koverman was fiercely on Judy Garland's side, but Maud had no idea how she would feel about Maud trying to interfere with creative decisions.

"They're planning to cut the rainbow song from the picture," Maud began. "Some of the boys asked me to come up and talk to Mr. Mayer. I'm not sure if it will work, but I told them I'd try."

"They want to cut the rainbow song?" Ida asked. "But why?"

"The film's running time is too long, apparently," Maud said. "And I think it should stay in because—"

"You don't need to tell me why. It's because that girl needs that song—it's going to be the thing that makes her into a star!"

"Okay, so what should we do?"

"Listen, go on in and talk to him. Just remember, he's a hardhead about business, but he's as sensitive as they come."

Maud entered the blinding-white inner sanctum of the M-G-M Studios for the second time. Louis B. Mayer sat at his massive white desk. Just like the last time, he didn't even glance up when she came in, but continued flipping through a bound script.

"Mr. Mayer," Maud said.

"Sit down," he said gruffly, still without looking up. "I'm in the middle of something."

Maud sat perfectly still and waited for what seemed like a long time.

"Now, Mrs. Baum, what can I do for you?"

"I've heard that you are planning to cut the rainbow song from the film."

"Already done," he said. "Preview was a big hit, but the song dragged the action down. Too slow. Too sad. Too unbecoming to have a star singing in a barnyard."

"But can't it be undone?" Maud asked.

"Can't be undone. This decision was made at the highest level.

Out of my hands. We're in the business of making money, and the picture was too long."

"Are you sure?" Maud said. "Because—"

Mayer held up his hand, then returned to perusing his papers. "Will that be all?"

Maud stood up to go. She turned away and took a few steps toward the door. Defeated. Surely the movie would be good enough without the rainbow song. How had she gotten so convinced that the song was Frank's voice, alive again, pouring out into the world? Hogwash and superstition—that's what it was. She was getting soft—she, who had always believed that magic was what you created from hard work and persistence, not something you plucked from thin air.

But an odd sensation, like a hand upon her shoulder, made her stop. She spun around and faced Louis B. Mayer.

"Do you remember when I first came in here?"

He looked up. "Yes, Mrs. Baum, I do."

"I came because I wanted to make sure that my late husband's story was in good hands. I told you that many people think of Oz as a real place. That you had a duty to those people to make that place come alive."

Mayer was still watching her.

"And you know what? I've watched your studio create magic using cameras and paint and glue and machines. I saw how you took the miniature house and filmed it dropping from the air, then reversed that film so that the house seemed to be flying up into the air."

"Clever, wasn't it?" Mayer said.

"And I saw how you created Munchkinland for real. I walked through it myself and knew that this must have been what Frank himself saw running through his mind when he was writing it. There was magic afoot here in the studio. True movie magic, and you made it, out of giant fans and painted sets and photographic wizardry."

Mayer was smiling and nodding his head in agreement.

"But there's more to making magic than that," she said. "There's a giant beating heart at the center of this story. That heart is real, and that heart sounds through this picture, through these songs, and then when Frank's jacket turned up on the set—I knew he was with us."

Mayer was looking at her, really looking now, and listening. "When your husband's jacket showed up on the set, I knew. I just knew," he said, sounding excited. "We try to make magic every single time. Sometimes we hit, and sometimes we miss. But that jacket. I knew it was an omen. I pressed and pressed and pressed to get more money from New York—do you know we spent almost three million dollars on this project? It has *got* to be a success."

"So you do understand."

"Of course I understand," he said. "The picture is great. The song's gone. It was too long." He gestured a dismissal. "Have a nice day, Mrs. Baum."

As if on cue, Ida Koverman swung the door open.

"You have a visitor, Mr. Mayer."

Judy Garland walked through the door.

"Well," Mayer said, lighting up. "If it isn't my little hunchback."

Behind her came the piano player.

"Do you mind?" Arlen crossed to the white grand piano at the other end of the office. "Did you know that this melody came to me when I was outside Schwab's drugstore?"

"I did not," Mayer said, leaning forward in his chair, intrigued.

"That was the last trolley stop," Maud said. "Back in 1910. The exact spot where Mr. L. Frank Baum first stepped onto the soil of Hollywood."

"You don't say." Mayer stood up, came out from behind his desk, and crossed toward the piano, where Arlen was settling himself on the bench, placing his right foot on the sustain pedal.

"Let us just do it one more time for you—you'll see, it stands alone," Arlen said. "You don't need the backdrop, or the orchestra. Just listen."

Judy's face, without the heavy stage makeup, looked younger; her hair was pulled back in a plain headband, and she wore a navy blue sailor dress, bobby socks, and scuffed loafers. It was as if the movie starlet had been replaced by an ordinary teenage girl who could pass you on the street without attracting notice. The piano player trilled through the opening chords, and then Judy, softly and simply, began to sing, her hands clasped in front of her. But as her voice soared and filled the room with its clear, strong notes, a glow developed around her, until the light appeared to shimmer. Her arms spread out in front of her, as if the song could not be contained in her small body so she gestured wide to give it room. With everything else stripped away—the lights, the makeup, the cameras—her voice became the simple, deep, plaintive, unadulterated sound of longing.

Soon tears glistened in Mayer's eyes. He crossed the room, fully under her spell.

When the song ended, he started to slip his hand over the girl's shoulder, but she deftly moved away, positioning herself close to Ida Koverman.

"You see," Maud said. "We think the song is a message from the author himself. It might be bad luck to cut it."

Mayer pulled a hankie from his breast pocket and blew his nose. He looked at each of them, one by one: first Arlen, then Judy, then Ida, then, at last, resting his eyes on Maud.

"It's not that I'm superstitious, but what with the jacket, what with all of the money we've put into this thing, I don't want to bring us bad luck. . . . And besides, that song—it's goddamned beautiful. You know, I don't tell this to everyone, but I quit school at age twelve. Had to. Needed to earn a hard living the hard way. See these hands? They were covered with calluses. Was colder than you can imagine up in New Brunswick, Canada. I'd get up long before the sun came up. So cold, so deathly still, and I was always hungry, and I was always thinking that there had to be a better place somewhere," Mayer said.

He contemplated the group for a few minutes. Then he crossed to his desk, picked up the telephone.

"Get me the editing room," he said. He waited a moment. "This is Mayer. Production 1060. Put the rainbow song back in."

———

ON THE WAY OUT, Maud grabbed Judy's arm and pulled her into the ladies' room.

"I don't know if I'll ever see you again," Maud said. "You are going to be a big star. So famous that you won't even remember my name—and that's all right. But there is something I want to tell you, and I don't want you to ever forget it."

"Okay," Judy said, her voice serious.

"You were born with a gift. A gift so giant that it scarcely fits in your body. You don't know why you have it, and neither do I, but you have it. I lived with someone like that. It was my husband, Frank. He didn't even call himself an author—he said he was the Royal Historian of Oz, just writing stuff down. But I want to tell you something right now: it's not magic. It's you. It's your hard work, it's your gift and what you put into it. You have the power to move hearts, and that is not magic at all."

"But . . ." Judy's lower lip was quivering. "There is magic. I saw it. What about the jacket?"

Maud laid her hand upon the girl's arm. "That wasn't magic, my dear. That was nothing more than a publicity stunt. Do you know how many old jackets there must be kicking around like that? Sure, it looked like it could have belonged to Frank, and it was made by a Chicago tailor he used to use. It was similar in cut and style, but there was no way for me to know if it was really his. The name tag was illegible—only wishful thinking made it look like Frank's name."

"So you lied, Mrs. Baum?" Judy said, her voice shaking. "You let everyone believe it was magic when it wasn't?"

"Oh, but it was magic—just not the way you're thinking of it. Magic isn't things materializing out of nowhere. Magic is when a lot of people all believe in the same thing at the same time, and somehow we all escape ourselves a little bit and we meet up somewhere, and just for a moment, we taste the sublime."

"Well, that's just rotten," Judy said, now in tears. "I thought you could help me contact my father. I *believed*, and now you are telling me that it's not true."

Judy wiped her nose with the back of her hand. She stuck her hand into the pocket of her dress and seemed to be fishing around for something. She pulled it out and held it up on the palm of her hand.

"So then how do you explain *this*?"

Judy was holding a yellowed, crumpled piece of paper. Maud's mouth went dry.

"What is it?" she said, trying to keep her voice steady.

Judy smoothed out the scrap of paper. She read aloud:

> "The Rainbow King's daughter sprang from her
> seat and leaped on the arched bow that awaited
> her. Dorothy could no longer see her but blew
> kisses toward her with one hand and fanned
> goodbye with the other. Suddenly, the end of the
> bow slowly lifted from the earth and its colors
> ascended, fading into the clouds, and she,
> along with the bow, were gone."

"Let me see that!" Maud said.

Judy dropped the brittle scrap of paper into Maud's palm. Maud's knees were shaking. She recognized her husband's distinctive back-slanted hand.

"Where did you get this?"

"In the pocket."

"The pocket?"

"Of the jacket. Remember when you found me in the wardrobe room, wearing the jacket? I stuck my hand in the pocket, and there was a hole in it. I reached down inside the lining, and I felt this little wad of paper. And when I read it, I knew it was her."

"Who?" Maud asked, her voice trembling.

"A girl from the other side of the rainbow. That's how I knew how to sing the song. When I sing it, I can bring my daddy close to me—he's looking down at me. He's just on the other side of the rainbow."

Maud gazed at Judy with wonder. She reached out and drew her into an embrace, then held her at arm's length and regarded her anew.

"I think that somewhere," she told Judy, "there is a little boy or a little girl who is feeling sad and hopeless right now, and when they hear you sing, they are going to dream of a better world. And that—that is magic."

BACK IN THE LOT, Maud found her car parked aslant. She looked around for the security guards, but they appeared to have given up the search. As she was driving home, it started to rain. Approaching her house, she was so startled that she almost crashed her car. All of a sudden, a giant rainbow had appeared in the sky. It seemed to end in the garden behind Ozcot. She blinked and it was gone. But it didn't matter. Frank, at last, had sent her a sign.

HOLLYWOOD

August 15, 1939

B RIGHTER THAN CELESTIAL BODIES, THE GIANT LETTERS of the marquee lit up the sky above Hollywood Boulevard, casting stripes of gold across the faces of the crowd. Four deep, they lined the street, crowding the velvet ropes. In the sultry August night air, the scents of Tabu perfume, sweat, and floral-scented powder twined together, the essence of hope and yearning.

Black Packards glided up, uniformed chauffeurs whisked open polished car doors, and the crowd sucked forward, pulled as if by planetary force. As elegantly clad men and women stepped out onto the red carpet, an explosion of photographers' lights flashed and popped, as if each star were followed by a comet's blazing trail.

MAUD COULD HAVE WALKED the five blocks from Ozcot; none-theless, the studio had insisted that she arrive at the theater in a chauffeur-driven limousine. In 1910, Maud had finally used her inheritance to build their family home in Hollywood. When they had arrived here, it had been just a sleepy town, and look what it had become—a modern land of enchantment, the most glamorous place on earth. Folding her gloved hands in her lap, Maud reminded herself that she was not picking up the tab for any of this. She had never stopped counting pennies, tallying up expenses. Force of habit. She was too old to change.

Such a crowd had gathered at home to see her off—the boys, their wives, the grandchildren. She pictured Kenneth, her baby, grown so like his father, with his erect bearing and twinkling eyes, fussing over her, helping her to the limousine, leaning in to kiss her on the cheek, and whispering in her ear, "Father is certainly loving all this fol-dee-rol." But Maud was traveling to the premiere unaccompanied—only a single ticket had been allotted for her, the other seats given away to Hollywood luminaries and the press. Just as well, she thought. This was something she needed to do alone.

Maud had seen the marquee before, in the light of ordinary day, the giant letters spelling out M-G-M's AMAZING "THE WIZARD OF OZ." She passed it on her way to the market and the pharmacy. Over the past few days, she had watched as workers assembled rows of bleachers on the street, backed by an additional neon sign on a large scaffolding that loomed over the boulevard. Even now, with the electric lights transforming the night sky, Maud perceived the artifice that lay behind all this—the scaffolding where the neon was affixed, the false-fronted opulence of the grand cinema palace. To see the ordinary, to avoid being bedazzled by spectacle—this was her gift. Each time she passed, she hoped to find Frank's name spelled out in lights. Each time, as she noted its absence, she felt a whisper of disappointment.

But tonight, as her limousine rolled up Hollywood Boulevard toward the ornate façade of Grauman's Chinese Theatre, she felt a flutter of excitement. The gaudy Chinese pagoda housing the movie palace stood out against the dark sky, its copper-topped turrets outlined with thousands of brightly colored lights. Adding to the spectacle, the powerful beams of searchlights crisscrossed the darkness, as if to warn the heavenly bodies to know their place— second to the stars that blazed here on earth.

The chauffeur swung the door open and offered her a hand; she felt unsteady, momentarily blinded by the brilliant lights, an old lady among the young. The crowd pressed toward her, the fans' excitement like a physical force, but no one recognized this woman, approaching the end of her eighth decade, with her gray hair pulled back sharply from her face, wearing sturdy walking shoes and a dated dress. Their eyes flitted toward her, then away, already greedy for the well-known personalities who would emerge from other cars.

Maud didn't care whether they recognized her. Chin aloft, back straight, she knew who she looked like now: like her mother, Matilda, when she'd stormed the dais at the nation's centennial in Philadelphia. Oh, if only Mother could have witnessed this—if only Matilda and Frank could have stridden with her, arm in arm, to see how what once was only imagined could now be brought to life.

Tonight Grauman's famous forecourt, decorated with the hand-prints of movie stars, had been transformed into a cornfield. A nice touch. Frank would have liked that. A handler at her elbow ushered her forward to stand for a photo in front of a cornstalk. She smiled.

Inside the grand movie palace, Maud scarcely noticed the elaborate adornment, the Chinese lanterns and hand-painted silk screens. The usher escorted her to her seat of honor. Settling into the red velvet cushioned theater seat, she closed her eyes, turning inward, summoning her mother and father, her dearest Frank, her sister, Julia. Without each one of them, this glorious moment in this grand cinema palace would never have occurred. And yet, here she was, alone.

The lights flashed, then dimmed as people hurried to claim their seats. The chatter subsided.

Maud folded her hands in her lap and sat, utterly still, as the curtains parted, the veil lifting between this world and another.

A credit appeared on the screen in large white letters, floating over a backdrop of puffy cumulus clouds that blew across a gray sky.

FROM THE BOOK

by

L. FRANK BAUM

The words tumbled off the screen, and Maud saw a sepia-toned road stretching off toward the horizon, and a little girl and her dog, running away.

Daughter of her heart. Forever young.

AFTERWORD

MY OWN STORY ABOUT DOROTHY BEGAN IN 1965 WHEN I was four years old, living in a suburb of Houston with my family. The owners of a local television store opened up after hours and invited the neighborhood folk to come watch the annual network screening of *The Wizard of Oz* on one of their brand-new color TVs. Like so many other people, I've never forgotten the first time I saw this legendary film. And as did so many others, I felt that the character of Dorothy belonged just to me. In the 1960s, sandwiched between two brothers, I knew that girls were not equal to boys—we couldn't wear pants to school or play on sports teams. I figured out instinctively that Dorothy was the kind of little girl I wanted to be— one who could stare down a lion, melt a witch, tame a wizard. From that day forward, Dorothy became my imaginary friend.

About six or seven years ago, I was reading *The Wonderful Wizard of Oz* aloud to my son when I found myself wondering about the author. Why was I so familiar with his creations yet knew nothing about the man who had created them? And then when I read about him, I suddenly felt as if I understood why this man, in particular, had created one of American literature's most spunky and enduring female characters.

Baum's wife, Maud Gage Baum, was a tour de force, completely unlike most Victorian women. Not surprising: Maud was the daughter of one of the nineteenth century's most outspoken advocates for the rights of women. In 1876, Maud's mother, Matilda Joslyn Gage, helped to pen a Declaration of the Rights of Women and marched, uninvited, onto the dais of America's centennial celebration to hand the document to a startled Senator John Ferry, then acting vice president, with her close friends Susan B. Anthony and Elizabeth Cady Stanton at her side. Matilda fought for women's access to higher education, helping to ensure her daughter Maud's place as one of Cornell University's first female undergraduates. And yet Maud chose to defy her formidable mother by running away with an itinerant theater man named L. Frank Baum, demonstrating the very independence of spirit that her mother had taught her. Maud never regretted her decision. Theirs was a great love. Frank and Maud remained devoted partners throughout the rest of their lives.

But it was not until I stumbled across a 1939 photograph of Judy Garland and Maud Baum seated next to each other, reading *The Wonderful Wizard of Oz*, that I realized I had found a story to tell. Maud Gage was born in 1861, shortly before the first shots were fired at Fort Sumter, sparking the Civil War. When I learned that Maud, aged seventy-eight, had met Judy Garland, aged sixteen, on the set of *The Wizard of Oz* in 1939, I needed to know more. How had this meeting ever come to pass? What might they have talked about?

When a reader is enjoying a historical novel, she is likely to wonder how much of the story is drawn from real life. In the case of *Finding Dorothy*, I have altered some dates and names for clarity and plot development, but most of my story is based on known historical fact. Before writing a single word, I turned to biographies and diaries, letters and photographs to help me reconstruct the Baums' lives. I found that Frank Baum's inspirations for *The Wonderful Wizard of Oz* have been well documented. You find in Baum's book the witches his mother-in-law wrote about in her well-regarded though radical tome *Woman, Church and State*. You find in the novel the scarecrow that haunted Maud's childhood, and shadows of the Tin Man in Frank's years selling axle grease for a firm called Baum's

Castorine Company. If you are interested in reading more about L. Frank Baum's life, there are several excellent biographies, including *Finding Oz: How L. Frank Baum Discovered the Great American Story*, by Evan I. Schwartz; *The Real Wizard of Oz: The Life and Times of L. Frank Baum*, by Rebecca Loncraine; *L. Frank Baum: Creator of Oz*, by Katharine M. Rogers; and *Baum's Road to Oz*, edited by Nancy Tystad Koupal.

But when it comes to the inspiration for the character of Dorothy, no clear consensus emerged. The Baums had no daughters. Some have speculated that Frank named the character after one of Maud's nieces, T.C.'s daughter, Dorothy Gage, who died in infancy in 1898, but I found this theory less compelling when I discovered that Frank used the name Dorothy in a story called "Little Bun Rabbit," which was published in 1897, before Maud's niece Dorothy was born. In that story, the character Dorothy is described as a gentle little girl living on a farm who was so kindhearted that she was able to talk to animals. So, perhaps Maud's little niece, who lived only five months, was named after Baum's character, not the other way around.

But there has long been a consensus among Oz scholars that Baum's vision of Kansas was modeled on the prairie town of Aberdeen, then part of the Dakota Territory where Maud and Frank arrived just as a farming boom was turning to bust. In particular, Baum seems to have drawn inspiration from the hardscrabble life of Maud's older sister Julia and her husband, who staked a claim in LaMoure County, Dakota (later North Dakota) in 1884. The Carpenters lived on a harsh and unforgiving homestead just as the drought was making it almost impossible to eke out a living from a government claim. Julia's handwritten diary, which I located in the collection of the State Historical Society of North Dakota, provided me with many details of her life, including her struggles with her health, with the harsh environment on the Dakota claim, and with the death of her son Jamie when he was an infant. Her husband was nearly ten years her junior, an alcoholic, a harsh man, and a poor farmer. Julia carefully recorded lists of her Christmas gifts, her children's teething and illnesses, the unrelenting burden of her work, and her dreadful loneliness in an isolated shanty with none but the wolves and the distant stars for company. But much was left unsaid—such as a haunting entry from one bleak midwinter day in 1888, when she wrote simply, "What a terrible night!" Within those margins, I've fleshed out her story.

After losing their farm, the Carpenter family was able to relocate, first to the small town of Edgeley, where Magdalena got a chance to attend school, and later to Fargo, North Dakota, where Frank set up his brother-in-law in the insurance business. Their material life improved considerably, but James Carpenter remained an unhappy man, eventually committing suicide at the age of sixty. Julia Carpenter suffered from health problems throughout her life, although she remained dedicated to the Christian Science faith, which forbade her from taking medicine. But her mental health also remained precarious, and she died in a sanatorium. Magdalena graduated from the University of Wisconsin in 1909. Her daughter Jocelyn Burdick, Matilda Joslyn Gage's great-granddaughter, was the first woman to serve as a United States senator from North Dakota.

Maud's own life—the unconventional childhood with Susan B. Anthony and Elizabeth Cady Stanton as frequent visitors in her home, the hazing she suffered at Cornell, her near-fatal bout with childbed fever, her work as a seamstress to support their family, and her close relationships with her mother, sister, and husband—is based on historical fact. Maud had four boys, and she did at one time ask her sister if she could adopt Magdalena, an offer her sister declined. She certainly pined for a daughter in many of her letters. The Baum family did visit Chicago's famous White City on more than one occasion, and many researchers believe that it served as an inspiration for the Emerald City. The dedication to *The Wonderful Wizard of Oz* reads: "This book is dedicated to my good friend and comrade. My Wife." Frank Baum died in 1919 at the age of sixty-two of complications from gallbladder surgery. A bankruptcy in 1910, after Frank's early foray into the nascent film industry, had led to Maud consigning the rights of *The Wonderful Wizard of Oz* to their creditors. Yet Maud still had the money to build

Ozcot, the Baums' first permanent home, thanks to her inheritance from her mother. After Maud's death, Ozcot was razed to make way for a nondescript apartment building, but the Baums' home in Aberdeen, South Dakota, still stands.

Finding Dorothy streamlines Maud and Frank's life stories, skipping over some events in their long life together. *The Wonderful Wizard of Oz* was Frank's first full-length book, and the one that brought lasting prosperity to his family, but he published two other books of nonsense poetry before its publication. In the interest of simplicity, I left out several close family members. In addition to T.C. and Julia, Maud had another older sibling, Helen. In addition to Magdalena and Jamie, Julia had another son named Harry. T.C. had another daughter, Matilda Jewell, as well as two daughters who died in infancy.

If you would like to learn more about the creation of the classic film *The Wizard of Oz*, I would recommend *The Making of the Wizard of Oz*, by Aljean Harmetz. "Over the Rainbow" was almost cut from the film after a sneak preview. Many of the people associated with the film later took credit for saving the song. Yip Harburg, who wrote the lyrics for "Over the Rainbow," later wrote the songs for a successful Broadway play, *Bloomer Girl*, whose story was inspired by women's rights activist Amelia Bloomer, a contemporary of Matilda Gage's. Harburg was blacklisted in the 1950s after refusing to cooperate with the House Un-American Activities Committee.

Did Frank's jacket really appear on the set of *The Wizard of Oz*? The unit publicist never backed away from her story that the jacket worn by Frank Morgan during the Kansas scenes was purchased in a secondhand shop by someone in the wardrobe department and was later authenticated by both Maud Baum and the Chicago tailor as having belonged to L. Frank Baum.

Judy's life, her difficulties as a child actor, and the story of her father, whose experiences living as a closeted gay man in the early twentieth century caused her family to be run out of their small-town homes on several occasions, are all drawn from historical fact. The ruthless treatment she received at the hands of studio executives, the studio doctors who plied her with pills, her pushy stage mother, her father's death in a hospital while she sang on national radio, and instances of sexual harassment at the studio all come from documented sources. Arthur Freed may or may not have molested Judy, but he did expose himself to Shirley Temple when she was only eleven years old. "Over the Rainbow" was Judy's signature song, the touchstone she returned to again and again—but, tragically, Judy Garland never did manage to find that peace for herself. In her own words, "I tried my *damndest* to believe in the rainbow that I tried to get over and I *couldn't.*" And yet, it was her role as Dorothy and her rendition of "Over the Rainbow" that cemented her place in immortality.

The Wizard of Oz debuted in 1939 to generally positive reviews and moderate box office success, but it was not the top-grossing film of that year. After its debut on television in 1956, however, it was screened yearly on network television until 1980, and viewing the film became a beloved holiday tradition for an entire generation, making *The Wizard of Oz* one of the most-viewed films of all time. "Over the Rainbow" was voted the No. 1 song of the twentieth century by the Recording Industry Association of America and the National Endowment for the Arts.

ACKNOWLEDGMENTS

IT OFTEN FEELS AS IF AN AUTHOR GETS TO PLAY THE WIZARD while an army of hardworking people behind the scenes whisper, "Pay no attention to the man behind the curtain." This is my place to thank the many, many people without whom this book, and none of my books, would be possible. It is an understatement to say that I'm grateful that with their help I'm able to spend my time doing the thing I love the most in the world—making up stories.

I think the greatest joy for an author is to be given the opportunity to publish several books with the same people, especially when those people are as awesome as the team at Ballantine. Thank you so much to Ballantine Bantam Dell publisher Kara Welsh, deputy publisher Kim Hovey, and editor in chief and associate publisher Jennifer Hershey for their unflagging support. For their painstaking attention to detail and sagacious suggestions, thank you to production editor Steve Messina and copy editor Bonnie Thompson. For the book's beautiful jacket and interior design, I'm grateful to Lynn Andreozzi and Barbara Bachman. As always, I am so grateful to Cindy Murray, deputy director of publicity, and Quinne Rogers, director of marketing, for their cheerful, creative, and ingenious strategies for figuring out how to connect a book with its audience. I am greatly indebted to the entire team in sales, who have shown me time and again that they truly do care about every single book and author.

It is difficult for me to adequately express my gratitude to my wonderful editor, Susanna Porter. Not only does she have keen editorial skills, but she puts in a huge amount of work helping to hone each manuscript. Her perceptive understanding of character helped me to deepen my story and stay true to the strong women I was writing about. I also owe thanks to Emily Hartley, whose helpful and insightful input on an early draft reminded me of the importance of love.

As always, I'm indebted to my agent, Jeff Kleinman at Folio Literary Management, who encouraged me to write fiction again, and whose unflagging and contagious enthusiasm for this story buoyed me through the writing process. I'm also very grateful to Jamie Chambliss at Folio, whose astute editorial feedback early on helped point me toward the emotional heart of the story.

There were many people who read early drafts of the manuscript and whose feedback provided key insights to me. In particular, my children aided me in so many ways—Nora, who helped me to figure out who Dorothy was; Hannah, who came up with the wonderful title; and Willis, who led me to discover Frank and Maud's story in the first place through his enthusiasm for *The Wonderful Wizard of Oz*. Thanks to my mother, Ginger Letts, who patiently listens and rarely criticizes.

For assistance with the L. Frank Baum Collection, thank you to Shirley Arment at the K. O. Lee Aberdeen Public Library, and thanks also to Michael Swanson at the State Historical Society of North Dakota for providing me with a copy of the Julia Gage Carpenter diary.

Writing can be a solitary profession, and I could not survive it without my dear writing friends who celebrate every success and mourn every missing comma with me: Tasha Alexander and Andrew Grant, Jon Clinch, Karen Dionne, Renée Rosen, Danielle Younge-Ullman, Jessica Keener, Lauren Baratz-Logsted, Melanie Benjamin, Sachin Waikar, Keith Cronin, and Darcie Chan.

For every reader who passes along book recommendations,

writes reviews on Amazon and Goodreads, or takes a chance on an unfamiliar author, I'm eternally grateful. For every librarian and bookseller, I consider you my heroes. For all the book club members, you are part of the big extended family of book lovers. Without readers, there are no writers.

To every member of my family, I am eternally grateful for your love and support.

And last, I'd like to honor the memory of Matilda Joslyn Gage, who fought so hard for women's right to vote so that future generations could benefit from her efforts; L. Frank Baum, whose story and characters have endured more than a century and inspired countless other artists; Judy Garland, whose great talent has continued to spark joy for so many; and Maud herself—the woman behind the curtain!

READING GROUP MATERIALS

QUESTIONS AND TOPICS
FOR DISCUSSION

1. Almost everyone remembers watching the iconic 1939 film, *The Wizard of Oz*. Share your special memories of watching the film. Did you see it in a theater, or on television? What is some detail from the film that has stuck with you? Did reading *Finding Dorothy* make you want to watch the film again?

2. Did you ever read *The Wonderful Wizard of Oz*, the book? Before reading *Finding Dorothy*, how much did you know about the author's life? Do you think it's surprising that the story is so much more well-known than its author?

3. *Finding Dorothy* is told from the perspective of Baum's wife, Maud. Why do you think the author chose to tell the story from her point of view? How did you feel about that choice? Did getting to know Maud help you understand more about how *The Wizard of Oz* was created?

4. In *Finding Dorothy*, we first meet Maud as an elderly widow, struggling to get people to pay attention to her so that she can preserve her husband's legacy. Then later we meet Maud as a girl. Did young Maud grow into the kind of woman you expected her to be? What do you think it was like for Maud to try to have an influence at the studio? Do you think it was harder for Maud, as an older woman, to make her voice count? Have things changed for women in this respect since Maud's day?

5. In *Finding Dorothy*, the author drops lots of hints about where Frank got his ideas for *The Wonderful Wizard of Oz*. What was

your favorite thing you learned about the real-life origins of the story? What surprised you the most?

6. Frank and Maud had four boys, but they never had a daughter. Why do you think Frank's most famous character is a little girl? After reading *Finding Dorothy*, who do you think was his inspiration for the character of Dorothy? To what extent do you think authors base their stories on their own lives?

7. Loving, creative, cheerful, optimistic, and fun: these are all qualities that could describe Frank Baum. But he was also an impractical dreamer, prone to wild schemes that didn't always pan out. What was it like for Maud to be married to such a man? Were you surprised that she was so loyal to him? If Frank and Maud were a 21st century couple, how do you think their relationship might be different? Or would it be the same?

A Q&A WITH AUTHOR
ELIZABETH LETTS

The Wizard of Oz is one of the best-known and best-loved American stories, and yet the life of author L. Frank Baum is not well-known. What drew you to this story, and why did you tell it from the point of view of his fierce, loyal, and independent wife, Maud Gage Baum?

I've always been a fan of the 1939 Wizard of Oz movie, which I watched every single year when it came up for its annual showing on TV during my childhood, and I also read all of the Oz books as a child, but it had never occurred to me to wonder about the author and his life until I was reading the book to my son about six or seven years ago. As I was reading, I got the feeling that there was something wonderful and kind of subversive in *The Wonderful Wizard of Oz*—particularly in the female characters—the witches, and of course Dorothy, and so I started to wonder about the author. Who was he? Why was he only known for writing this single series? And where had he developed his unusual way of looking at the world? Out of curiosity, I looked him up, and that was when I realized that he was married to the daughter of one of the 19th century's most outspoken advocates for the rights of women. Suddenly, I saw the story of the Wizard of Oz in a whole new light. But the story didn't break open for me and demand to be written until I saw a picture of Maud Baum and Judy Garland together on the set of *The Wizard of Oz*. Maud was seventy-eight years old and had been the steward of the Oz legacy since before Judy was born, and Judy, who became a giant international icon, was just stepping into the role that would come to define her. What did the two of them talk about, I wondered. I realized that Maud, to whom the book was dedicated, had been the inspiration behind much of it, and had been able to work behind the scenes to leave her own imprint on the movie.

You mention Maud's mother, Matilda Joslyn Gage, who was a famous suffragette who worked alongside Susan B. Anthony and Elizabeth Cady Stanton, and yet she is not as well-known. Why has her name been lost to history and how did she influence Maud?

I have long had an interest in the late 19th century women reformers, and so I myself was surprised to learn what a towering figure Matilda Joslyn Gage was in her time. As president of the New York State Women's Suffrage Association, and editor of an influential newspaper called *The Citizen and Ballot Box*, Gage was just as influential as her two close friends and colleagues Stanton and Anthony—but eventually, there was a rift between Anthony and Gage, and Gage's contributions were largely written out of history. And yet, Matilda was a huge formative influence on her daughter Maud, and had a close relationship with her son-in-law Frank Baum, and so clearly, Matilda's ideas did in the end go on to have a tremendous impact, through the story that has been called "America's first home-grown fairy tale."

Frank Baum died in 1919, but Maud outlived him, and in 1939, when The Wizard of Oz *was being filmed, she had a role as a consultant on the film. How involved was she really?*

Sometimes when researching a story, I come across something that strikes me as unusually poignant, and this was the case with the making of *The Wizard of Oz* movie. Frank Baum always had a fascination with gadgets. In the 1880s, he purchased an Eastman camera, one of the earliest portable film cameras, and took up photography when it was a brand-new phenomenon. Later, he guessed at the potential for moving pictures, actually putting on an Oz-themed production using hand-colored glass slides that is now remembered as an early precursor of cinema. Frank and Maud moved to Hollywood in 1910, when it was just a rural hamlet, and Frank became involved in the early film business, even founding a studio called the Oz Manufacturing Film Company, which was not a success. So, I thought a lot about how Maud must have felt when everything that Frank had been able to imagine at last came to pass and *The Wizard of Oz* went into production at MGM, Hollywood's premier movie studio. What a sense of duty she must have felt—to be alive to see his dream through. I think where the novelist really comes to the fore is in a situation like this. Maud acted as a consultant on the film, but little trace of that role remains, and so it was up to me to imagine and intuit how that went. I do believe that the reason the film was so fantastically successful was that they managed to capture the magical, whimsical essence that Baum wrote into the book.

In your book, you write about the young Judy Garland and her relationship with Maud, as well as the often heartless treatment she suffered as a girl working in the studio system. How much do you know about their relationship, and were things really so tough for Judy?

Judy Garland is truly one of the great movie stars of the 20th century, and her role as Dorothy in *The Wizard of Oz* was the one that catapulted her to stardom. "Over the Rainbow" became her signature anthem, but heartbreakingly, Judy never found personal happiness in her own life, succumbing to drug addiction at the age of forty-seven, an addiction that started when she was a child actor plied with pills – what she called her "bolts and jolts" – by studio doctors. But during the filming of *The Wizard of Oz*, she was just a girl. Tremendous pressure was put upon her—the giant budget, the high stakes—and she was a child actress playing among seasoned adults. There was a refrain from "Over the Rainbow" that was eventually cut from the final movie, but an audio clip survives, and it is gut-wrenching to listen to as Judy sobs as she sings. Maud was not able to save Judy—but I do believe she would have done whatever she could have to help her, and that is the heart of the story.

You've written non-fiction before. How much research did you do for this book, and how do you find fiction and non-fiction to be different?

I'm a great lover of history, and have written several non-fiction history books. But I also know that sometimes only fiction can get to the emotional truths of the past. To understand your characters and their place in the world, you have to dig into the historical record, but so much is left unsaid. You know where people went and what they did—it's the novelist's job to try to imagine how they felt about it. As an avid reader throughout my life, most of my most vivid impressions of history come from fiction, and this is the spirit that I tried to bring to this book. But there is something uncanny about immersing yourself in the lives of real people. Especially while writing this story, I always had the sense that Frank and Maud Baum were close to me—Frank Baum believed there were other worlds, separated from our own by just a flimsy veil, and all we needed to do was push aside that veil and we could see them, and that is a lot what it feels like to write fiction. There are times when you feel as if the characters are coming alive and telling you what to write. A week ago, I saw a beautiful rainbow that seemed to point straight down directly across the lake from the house where I was staying. One of my kids said, "I think Frank just stopped by" and that's just how it felt to me.

Which part of the story resonates with you the most?

Before I became a writer, I had a career as a nurse-midwife, and so when I came across the fact that Maud Gage had suffered from severe peritonitis after the birth of her second child, it made a huge impression on me. Even today, with modern health care and anti-biotics, peritoneal sepsis is a severe, life-threatening condition (though, fortunately, very rare.) Given my background working in the field of maternal-child health and my own experience juggling a career with being the mother of four children, I was particularly attuned to how the experiences of childbirth and infant death would have had a profound impact on the lives of Maud and her family.

What is it about The Wizard of Oz *that gives it such an enduring appeal?*

One thing I discovered in writing this book is just how incredibly huge *The Wizard of Oz* was in its time. The only thing I could really compare in the modern time would be the Harry Potter phenomenon. *The Wonderful Wizard of Oz* spawned thirteen sequels written by Frank himself, followed by twenty-one more written by Ruth Plumly Thompson, the author appointed by Maud to continue the series. An original Oz book was published every year before Christmas between 1913 and 1942. Just a couple of years after its original publication there was a massively popular Broadway play, and since then, the number of Oz spin-offs has been staggering. One hundred and twenty years after its original publication Baum's imaginary world is still going strong. Now, Oz permeates our culture in so many ways—you can scarcely read a newspaper, watch a TV show, or even have a conversation without an Oz reference being thrown in somewhere. Dorothy, the Wizard, the Scarecrow, the Lion, the Tin Man, and the Good and Wicked Witches have danced right off the page and earned enduring places in our collective imagination. It is one of our greatest cultural touchstones. To me, Maud and Frank have such an American story—they were hard-working dreamers who also faced hardships, but eventually prevailed, and I think we all see ourselves in the Oz characters, and especially in Dorothy, who presented a courageous image of what a girl could hope to be.